THANK
YOU
for
LISTENING

ALSO BY JULIA WHELAN

My Oxford Year

THANK YOU
FOR
LISTENING

A Novel

JULIA WHELAN

AVON

An Imprint of HarperCollinsPublishers

P.S.™ is a trademark of HarperCollins Publishers.

HarperCollins books may be purchased for educational, business, or sales promotional use. For information, please email the Special Markets Department at SPsales@harpercollins.com.

FIRST EDITION

Designed by Diahann Sturge

Headphones line art © Singleline / Shutterstock
Open book line art © Olga Rai / Shutterstock
Emojis throughout © Cosmic_Design; popicon / Shutterstock

Library of Congress Cataloging-in-Publication Data has been applied for.

ISBN 978-0-06-309556-4
ISBN 978-0-06-324315-6 (hardcover library edition)

22 23 24 25 26 LSC 10 9 8 7 6 5 4 3 2 1

Praise for
Thank You for Listening

"Mix Julia Whelan's storytelling ability and smart banter with a cynical romance audiobook narrator who won't trust a happily ever after and what do you get? Pure magic."

—Jodi Picoult, *New York Times* bestselling
author of *Wish You Were Here*

"A fun—and sometimes—steamy glimpse into the world of audiobook narration from the queen of the medium."

—Catherine McKenzie, *USA Today* bestselling
author of *Spin* and *Hidden*

"An absolutely exquisite story that made me laugh out loud, weep on multiple occasions, and stare off into the yonder wondering how Julia Whelan's fabulous mind works. . . . God, what an electric read!"

—Robinne Lee, author of *The Idea of You*

"*Thank You for Listening* is a novel of great wisdom and depth, and it's also sparkling, sexy, and fun. We are lucky readers to have this book."

—Allison Larkin, author of *The People We Keep*

To those we have loved.
Particularly partners.
Particularly mine.

THANK
YOU
for
LISTENING

 # PART 1

All of literature is one of two stories: a man goes on a journey or a stranger comes to town.

—Leo Tolstoy

Prologues are like flirting: there's a time and place. But sometimes you just need to push the reader up against the wall and stick your tongue down their throat.

—June French, *USA Today* bestselling author of the Love Comes Hard series, as told to *Cosmopolitan*

CHAPTER ONE

"A Woman Goes on a Journey"

THINGS WERE HEATING UP WITH NO POSSIBILITY OF COOLING DOWN. Not this time. She could see it in his eyes. His pupils were throbbing. The gentleman of the last three weeks was gone. He was now anything but gentle. He was all man.

Their eyes were locked and loaded. He raised his hand and flattened it against her white silk blouse. Her heartbeat grabbed at it. He kissed her, hotly, wetly, then took hold of her straddled hips and lifted her off him. She gave a startled cry as he flipped her—

"Something to drink?"

—onto her back on his expensive crepe de Chine couch.

"Ma'am?"

"We shouldn't be doing this," he growled. "You're my intern. And Grandfather insists I marry Caroline."

"Something to drink?"

The long-suffering tone broke through and Sewanee Chester, startled window seat occupant, whipped off her noise-canceling headphones as if they were on fire. "What? Sorry! What?"

"Something to drink?"

"Uh. Just water. Please."

"Ice?"

"Uh, just—please."

She dropped her tray and the flight attendant passed her the water. Before Sewanee could thank her, the woman on the aisle turned to her daughter in the middle seat and asked, in the squeaky, love-dripping voice used interchangeably for pets and children, "Anything to driiiiink?"

"Juice!"

"What kiiiiind of juice?"

Sewanee slipped her headphones back on and realized she hadn't stopped the audiobook. The blouse was off now. She sighed, paused it, connected to the in-flight Wi-Fi, and texted Mark:

Good morning. I hate you.

She hit send and sipped her water.

Twenty seconds later, he replied:

I gave you one of the well-reviewed ones!

SEWANEE:

His pupils are throbbing, Mark. His PUPILS.

While Mark typed (bubbles, bubbles, bubbles . . . he was pushing seventy, she cut him some slack), Sewanee drank.

MARK:

Don't be a snob. Not all of us have English prof fathers honey.

SEWANEE:

this has nothing to do with snobbery. OR my father. This has to do with ANATOMY.

Mark ignored this:

> Really appreciate you filling in.

SEWANEE:
> Anything for you. How's the foot?

MARK:
> Still broken. How's you?

SEWANEE:
> I want to change the name of the panel.

MARK:
> What's wrong with Faking it: Narrating Love and Sex in Romance Novels?

SEWANEE:
> I was thinking . . . Narrating Romance Novels: How to Give Good Aural.

She finished the water, tipping her head all the way back. The ice cubes mounted their escape, ramming her teeth so forcefully water shot down her neck and onto her shirt.

"You spilled!"

Sewanee smiled tightly at the child while setting her cup down in the circular playpen at the corner of the tray. Had that little lip ever prevented cups from overturning during turbulence? She wanted the numbers on that.

MARK:
> I know how you feel about Romance but you'll get threw this. Just please take it seriously.

SEWANEE:

*Through.

Over the PA, a male flight attendant announced, "Ladies and gentlemen, I know we just finished service, but in a few minutes, we'll be starting our descent into Las Vegas. At this time, we'll need you to put away all electronic devices—"

Sewanee looked down at her phone. Mark had finished typing.

MARK:

The fans are insane. You should see the facebook groups. You don't no.

SEWANEE:

*know. We talked about this. I get it.

MARK:

ducking autocorrect! This is BiblioCon! 50K attendees and the Romance pavilion is at least a third of them.

"Ma'am, I need you to put up your tray."

Sewanee did.

"I also need you to put your seat up."

"It won't go up." Sewanee kept typing into her phone.

The flight attendant reached across the mother and child to yank Sewanee's seat forward. The little girl turned to help her for a moment, then threw her sticky hands up in defeat. "It won't go up!"

"Thank you," Sewanee muttered.

"Welcome," she replied.

SEWANEE:

Mark, I said I get it. Big! Yuge! You get a book and you get a book and you get a book!

MARK:
And don't forget to enjoy yourself,
Oprah. Vegas, Baby! LOL.

Sewanee pulled up her e-mail and rechecked the overwhelming number of BiblioCon events. She narrowed it down to Romance programming and shuffled through author talks, signings, cocktail hours, and a silent auction for charity. She laughed out loud at one highlighted item: dinner with a male cover model. She then perused the plethora of panels on offer: Crossed Swords: Writing M/M Romance When You Don't Have a Sword of Your Own; How to Write Period Clothing and How to Take It Off; and, of course, her own panel on audiobook production that Mark—her mentor, boss, and landlord—would have been moderating himself if he hadn't run over his foot with his own car two days ago. That red Karmann Ghia, Sal, was the closest thing Mark had had to a long-term relationship since he'd fled San Francisco in it fifteen years ago. After his partner, Julio, died.

She'd been happy to help him out with BiblioCon, but there were two problems. Maybe three. While she was essentially Mark's Girl Friday, helping him run the recording studio he operated out of his home in the Hollywood Hills in exchange for living in its hillside guesthouse, she wasn't an audiobook producer like Mark; she was a narrator. The second problem was she was a narrator who didn't narrate Romance. She'd done it in the beginning when she was cutting her teeth, recorded it under a pseudonym as many narrators did, but once her career took off, she'd retired her alias, quit Romance, and never looked back. Lastly, she wasn't even a fan of the genre.

She didn't belong in the Romance pavilion.

She double-checked the info Mark had forwarded her. She had nothing until tomorrow. The panel in the morning, then booth duty on the general convention floor for the rest of the day, answering authors' questions about audiobook production. A quick flight back on Sunday afternoon. An easy forty-eight hours of her life. Plus, she got to be in Vegas at the same time as her best friend, who had also been roped into attending the conference. But for very different reasons.

"Are you a pirate?"

Sewanee startled, turned to the little girl, and found her staring.

The mother startled, too. "Hannah!"

"She looks like a pirate."

The mother took her child into a hug, conveniently muzzling her. "You'll have to forgive her. She's four."

"I'm almost gonna be five!" Hannah sounded like she was arguing into a pillow.

"It's okay." Sewanee gave her an indulgent smile. "No, I'm not a pirate."

Hannah wriggled out of her mother's chokehold and turned fully to Sewanee. "But you have a patch on your eye."

"Hannah." Sharper this time. By Los Angeles parenting standards, it might have been considered stern. She pivoted toward her daughter, scooting to the edge of her seat, loosening her seat belt, getting *directly in front* of her child and *on her level*, as she'd probably been coached to do. A teaching moment was upon them. "We don't ask strangers personal questions, sweetness. You're so, so, *so* smart, and I cherish your curiosity, but we respect people's privacy, mmkay?" The high-pitched pet voice was back.

Hannah turned toward Sewanee again. "But why do you have it?"

Her mother turned her back around. "Now, see, Banana Bread, that's a personal question, isn't it?"

"Don't call me Banana Bread, I told you. I hate it."

"I'm sorry."

Hannah wriggled back to Sewanee. "Are you hurt?"

One more Hail Mary, "Hannah!" But Sewanee was used to this line of questioning. She supposed it was refreshing that, at the moment, it wasn't coming from a drunk guy in a bar.

"Nope. Not anymore."

"But, but, if you're not hurt, why is it got—"

That said, Sewanee's patience extended only so far. "I'd love to keep talking to you," she said, tapping the Bluetooth headphones around her neck, "but I need to finish my work." She glanced at the mother for parental assistance.

"Oh, of course! Four is just such a curious age—"

"Five!"

Sewanee shook her head. "It's totally fine. I'm just on deadline and if I don't finish listening to this, I could end up looking for a new job."

Blame the improv background, the acting training, a childhood living in stories, but Sewanee could lie. Easily. To herself as much as anyone else. She lifted the headphones off her neck and secured them over her ears. She pressed play on her phone. No sound. She turned up the volume. Still nothing. She turned it all the way up.

In her peripheral vision, she saw the mother clasp her hands over Hannah's ears, pull her into her narrow chest, and bug her eyes at Sewanee.

No.

God, no.

She ripped the headphones off in time to hear, at full volume:

"He thrust her legs apart, splaying her open, exposing her secret place to his throbbing eyes. Already pulsing, glistening, her generous—"

Sewanee stabbed so fiercely at the pause button the phone shot to the floor. She scrambled for it, the audiobook continuing:

"'Say it,' he growled. 'I want to hear you say it.' He gave her one quick, teasing lick. She moaned. 'Say you want my—'"

The phone had fallen under Hannah's dangling, light-up Disney-princess sneakers. Sewanee grabbed it, jerked upright, and—in three stabs—stopped the audiobook . . . just after the word "cock."

She stared down at the phone, ignoring the glare drilling into her temple. She took, what she hoped, was a casual-seeming breath. Then, as if nothing had happened (denial was another skill she'd honed), she turned fully away from mother and child and looked out the window.

Once she'd focused, actually took in the view their descent offered, she concluded Las Vegas had a rather flaccid look during the day. All that nighttime neon was like Vegas Viagra.

She shifted in her seat. Who takes a kid to Las Vegas, anyway? she thought righteously, if irrationally. Great parenting. She knew mothers like that. Hell, she had a mother like that. Soft, over-loving. She'd been raised the way Hannah was being raised. West side of L.A. (you could tell by the mother's ropey yoga arms, her rootless dye job, her thoroughly moisturized skin), schools with *feelings*, parents who wanted the best for their child while ensuring their child was the best. Who said you could be anything, do anything, dreams do come true, you're special, you're anointed. Just be *nice* to everyone, *respect* everyone, tell the truth, work hard, and everything will fall into place. You will live happily ever after.

Well, good luck with that, Hannah.

Because this is how it actually goes.

A stunningly average woman the wrong side of thirty on her way to Vegas, wearing an eye patch, sitting in a broken seat, listening to porn.

CHAPTER TWO

"The Best Friend"

SEWANEE ASSESSED HERSELF IN THE GILDED MIRROR OF THE VENE-tian's elevator. Unwashed hair, saggy jeans, rumpled T-shirt, zip-up hoodie with some unidentifiable breakfast-y stain near the zipper. No wonder the woman who gave her the key at the VIP lounge had looked confused.

When the elevator doors opened on the thirty-fifth floor, she followed signs to the right. Stopping at the correct door, she slipped her backpack off (carefully—her right shoulder still screamed sometimes) and set it on top of her roller bag. She opened the door with the key card.

A marble hallway beckoned her. She glided down it, passing a powder room larger than her guesthouse bathroom. On the opposite side, a butler's pantry/bar that could have serviced the entire hotel. Eventually she was standing in the middle of a sunken ultra-modern marble living room with floor-to-ceiling windows overlooking the Strip.

"You made it!"

She pivoted left, looked down another long hallway, and saw the bathrobed and barefoot two-time Golden Globe–nominated, one-time Oscar-nominated (they didn't talk about *that* discrepancy), L'Oréal spokesmodel, and UNICEF ambassador, Adaku Obi sprinting toward her.

Before Sewanee could respond, Adaku was upon her, wrapping her in a fierce, all-encompassing hug. Adaku's hugs always began with swaying, moved into meditative stillness, and ended with deep yoga breathing. The girl knew how to stay in the moment. Even if it was only for a moment.

Adaku pulled back and smiled big. "Isn't this insane?! It's ginormous! Stupid!" Adaku had always spoken in exclamatory bursts, but the tempo had increased, Sewanee had noticed, in direct proportion to her success. "And guess what?! You'll never guess so I'll tell you. There're two bedrooms!" She gave Sewanee a teasing push.

Sewanee pushed her back. "Only two?"

Adaku guffawed and pushed her again. "That I've found so far! Now you have to stay with me!"

Sewanee scanned the sprawl. Shook her head. "Mark already paid for my suite at the Rio."

Adaku gave her a look. "Aren't all the rooms at the Rio 'suites'?" She finger-quoted the last word.

Sewanee reached for her hand, smiling. "I can't leave Mark with a bill for a hotel I didn't use."

"How much is it?"

Sewanee squeezed Adaku's hand, shook it for good measure. "No, no, no. You know I hate that." Off Adaku's pursed lips, she added, "Don't do the face."

"What face?"

"You know exactly what face."

"I don't know what—"

"A!" Sewanee dropped Adaku's hand and walked to the window. Dammit. It was a spectacular view.

Adaku was starring in a film based on last year's number one

New York Times's bestselling book. She was doing a main-stage interview with the author, a VIP meet-and-greet, an autograph hour, and some international press junket thing. No sideshow Romance pavilion for her. At BiblioCon, she herself was the main event.

In the window's reflection, Sewanee watched Adaku come up behind her and spread her arms out, a queen addressing her people far below. "We're living the dream, Swan! I've got bottle service at the club, a limo on standby, a freaking butler at my twenty-four-hour beck and call!"

Sewanee paused. Adaku, born and bred in the white Chicago suburbs, third daughter of two lovely but demanding Nigerian doctors, was finally allowing herself to enjoy her hard-won accomplishments. It had been a long time coming. People thought success happened faster than it did. A best-supporting-actress nomination did not come with a swag bag of private jets, penthouses, and Porsches. Adaku had *just* bought her first house, a two-bedroom bungalow in Echo Park, thanks to the L'Oréal money. This was the first time the red carpet had been rolled out to this extent. Adaku Obi was starring in a film and the studio wanted to make her happy.

So it was earned. And, yes, it was fun. But Sewanee wanted to urge caution. To slow her down a bit. Tell her that life was subject to change without notice. But she squashed the impulse and used a move out of Adaku's own playbook: when she couldn't say what she wanted to, she changed the subject. "I'm sorry, why aren't we drinking champagne right now?"

Adaku barked her signature laugh and squeezed Sewanee's shoulders. "Because it's chillin' in the fancy Sub-Zero fridge!" As she scampered off, she yelled over her shoulder, "They gave me Cristal!"

Sewanee turned back to the window and gave herself a good,

firm, mental shake. She was happy, genuinely, for her friend. This had nothing to do with Adaku. Adaku wasn't the problem.

She heard the *pop* of the cork, the glug of the pour, and the posh little patter of Adaku's bare ballerina feet on the marble behind her.

She turned away from the window and Adaku handed her the glass of bubbly, looking Sewanee directly in the eye. "To our dream coming true."

Sewanee toasted her and took a large swig of the best champagne she'd ever had.

"Okay! What do we want to do? I have that dinner I told you about but I'm free until then. Let's get this party started!" Sewanee knew, because she knew everything about her best friend, that while anyone who found themselves in Adaku's whirling dervish of a presence would swear otherwise, she had never done cocaine.

"Whatever you want! I can't check in until three o'clock so . . ."

Adaku rolled her eyes and Sewanee could see another argument for ditching the Rio forming, so she quickly said, "I have to do some work tonight, so let's have fun but not too much. Tomorrow night, I'm all in. Speaking of, I brought five hundred dollars and I'm putting it on red or black. Haven't decided which yet. Who knows, maybe I'll get lucky."

"Oh, you're getting lucky if I have anything to say about it! It's been way too long." Adaku held up her glass again. Sewanee clinked it, chuckling, and they both said, simultaneously, effortlessly, freely, "I love you." They sipped and the bubbles felt like Pop Rocks on Swan's tongue and, suddenly, she was content. That's what A did for her.

Adaku set her glass down on a side table Sewanee thought might have been a sculpture and clapped her hands together. "So! I have to do a phone interview in ten minutes, shouldn't be more than half an hour—at least my publicist promised it wouldn't be—and then we hit it!" She refilled Sewanee's glass while saying, "You take this, go luxuriate in the spa"—she pointed down yet another long hallway—"fix yourself"—she looked Swan up and down—"and get ready to *partaaay*!" She twirled out of the room on the last word like Stevie Nicks, champagne sloshing out of her glass and splatting on the marble.

Sewanee smiled and walked down the other cavernous hallway, stopping in her tracks at the door to the bathroom.

Oh, okay. It was an actual spa. There was a steam room, a sauna, and a massage table all surrounding a Japanese soaking tub. She wasn't sure where to go first. The tub called to her, so she stripped down—eye patch and all—and slipped into the perfectly regulated 104-degree water.

As she adapted to it, her mind wandered back to the studio apartment in Washington Heights. The one she had shared with Adaku when they were in school. The one where they had huddled together under blankets when the furnace had gone out and played the "when we're famous" game. Julliard had been sucking them dry, financially and emotionally, but they'd had a bottomless well of optimism that could only come from youth and inexperience. When we're famous, we'll eat sushi every night. When we're famous, people will stop us on the street and say how much they love our work. When we're famous, we'll have reliable heating. When *we're* famous.

Not you. Not me. We.

Sewanee hadn't known then how quickly a dream could become a thing that mocked you.

TURNED OUT, VEGAS by day was not as flaccid as Sewanee had thought. She and Adaku had already window-shopped and people-watched, and they were now tucked into two club chairs in a beautiful bar somewhere in the Venetian's Grand Canal Shoppes, sipping something expensive. Free, but expensive. Once Adaku had signed a cocktail napkin "To Roy, Always Adaku," their eager server had upgraded their vodka sodas to something sweet dusted with gold flake. "Do we need to worry about heavy metal poisoning?" Sewanee joked once he'd left. Adaku had sniffed the surface of the drink, said, "But, what a way to go," and took a sip. Sewanee followed suit.

"So, how's BlahBlah doing?" Adaku asked.

"Oh, you know," Sewanee sighed. "Physically, she's okay. Mentally? You ever seen *Memento*?"

Adaku grimaced. "Is she . . . does she still remember who you are?"

"Oh, yeah. I started bringing her my audiobooks and I think hearing my voice when I'm not there helps her remember me when I am."

"Amazing. And how about your dad?"

"She remembers him, too. Unfortunately."

Adaku chuckled. "I meant how *is* the old bathrobe?"

Sewanee guffawed, they set their empty glasses down, and Roy appeared, as if he'd been waiting in the wings for just such a cue. "You guys doing okay? Or do we need some more gold for that?"

"My bartending magician!" Adaku flirted. "Abracadabra, please!" She held up both empty glasses.

"Your wish is my command." Roy relieved her of the glasses. "Back in a flash." He made a *whooshing* sound as he left, presumably vanishing.

"Is there anything you can't get a man to do?" Sewanee marveled.

"Commit?" As Sewanee laughed, Adaku turned her attention

to the room, scanning it, radar looking for a blip. "Speaking of men, see anyone cute?"

Sewanee didn't look. "No."

"Come on! We're in Vegas!" Adaku leaned in, grinning devilishly. "What happens in Vegas, stays in—"

"Only if you use protection." Adaku chuckled, but Sewanee made a sound like a hissing cat. "I think I have a gold flake caught in my throat."

At that moment, Roy reappeared, making the same *whooshing* sound, and Sewanee stifled her hacking.

"He appears!" Adaku exclaimed. "Roy the Remarkable!"

"What else can I conjure for you ladies?" he asked, through his Vegas grin.

Adaku caught Sewanee's eye. A silent conversation ensued. *How about him?* Adaku asked. Sewanee imperceptibly tipped her chin down. *No.*

Adaku ignored her, turning to Roy. "By the way, this is my best friend, Sewanee."

"Shauney?"

"No, SWAH-nee. Like swan the bird and knee the joint."

Sewanee cringed. "Call me Swan. Like the bird. Forget the joint thing."

"This is the cool name table, huh?" He offered a little windshield wiper wave. "So, Swaaaan, you somebody, too?"

"Uh, yes." She cleared her throat one more time. "Aren't we all?"

"Ha!" He finger-gunned her, making yet another sound. "*Pew pew.* I meant, you famous, too?"

Adaku leaned in. "She's the greatest living audiobook narrator on the planet!"

Sewanee held up a hand. "That's not—"

"Audiobooks?" Roy's eyebrows shot up. "Dude, that's my jam! You done anything I would have listened to?"

She sipped her cocktail and discovered the secret to dislodging gold flake was, apparently, more gold flake.

Meanwhile, Adaku said, "You've heard her, trust me. She does, like, every big book! She's won every award that can be won! Have you listened to *Them Hills*?" Sewanee had to give Adaku credit for sizing this guy up. If there were any book she'd narrated that he'd probably listened to, it was going to be last year's hyper-masculinized best-selling Western. *Butch Cassidy and the Sundance Kid* told from the woman's perspective.

He lit up like a slot machine. "Dude! Dude! That book rocked! That was you?"

She presented herself awkwardly with her hands.

Roy peered at Sewanee, seeing her anew. "You crushed it! Wait, so did you meet the guy who played Butch and Sundance? Do you, like, record together?"

Adaku and Sewanee looked at each other then back at Roy. Adaku said, "What guy?"

"The guy! The guy who voiced the guys."

Adaku and Sewanee looked at each other again. Adaku said, "That wasn't a guy."

"No, the Butch-and-Sundance-guy guy."

"Ohhhh, that guy. Yeah, he wasn't a guy." Adaku was enjoying this a bit too much.

"*Who* wasn't a guy?"

"The guy reading."

"Wasn't a guy?"

"Nope."

Sewanee intervened before Adaku short-circuited Roy. "What she's trying to say is, it was me."

Roy took a moment with this. An extended moment. He narrowed his eyes. "Oh, I see." He turned to Adaku. "You think I think she did the whole book, *including* the guys!" Roy guffawed. "No way I would have thought that! But I can understand how you would think I thought that."

Adaku's head jerked around on her neck like a malfunctioning robot. "Well. Glad we cleared that up!"

Roy turned back to Swan. "So, who was the guy?"

Sewanee considered making up a name and moving on. Adaku was no help at this point, having submerged her laughing face in her drink. She'd give it one more go. "Roy?" Her tone was kindergarten teacher. "The guy? The guys? Were me."

Roy threw his head back. "Not you, too! The guy—"

"Roy?" Same tone. He looked at her again. "When I recorded *Them Hills*, the . . . book people? Had me do all the voices. Butch and Sundance included."

Silence. "All the voices?"

"All the voices," Sewanee repeated.

Roy stilled. Then tilted his head. He looked like a Labrador waiting for a command.

She dropped her voice to a place that was second nature at this point. "'Someday, Butch, you're gonna die and then you'll realize you never really lived.'"

Roy stared at her.

Sewanee took a sip of her drink, waiting.

Finally: "Dude."

Adaku banged the table. "Amazing, right?!"

The sound snapped Roy out of his confusion. Now he was awestruck. "How do you do that?"

Sewanee waved him in and spoke quietly, mysteriously. "Keep it to yourself. Know what I mean?"

He looked as though he had been allowed to peek behind a curtain. He slowly bobbed his head. "Riiiight. Totally." He winked knowingly and headed back to his post at the bar.

Adaku took a moment. Then shrugged. "Okay, so not him!"

"HIT ME!"

They'd landed at a blackjack table. Adaku was playing, Sewanee was watching.

The dealer turned over the next card. "Twenty-one."

"Bam!" Adaku pulled Sewanee down into the seat next to her. "Come on! Play!" She pushed a stack of $25 chips in front of her and said to the dealer, "She's playing."

"Not with your money."

"Shhhh. Ten minutes! Ten little minutes! I'm on a roll. Then we'll go find your roulette wheel."

"I have prep work to—"

"The books aren't going anywhere, Swan."

The dealer said, "Card change, ladies. It'll be a couple minutes."

Relieved, Sewanee sat back.

And sensed two guys skulk up behind them.

"'Scuse me?" The taller one tapped Adaku on her shoulder.

Sewanee watched her pull away from the touch even as she turned to them with her stock yes-it's-me smile. "Hi!"

"Holy crapolla. It *is* you! We wasn't sure."

"*I* was sure," his shorter companion put in. "Acura Oboe!"

Sewanee sighed audibly and got Adaku's foot in her shin.

Adaku smiled bigger. "Adaku Obi."

"Yeah." The taller one snapped his fingers. "I'm Chuck. This waste of space is Jimbo."

Chuck had a glassy glint in his eyes Sewanee didn't like. He kept staring at Adaku. "I gotta tell ya, between you and me?

You remind me of this—" He turned to his friend. "Jimbo, you remember Sheniqua?"

Jimbo snorted. "Do I remember Sheniqua."

Sewanee would never get used to it, the things some men thought they could say. Roy was harmless. But these two? These two were trouble before they ever showed up, wherever they showed up, and particularly in Adaku's case. As Sewanee debated whether to step in, she placed their accents. East coast. Not New York, not the boroughs. Definitely not Boston. Jersey. Probably the shore. Badda Bing.

"Hey, so." Chuck dropped a hand on the back of Adaku's chair, leaning down. "Don't take this the wrong way, but do you like white guys?"

Sewanee stood up and said, "Okay," as Adaku said, lowly, sharply, "Don't."

Chuck lifted both meaty hands. "I'm just sayin'!"

Jimbo chuckled. "We've had a little too much of a little too much, if you know what I mean." They fist-bumped. Sloppily.

Sewanee knew there had been a window, a small window, a few years ago, when being recognized had been enjoyable. Now, it felt like surveillance.

Adaku caught the pit boss's eye. That was all it took.

Chuck, oblivious, stepped closer to Adaku. "You're special. That 'it' thing. You twinkle. All mischievous and shit."

"Mischievous," Sewanee said in that well-trained voice of hers, which, despite its low volume, made people listen. "Miss. Chi. Viss."

Chuck looked at her for the first time, surprised to find her there. "Dat's what I said."

"No, you said, miss-CHEE-vee-us. It's MISS-chi-viss."

"So?"

"Mis-chi-viss is a word. Miss-chee-vee-us is not."

Chuck struck a theatrical pose of contemplation, stubby finger on his scruffy chin. He turned to his buddy. "Hey Jimbo, is 'bitch' a word?" He looked back at Sewanee. "I say dat right?"

As they laughed, two large men appeared. One took Chuck by the elbow. "Gentlemen, please come with us." There were brief protests: We didn't mean nothing; just having some fun; way to treat your fans; you ain't hot shit, you know. But they were already on their escorted way toward the nearest exit.

Sewanee sat back down. She looked at Adaku and said, "Okay, so not him!" They were sharing a rueful smile when Chuck took one final, loud shot over his shoulder:

"Yo, bitch, catch ya back at Treasure Island!"

ADAKU HAD INSISTED on taking Sewanee to the Rio in the limo. She'd checked into her fourth-floor room, threw open the curtains to reveal a sumptuous parking garage view, made a cup of tea, put on the Golf Channel—her favorite source of white background noise—and worked. First, she went over the questions Mark had given her for the panel tomorrow morning.

Then she began prepping a book she was recording in a few weeks, making word lists and finding the correct pronunciations, identifying the emotional arc of the story, marking breath points in syntactically challenging passages, mapping relationships between the characters, and developing voices and accents. Book prep had become as relevant to her as rehearsal had once been for performing a play or researching a character before shooting a film. But Sewanee Chester hadn't stepped on a stage or in front of a camera for seven years.

After a few hours, she sat back, realizing she was hungry, and absently fiddled with the elastic of her eye patch above her right ear as if it were a lock of hair. In the beginning, she'd taken it off whenever she was by herself. Now it was just another part of her. She picked up the phone and treated herself to room service.

Then did something she hated: went on Facebook.

She had let her activity lapse after the accident. Too many sympathy posts and then, seemingly overnight, not enough. While people posted photos of their engagements and weddings and first dogs and first houses and first kids and now second kids, the last picture she'd been tagged in had been from the hospital. Adaku by her side, both sporting cheeky thumbs-up. She was frozen in time like that.

But then Mark had gone and said: Romance audiobook fans are insane, you should see the Facebook groups.

So she went to Dixie Barton's page, a narrator friend who had made a career doing Romance and would be on the panel tomorrow. Her real name was decidedly *not* Dixie Barton, but Alice Dunlop. Alice had chosen the pseudonym Dixie Barton because she'd been a famous burlesque dancer in the 1940s. Sewanee looked at the groups "Dixie" belonged to:

Romance Rosies.

Midnight Riders.

All Things Romance.

She clicked on the one with the most members—twenty thousand?!—and slipped into another dimension.

There were at least fifty posts a day, some heralding new releases ("book 14 in the Katy Totally Did series is out today! Come to mama!"), some espousing love for a specific book or narrator ("I've started hearing Joe Kincaid's voice in my dreams"), and some asking for recommendations ("anyone got a funny m/m/f threesome book? Must be FUNNY"). Authors were members of this group and narrators were, too. But mostly, it was the fans.

Fans who, Sewanee discovered as she scrolled through the page, could listen to a book a day. Fans who made devotional videos to their favorite narrators. Fans who impatiently waited for a narrator's next book because they had already *listened to their whole catalogue.*

Sewanee knew how popular Romance novels were (it wasn't just a category, it was a *pavilion*, after all), but she was surprised to see narrators had their own following. The fans loved the women . . . but they revered the men. And it seemed one in particular, Brock McNight, was the reigning king. The lack of subtlety in the comments made it obvious. "All hail!" and "our resident unicorn" and "Brock McNight! I want you to read this section to me while I go down on you!"

Hokay then.

Sewanee knew there was no way Brock McNight was his real name. The explicit nature of these books led many narrators— much like the books' authors—to use pseudonyms. It was an industry norm and everyone had his or her own reasons for doing so but, like a society of magicians, they were all sworn to secrecy. A pinned post at the top of the page promised that any listener who "outed" a narrator without their permission would be kicked out of the group.

Good.

Mark was the person who'd first suggested Sewanee do audiobooks. They'd been seated next to each other in a thirty-seat black box theater at a mutual friend's showcase and seemed to be the only two people in the audience not impressed by the tortured writhing onstage. After a two-minute conversation at intermission about audiobooks, he gave her his card, said she'd have to start in indie Romance, and that she should pick an alias. She'd chosen her stripper name. Using the classic middle school algorithm, she combined her first pet (Sarah, a black Lab as loyal as she was stupid) and the street she grew up on (Westholme, a half mile from the UCLA campus where her father taught). Sarah

Westholme sounded realistic. Some narrators went the other way. Fluffy Foxtrot. Dick Long. And in the case of a very gay, very Liberal narrator she adored who only recorded queer erotica, Lindsey Graham, because "let the bastard come after me, I dare him."

The industries—both audiobooks and indie Romance—had grown so much since she'd "retired," Sewanee was sure Sarah had faded into obscurity. But she put her old alias into the Facebook group's search bar to see if she existed.

Boy, did she. She was an enigma. The White Whale of Romance. The posts told her as much:

> Why isn't she narrating anymore?

> What happened to her??

> OMG, she was my absolute favorite, why 😭???

> No one does guy voices like her! Shadow Walkers?! It doesn't get better than SW reading June French!

Shadow Walkers was the last Romance series she'd done and she'd loved those books. But, then, it was June French. What was there not to love? In the '90s, June had been an iconic Romance author helping to define the category. When she went indie with the Shadow Walkers series, she'd hired Sarah to do the audiobooks and they'd exploded.

June was the one Romance author Sewanee had felt bad about abandoning. They'd worked well together, exchanged thoughtful e-mails that made Sewanee feel they probably would have been friends in real life. She recalled even telling June—in abstract terms—about what had happened to her, why she wasn't acting on-camera anymore. When she'd heard only a few weeks ago that June had died—a shock wave still working its way through

the audiobook community—the news had hit her in an unexpect-
edly tender place.

The knock on the door startled her. For a moment—brief, but
still—she imagined herself in a June French novel. What adven-
ture might she find on the other side of the door?

Oh, right. Food.

She snapped the laptop closed, popped up, and adjusted her
eye patch before opening the door to a man who would never
grace the cover of a Romance novel, not even in his prime thirty
years ago. He wheeled the food into her room, she signed the bill,
tipped him well, and closed the door.

She uncovered the plate and found cold French fries, a day-
old bun, a possibly older burger, and garnish she suspected had
been taken off another, discarded dinner.

Fantasy over. Reality had arrived.

CHAPTER THREE

"The Stakes"

THE NEXT MORNING, AS SEWANEE DEBATED HER LIPSTICK COLOR FOR the panel, she found herself staring into the bathroom mirror, eye patch off. It didn't matter how accustomed she'd become to it, she couldn't help looking at it. Every time as if it were the first and every time hoping it were the last.

The space where her right eye had been was curtained with skin that looked as if it had been burned. It hadn't. It was simply the effect of not enough skin to cover too much surface. The long, jagged scar that accompanied the drape went from the middle of her right eyebrow down over the highest point of her cheekbone. Like the mouth of a river, it dumped itself into the estuary of her cheek's hollow.

She looked down again at the lipstick. Red. Definitely red. Be bold.

Her cell phone, resting on the counter next to her, rang.

She glanced at the caller ID: Seasons. Her grandmother's assisted living facility. No matter how many times she had seen "Seasons" on her screen over the years, her stomach tightened. In recent months, the tightness had worsened in tandem with Blah's mental state. "Hello?" she answered.

"Sewanee?" the familiar voice asked.

"Amanda. Is everything okay?"

"Well, we had a bit of an incident."

Sewanee turned around, leaned against the counter. She imagined spark-pluggy, capable Amanda behind the desk in her tidy office, Christmas sweater probably over the back of her chair, frizzy gray-black hair pushed back by a reindeer-antlered headband. "What happened?"

"Sorry to bother you. We reached out to your father, but he hasn't returned our call."

Typical. "It's fine, what's going on?"

"Well," she sighed, "BlahBlah left her room last night." Even the caretakers had adopted her grandmother's nickname. Barbara had never wanted to be called "grandma" or "nana" or any other "ancient-sounding familiarity." But a young Sewanee couldn't say Barbara. The best she could manage was BlahBlah. Sewanee's father had thought it fit his loquacious mother perfectly, so it stuck. "One of our orderlies found her in the common room at two thirty this morning. She believed she was at a hotel in Tennessee getting ready for her debutante ball. She thought the orderly was her escort."

Sewanee closed her eye. "How is she this morning?"

"She woke up having no memory of last night. Was her usual bubbly self at breakfast."

"Okay," Sewanee breathed, tipping her head back. "That's good. Right?"

"Yes, but the thing is, we had to put her on lockdown for the rest of the night, for her own safety. Her circumstances have advanced, necessitating we evaluate future care requirements."

"What—what does that mean?"

"We believe that, in the somewhat near future, we'll need to transition her to our memory care side."

Sewanee had seen the big, locked door. She recalled vividly

the red-lettered sign above it: MEMORY UNIT. KEEP DOOR CLOSED AT ALL TIMES. It was off the hallway that led to the bar. Yes, Seasons had a bar. And a yoga room. The place was designed to look like a Hollywood back-lot version of 1950s Americana: the main hallway, Main Street; the salon boasted a barber shop pole; the little market had a soda fountain counter and jukebox. It unnerved Sewanee, the Disneyfication of dissolution. But it made Blah happy. And being located in Burbank, right across from Warner Bros. Studios and next to the Smoke House, it was full of Show Folk like her grandmother.

That was why Blah had chosen it after her sister, Bitsy, with whom she'd been living, had died.

While other assisted living facilities took their residents on field trips to the mall or a museum, Seasons' field trips consisted of movie nights at Hollywood Forever Cemetery to watch classic films outside ("and to visit old friends," her grandmother liked to joke). They went to sitcom and talk show tapings. They had a happy hour Friday night that was open to the public and Swan would be there for most of them, drinking a martini with Blah and her pals.

When they'd first toured Seasons four years ago, Amanda had assured them if and when the time came for a transfer to memory care, Blah wouldn't be isolated from the world she'd enjoyed; she would still participate in the activities of the assisted living side, if she wanted. If she could. Both Sewanee and Blah had brushed this off at the time. Neither seriously entertained the possibility of BlahBlah—gossipy, cackling, bright-eyed, sailor-mouthed, song-and-dance BlahBlah—needing locked doors and twenty-four-hour monitoring.

"Would you like me to keep trying your father or would you prefer to contact him?" Amanda asked.

"No, I'll get hold of him."

"Okay. Please have him call me as soon as you do."

"Absolutely. Thank you, Amanda."

Sewanee hung up and immediately brought up her father's number.

She paused.

She sighed deeply and called.

"Sewanee, I don't have time to chat, are you okay?"

"I'm fine." Not that he was really asking. And not that he really didn't have the time. Which made it impossible for Sewanee *not* to goad him by saying, "I just wanted to have a long heart-to-heart about our hopes and dreams, Dad." Sarcasm was her best offense against his unrelenting self-protection and she wielded it expertly.

"Is there something you want?"

"Yes. When your mother's assisted living facility calls, I want you to pick up."

The smallest pause. "Is everything okay?" he asked, parroting exactly what Sewanee had asked Amanda. But the difference was in the tone. She knew tone. It was her job to know tone. His was distracted, impatient. But—and this was what struck her—almost hopeful everything wasn't, in fact, okay. It turned her stomach.

"No," she answered, swallowing. "There was an incident last night, nothing serious, but it prompted Amanda to tell me—tell you—that Blah needs to go into memory care. So, Amanda has to speak with you."

"Why?"

Sewanee paused. "Why? To discuss . . . literally everything?"

"Her hopes and dreams?"

Sewanee didn't respond to the quip and Henry didn't continue. When the silence grew too long, Sewanee said, "I was planning to visit on Monday, for lunch." Still nothing. "Why don't we meet there?" If it weren't for the sound of his swallowing—what Sewanee assumed was coffee—she would have thought they'd been disconnected. "Dad?"

A slight chuckle. "There's no need for that. You go ahead and have your luncheon, you ladies figure everything out, and we'll talk after."

"Okay. I'll call you Monday evening." More silence. "Would you like to at least know what happened—"

"Swan, we'll talk Monday, I have to go." He hung up.

BIBLIOCON LANYARD AROUND her neck, Sewanee hustled and dodged her way across the massive convention floor like a running back going for the end zone. The number of attendees was astonishing. For someone who spent a good portion of her working life with headphones on, hearing only the soft hush of her own voice in her ears, who prized, above all else, absolute quiet, the ambient din of the room made her shoulders creep up her neck.

Her phone vibrated in her pocket, just once, a text.

ADAKU:
You here?

SEWANEE:
Yep. On my way to panel.

ADAKU:
Come to the green room for a sec.

SEWANEE:
There's a green room??

ADAKU:
Northwest corner.

SEWANEE:
What am I, Magellan?

ADAKU:
By the Starbucks. Under the poster of me.

Sewanee swiveled her head around the room. She located the poster for the movie *Girl in the Middle*—a stop-action close-up of Adaku's face looking from left to right—and shuffled over. She quickly texted:

Only have 10 mins.

ADAKU:
Only need 2.

After finding the door and having her ID checked against the name tag hanging from her lanyard by the super-sized man guarding the room, she was ushered into the exclusive holding area, where Adaku was waiting for her, a to-go cup of coffee outstretched.

"Bless you," Sewanee said, taking it.

Without a word, Adaku grabbed her hand and dragged her down the hallway into a women's restroom. She quickly checked the two stalls, making sure they were empty, then practically leaped over Sewanee and deadbolted the door behind them.

"What's up, you kill someone?" she asked, taking a gulp of coffee. Adaku clasped her hands together but couldn't seem to speak. Sewanee peered at her now. "Is this good or bad?"

A sound escaped Adaku that would set dogs howling. "It's good, Swan. It's so good. It's In-N-Out good."

Sewanee knew if Adaku were allowed one dying request, it would be a Double-Double from In-N-Out Burger. Adaku was buzzing like a lightbulb. Sewanee began to buzz, too. "What?"

Adaku wrung her hands. "That Lysistrata-in-the-jungle project I was telling you about?" Sewanee nodded. "I hit a milestone. The big one."

She stilled. "*The* big one?"

Adaku's chin trembled. "*Our* big one."

Sewanee could take comfort, later, in the fact that her *first* impulse, her *instinct*, had been happiness and not a finger-snap of jealousy. The smile that happened was real, the shout that erupted from her was genuine, the tears that followed were joyful. They giggled and they cried and it was impossible to tell, after a certain point, which was which. A wintry mix of emotions. Sewanee threw her arms around her friend, the only true one she had left, the most constant thing in her life, and felt Adaku's heart beating rapidly against her own.

"A million dollars," Adaku whispered, trembling. "A million goddamn dollars."

"You did it!" Sewanee squeaked.

Adaku pulled back, took Sewanee's wrecked face in her soft hands. "We did it! In that shitty pizza joint on 181st—"

"You dare malign the memory of Tony's?"

Adaku's tears coated her smiling lips. "Over our $2.99 two-slice-and-a-Coke special, we promised. One of us would get a cool mil before thirty-five."

Sewanee pulled her close again and felt tears overtake the laugh, her throat tightening. "You did it. You—" She abruptly shoved Adaku away. Playfully, she was sure. "God, I'm so proud of you!"

Adaku wiped her face. "I mean, after taxes and commissions it's like four hundred thousand dollars, but—"

"Oh, well then never mind."

They looked at each other for a quiet moment. Adaku's eyes clouded. Her face turned earnest. "We both know you would have gotten this ages ago. If that motherfu–"

"You win, I win, we win, remember?"

"But it's so unfair–"

"Don't," Sewanee demanded, taking Adaku by her shoulders. "You're getting paid a million dollars to star in a film."

Her smile returned. "I just got the call and you're the only person I wanted to share it with. I'm so glad you're here!"

Sewanee stepped back and held up her hands, like a sooth-sayer fending off a vision. "I see . . . I see copious amounts of champagne in our future." Adaku laughed. "But right now your two minutes are up and I'm going to be late."

Adaku jumped forward. "Of course, of course! Sorry." She unlocked the door. "What do you want to do tonight? I was thinking–"

"Whatever you want!"

"Can I convince you to go to a club? The bottle service–"

"Yes, all of it, babe, I gotta go!"

Adaku flung open the door. "Go, go! You're going to be late! How many times do I have to tell you?"

Sewanee laughed, gave Adaku's arm a firm squeeze, and bee-lined away.

As she hustled down the hallway, she felt her jaw lock.

As she reentered the convention floor, she felt her chest tighten.

As she found her way to the Romance pavilion and located the correct ballroom for the panel, one word pounded in her head. Why. On a loop. Why. Why. Why.

This was how quickly her mental state could change. This dangerous, invisible undertow was the one thing in this life that still scared her, made her wonder if she was wrong to have forsaken medication after the first year, to have given up on therapy earlier than that. Because this wasn't good. Because in her mind, it was seven years ago and she was lying in that hospital bed wondering why they had bothered saving her.

THE BALLROOM WAS filled to overflowing with authors and fans. They were sitting on the steps, leaning against the walls, propped on their friends' laps. The well-chosen panel—smart, talented people who had upended the childhood dictum to be seen and not heard—had kept the room engaged. There was Alice Dunlop aka Dixie Barton; Mildred Prim, a Royal Academy of Dramatic Art–trained septuagenarian Brit with an obsessive following from the famous Highlander series she'd narrated for the last twenty years, who simply used her ironic maiden name for Romance; and Ron Studman. Ron was one of the few Romance narrators who relished being seen, because he wanted people to know that even if you were more than middle-aged, with an ever-increasing waistline and an ever-decreasing hairline, you could be a sex symbol, too, if you had the goods. And the goods, in his case, was his voice, and the fans loved him for it.

Ron currently had the crowd eating out of his hand. There were catcalls from a group of women in the front row when he did the voice he was best known for: a sexy Irish vampire named Seamus.

Sewanee had covered everything Mark had asked her to. *Why do you think audiobooks are booming right now? How do you prepare to record a book? What is the best approach when recording a sex scene? Why people who out a narrator's pseudonym should be publicly drawn and quartered.* It was time to wrap it up, so she asked a question that would give the panel one last opportunity to shine. *Why are Romance novels so popular?* As each member answered, Sewanee's spirits rose. She had done her job and done it well. Mark would be happy and the organizers pleased. She was looking forward to the night ahead with Adaku, who deserved to be celebrated, who deserved every goddamn ounce of success she was enjoying.

Ron was the last panelist to answer and, being Ron, didn't disappoint. "Women are discovering the full extent of their pleasure. Shame is a thing of the past! Happily ever after is possible. It might even be sitting right in front of your eyes!" Then he winked at the audience.

"All right," Sewanee said to the room. "Thank you, panelists, for your insights. We have a few minutes left, so let's open it up to questions."

One of the women in the front row jumped up and asked Ron if he'd sign her chest. Hoots all around. Ron obliged.

A woman a few rows back stood, took the mic. "Hi. I think I speak for all of us when I say: Who is Brock McNight?" The crowd cheered. "Seriously! We have to know."

Ron made a show of zipping his lips and the rest of the panel shook their heads.

The next question was also about Brock McNight. As was the next. Then Sewanee said, "Any non-Brock-McNight-related questions?"

Someone had a question for Sewanee: "Do you narrate Romance?"

"No." She realized it came out more emphatically than she'd intended. She beamed and pointed to the panel. "I leave that to the experts."

"Sewanee does all the tough books," Ron chimed in. "The ones no one else can touch. Fantasies with three hundred characters, war sagas with twenty different accents, the Classics, literary doorstops. The longer the better, the bigger the better, she does them all."

"That's what she said," Sewanee quipped and the audience laughed. She'd learned long ago to leave them laughing; Blah-Blah had taught her that. "Okay, so how about one more round of applause for our wonderful—"

Sewanee noticed a young, barrel-curled blonde stand and smooth her pretty sundress. She called out, "Sorry, y'all! One quicky little question?"

Sewanee glanced at the clock on the back wall as the floor mic made its way to the woman.

"Thanks so much," the woman said. "And thanks so much for taking the time to come talk to us?" She had a significant Southern drawl. So significant Sewanee wondered, briefly, if she were putting it on. High, nasal, and with the propensity to up-talk. "Um, my question is? What's the best way to get into the business?"

"I can give you more info at the booth," Sewanee answered, "but once you've got a draft of your book you should be thinking about audio—"

"Oh, no!" the woman giggled. "I'm not an author! I'm an ac-tress?"

Sewanee stalled, her brain misfiring.

Ron took the wheel. "Well, first thing you should do"—he leaned into the microphone and dipped into his Irish vampire voice—"is come see Seamus after the panel."

"Ron," Sewanee scolded, "Seamus on you!" The audience laughed. "Okay, everyone, thanks for—"

"I mean, I love reading?" The girl tucked her hair behind her ear and continued. "And I'm taking some acting classes in L.A.?" Oh God: they had one of those *this isn't a question so much as a comment* people on their hands. "And, like, I don't know, it just seems like the perfect job?"

Once again, a panelist saved Sewanee from having to respond. "Well," Mildred began, "I tell people the best thing one can do, if one thinks this job might suit, is to go into a windowless room and read a book aloud, stopping at every mistake and starting again at the top of the sentence. Do this for eight hours and see if you still think it's the perfect job."

The audience chuckled. Sewanee silently thanked Mildred for the reality check.

"Listenin' to y'all has made me realize," the girl continued—continued!—"narrating Romance'd be real neat."

Sewanee's morbid curiosity got the best of her, as if slowing to pass a car accident on the freeway. "Why?"

"Well, using my acting skills and all, I could bring hope to people?"

"How?"

"By—by what I just said? By audiobooking Romance? How great would it be to help the world know love will always find a way, it'll all work out, that we can truly live happily ever after?"

Sewanee fortified herself and tried not to sound condescending. "That would be great, if it were true, but . . . probably best we leave it there."

The girl made an adorable pouting face. "Sounds like somebody could use a little of that hope?"

Straw, meet camel's back.

"I have hope. Real hope, not false hope. Romance novels are a wonderful escape, but—" Sewanee took only the smallest beat—certainly not long enough to consider the polity of what she was about to say—before continuing, "Look, you want to give people something, give them the truth. Level with them. Romance novels are not real life, love is not a God-given right, being an actress won't make life better—in fact, it might make it worse—and happily ever after is bullshit."

Someone was waving frantically at the back of the ballroom, a woman wearing a T-shirt with the convention's logo on it and holding a clipboard. She tapped her wrist in a manner that struck Sewanee as vaudevillian. Which broke the spell.

She looked out into the silent crowd, what she'd said settling over the auditorium like suffocating ash from a volcano.

Shit.

She took a measured beat. "I heard someone say that earlier on the convention floor and I couldn't believe it. I mean, what do we think? Is HEA a bunch of BS?"

"No!"

She'd recaptured them. "I'm sorry, I don't think they heard you over in the snob pavilion! Is it bullshit?!"

A reverberating, room-filling response: "NO!!!" The audience clapped and cheered.

Another Blah-ism? Get the audience on your side.

Over the applause, Sewanee shouted, "Thanks, again, to our panel and remember we'll be signing for the next hour at booth 2186! Have a great day!"

AS THEY ARRIVED at the end of the allotted hour, the activity at the signing booth slowed. Ron came over and gave Sewanee a hug, said he was off to the casino for a Scotch and soda and some Let It Ride. "You should get a drink, too," he said, affable, lovable, wink-able Ron. Sewanee heartily agreed. Mildred stood, cracked her back, and patted Sewanee's hand before leaving.

Alice, however, pulled Sewanee behind the curtains of the booth and looked her right in the eye when she said, "Swan."

"I know."

Alice exhaled and put a hand on her motherly hip. "You saved it, you did. But hon . . . everything okay?"

"Yeah, no!" Sewanee chirped. "It was just that girl, with that *voice*, thinking she could—"

Alice shook her head. "Not our job to tell her. She'll be selling essential oils on Instagram or something within the month. But I don't think she was the issue?"

"I mean . . ." Sewanee looked down, shook her head, and took a breath. "I've been . . . a little off. Lately." She felt Alice peering at her.

"You know, I like Romance novels. And not just narrating them. Reading them."

Sewanee glanced up.

"Ten years ago, when I was empty-nesting, I found out Bob was having an affair, and we were going to lose the house, and then my mom got sick, and *then* they found a lump . . ." Alice's hand touched her chest, the top of her right breast. "More than anything else, I wanted to believe that there could still be a happily ever after for me. It was actually kind of religious." Sewanee opened her mouth, but Alice continued, "Relax, I'm not getting weird."

She took Sewanee's hand. "You're amazing. You're talented and kind and you have shoveled a ton of shit in your young life and I don't blame you for being cynical. But you don't know how things are gonna go. And that cuts both ways, good and bad. So you just have to trust it'll work out in the end."

Sewanee searched for a wry, sarcastic comeback that would dismantle Alice's argument. Something her father might say. But there wasn't one.

So she said nothing.

CHAPTER FOUR

"The Makeover"

"LET'S SEE!" ADAKU CRIED, KNOCKING PERFUNCTORILY ON THE DOOR to the suite's second bedroom before walking right in.

Sewanee stood in the middle of the room. She did an ironic twirl.

Adaku's hands came to her mouth. "Swan," she breathed through her fingers.

Sewanee turned back to the full-length mirror.

She looked good. She looked hot. She looked like a different person.

After she'd closed up the booth around 4:00, she'd walked briskly to the nearest bar for the Last Word she'd been drinking in her mind since 11 A.M. when Ron had suggested she get a drink. But the bar hadn't had the necessary ingredients. So she'd gone back to her room, intending to grab her stuff and head to the Strip, to a bar that knew what it was doing. Instead, she'd fallen instantly asleep and woke an hour later to a text from Adaku telling her to be at the suite by 6:00. She showered quickly, threw on the modest outfit she'd brought to go out in, put on her eye patch, and cabbed to the Venetian.

Adaku had been waiting with a hair and makeup artist and a stylist with three designer dresses in Sewanee's size. She'd protested halfheartedly, but the truth was Adaku's instincts always bordered on clairvoyance. She knew what Sewanee needed before she did. For reasons she hadn't quite parsed, Sewanee wanted to be something more tonight, something different, something slightly less . . . her.

The stylist, wanting to get in good with Adaku, had done a speedy alteration of Sewanee's selection: a bodycon dress that managed to flatter her curves without drawing her perfectionist attention to the extra fifteen pounds she wished weren't there. That used to not be there, before her job involved sitting for the length of a hundred pages a day.

Sewanee had enjoyed being "put through the works," having hair and makeup experts descend upon her with the sole purpose of making her look her best. It had been so long. Now, her auburn hair was styled in a sweep, parted on the left, the bulk of it swooping over her eye patch and down over her right shoulder. Her left eye, her mother's glacial blue, was slightly smoky. She had red lips and defined cheekbones. Contouring. Bronzer. A thicker brow. And boobs! Where had those come from?

Even to Swan's constantly critical eye, she looked stunning.

"Yes!" Adaku clapped. "Come through, lips! Come through, hips!"

Sewanee focused on her friend's gleeful face. "I can't thank you enough, A."

"Oh, please. I didn't do this for you, I did it for me. Now everyone will be looking at *you* instead."

Sewanee's mood had lifted, a fog burned off with the warmth of the sun.

Adaku was her sun.

"And you!" Sewanee exclaimed, walking over to her. Adaku looked gorgeous per usual in a short romper of silver sequins, ankle-height zippered heels, and a deep burgundy lip. Her hair had been straightened into a jaunty bob, made shiny by the co-conut oil finishing serum her usual stylist had designed specifi-cally for her. "You look like a million bucks before taxes and commissions." They laughed and, when Adaku looked at her with Pygmalion pride, Sewanee pulled her into a hug. "It's stu-pid, but I do feel better."

"Playing dress-up occasionally is necessary."

The suite's doorbell rang and Adaku pulled out of the em-brace, jogging from the room. Sewanee took one more look in the mirror and followed after her, hearing Adaku open the door, thank someone profusely, and close it.

The sight in the foyer stopped her.

"Why—what are my bags doing here?"

Adaku, a fresh bottle of Cristal braced inelegantly between her thighs, fingers speedily dispensing with foil, merely smiled that silver screen smile that was impossible to argue with. "You've checked out of the Rio."

Pop.

"LEAVE IT TO you to find the one bar in all of Las Vegas with books in it."

They were ensconced in a library-themed bar somewhere on the perimeter of the Venetian's casino floor, sitting on a deep chesterfield sofa in front of a fireplace that didn't give off any heat, surrounded by heavy mahogany bookshelves full of non-descript antique hardcovers. Sewanee was sure the books were fake. It was the Vegas way: everything was meant to seem real, but wasn't. Tonight, though, she didn't care. It was all part of the fantasy.

Their waitress stopped by the table. "Another, Ms. Obi?"

"We're good for the moment, thanks!"

"Signal if you want anything else, anything at all." She gave them a toothpaste commercial smile and went on her way.

Adaku nodded toward a man who had just walked in. "What about him?" It was not the first time she'd said this tonight.

"Why don't I stand by the door with a net?" Sewanee smirked and took a sip of her Last Word. "A, seriously, I'm not gonna hook up with some rando. Tonight's about you and—"

Adaku's phone buzzed. She glanced at it. "One sec, sorry. Manager." She picked up. "Hello? Manse? Manse—can you hear me?" She plugged her ear with a long, well-groomed finger. "Hang on—yeah, I know, one minute." She stood, made apologetic eyes at Swan, and hustled out of the bar, likely toward a quiet bathroom hallway.

She returned five minutes later looking sheepish. "So!" She sat, but on the arm of the chesterfield, perched like a bird about to take flight. "Don't hate me," she began.

"They up the offer to two mil?"

"I have to go."

"Okay." Sewanee reached for her purse.

"No. To L.A. Tonight. Like, now."

Sewanee shook her head the way a cartoon character did a double take. *Brrrroing!* "What?"

Adaku grabbed her drink and polished it off. "The Angela Davis biopic I was telling you about? I want it. But the exec producer doesn't think I'm right for it. He lives in Paris or Florence or something so I haven't been able to get to him. But he's flying back from Hawaii through L.A. tonight, landing in ninety minutes. Manse told the exec's assistant about the jungle movie, his assistant e-mailed him while he was in the air, and he's agreed to meet me for a drink."

"Wait, you're meeting him at LAX?"

"Yes. There's a Southwest flight leaving in forty-five minutes. So, this is me, going." She bent over, kissed Sewanee's cheek. "Back by midnight."

Sewanee's eye bugged. "You're coming back?"

"We're celebrating! Return flight's already booked!"

"A, you don't have to—"

"You've got a dinner reservation at the celebrity chef steak house in half an hour, bottle service at the club, a driver. Put everything on the room! Find someone to join you! See you in four hours! Leaving!"

Before Sewanee could respond, Adaku was on her way out. As she passed the waitress, she pointed at Sewanee and her drink, clearly ordering her another.

Sewanee sat back. She took a breath.

She already felt awkward sitting in the bar alone, looking like she was waiting for a prom date—or even, she thought, glancing down at her cleavage, a customer. Before she could tell the waitress to cancel the drink order, she'd arrived back to deliver it, as if Adaku had some FastPass lane at the bar reserved solely for her.

She gulped down a good portion of it and thought.

Why would she go to dinner by herself, go to a club by herself, be driven around by herself? Ridiculous. She'd go upstairs, have some coffee, finish prepping the book, and wait for Adaku to come back. She'd have this last drink and close out.

She caught the waitress's eye and made the universal hand gesture for *check, please?* And sat back, waiting. Drinking. Drinking until her cheeks began to warm and her shoulders began to loosen and the bar took on a slightly sexier cast, as if a filter had been applied to the whole room. Before she was officially tipsy, she did the thing she'd been trying to find the time to do all day. She called her grandmother.

"Hello?" Sewanee could hear the familiar click of her grandmother's rings on the plastic receiver. She'd tried to get her to use a cell phone, but the buttons were too small and she'd somehow dial international numbers and then lose the thing in the couch, and anyway they were back to a landline.

"Hi, BlahBlah!" There was a half second of silence, which prompted her to quickly add, "It's Sewanee," before her grandmother could reveal she hadn't known that.

Her voice immediately warmed. "Dollface! How's my favorite girl?"

Sewanee's smile was equal parts relief and joy. "I'm good. I'm still in Las Vegas."

"You're in Las Vegas? I didn't know you were in Las Vegas."

She did. Or she had, anyway. "I'm here for a conference."

"Well, I hope you're finding time for fun." The texture of her grandmother's voice was the result of every cigarette she'd ever smoked, every martini she'd ever drunk. While she retained none of her Tennessee accent (she belonged to the generation of actors whose regionalisms had been drilled out of them), she still carried a Southern dignity and propriety. She swore and drank and partied in her day, but goddammit, she did it *elegantly*.

"Your grandfather took me to Las Vegas once."

Sewanee had heard this story many times before and recently. But this was how it went these days and she knew to go along with it. "Did you enjoy yourself?"

"What a night we had! We saw the Rat Pack. Frank, Dean, Sammy, and . . . oh. I can never remember the other one."

"Isn't it Peter something?" Amanda had told Sewanee to make Blah use her memory whenever possible, instead of just supplying answers.

"Yes! Yes! Lawford, Peter Lawford." She muttered, "He was

never that important anyway. He didn't do anything. Anyway, after the show, Marvin took me backstage—it was the Sands Hotel—and introduced me to Frank and Dean. And of course Sammy and . . . shit! Who's the other one? Doesn't matter. Frank took my hand and asked me what I thought of the show and I came right out with it, I said, 'You should have a lady up there.' Marvin was mortified—he's always mortified—but Frank and Dean, they laughed their tooshes off!" Blah's chuckle became a hacking cough. "Frank's hand is softer than I expected."

Sewanee noticed the shift from past tense to present and she tried to guide her back. "Didn't Grandpa know Sinatra?"

It worked. "Oh yes. Frank had done one of Marv's early pictures, you know, so they went way back. He was awfully sorry for all that McCarthy business. Frank, not Marv. That sonofabitch. McCarthy, not Sinatra." There was a pause. "Do you want to come over, Dollface?"

"I'm in Las Vegas."

Blah clucked her tongue. "Christ on a crutch, you just said that. I swear, this old tackle box of a head is nothing more than tangled up lines, lures, and sinkers. Getting old is for the goddamn birds."

Sewanee smiled. "I'll come by on Monday for lunch, okay?"

"I wouldn't if I were you. It's chicken salad day."

"I love you, Blah. See you Monday."

"Love you, Dollface. Now go have fun. You're only young and beautiful once. Make the most of it."

"We'll see—"

"Do it, Swan!" There was a pause. "When can I see you?"

Sewanee took a patient breath. "How about Monday?"

"What's today?"

"Saturday."

"Perfect! Though, fair warning, Monday's chicken salad day." She made kissing sounds into the phone and hung up.

The waitress appeared with the bill (tucked like a bookmark into a real hardcover—*Jane Eyre*, she noted) and Sewanee thanked her. She took another sip, leaned over the low table, opened the book, and heard, from above:

"Hi."

CHAPTER FIVE

"The Notorious Rake"

SHE LOOKED UP. A RATHER STRIKING MAN STARED DOWN AT HER, hands on his hips. "Uh. Hi."

"You can't be leaving. We just met."

Now *that* was a smile. It rendered the cheesy line charming.

Oh, God. Swan wasn't ready for this. This lanky-limbed, broad-shouldered, tanned-wrinkles-at-the-corners-of-his-eyes, eight-o'clock-shadowed, tall-iced-umbrella'd-cocktail of a man.

She made a point of looking back at the bill, but he said, "May I?" and before she could answer, he sat down on the opposite end of the long chesterfield, leaving a respectful distance between them. "Cheers," he said, and for a stupid moment she thought he was toasting her. But when she looked up at him, he was gazing out into the room. "It's crowded, yeah?" And she realized he hadn't been toasting her; he was British. Cheers as in: thanks. Cheers as in: I don't need your permission, but I'm a gentleman so I asked anyway. Cheers as in: buckle up, toots.

Sewanee returned to the bill, but he loomed in her peripheral. She took a swig of her drink and set it down.

He signaled to the waitress. He unbuttoned the jacket of a nice suit. He loosened his oxblood tie. He shifted his body toward her, tucking one foot behind the opposite knee, throwing an arm over the back of the couch. He moved with a feline simplicity, a traffic cop expertly directing cars in multiple directions, all while asking, "What are you drinking, then?"

Hearing more of the accent, Sewanee revised her previous assessment. Irish.

Maybe she'd been jaded by men like Chuck and Jimbo and the others that came before them, but her defenses were up. So she adopted the accent of the girl at the panel, giving herself some distance, some cover. "Gin."

"A dry gin, it seems."

She glanced at her glass on the table in front of her. It was empty. She'd finished it.

"Vegas bars. Charging for air."

Sewanee bit back the grin she felt beginning. She sought something else to focus on. There were only so many times she could examine a bill. But then Mr. What-the-Hell-Is-Happening asked, "What would you say to a quick drink?"

"Actually," she began, uncrossing her legs only to cross them again, this time away from him, "I have to—"

"It's all I'm good for." The waitress appeared. "Seriously." He gave the waitress *that* smile. "What's the news, lass?" Then, back to Sewanee, "Gin martini, is it?"

The waitress picked up Sewanee's glass. "She's actually having the Last Word."

He looked at Sewanee. Directly at her. "As she should. And so shall I."

The waitress paused. "You know what it is, right? I mean, she's the first person to order it in months. It's—"

"Equal parts green Chartreuse, lime juice, and maraschino liqueur—do you use Luxardo? The Luxardo family's been making it since 1821—oh, and one of their little black cherries for garnish."

Sewanee grinned to cover her surprise and drawled, "You forgot the gin."

"Just giving you the last word."

This guy's smirk put a young Harrison Ford on notice.

Sewanee passed her the signed receipt, including an excessive happy-holidays-someone-else-is-paying tip, and the waitress said, "Carter will bring them right out."

She left and Sewanee sat back on the couch, deciding to enjoy this, whatever this was. "You're good."

"Engh, I'm an arse, I promise, just wait."

Maybe it was his easy manner. Maybe it was the broad chest underneath that dress shirt. Maybe it was the accent, even for her, someone who could do the accent herself. Maybe it was as simple as a nice man in a nice suit. There were a few reasons this was working for her.

But why was it working for *him*? Why had he chosen her? She realized her hair had fallen forward in a way that obscured her eye patch. She hadn't done it intentionally. What was intentional, however, was how she deliberately pushed her hair back now. She faced him head-on, hiding nothing, challenging everything.

He didn't flinch. He didn't blink. He just smiled again. "So, whaddaya say we get to know each other a wee bit?" He gazed out into the bar and said, dryly, "Or we can find the nearest chapel, as you're obviously mad for me."

She snorted.

"Right, I'll go first. Here's what you'll be wanting to know." He shifted his body in a way that effortlessly brought him closer to her. "I'm flying to Dublin in three hours. My bag is checked with the host and I'm happy to show you the claim ticket, if you wish. That takes care of any possible funny business. I'm here for one drink with a beautiful woman to distract me from the disaster that was today. Las Vegas is supposed to be craic, yeah? Well, I've been here thirty-six hours and it's been absolute shite for the entirety of them."

"It hasn't been great to me, either."

Vindicated, he slapped his knee. "It's false advertising is what it is!"

"You want to speak to Vegas's manager?"

"Nah. This is the chat I'm wanting to have." There was a brief someone-say-something moment and a narrow-shouldered, elvish-looking server appeared and set their drinks down. "Impeccable timing, mate." The server blushed slightly. This man's effect was universal. He turned to Sewanee, lifted his glass. "To . . ." His face went blank. "Vegas? No, that's idiotic. To life? No, that's horrid. To . . ."

Sewanee leaned forward, caught his eye. "To," she said.

He smiled again. "We'll leave it at that, then. To."

They clinked glasses and took a thoughtful sip. When they were done, she set down her glass, looked at him. Raised her eyebrow. *Well?* He gazed steadily back at her. A verdict had been reached. "Perfect. I believe I'm in love," he said, right at her.

Something deep inside of Sewanee twitched, once, like the flank of a hibernating bear. She looked away. The Irishman brought her back to him, setting down his drink and reaching out his hand. "Nick."

She took his hand, debated for about half a second. "Alice."

This wasn't real. None of this was real. She didn't feel like herself tonight so why should she *be* herself tonight? He had a good handshake. He had good fingers. She checked them for a ring. Only one, on the middle finger of his right hand. Odd placement, but safe.

She pulled back and reached immediately for her drink again. "Where are you from?" she asked. Although she had adopted the accent of that girl from the panel, she was careful to leave out the nasality and grating uptalk because . . . just no.

"Ireland." At her eye roll, he chuckled. "That obvious? Dublin."

Sewanee cocked her head at him. "North or South?" He cocked his head at her. "Your accent."

He smiled wider. "What about it?"

"It's muddled." Honestly, Ron's vampire Seamus sounded more authentic.

"Well, if you must know, Henry Higgins, I grew up all over the place. Divorced parents." He plucked up his drink, took another sip. "You?"

"Texas."

He made a doubting face. "Sounds more like East Virginia to me."

"Do you think there's a state called East Virginia?"

"Well," he said, taking another sip. "There's a West Virginia."

This shouldn't have been as charming as it was. But a few Last Words in . . .

BlahBlah was right. Swan should make the most of it. She was in a designer dress, perfectly coiffed, Adaku would be back in four hours, and he was leaving in three. It was a Cinderella-at-the-ball situation. Everything would be over by midnight, but in the meantime . . . do it, Swan.

"I know I said one drink, but I'm thinking we've got more to say. Shall we get another round started?" Nick asked her.

If Adaku were perched on her shoulder, Sewanee knew exactly what she'd say right now: Him!

"Hold that thought." She picked up her phone. "I just got a text." She hadn't. She pretended to read it. She didn't. "Ah. My friend. She can't make it to dinner. Bummer." She looked back at Nick and something passed briefly across his eyes. Nothing meaningful, but something all the same. He looked away, held the coupe glass up to the light emanating from the crystal chandelier above them, and rolled the stem between two of those fingers. Then he plucked up the toothpick sitting in the drink, put it to his mouth. He slowly slid the black cherry off with his lips.

"So," she heard herself say, "I have a reservation at a place with tremendously thick steaks and bottles of wine that cost more than my monthly car payment and I'm going to charge everything to my friend's expense account." She quickly added, "She told me to. In the text. I would never just do something like—" *stop talking* "—do you have the time to join me?"

Nick smoothly turned, caught the server's eye. "Check, please, thank you so much." He looked back at Sewanee, toothpick rolling to a languid stop in the right corner of his mouth. "I'm starving."

She picked up her own toothpick, considered the cherry. "Me too," she said, and slid it into her mouth with her teeth.

CHAPTER SIX

"What Happens in Vegas"

"SO, NICK. WHAT DO YOU DO?"

He had just put the last shrimp into his mouth. "Best shrimp cocktail I've ever had." He apparently had no problem speaking with his mouth full, another thing Sewanee found inexplicably charming.

She chuckled and leaned back. "So good."

Nick swallowed and leaned forward earnestly. "*So* good. And as large as baby lobsters. Big shrimp! The most delicious oxymoron."

Yes, inexplicably charming.

A busboy cleared away the destroyed remains of the appetizer and Sewanee appreciated how the candlelight danced on the table's glass top. She appreciated Nick's toned forearms resting on it, revealed after he'd pushed his sleeves back when the food arrived. She appreciated the swimmy feeling in her head, the glint in Nick's hazel eyes, the way her body felt in a dress she'd never buy.

Before she could reiterate her question, the sommelier arrived with a bottle of wine. He poured a splash into a large Bordeaux glass and nudged it to Nick, who passed it to Sewanee, wordlessly correcting the somm's gendered assumptions about who was making the decisions tonight. She thrilled at the simple gesture and said to the sommelier, "Can he have some, too?"

"Certainly!"

Once Nick was holding a glass, they tipped them toward each other, gave a delicate swirl, breathed in the aroma, and took a sip. There was a pause as they chewed the wine. They swallowed in sync, the way two people would reach for the other's hand simultaneously.

They said, at the same time, "Wow." They laughed. Then repeated, louder, "Wow," and laughed again.

Sewanee looked back to the sommelier. "Amazing. Thank you. Would you decant it, please?"

"Of course. Right away." He left them.

Sewanee finished her taster and sighed happily, giving silent thanks to Adaku.

Nick watched her. "Decant it, eh?" He took the rest of the wine into his mouth.

"It's a bit tight. It needs to open." She watched him swallow. "So what is it you do?"

"Why are Americans always asking, 'what do you do?'"

Sewanee grabbed some bread out of the basket and slathered it with what the waiter had described as "malted ghee." She suspected it was just honey butter. "It fills the gaps in conversation."

"Thank God for that, because uncomfortable silences have been a real bother tonight."

There hadn't been any lull in the conversation. They'd bantered and prodded and downright delighted each other for the last hour.

The sommelier returned with their decanter, poured two healthy glasses, and left again.

"I'd think," Nick said, taking a sip, "asking 'what do you like to do' would be a better way of actually getting to know someone."

Sewanee cocked an eyebrow. "Bless your heart. Stop evading."

Nick guffawed. "I'm not evading! It'll just bore you." He grabbed some bread. "I work for a VC that buys and sells companies."

"So, finance."

"Now, try and contain your excitement, please, I'm not done yet." Nick leaned in, mock-whispering, "I'm the closer. It takes a good amount of charm to close a deal and in case you hadn't noticed, I'm quite charming."

"I hadn't, no."

"Huh, it's usually the first thing people notice about me." Grinning, he took another swallow of wine. "What's the first thing people notice about you?"

"My wit," Sewanee deadpanned.

"It is wonderfully dry." He held up his glass. "Like a fine wine. But it wasn't the first thing *I* noticed about you."

"No?" Sewanee drawled.

"No. First thing I noticed was your mouth."

Sewanee ignored the hum that went through her at that. "Really."

Nick paused with the glass at his lips, looked thoughtfully out into the restaurant. "No, you're right. It was your legs. Your head was down at the time. So, chronologically . . ." He looked at Sewanee over the rim of his glass.

She leveled her gaze at him. "You can ask."

"What do *you* do?"

"Not that. Go ahead. Ask about the eye patch you've so graciously avoided asking about."

Nick looked baffled. "I haven't avoided asking about it, or anything else for that matter. It wasn't a topic of conversation. Much like your legs, which hadn't come up until a moment ago."

She could see why he was good at what he did.

He continued easily, buttering his bread, "An accessory? A statement piece? Like a fake tattoo or lens-less spectacles? This is Vegas, after all."

"No."

"All right, then. Not temporary?"

"No."

"Well, then."

There was a silence. The first true silence between them.

Sewanee leaned forward. "You're not curious?"

Nick shrugged, pouring them both more wine. "'Course I'm curious. The same way I'm curious about what's under that dress, because it's you and I'm curious about you, but satisfying that curiosity isn't in the cards for us tonight." He set the decanter down and stared at the tabletop for a moment.

"Can I say, though?" He leaned so far forward their faces were less than a foot apart. And then he looked up at her. His eyes had brown flecks. "Cover up whatever you please for the world, but in intimacy? Hide nothing. In intimacy, everything is beautiful. So, what *do* you do?"

Sewanee didn't hear the question. That is, she heard individual words that formed a question, but she didn't hear what was asked. It came to her on a delay. In the ensuing silence, she picked up her glass and took a drink, *mmm*-ing about the wine, stalling, regrouping.

She had already given him a false name and Texas twang. It was too late to drop the charade, so she continued the deception. "I work in publishing." She knew enough about books and how they worked. She *did* sort of work in publishing, after all. She could sustain this until he left. "I'm an editor."

"Ooh. Clever lass. And what kind of books do you edit?" She sighed, debating whether she truly wanted to go down this road. Nick interpreted the sigh differently. "Are you about to bore *me* now? What are they? Technical manuals? Microbiology text-books? Something horribly dry, like that wit of yours?"

"The opposite, actually."

"Can't say I've ever heard of a wet read." He took another sip of wine.

There was nowhere to go but straight ahead. "I edit Romance novels."

He nearly did a spit take. He swallowed roughly and choked out, "Grand."

Their steaks appeared. Food, yes. Food was a good idea. She'd lost track of how much she'd had to drink.

"Jaysus," Nick murmured, cutting into his steak, "you are a curious one. Where on earth did you come from?"

"East Virginia."

He laughed and pointed his steak-tipped fork at her. "So, let me get this straight." He popped the bite into his mouth and groaned lasciviously. The sound did not go unnoticed. "By Romance novels, do you mean . . . oh, who's your man with all the movies? *The Notebook* guy."

"Nicholas Sparks. No. He writes love stories."

"Love. Romance. What's the difference?"

Sewanee was kicking herself already. Why? Why had she done this? "So, there's Fiction, right? Love stories are fiction."

"I'll say," Nick said wryly.

Sewanee laughed. "Just remember: you asked. So, under the umbrella of Fiction, there's Women's Fiction. Usually written by women, about . . . life. You can win, you can lose, you can die. You know, real, human things universal to everyone."

"Then why the hell's it called Women's Fiction?" Off Sewanee's pursed lips, Nick nodded. "Right. Sexism. Continue."

"Then there's Romance. There has to be two things for Fiction to be considered Romance."

"Is there going to be a test later, because I don't have a pen."

"One: there has to be a happy ending. Boy gets girl, boy loses girl, boy gets girl back. Usually some groveling is involved. The beast is tamed, all obstacles are overcome, true love finds a way."

"A fairy tale."

"Exactly," Sewanee murmured, thinking briefly of the panel earlier today. Which somehow felt like a decade ago. "In fact, there's an acronym for it. HEA."

"Happily ever after?"

Sewanee smiled and took a bite of steak. "Who needs a pen?"

Nick chewed thoughtfully. "Are they popular, these Romance novels?"

"They make up about thirty-five percent of all fiction sold."

He snapped his head back. "I should be publishing Romance novels! Know any good editors?" He glanced at his plate. "This steak, by the way."

"It's obscene."

"It's a testament to your company I'm even talking right now and not dragging this off into the corner like a feral hyena." Sewanee laughed and took another decadent bite. "And what's the second thing? About Romance novels?"

"It has to be about two people falling in love." Sewanee paused, remembering some of the books she'd recorded as Sarah. "Well, actually, now it can involve more than two people. But it has to be about love."

Nick thought about this. Tapped his empty fork on his plate. "How's that different from a love story in Women's Fiction?"

"The HEA."

"Right. So, Women's Fiction can't end happily?"

She was so out of her depth here. She whirled her hand, reached for her wine. "The lines are blurred—it depends. It's about marketing. Mostly." She had no idea if that was true.

"That's it?"

"Well." She swallowed. "Also. Usually—not always, but almost always—I mean, it's what the genre's known for, but *usually* . . ." Now he was peering at her. "There's sex. On the page. Lots and lots of page sex."

"Ohhhhhh." He elongated the vowel to the point of absurdity. "Smut. Trash. Filth. Heaving bosoms. Throbbing members and the like."

"We've stopped using euphemisms in the last thirty years, but—"

"The kind of books your spinster aunt wraps in a paper bag and tucks away in her nightstand drawer?"

Sewanee shook her head. "You'd be surprised who reads these books." She took another sip of wine. "You know who *should* read these books? Men. If they really wanted to understand what makes women tick."

Nick wiped his mouth with his napkin. "Or we could just ask. What makes you tick, Alice?"

Sewanee cycled through possible replies in her head, all sarcastic. Then she stilled. She didn't have an answer. It had been too long to know. So she deflected. "What makes *you* tick?"

"Curiosity," he answered without hesitation. "I don't understand people who stop. Who go, I'm good right here, no more for me, ta. You know that parable, the bloke dying of thirst who goes to the well?"

"And won't risk looking into it to see if there's water, because he couldn't live with the disappointment?"

"So he dies of thirst. *Womp womp.* Me? I'd be looking in that well for sure. I have this painting—and I'm not one of those art people, but I have this one painting—of a path that disappears 'round a bend. Because I always have to go 'round the bend. *Must* do."

"Like the next page of a novel."

"Like the offer of dinner with a beautiful woman."

"God, you're good."

"A woman who says, with oblivious innocence, 'It's a bit tight. It needs to open.'"

Sewanee's brow furrowed. "Well, it was. It did."

"Ay. But you can bet I wasn't thinking of the wine when you said it." He looked quickly at her dress then had the grace to look away. He muttered, almost to himself, "If I knew you better I s'pose I'd be ashamed." After a moment, he dared to look at her. "But I don't. And I'm not."

Sewanee unconsciously licked her lips. "Well. To assuage your curiosity? I am and I don't." The retort flowed from her as smoothly as the wine from the decanter.

Nick stilled, untangling her comeback. She saw the moment it clicked. His eyes bulged and an uncontrolled laugh burst out of him. "Jaysus." He threw his napkin on the table and slow clapped. "I'm done. You win."

"Were we playing a game?"

"Always."

"And you like to win?"

"Who doesn't?"

Smiling, they both sipped their wine. She saw him glance at his watch and said, before she thought better of it, "Do you have to go?" She was surprised to find her voice hoarse. She quietly cleared her throat. Good thing she didn't have to record tomorrow; nothing dried her voice out like red wine.

"Not this second. But soon."

Resigned, Sewanee signaled the waiter for the check.

"I'm curious," Nick said. "Do they talk to each other in these Romance novels of yours or just get straight down to business?"

"Of course there's talking. Talking is foreplay. The other stuff doesn't work without the talking."

He smiled slowly. "You don't say."

FULL OF STEAK, truffled potatoes, and Margaux, Sewanee and Nick giggled their way out of the restaurant and onto the casino floor. Nick dragged his weekender roller bag and slim briefcase behind him. On impulse, she looped her arm through his, just another couple strolling through a Vegas casino, slightly over-dressed, slightly drunk, slightly inclined to make bad decisions. Then something caught Sewanee's attention and she slowed.

Nick followed her gaze. "Are you wanting to play?"

She bit her lip. "I'm not sure. I mean, I came with five hundred dollars and told myself I'd make one bet. All of it on red or black."

"Right." He moved toward the roulette table. "I want to see which one you choose."

She tugged him to a stop. "I think I'm a little too tipsy to enjoy the win. And not tipsy enough to handle the loss." She moved to leave.

He didn't budge. "C'mere to me and listen?" She nodded benevolently. He took a breath. "This isn't dire. This isn't life and death. Either way you're walking away from the table. The excitement's in the play, yeah? That's what we're doing here." He stepped closer. "You came with five hundred dollars to lose. You could have lost it in the jacks, slipped out of a pocket, into the toilet, never to be seen again." He paused, gazed into her eye. "Surely you've lost more important things before than five hundred dollars."

For a moment, she blinked at him. Then she said, "You're right, you are an arse," and walked straight to the table.

She opened her purse, pulled out a small billfold, took out the whole of the cash in it. *Do it, Swan.* She put the bills on the table and the croupier changed them into chips. "Place your bets, place your bets," he called.

Nick came up behind her, the front of his body hovering like a polarized magnet at her back. Without hesitation, she put all her chips on red. Nick whispered in her ear, "Win or lose?" She would have answered immediately were it not for his voice traveling from her ear, down the inside of her neck, dropping into her chest cavity with a free-falling thunk and then pooling, seeping, into the part of her that had been swelling since dinner. She found her voice. "Win or lose."

The croupier took the little white ball and released it with a practiced flourish. "Final bets, please."

They watched the ball go around.

"No more bets, no more bets."

As the ball circled the wheel, Sewanee felt Nick inch further forward. "Why red?" he murmured.

"The steak. The wine. Your tie. My lips."

The ball circled.

Around.

Around.

Around.

As the ball slowed, she leaned further over. It bounced around; black 35; red 7; green 00; black 17; red 14. And stopped.

Red 14.

Sewanee didn't jump up and down. She didn't scream. She simply turned to Nick, eye wide, lips parted, and said, softly, "That was incredible."

That made him laugh. "You're incredible."

She kissed him. It began as a *thank you* kiss, something pure and almost infantile.

But it lasted long enough to reach puberty.

Nick moved deeper into her as though they had known each other for years, his hands finding hers at her sides, his mouth soft and firm and warm and powerful and everything good she'd forgotten existed in this world.

When he pulled away and she opened her eye, she found him smiling down at her. "You should collect your winnings," he whispered.

"I already did."

His laugh propelled them apart. The croupier exchanged Sewanee's chips for a single $1,000 one that she dropped into her purse. Nick took her arm, steering her toward a quieter corner of the casino. Well, as quiet as a Las Vegas casino corner could be on a Saturday night.

They were both breathing heavily. His eyes looked slightly glassy and his tie was askew and her legs shook a bit and just as she said, "I don't want you to go," he said, "I don't want to go."

They broke. They laughed. Kept laughing. They laughed so hard, they bent at the waist. She pushed him gently, so he pushed her back and she tottered in her heels, crashed into a swiveling leather chair in front of a slot machine, which just made them laugh harder. Why? This wasn't funny. Nothing about this was funny.

But it was playful. It was sexy. It was a level of intimacy she had imagined, but never experienced.

Seconds ticked by. A minute. Their breathing steadied. They straightened. Nick stepped toward her and took her face in his hands. They smiled weakly at each other.

Eventually his hands fell to her shoulders. "I'm guessing you don't often find yourself in Dublin?"

She shook her head. She had to remind herself to use the Texas accent when she answered: "I've never found myself anywhere."

She heard how this sounded, so added, "Never been there, actually."

He seemed to come out of a trance. He slid his hands down her arms and dropped contact. He took another breath.

She cupped her elbows, holding herself, suddenly cold. "Maybe this is better," she said.

"How's that?"

"Maybe this is the whole story. I mean, what are the chances?"

"Of what?"

"Of this being as good as we imagine it would be."

He grinned at her. "But what if it were?"

She bit her lip.

Roys she could handle. Chuck and Jimbos—Jim and Chuckbos?—she could deal with. Nick was singular. Entirely uncharted waters.

On the one hand, Sewanee was ready for him to go, for the evening to end. Curtain closes, house lights come on, makeup comes off. On the other hand, she was ready to drop the phony accent, the fictitious persona, and make everything real. Curtain opens, lights dim, everything comes off.

But that was impossible.

So instead, she said, "How would you write the rest of the story?"

"Whaddaya mean?"

She stepped forward. "There *is* a quiz."

He pointed a finger at her. "I knew I needed a pen."

"What's the Women's Fiction ending? And what's the Romance one?"

He laughed. "Right. Grand. Here goes." He took a deep breath. "Women's Fiction—I want it on record I still hate the name."

"Get in line."

He paused. "I wrestle with my decision to leave. I'll hate myself forever, but I do it. I probably have a fiancée. And there's probably a war on. We live completely different lives, struggle with the unfairness of it all."

Sewanee was smiling so wide her jaw ached.

"Thirty years later, we cross paths." He gestured at the casino. "We're back here. So much has happened. So much sacrificed. And yet, here we are, together at last."

Sewanee tilted her head. "*Engh*," she began, but Nick held up a hand.

"But. I've some mysterious disease for which there's no known cure. And I *die*. No HEA!" Smiling victoriously, he held out his hands as if he'd set a beautiful table and wanted her approval.

Sewanee chortled. "Bravo! And the Romance version?"

"This one's easy." He stepped closer. "I blow off my flight. We go upstairs. What happens is . . . well." He whispered huskily, "Page sex." She laughed. "A fantasy come to life, isn't it? Next day, we part, but you . . . you're preggo, aren't ya? Cut to: One Year Later. A job across the pond. You bundle up your—our—infant son and show up to your first day of work and your new boss is, wait for it now . . . me. Shocking, I know. You don't tell me about our son—I don't know why, exactly, but you don't—and we agree to conduct ourselves properly at work. Then. One day. My desire overtakes me and I want, nay, I *must* have you."

Sewanee giggled, her cheeks pinking. Nick stepped even closer. "I drag you into my office. Lock the door. Sweep everything off the desk, all man-like, lots of growling. I pick you up, set you down on it, right there on the edge. I push up that skirt that's been driving me mad, open your—"

"Okay, okay, Mr. Fast Learner. I get the picture."

"You sure?"

"Tease."

"You have no idea."

Sewanee took the deepest of breaths. "Then what?"

"Well. After that there's no way you can continue to work for me. So you quit. I chase after you and . . ." He looked past her shoulder, thinking. "And . . . I offer you money—because I'm a billionaire, of course—money to start the nonprofit you've dreamed of starting. Something with kittens. But then I hear, off in another room . . . Is that the cry of a forlorn kitten? Or is that a *baby*?!"

"Oh no," Sewanee gasped.

"You have a *baby*?! You slut!"

"I tell you it's yours."

"Jaysus no, not yet. Because you see how I react and I'm an utter wanker—sorry, I forgot to mention that—"

"It was implied, it's always implied."

"So I go to my penthouse or castle or some shite and drink myself absolutely rat-arsed. And then . . . and then . . ." Nick blinked helplessly at her.

"You have a brother."

"I have a brother! A billionaire brother! And . . . ?"

"And he knows the truth about the baby."

". . . How?"

"Because you work together—"

"At the money factory!"

"And after meeting me he puts two and two together."

". . . How?"

"Because."

"Right. And I finally realize the error of my ways and I come beg your forgiveness."

"Grovel!"

"I come *grovel* your forgiveness."

"And I accept your grovel. Because all my dreams have come true."

"And we fix everything that was ever wrong with us and we live—"

"Happily. Ever. After," they finished in unison.

"Grand," Nick breathed, looking at her in a way that made Sewanee feel like his hands were everywhere on her body at once. She held his gaze. Then he looked down at his shoes. Then at his watch. Then he stuck out his hand. "Alice."

She took it. "Nick."

"I leave you as I found you."

Hardly, Sewanee thought.

Nick stopped a passing cocktail waitress. "Excuse me? Which door do I go out of to get a taxi?"

"Where are you headed?" she asked.

"Airport."

"Not tonight you're not."

"Pardon?"

"Airport's closed. Can I get you something to drink?"

"What? No, no thank you, what do you mean the airport's closed?"

"Snow. Can you believe it?"

"Sorry, *snow*?"

Sewanee stepped over. "Since when does it snow in Las Vegas?"

"Like, never," the waitress replied. "Last time I was in first grade and we got a snow day. It was awesome."

Nick and Sewanee both took out their phones.

"The airline sent a text an hour ago." He looked at his luggage as if it might have more information. "I need to get a room."

"Ooh, yeah, that's not gonna happen." The waitress rested her tray on a cocked hip. "Just heard we're sold out tonight."

"What? How?"

"Take a fight night at MGM, Beyoncé in concert, and that book convention thing and the town's nearly at capacity. Cancel a few hundred flights on top of that?" At Nick's stricken look, she tapped his forearm. "You want that drink now?"

"No, no thank you."

"Well, casino'll be poppin' all night! Good luck!" She beamed and left.

Sewanee, still looking at her phone, mumbled, "All flights are canceled. In and out. My friend can't leave LAX."

Nick raked a hand through his hair. "I haven't pulled an all-nighter since uni." He laughed. "Snow?! Really?"

"Okay," Sewanee muttered, putting away her phone. "I'm about to do something and I don't want you to take it in any way that could be . . . whatever. I have a room."

He raised an eyebrow. "Is this your turn at the Romance version?" She snorted. "Let me guess. There's one very small bed."

"Two, actually. Very large beds. In very large rooms. Very large separate rooms. It's all very large. Hotel-room-from–*Rain Man* large." She impulsively created a bit more space between them. "I'm comfortable offering you a place for the night. But only if you're comfortable."

"I'm comfortable. But are you comfortable? You're awful kind, but are you—"

"The place is so big I could be sleeping in another state. It's fine. I'm fine. If you're fine."

"I'm fine!"

"Then we're good." Sewanee straightened. "You're good?"

"Good." Nick nodded. "After you."

He followed Sewanee through the casino and around the bend.

SHE LET NICK enter the suite first. The butler had been by to turn on some lights. Low. Moody. Sexy. Nick took in the expanse of the room before taking in the view. He smirked at her. "This'll do, I s'pose."

He ventured deeper into the space, into the living room, his broad back silhouetted against the window. "It's a bit magical, isn't it?"

"Yes," she answered as she moved toward him, rounded his right side, and looked out into the neon night. The flashing colors of the city, like gels on theater lights, continuously shifted the tint of their faces. They stood side by side, staring out the floor-to-ceiling windows. Beyond the ghosts of their own reflections, the Strip lay sprawled, a white blanket collecting over it. Soft flakes confettied from the sky. It was a sight Sewanee knew she would never forget.

Nick murmured, "I want to say something. Something profound. Poetic. Spirit of my ancestors and such. But for the first time tonight, I have no words."

"You've run out of foreplay?"

"Cheeky." More silence. "It looks like a pointillist painting, doesn't it? That's it. That's all I've got."

"Well. Que Seurat, Seurat."

He threw back his head. Then his laugh melted like the snow hitting the window, sliding down the glass, and she watched, in the refracted reflection, his eyes slide down her body in kind. "I'm fairly confident this is as close as I'll ever come to being in one of your novels," he murmured. "This must be some sort of trope, yeah?" He waved his hand about, taking in the room, the lights, the falling snow. Her.

She continued looking out. She felt as though everything she was wearing—every last thing—had slipped off her. She had never felt this way. She had always wished she would. "Guess what it's called."

"Something epic, I'm sure. Divine Providence? Celestial Intervention?"

She chuckled. She finally turned to face him. "It's called Snowed In."

PART 2

Forget your personal tragedy. We are all bitched from the start and you especially have to be hurt like hell before you can write seriously. But when you get the damned hurt, use it—don't cheat with it.

—Ernest Hemingway

It's always the men, isn't it, talking about writing from a place of pain. Maybe try writing from joy. We get it, the world is hard. Which is precisely why I write: to escape it. Calm down with this tortured artist shit already, my God.

—June French in *Cosmopolitan*

CHAPTER SEVEN

"The Offer"

SEWANEE CARRIED THE LAST TWO BOXES OF KEURIG PODS INTO Mark's garage. His beloved Karmann Ghia, Sal, took up one side and the other had two shelving units with a narrow pathway between them. Every inch accounted for, like an aisle in a New York grocery store. The shelves were stocked with paper goods, bottles of caffeine-delivery-vehicles, bulk bins of assorted snacks, and spare recording components: extra mics, cables, preamps, mixers.

As Sewanee slid the boxes onto the uppermost shelf, standing on tiptoe to do it, the tightening of her calves and arching of her feet sent a rush through her body. Her eye fell closed and she was lying in cool sheets, back bowed, her head turned to the side in pleasure, watching the snow fall outside. She opened her eye and the snow was still falling, right there in the garage.

Dust. Dust from the disturbed shelf.

Telling herself to get a grip, she quickly finished her task and walked through the connecting door into Mark's house.

"Mark's studio" was perhaps more accurate. His personal living space had been reduced to one room off the kitchen that housed a queen bed and a desk almost as large. The rest of his home was all business. A kitchen with two Keurigs, three microwaves, a kettle on the stove and an electric one on the counter, an entire cabinet of tea, snacks laid out daily by Sewanee, and what felt like hundreds of cups to her, the person responsible for cleaning them. There was an oversized fridge, full of every kind of milk and milk substitute, condiments and sauces, and a produce bin consisting entirely of the audiobook narrator's secret antidote to mouth noise: green apples. No one knew why they worked (Acidity? Tannins?), but they did. Alice had once proposed they all get green apple tattoos until someone—probably Mark—had pointed out green blobs would look like a disease.

Each of the four bedrooms upstairs had a booth and sound-board in them. The living and family rooms had been taken over with workstations for the editors and engineers Mark kept on staff. Even now, on a Sunday night, there was a low-level buzz of activity as two editors hunched over their desks, headphones on, reading along to the recording they were listening to; stopping when they noticed a mistake, marking the script, and preparing a package of pickups for the narrator. Sewanee noticed the newer engineer tapping out a perfect drum beat on his thigh with a pencil while listening to the recording. So, another musician, then. This was not unusual. Most sound engineers came into the industry through the music door.

All these guys (they were mostly guys) were young and enjoyed the communal friendliness of the studio. Of being above it all in the Hollywood Hills, of grabbing a drink with the others down on Franklin before heading home. More than one band had formed in Mark's living room over the years.

Most days, Sewanee felt like a House Mother at a frat. If the frat were full of nice, mildly-alt sound nerds.

She passed by the two editors without being noticed. That changed when Mark called out from his office, "Swan!" He'd heard the garage door. He heard everything.

She walked into his bedroom/office and found his lanky, sinewy-fit form sitting at his desk, casted foot propped up, peering at his computer monitor over the tops of his wire-frame glasses.

"Hi!" she chirped. "I stopped by Costco on the way home from the airport, replenished the K-Cups. I went to the one they opened up on Sherman Way? Man, that whole area is growing, huh? And how great is it flying into Burbank? I don't know why anyone would ever use LAX. How's the foot?"

Now he was peering at *her.* "Is this caffeine or cocaine?"

"I'm excited to see you is all."

"And I'm excited to see you."

"So." She swallowed. "I'm sure you'd like me to catch you up on Vegas."

Mark exhaled sharply. His face turned somber. "Just unbelievable."

Sewanee stilled. "What do you mean?"

He shook his head. "So tragic."

"What?"

"What? It's all over the news!"

"The snow?"

"The snow? No, the actress!"

Sewanee grabbed a chair and sat down. "Okay, seriously: What are you talking about?"

"I don't have all the details, but some wannabe actress went thirty-eight floors and didn't take the elevator, if you know what I mean."

Sewanee's mouth opened, but nothing came out.

Mark continued, "All they know so far is she was there for the convention. I think they said she was from East Texas. I can't believe you don't know about this."

A few words spattered out. "I . . . I didn't—I don't know what to say."

"Well, she did! Apparently she was screaming all the way down, 'Happily ever after is bullshit!'"

Oscillating between suspicion and panic, Sewanee sputtered, "Wait—you are—did—how—what—"

Mark burst out laughing. His full swoop of silver hair flopped into his face; his Clint Eastwood crow's-feet crinkled.

Sewanee crumpled over in the chair. "You asshole! You absolute raging asshole!" She snapped her head up. "How did you know about her?"

Mark wiped at the tears in his eyes. "Alice was in this morning and told me about your little exchange. I couldn't resist."

"God, you are such a dick!" She stood up. "I have work to do." She started for the door.

"You make it too easy! Wait, don't leave yet, I have something to talk to you about."

"That's okay, I already own a piece of the Brooklyn Bridge." She continued out the door.

"Swan! I'm serious, come back. I'm sorry, but it was payback. Remember your little tour de force last month? 'Mark, oh my God, did you see Sal's passenger side?' You know how I feel about my Ghia. Now we're even."

She turned around and stomped back into his office, striking a defiant pose in front of him, arms crossed. "What?"

"Have a seat."

"I'm fine standing."

"Good, I want you to stand."

In spite of herself, she huffed a laugh. This was their relationship. They played, they poked, they tested, but they were there for each other whenever either needed it. Or simply wanted it. They had done more for each other than either would ever say, mostly because they didn't have to. They worked because they loved each other the way two people could when attraction was off the table.

"You got an offer," Mark said.

"Okay?" This wasn't unusual. Most of the time, offers came to her directly, but occasionally someone couldn't find her and they reached out to Mark. But the way he was smiling made her suspicious. "What?"

"It's . . . fitting."

She knew. She just knew. "It's a Romance novel, isn't it."

"Yes. But no."

"Mark."

"I'm not being cagey. It's just different." He clasped his hands. "You remember June French?"

"Of course. She gave me my start. Back when I did Romance. Which I no longer do."

"She died recently."

"You're clearly very broken up about it."

"You knew?"

"I knew. But can you imagine if I didn't and that's the way you told me?"

"You're not gonna make this easy, are you?"

"After *your* little tour de force, no."

He rolled his eyes. "Well, her very-much-alive producer reached out. There's a project she penned that never saw the light of day. She had wanted Sarah Westholme to—"

"Still don't do Romance."

"Swan, hear me out." He leaned forward, brought up the e-mail on his computer, cleared his throat, and dipped into his narrator voice. The voice that read political histories to the masses. The beloved voice of Dad Literature everywhere. "'Dear Mark, my name is Jason Ruiz and I am working with June French's estate to produce an audio version of her final project. I am trying to get in touch with one of June's narrators, Sarah Westholme. I've been told you might be able to connect us.'"

"If only I still did Romance."

"Shhhh. 'It's a bit outside the box and June wrote it with Sarah in mind. She was June's favorite narrator and also a fan favorite.'"

"That's sweet. But I don't do—"

"Will you shut up?" He was smiling, but he meant it. "'The project will be dual narration. June had intended to serialize this new novel into hour-long episodes released on a weekly basis and distributed through her platform.'"

"Smart," she observed. "Too bad I don't do—"

"I swear to God, Swan— 'The whole series will be around eight hours long, split evenly between Sarah and the male narrator. I am aware Sarah no longer records Romance . . .'" Mark read with strong emphasis, "'but June wanted her one more time for this ambitious and unique project and was prepared to compensate her handsomely.'"

Sewanee sighed. "Mark, you know it's not just about the money."

"Handsomely, Swan. Paul Newman/Robert Redford/the-kid-from-*Outlander* handsomely. This goes way beyond the standard flat session fee."

She threw up her hands, preparing to be unimpressed. "How far beyond?"

Mark went back to the e-mail. "'We are prepared to offer Sarah thirty-three percent of the gross revenue. While we don't know how much this will be, in the interest of full transparency, subscribers will pay ninety-nine cents an episode and we currently have twenty thousand pre-orders and we haven't even announced the narrators yet. We have a commitment from the male narrator . . .'" At this, Mark glanced up, lips smugly pursed, and said, "'Brock McNight, who has never done a June French book before, though fans have clamored for it. I know having these two powerhouses doing the project will increase the downloads exponentially. It is a great sadness that June can't'—yaddyyaddyyahdah—'please forward this to Sarah and I would also ask that you keep this confidential. Thank you for your time. Jason.'" Mark sat back and laced his fingers across his trim stomach. "Your turn."

Sewanee sat back down. She stared at Mark across the desk. He waited. Eventually, she said, "I'm not usually motivated by money, but this . . . I have to admit . . ."

"I did some math, just back-of-the-envelope, and my recommendation? Get motivated."

"I don't do Romance—"

"Say that one more goddamn time—"

"You didn't let me finish! I don't do Romance . . . but I'll think about it."

Mark slapped his desk. "That's all I wanted to hear. Unless you have anything juicy to dish about Vegasland?"

Caught off guard by the topic change, her cheeks flushed traitorously. Mark clocked this, raised his eyebrows. "Ms. Chester!"

Her embarrassment was palpable. "I'm glad I went and I'll leave it at that." She stood up.

Mark raised his hands. "You don't want to tell me about Studman's prowess in the bedroom, you don't have to."

Sewanee's mouth dropped open in mock-outrage. "I told Alice that in *confidence*!" He laughed and she stood for one more moment before saying, "Thank you. For everything. Don't know what I'd do without you."

"Be a broken, sad mess," he said buoyantly.

She turned to leave, but then walked back and hugged him.

ON THE DAYS life prevented Sewanee from getting to the gym, she comforted herself knowing she'd at least walked down from her casita to Mark's house and back up: sixty-four hillside steps each way.

Tonight, she also carried her luggage, so there was that.

She let herself in and flipped on the living room light, set down her suitcase, and ran her sleeve over her brow. She shook off her hoodie and crossed to the sliding door on the opposite side of the room, pulling it open, letting the mild December evening air refresh the tiny space.

She took a moment to step out on the balcony. Mark's house enjoyed a spectacular view of downtown L.A. and the surrounding vista. The guesthouse shared the view, but those sixty-four gym-skipping steps gave her an even greater sense of the expanse.

Hollywood down in front. To the right, the dam of the reservoir peeking out. Further beyond, the twinkling lights of the city. Occasionally, a searchlight at Grauman's Chinese Theatre or the Egyptian or an awards ceremony at the Dolby would scan the sky, but not tonight. It was a quiet Sunday evening. Lines of white headlights and red taillights demarcated Highland and Cahuenga and Vine, all running to and from the 101 freeway like parallel stripes in a tartan plaid. In the distance and slightly to the right, the lights simply disappeared, fell off, giving way to the Pacific. The pièce de résistance laid in wait behind her. She walked to the left side of the balcony and turned around, looking up the hill to the Hollywood sign, looming larger than most people ever got to see it. The sight always made her feel at home.

Tonight, there was a marine layer on the west side and a little smog on this side of town, so the sunset was less a bowl of bright sherbet and more a slowly expanding puddle of spilled strawberry milk shake.

Sewanee never took any of this for granted. It was a view

people paid millions of dollars to see every night and she got it for the bargain price of running the studio.

She went back inside, into the small galley kitchen—still boasting flamingo-pink tiles from the 1930s—and put the kettle on. She went into the cozy living room, turned on the TV, clicked through to the Golf Channel. She quickly unpacked, came back into the kitchen as the kettle began to whistle, and made herself a cup of ginger tea in the Tea-For-One combination cup and mini teapot her mother had given her when she'd graduated from Julliard. Marilyn had wanted her daughter to remember that being alone, being on her own, didn't mean she had to be lonely. It was a symbol of independence and she loved it.

Finally, she settled on her love seat, curled her legs under her, and took stock of her life.

How much could possibly change in twenty-four hours?

She'd once known the answer to that: everything. But this time was different. This time wasn't immediately tangible. This was more like a seed had been planted; the change was in the offing.

She picked up her phone in an effort to change the channel in her brain and noticed she had a WhatsApp message from her mother. She clicked on it.

> Santorini today. Beautiful. Lots of young, drunk people stumbling around. Reminded me of UCLA on the weekends. 😄 Here for a week. Let's video call soon. Love you. Hope Vegas was fun. Did I see it snowed there?

> P.S. Stu is making me send this photo.

Attached was a picture of Marilyn mid-bite of a gigantic gyro. It wasn't flattering, but it was spirited and joyful and Sewanee had such a rush of missing her mom she felt for a moment she had been transported, was sitting at the table, enjoying the fragrance of her mother's cherry blossom perfume.

She checked the time; there was nothing she wanted more than to talk everything through with her mom. Like any mother and daughter, they'd had a long, circuitous, often conflicted journey, but their roads had reconverged just in time for Marilyn to leave on an actual journey. She was happy for her mom, but it was tough in moments like this: it was the middle of the night in Greece and Sewanee was forced to rely on herself.

The job, she thought. Let's start there.

She knew how ridiculous her deliberation was, she'd seen it on Mark's face. She knew any other narrator would open a vein to make this kind of money. Opportunities like this never came along.

So what if she didn't believe in the way Romance novels portrayed life? She wasn't the gatekeeper of reality. She could believe whatever she wanted and get paid a ton of money to let other people believe whatever they wanted. This project didn't represent her personal point of view any more than the Sci-Fi or Fantasy or Speculative Fiction she recorded did.

A text came in from Adaku:

> You make it home??

SEWANEE:
> yes. Your luggage is in my car. Wanna come by tomorrow night?

> **ADAKU:**
> not good. Tuesday night?

SEWANEE:
> yup.

ADAKU:

and I want to hear EVERYTHING

Sewanee chuckled. She'd texted Adaku around 2 A.M. telling her she'd met someone. Actually, her exact words had been: sorry I ruined your makeover and she'd attached a picture of herself sitting on the end of the bed, clutching a sheet to her chest, eye patch off, smudged makeup, smeared lipstick, rats' nest hair. A napping naked Nick in the background. He'd woken up five minutes later and the night had continued.

Sewanee texted:

Promise.

And set her phone down.

Tomorrow she'd go to Seasons, check on Blah, talk to Amanda, talk to her father.

She finished her tea and let the cup rest in her lap, looking out into the night at nothing in particular. The residual warmth of the cup seeped through her skirt and she opened her legs to the heat, soothing the pleasurable tenderness there. She began drifting. She was in a bed, a man's head pressed into her neck. He turned his face and brought his mouth to her ear and whispered, "Beautiful. Everything beautiful."

AFTER A LUNCH of iced tea and chicken salad, Sewanee and Blah-Blah headed back to her room.

Blah made her way in, Sewanee right behind her in case she lost her balance. But once they were inside, Blah closed the door as Sewanee headed over to a small couch opposite her grandmother's favorite rocking chair.

"Pssst!" Blah hissed, and Sewanee turned around to see her

pointing at the door. "Can you believe Mitzi? What a job they did on her!" she stage-whispered, though they were alone. "You call that a face-lift? I call it a felony!" Blah cackled her way to the small kitchenette that contained a minifridge, a coffeepot, and a microwave. "Jesus H. Christ, what a botch." Blah grabbed a package of Mallomars off the counter. "She used to look half-decent, now she looks indecent." Blah's humor was a remarkable holdout of her dwindling acuity and Sewanee had a feeling when the jokes no longer existed, neither would Blah.

She chuckled. "It's not that bad, Blah."

"She should have left bad enough alone. You hungry? You want something, Doll? A Mallomar?"

"No, thanks, I'm stuffed."

"Me too, me too." Blah put the Mallomar she'd taken out back into its plastic cradle.

BlahBlah never ate. Not really. While a cookie was always close by, she didn't eat full meals. When pressed, Blah would claim it was because she'd been born during the Depression, but Sewanee knew the studios had drilled it into her. Now, she still didn't eat, as if tomorrow she might be asked to strip down to a bikini for a screen test.

Sewanee and Blah sat down. Blah rocked in her chair with a rhythm established over a lifetime. She'd been nursed in that chair and had nursed Henry in that chair and now she appeared ageless in it. Sewanee watched her go back and forth, seeing simultaneously a little girl whose feet didn't touch the ground and an old woman who carried that little girl through all of her ninety-two years.

"Are you hungry? Do you want something?"

"No, thank you. I'm stuffed."

"Me too, me too."

"The chicken salad was pretty good today."

"I hate chicken salad. I like tuna."

"Right, I forgot."

"Your memory is shot, Doll." Blah winked.

They both smiled again, and Sewanee felt the lull in conversation begin. Blah's jokes aside, the conversation didn't flow as it once had.

Sewanee had first noticed the change about a year ago. Blah would forget they'd talked on the phone. Then she'd forget the movie they'd gone to see, or the art exhibit, or Adaku's birthday party. Then she had trouble remembering why she'd moved into Seasons. Sewanee would remind her that her sister had died and that Blah had needed to move out of the house so Bitsy's kids could sell it. Interestingly, all her memories of being in the house were as a guest, even though she'd lived there for over thirty years. Henry considered this wishful thinking: in Blah's mind, she preferred the version of herself with the elegant party home in Beverlywood, not as a lodger in her sister's petite Sherman Oaks ranch. Maybe he was right.

"Are you hungry, Doll? Do you want something to eat?" Blah repeated for a third time.

"I'm good." The slow deterioration had been challenging, but this recent acceleration was terrifying. She had to find out if Blah was aware it was happening to her. "How's your memory these days?"

"I don't know, what's today?"

Sewanee gave her a smile, but said, "Seriously. Is it difficult to remember things?"

She rolled her eyes. "I'm old, everything's difficult."

Sewanee wished she didn't have to ask the next question. "Do you remember what happened on Friday night?"

Blah got a good rock going. "Did something happen?"

"Carlos found you in the common room in the middle of the night."

"No, he didn't."

"He did, Blah. According to him, you thought you were in Tennessee, getting ready for your debutante ball."

Blah went silent. Sewanee went silent. The look that traveled between them was everything Sewanee needed to know.

Blah made her way to her feet. "Want a Mallomar, Doll?"

"No."

She whispered, "Did you see Mitzi's face-lift?"

"Blah—"

"How's your mother?" She retrieved a Mallomar from the package sitting on top of the minifridge in the corner. "She should come for lunch sometime."

Sewanee watched Blah nibble at a corner of the cookie. "She doesn't live here anymore."

Blah stopped nibbling. "Since when?"

"Since the divorce."

"What divorce?"

Was she serious? "Mom and Dad's."

"Of course, of course. There are so many these days!" Blah laughed. She took another cookie and returned to her rocker. "Did she go home?"

"For about a year. To take care of Nana before she died. Then she met Stu."

BlahBlah nodded and nibbled. "Stu's an unfortunate name, but Stus are always nice. How did they meet?"

"It's a good story. Wanna hear it?"

BlahBlah set her half-eaten first cookie down on the coffee table, keeping the second one in her other hand. She sat back. "I love how you tell stories."

Sewanee sat back, too, fingering the fraying arm of the couch. "So after Nana died, Mom cleaned out the house and had a garage sale. And in the middle of making change, she noticed a man loitering by an old Victrola in the driveway."

"Marv's old Victrola?"

"No, Nana's. But you're right, you had a Victrola, too. Anyway, she went—"

"What happened to mine?"

"I—I don't know." Sewanee hadn't seen it since Bitsy's house. She could ask Henry about it.

But Blah didn't seem bothered by the mystery. She took a bite of the Mallomar she was holding, the half-eaten one forgotten on the coffee table.

"So, Mom went up to the man. 'Can I help you?' And he says, 'I can't believe it, we used to have this exact model growing up. Do you happen—'"

"Jeez louise, everybody has a Victrola?"

This made Sewanee laugh. "I guess so. Anyway, he asks if she has any records—"

"She doesn't have records? I have records. Somewhere."

"No, she—she had records. She opened up the cabinet and pulled out a whole bunch of old 78s. He flipped through them and then stopped and said, 'May I?' Mom nodded and he started cranking the old Victrola, wound it up good, and put a record on the turntable. Ella Fitzgerald started singing."

"Oh, Ella Fitzgerald! Which song?"

"'I'll Chase the Blues Away.'"

"Golly!" Blah started singing it. Her voice had thinned to a crackle, but she could still trill. "'I'll chase the blues away . . .'"

"That's the one. And he asked Mom to dance. Right there in the driveway. She was in sweatpants and a bleach-stained T-shirt and before she knew it, she was crying and they stopped dancing and he just held her. When the song stopped playing, they pulled apart, and he said, 'I'm Stu,' and she said, 'I'm Marilyn.' And they've been together ever since."

"Still in Seattle?"

It was Portland. Her mom was from Portland, but to be fair, BlahBlah could never remember that; she'd always thought it was Seattle. "No. Stu'd recently retired from Nike. He'd never been married, never had kids, and had gotten high up in the company. High up enough to buy an apartment on one of those cruise ships that have condos on them?"

"Cruise ships have condos?"

"These do. And you can get on and off whenever you want as it travels all around the world. They've been on board for about a year."

"How perfect! Can I get one?"

"Well, they're expensive."

"Oh, I'm sure they cost a pretty penny, but so what? It's like a fairy tale," Blah murmured. "And Mar deserves it." The way she said this made Sewanee believe that, for the moment, Blah remembered everything about her ex-daughter-in-law.

"She does. Yes, she does."

"And how's your other grandmother doing, with her daughter all over the world?"

"She . . . died, Blah."

Blah's face went slack. "Well! She should have said something!" Sewanee chuckled. What else could she do? "How's your mom handling it?"

She didn't know what to say. She just didn't. She wasn't going to retell the story. "She's doing fine."

There was a knock on the door and BlahBlah called out, in a bad Walter Matthau impression, "Ennnterrr!"

The door opened and Amanda poked her smiling head in. Sewanee had texted her at lunch, letting her know she was in the building. "You! Ever since you had me watch *The Sunshine Boys*! You get me every time. Am I crashing the party?"

Blah launched into the story about how Neil Simon once came on to her, which she did any time she quoted from *The Sunshine Boys* or *Barefoot in the Park* or *The Odd Couple*. She stood up. "Want a Mallomar?"

Amanda made a show of putting her hand over her stomach. "Ah, thanks, I just ate. May I steal your lovely granddaughter for a minute?"

Sewanee stood. "I actually have to get going anyway."

"Are you recording something?" BlahBlah asked, eyes lighting up.

"I am! A mystery." Sewanee waggled her eyebrows.

Blah looked disappointed. "You should record more love stories. We need more love in this world. Fewer criminals and evil and murder."

Sewanee went to her grandmother and hugged her. "When you're right, you're right." She pulled back and looked at her. "Friday happy hour?"

"It's a date, Doll."

Sewanee kissed her on the cheek and joined Amanda. Blah called after her, in a stage whisper, "Get a look at Mitzi on your way out! Talk about a murder!"

AMANDA TOURED HER through memory care and Sewanee had to admit she was impressed. It was nice. It was clean. It was quiet and comfortable and bright. But a ball of something unpleasant churned in her stomach the moment she'd crossed the threshold and she couldn't tell if it was worry or sadness or even a premonition. Of having to see less and less of her grandmother, no matter how much more she visited.

Instead of going back to Amanda's office, they walked outside in the garden, as if Amanda could tell Sewanee needed fresh air. "Well. What do you think?"

"It's great," Sewanee answered honestly. "Much better than I'd thought it would be."

Amanda smiled. "I appreciate that. We've won many industry awards. I don't know if you know this, but we were rated the number one assisted living facility in the city this year."

"I didn't know that! Barbara Chester can pick 'em." They sat down on a bench. "Dad will be glad to hear that, too. I'll be talking to him a little later. Is there anything else I should relay?"

"There will of course be a rather significant increase in the cost of care." Sewanee nodded. "She'll start out at Level 1, which is sixty-eight hundred per month." She didn't know for sure, but she thought that was about double what her grandmother was paying now. Amanda continued, "For each level of care added, it's an additional thousand dollars."

"So, what's the worst-case scenario? When someone's . . . here but not here?" Sewanee winced.

"The highest level of care is thirteen a month."

Sewanee's breath caught at that. "Wow. Okay. I mean, that's fine. Blah deserves the best. She is the best." Sewanee swallowed, surprised she had to hold tears back. "Sorry, it's—"

"No, please. None of this is easy." Amanda paused, giving Sewanee time to collect herself. "Last thing I'm obliged to say, and forgive me if I mentioned it when you all first toured the facility, but we don't have a Medicaid contract. So, there's no possibility of outside assistance."

Sewanee shook her head. "I'm sure that won't be a problem. What's the time frame for moving her?"

"It depends on Blah." Amanda pulled her reindeer sweater tighter around her and crossed her arms. "Had the incident on

Friday not occurred, I'd have thought she'd be fine for a while longer. But in these situations, days can feel like months. It's difficult to predict." Amanda took a moment. "If it were me, I would want to put her on the waitlist, to get the ball rolling. But it's obviously up to you. It will probably take a couple of months for a vacancy."

At Sewanee's silence, Amanda exhaled. "I know this is tough. I went through it with my mom."

"I'm sorry." Sewanee respected Amanda. She showed genuine concern and was caringly honest. She was a good woman doing her best in what Sewanee knew was a deeply flawed system. "I'll talk to my dad, though I'm sure he'll tell you to put her on the waitlist. Anything I can do in the meantime?"

Amanda smiled. "You keep reading those books. They get me through my commute. But I agree with BlahBlah. How 'bout a love story soon?"

SEWANEE SETTLED IN on her couch after a long afternoon of recording and a bowl of nourishing soup, and called her dad. She told him everything Amanda had told her, reporting in as he had requested, and then said, "So, all you have to do is make the call and she'll put Blah on the waitlist."

"Oh, is that all?"

"Yeah."

"Just one question: Where, exactly, did you ladies find the buried treasure?"

"What?"

Henry took a breath. "Four years ago, your grandmother, against my wishes, moved herself into Seasons. This is after I had found a perfectly suitable facility that accepted Medicaid, in the event she should live long enough to require care she couldn't afford. But she wouldn't hear it. It had to be Seasons."

"So?"

"So, I've had to stand by, watching her savings dwindle down to nothing. I've even pitched in over the last year. I bet she didn't mention that."

Sewanee held up a hand, as if he could see her. "Dad. Hang on. Doesn't she have Social Security? And what about that land in Tennessee she leases out for grazing? And I don't know, maybe some—"

"Buried treasure?"

"Stop with the buried treasure!"

"Nothing's left, Swan. She cleaned herself out. Her monthly income doesn't even cover what it costs now." He paused. "Which is why, instead of going to Seasons to get all the information I already possess, you could have tried asking me what was best—"

Sewanee groaned.

"Must you groan? If you have something to say, use words. Sounds are for animals."

Sewanee groaned again. Loudly this time.

"Sewanee—"

"You want words? Fine. You really can't afford to help her pay for this? Or are you just being vindictive?"

Henry laughed out loud. "Vindictive? You haven't earned the right to analyze me, sweetheart. I don't have a job. I don't have a house to mortgage. The lawyers wiped out whatever savings I had, your mother gets half my pension, and I have my own life to worry about." He snorted. "Maybe Marilyn's Sugar Daddy can help."

Sewanee took the phone away from her ear and almost threw it across the room. She brought it up to her mouth like a walkie-talkie. "Ask *my* mother's boyfriend to pay for *your* mother's care, that's your solution?"

"It was sarcasm." He had his condescending, professorial voice on. When he spoke again, he sounded impatient, done with this. "Look, this isn't your responsibility. I'll handle it from here."

She didn't like the sound of that, not one little bit. "What are you gonna do?"

"I know a place where she'll be comfortable."

Sewanee grew frantic. "Dad. No! She's happy at Seasons, everyone knows her, cares about her. She has friends. She has to stay there."

"People die, Swan. Decisions have to be made. It would be lovely if those decisions could be based on *feelings* but, unfortunately, they come down to money." Henry apparently heard how callous he sounded, because he added, more gently, "You think I don't care, but I do. I want you to know that. I wish you . . . these are hard things. Hell, I struggled over deciding what to do about Sarah."

Sewanee paused. "Sarah? Our dog? What are you talking about? There was no deciding. She was hit by a car and died."

"No, she was hit by a car and lived. But the surgery was going to cost ten grand, so we put her down." A long silence. "I'm now remembering we agreed not to tell you that."

"You killed Sarah?!"

"Noooo," he exhaled, "the driver killed Sarah. I merely decided not to intervene. She was twelve years old."

"So?!"

"So that's a good run. Ninety-two is a good run. Look, I'm not pushing her out to sea on an ice floe. This is what happens to millions of people when there's no money left. They go into the system."

"But the system is bad! Those places are bad!"

"Stop being histrionic, they're not the Dickensian hellscape you're—"

"You don't know that. You've hardly stepped foot inside Seasons let alone any other place. You're not going to be the one checking up on her, I can't even get you to go to Seasons for bingo night!"

"What does it matter if she doesn't know where she is?"

Sewanee couldn't exhale. "Dad."

"Swan. Honestly. What difference does it make?"

All she could say was, "I'll remind you of this conversation in twenty years."

"You're not hearing me. I'm trying to get you—"

"Goodnight." She hung up.

Hours later, Sewanee lay in bed unable to sleep.

She wanted to fix this.

She wanted everyone to be happy.

She wanted to be back in Las Vegas.

Eventually, around 4 A.M., she got up, showered, dressed, made tea to go, navigated the sixty-four steps to her car, and texted Mark:

Tell the June French people I'm in.

She drove the empty freeways to West Los Angeles, to the eight-unit apartment building off Bundy, where she sat in the car until a reasonable hour—six o'clock—got out, went to her father's door, and knocked.

CHAPTER EIGHT

"The Decision"

WHEN HENRY CHESTER WAS TWENTY-FIVE AND LIVING IN NEW YORK, his father's body was discovered slumped over his typewriter by a housekeeper, two fingers of Old Smuggler Scotch in the tumbler beside the carriage, three cigarettes in the Paramount Pictures ashtray—one still smoldering—dead from a heart that had simply given up.

Marvin had been a screenwriter. And Sewanee remembered Henry telling her the rapid tapping of typewriter keys (so like the ticktock of a perfectly balanced pendulum clock) emanating from his father's office had calmed a young Henry. It made him feel safe because his father was doing something, making something, being productive. But Barbara had been a performer, in the truest sense of that word. Onstage or off, she, herself, was always on. To Henry, she embodied the erratic unpredictability of an overwound clock.

Henry left Brooklyn to return home, to mourn his father, to pick up the reins and help a fiftysomething woman who had never taken care of anything on her own learn to take care of everything for the first time.

But Barbara resisted the help. She would handle it. The problem was, Henry knew she wouldn't handle it, she'd only pretend to. She'd *perform* handling it. After all this, everything he'd sacrificed to help her, Barbara was going to be . . . well, Barbara.

Eight months in, after she'd started dating a money manager Henry couldn't stand, could smell the bullshit wafting off the guy like cologne, he gave up. He'd gone into Marvin's office, poured some Old Smuggler, fingered the typewriter keys, and envied his father for taking the easy way out.

Within a few years, Eau de Fraud had disappeared, the house was foreclosed, and Barbara moved in with Bitsy and spent the next thirty years rebuilding a savings she'd burn through in four years at Seasons.

Sewanee was more than aware of how all this rankled Henry. She'd grown up with the sighs and the eye rolls and the thrown-up hands after every phone call. She felt bad for her father, but she felt worse for Blah. The time had come, a mere thirty-five years on, for this battle of wills to end. Someone needed to end it. That someone was apparently going to be her.

She could hear the shuffling steps of her beslippered father making his way to the door. Without unbolting the chain, he opened it a crack and peered out. Upon seeing his only child, the morning sleepiness in his eyes slid into concern. "Are you okay?"

"I'm great. I have something to tell you." Her voice sounded carbonated.

"Did you lose your phone?"

"Just open the door. Please?" Her tone when she said "please" granted her access. It was subservient enough, little girl enough, to persuade him. He closed the door and unlatched the chain with methodical undertaking, as if she were being let into a prisoner's cell. The door reopened; Henry had already walked away from it.

He was in his tattered bathrobe, as familiar to her as his face. He sat down in a patchy leather recliner that perfectly complemented the disintegrating robe. He was holding a cup of coffee so black it looked like a portal to another dimension. "You want a cup?" he mumbled. "It's yesterday's, but help yourself."

She went into the kitchen, quickly opened and closed the few cabinets looking for a mug. She found a dirty one in the sink and gave it a rinse. She poured some coffee into it and placed it in the small microwave with buttons so worn she had to guess at what she was hitting. As she waited, she looked around.

He hadn't always lived here. After the divorce three years ago, when they'd sold the family home, Henry had originally moved into a swanky high-rise apartment in the Wilshire corridor befitting a respected UCLA professor. Doorman. Valet. Gym. Sewanee had been so happy for him, for his fresh start. After all, she'd blamed her mother for the divorce (she *had* initiated it with zero provocation, as far as Sewanee knew) and back then she was daddy's little girl.

But the following year she'd found out she wasn't daddy's *only* little girl. Everything came out at once: Henry was losing his job, because he'd had an affair with a graduate student, which had started while he was still married.

They'd stood in that bourgie Wilshire apartment on opposite sides of the living room like two reluctant gunfighters. Had Marilyn known? Is that why she left? Yes, Henry admitted. But this whole thing was her fault. She hadn't been a wife, not really, not for a long time. She never appreciated him, all he'd given up for her, for their family. But the girl—Kelly her name had been—*had* appreciated him, had *revered* him. And yes, he'd been taken in, but she'd pursued him ruthlessly, and Sewanee would understand when she was older, how a starving man, etc., etc.,

etc. Sewanee had rejected this premise, talked about the power imbalance between teacher and student, but Henry had shouted, "Power imbalance?! Who's getting whom fired?!" She was the one who'd had the power! She'd used him!

Used him.

There was nothing left to say after that.

The ancient microwave's beep was more of a moan. Sewanee took the marginally warmed mug and walked into the living room. It was a short walk. There was an overflowing bookcase next to a futon couch. There wasn't a coffee table; there wasn't a lamp; there wasn't even a TV because Henry didn't "believe" in TV. There was just the futon couch, the beaten leather chair, Henry, his tattered robe, his black coffee.

Sewanee did her best to shelve her sarcasm, but it was a low shelf. "Like what you've done with the place."

"Sit."

She did, lifted the cup to her lips, blew gently, and took a swallow of blackness. She had come here with resolve, with excitement, with answers, and she would not let him diminish it. A significant smile opened up her face.

"Little early to look so chipper, no?" His tone could smother a forest fire.

Undampened, Sewanee said, "You don't have to worry about Blah anymore. I'm gonna pay for her care."

Her words hung in the air, a cluster of balloons waiting to be gathered up. But Henry let them drift. She assessed him in the silence. Still attractive for his age, a bit of a belly, some errant nose and ear hair, a little jowly, maybe, but Adaku had said once he looked like Gabriel Byrne and Sewanee hadn't been able to unsee it since. "Where, exactly, is this windfall of money coming from, Swan?" he eventually asked.

"I found the buried treasure!" She laughed, hoping Henry would join in. He didn't. "I got a voiceover job," she said, happily, adding another balloon to the still-suspended collection.

"A voiceover job."

"Yes. *The* voiceover job. A once-in-a-lifetime job that will cover the cost of her care. All of it!" A final balloon.

Henry looked into his coffee. His voice took on a worn quality, as if there were holes in it. "And you would take this once-in-a-lifetime opportunity to help secure your own future and throw it away on something this unnecessary, this frivolous?"

"First of all, my future will be fine, and second of all . . . Unnecessary? Frivolous? Really?"

"You can't know your future, Swan."

Pop.

"You don't know you'll be fine."

Pop.

"I would think you'd have learned that."

Pop.

Then, to himself: "I swear, talking to you is like talking to her."

And *pop.*

Now that her balloons no longer hung between them, she saw him clearly, even if nothing was, in fact, clear. "I don't get you," she gritted out. "I've tried . . . but I don't."

"Of course you don't." Monotone. Dead.

She shook her head. "Why can't you be happy? I'm doing this for you as much as for her. Why can't you see that? You're free. No one owes anyone anything. What else do you want?"

Henry wasn't looking at her. He was looking at the ragged hem of his bathrobe belt. "I don't want anything. Nothing, I want nothing." He gave his coffee a swirl and downed the rest of it.

"I don't understand. I came here so happy, so excited to tell you—"

"You're right, you don't understand me. None of you do." His voice had a shakiness, as if it belonged to a child left behind in a store.

The vulnerability surprised her, which was why it took her a moment longer to stand. When she did, she reached out to him and said the only thing she could think of. "Hand me your cup, I'll rinse it out."

He shook his head. "I'll take care of it. I'm not completely use— helpless, I'm not helpless."

"Dad . . ."

Henry got up and walked into the kitchen. She heard his cup land in the sink.

Sewanee gathered herself and went to the door. But when she opened it, she couldn't bring herself to cross the threshold. She stood there, going no farther out nor back in. She'd come to build bridges, not blow them up. Why couldn't he at least meet her halfway? She said, staring straight ahead, "I'd thought you might be thankful."

Henry scoffed, went back to his chair. "Appreciation is not something of which anyone in this family is capable."

The bitterness. She felt as frayed as his bathrobe. Her anger flared. Life hadn't gone as planned for any of them, but Henry got to be the lone injured party?

"Take care of yourself, Dad."

Just as she entered the freshness of the morning air, her father said, "You want to take your turn, go right ahead. But it won't matter. You'll see. Even with one eye, you'll see."

She could sense his regret even before the sentence had concluded, could hear it in the weakened, thinner reiteration of "you'll see." She waited a moment, a moment in which a normal person would say, "Forgive me. I'm sorry. That came out wrong." He said nothing.

She wanted to turn and face him. Scream at him. Walk back to him and loom over him in his stupid chair, yank off her eye patch and make him touch her scar, press his face to it, kiss it. Instead, she flicked away the tear that fell from her other eye and walked out. She left the door open.

THE WESTSIDE MORNING traffic was already at a standstill. Sewanee was in no mood to fight something else that morning, so she headed west instead of east. She needed the ocean. She needed space. She needed to breathe, having done so little of it since the moment she entered Henry's apartment. She easily found street parking she would never have found an hour later, grabbed the jacket she kept in the back of her car, and made her way to the cliffside walking path of Palisades Park. The nearest bench was occupied by a man cocooned in an overused sleeping bag, so she walked to the railing and leaned her elbows on it and looked through the morning haze at the ocean.

The sky was beginning to lighten. She inhaled deeply.

She allowed the thought of committing to the June French project to take root. She felt the rising sun on her back and closed her eye, letting the rhythmic sound of the waves caress her, letting the warmth and the breeze and the crashing surf carry her to a place a June French novel would describe in gleeful detail.

It was still slightly shocking she had these new memories to return to.

There'd been a few men since the accident, all casual, nothing relevant. Sex had been an exercise in nostalgia for her: a way to remind herself she could feel something. It hadn't been a *want*. Until Vegas. Until Nick.

"What a pissah!"

The voice was more intrusive than it might normally have been, given where Sewanee's mind had wandered. She tried to ignore it, hoping it would disappear as quickly as it had arrived.

"Sewanee Chestah! I'd recognize that backside anywhere!"

She hoped it wasn't who she thought it was. She really hoped it wasn't.

She turned around.

It was exactly who she'd hoped it wasn't.

A decade older. Shirtless. Oakleys on the back of his head. Spandex running shorts. "Oh my God," was all she could say.

"Just playin'," Doug Carrey said in that smoky trademark Boston accent. And then, predictably, he laughed. Doug had always laughed at anything he said whether anyone else joined in or not. "Damn, girl!" His eyes swept her body. "Look at you!"

She lifted her hands marginally at her sides, an unenthusiastic *ta-da*. He moved in for a hug, seemed to think better of it. "Ah, I'm all sweaty." So he kissed her cheek, grabbed her waist, and squeezed. It felt analytical, like he was measuring the reality of her body in this moment against what he maybe remembered.

He stepped back and pulled a voice. "Of all the gin joints, amiright?" It might have been charming were he not terrible at impressions. His Humphrey Bogart was closer to Gilbert Gottfried. "Shit, what's it been? Five years?"

"I think at least eight."

"No suh! Really?"

Really. Trust her, Doug.

"Well, you are wearing them well." That *Tiger Beat* cover grin resurfaced.

"You too," she said, then followed the lie with an unwritten law of Hollywood interactions: the stated recognition of an actor's success. "Tommy Callahan."

Back when they'd met, he'd been on the fast track to action movie stardom, but he overspent the money he'd made, lost his edge, and, desperate for cash, took a network family sitcom pilot that went to series. And now he would forever be Tommy Callahan, the Reformed Bad Boy Turned Single Dad Trying His Best.

She couldn't stop looking at him. He wasn't aging gracefully, was he? He wasn't getting craggy or jagged or crinkly; he was getting blurry.

And yet: men. They kept working.

"Yeah, it's a good gig." He laughed. She didn't know why, but she laughed along. "But I was sure if anyone was going big league it was you. Where'd you *go*? You like, *peaced*."

"Oh, I, uh . . . I've been doing a lot of voiceover."

He snapped his fingers. "Wicked smaht. Definitely the future. Everyone thinks they can just do it, but it's a skill. It's a whole nother talent. I'm getting into it myself."

Sewanee said, "That's great." But Sewanee thought, *now* we should be laughing.

"Not that you got a face for radio or nothing like that." He winked. Then he pointed at his eye, swirled his finger. "What happened here?"

"I had an accident."

Doug winced. "Yikes. I got a mascara wand in the eye once. Makeup girl was all worked up and someone banged the trailer door shut and—" he clucked his tongue "—direct hit. I had to wear one of those for a whole month. How long you in fah?"

Sewanee looked down at her shoes.

Eight years ago, this man had begged his way into her bed.

She'd made him wait months. She'd delighted in his every agonized text, the way he'd show up at the lounge where she worked and plant himself at the end of the bar just to watch her, the groans in the back of his throat when she'd let him kiss her. Theirs had been an age-old dance, a chase, a hunt, and its end hadn't hurt. It had been transactional from the beginning. He'd given her months of feeling worshipped, she'd given him a few nights of what he wanted, and then they were done.

And the whole of that entire relationship had been as exciting as one single thought about Nick.

"Spare a few bucks?"

Sewanee looked up. The man from the bench had made his way over to them, encased in his sleeping bag.

Doug made a show of patting his skintight shorts, "Ah, sorry, brothah." He looked at Sewanee, was already backing away. "This was dope. You still got my number, right? Give me a bell." He put his hand up to his ear, pinky and thumb extended. "We'll grab some Dunks!" He jogged away.

Yeah, no.

Sewanee reached into her jacket pocket, took out a few singles she'd left there for valet tips, and handed them to the man.

"Thanks. That guy on a sitcom?"

"Uh . . . yeah."

She supposed she didn't hide her surprise as well as she'd intended, because he preemptively offered an explanation. "I used to be an actor."

"Ah."

"He's a hack."

"Yeah."

The man stuffed the bills into his pocket, went back to his bench, and curled up underneath the bag.

Sewanee inched her way back to Hollywood, cleared the studio sink of morning-rush coffee cups, and found Mark in his office. She tapped the doorframe and he looked up, smiling wide.

"How's it feel to be motivated by money?"

AFTER A DAY of billing and a couple of hours in the booth, Sewanee was happy to hear Adaku's knock on her door. "Come in!" she called, as she finished pouring two glasses of rosé.

"This is why your ass is amazing," Adaku said from the other side of the kitchen wall, sounding winded. She rounded the corner and took Swan into a yoga hug.

She chuckled into Adaku's ear. "You work out with a trainer four times a week."

"And yet these stairs still kill me!"

"Well, here." She handed Adaku a glass of wine. She was about to ask how the drinks-meeting at LAX had gone, but Adaku launched into the story unprompted.

"So, the meeting started out awkward as shit. He had no desire to meet me let alone have a conversation." She took a quick gulp. "He says the typical producer stuff, I come back at him with everything I've got, and then he finally admits he doesn't think I'm 'culturally Black' enough to play Angela Davis."

Sewanee stopped mid-drink. "What the hell does that mean?"

"What it always means: nothing. They see you the way they want to see you. Black, white, tall, short, fat, skinny . . . you're condemned to it."

Sewanee pursed her lips. "How old is this guy?"

"*Too* old. Too *white*."

"Perfect person to make the Angela Davis story."

"Well, funny you should say that. I told him maybe he wasn't 'culturally Black' enough to be producing it."

Sewanee gasped, eye bugging. "OhmygodIloveyou, what did he say?"

Adaku lifted her glass and smiled. "I'm officially in the mix."

Sewanee laughed. "You are on a roll! Cheers." They clinked glasses and moved reflexively toward the porch. Unless it was raining, they never confined themselves to Sewanee's shoebox living room.

Adaku opened the sliding screen door for Swan, whose hands were full with glass and bottle. "Okay, now let's go! I want the full story! Every detail! No broad strokes, no glossing. I want to know the nitty, the gritty, and what he did to them titties!"

Sewanee guffawed and they sat down in the two stackable plastic chairs she'd secured at a garage sale for five bucks and which were light enough to carry up the hill. Then she spent half an hour telling a story that left Adaku open-mouthed, knee-slapping, and speechless. And Adaku was never speechless.

When she was done, Sewanee topped their glasses off. The silence was unnerving. "Please say something. You know what, actually, don't say anything. I did what I did and I have no regrets. A little out of character, I know, but . . ." At Adaku's receding chin, she amended, "A lot, a lot out of character, but A . . ." She put down the bottle, looked at her friend. "It was the best night I've had in years and not because of the sex."

Adaku raised a brow.

"Not just because of the sex."

Adaku assessed Sewanee. Then a slow, Cheshire smile filled her face. One word fell from her lips. "Damn."

Sewanee sprang up. "I need a snack." She dipped back inside and tried to get her nerves under control. Reliving the night had made it real, concretized it. It was now a story, one that had been shared with another person, open to scrutiny, available for opinion. Outside of her head it became . . . a lot. Maybe it *was* something to regret.

She grabbed the box of gluten-free quinoa cracker things she kept here for Adaku and went back outside.

Adaku took the folded side table leaning against the wall and placed it between their chairs as Sewanee resettled herself. "There's so much to unpack," Adaku murmured. "This isn't a suitcase, it's a steamer trunk."

Sewanee shook her head. "There's nothing to unpack."

Adaku bit her lip. "You really left? You both just walked away without any contact info? None?"

"I'd been lying about who I was."

"Yeah, but—"

"And, remember, he didn't offer anything, either, so chances are he wasn't exactly on the up and up." She dropped her face into her hands. "Oh my God. Who knows who he actually was? Jesus Christ, I can't believe—"

"Nope, unh-unh, stop. Don't ruin it. He was hot. You were safe." She leaned over, squeezed Sewanee's leg. "It's a happy ending."

"One of many," Sewanee mumbled.

Adaku laughed and sat back. She looked out at the view and sighed. Then gave Sewanee a side-eye. "The thing he did with the ring, though."

Sewanee groaned. "Don't."

Adaku held up a hand. "Just saying. Like something out of a Romance novel."

Sewanee sat forward. "Oh! That's another thing that happened." She told her about the June French project. How they'd made her an offer she couldn't refuse.

Adaku tilted her head. "I thought you were done with Romance."

"I was, but it's crazy money."

"Do you need money? Is something up?"

Sewanee knew if she told Adaku about BlahBlah, she'd want

to help. But Sewanee never wanted Adaku's success to rescue her from her lack of it. This was how friendships changed; hell, this was how families changed. How help became resentment. So she brushed cracker dust off her sweatpants and said, "There's only so much money I can ever make doing this job—there's a ceiling, no matter how in-demand I am—and this is a once-in-a-lifetime opportunity to cash in. Build a little cushion for myself, you know?"

Adaku looked out at the view again. "Makes sense."

"I mean, it'll be, like, eight hours of work. Maybe ten. It's insane."

"What's it about?"

Sewanee set down her glass and pulled out her phone. She'd told Mark to give them the old e-mail address she'd used for Sarah Westholme. The one she hadn't opened once since logging out of it six years ago. She'd resurrected it on her server and discovered—in addition to pages and pages of spam she was never going to wade through—three recent e-mail inquiries about this project. Which explained why the producer had reached out to Mark. At Mark's go-ahead, Jason had immediately e-mailed Sarah so they could work out recording details. Sewanee scrolled through the e-mail now, skipping over the "I'm so excited to be working on this together! Thank you so much!" part, then read aloud:

"'This dual-narration series is about a businesswoman who put her company on the back burner to help her husband while he was dying. After his death, she must now go about rebuilding both her business and her long-dormant sexuality. Five years prior, on the night before her wedding, she met an aspiring artist and, while their attraction had been undeniable, she faithfully refused him. But now she is free to seek him out, only to discover that he has not forgotten her, either. Furthermore, it turns out that bringing women's sexuality back to life happens to be his thing . . . he's a famous gigolo descended from Casanova who hosts wealthy women for "rejuvenating" weekends at his ancestral palazzo in Venice. She can't afford him, but they strike a bargain: he will give her his full VIP package–'" She looked at Adaku, held up her phone, tapped her screen. "It actually says 'package.'" She looked back down. "'–if she will use her connections to get his art in front of her very rich friends. It's a deal! But can these two wandering souls keep their transaction strictly professional?'" Sewanee rolled her eye at this.

Adaku clapped excitedly. "That's actually cute!"

"Sure, why not."

"It is! Who's the other narrator?"

"The alpha male of Romance. At least according to the audience at the panel." She said his name as if heralding the arrival of a king: "Sir Brock McNight!"

Adaku jumped up. "What?!" she screeched.

Sewanee looked startled. "Not you, too!"

"Swan! Like, ninety percent of my library is Brock McNight." She heard herself. "And you, of course."

Sewanee poured more wine, smirked. "But is his guy voice as good as mine?"

Adaku screeched again. "You've never heard his voice?!"

"You know I don't listen to audiobooks. Give me your glass?"

Adaku obliged and then fished her phone out of her back pocket. "I am about to introduce you to the man, the myth, the legend, the voice of my ever-loving dreams, Brock-talk-me-dirty-McNight."

Sewanee chuckled as Adaku perched on the edge of her chair and set her phone faceup on the folding table. Sewanee looked down to see a book cover that was nothing but a man's glistening bare torso. "Billionaire" was in the title.

As the audiobook began, Adaku took her glass back and

watched Sewanee's face intently, a kid who'd just handed her mom a new drawing.

The story opened like so many. Man sees woman standing across a room and catalogues her "assets." She had narrated so many of these opening scenes that for a moment she was distracted by the repetitiveness. But then. The voice hit.

By the time it had carved through the first paragraph, her eyes flicked to Adaku, who was still staring at her. Thirty seconds later, she'd gone slack-jawed and Adaku barely contained her smug mirth. Five minutes later, when the co-narrator started her section, when *the voice* was no longer present, Sewanee felt tantalizingly unfulfilled. It was a bite of chocolate when she needed the whole bar.

Yes, he had a great voice. Low, of course, and resonant, obviously, and the perfect balance of growl and breath. She couldn't imagine him narrating anything other than Romance; he'd be too distracting.

But as he described his body's reaction to seeing this woman, the way her mere existence affected him, he made the listener want to be her. Heat blasted from his vocal furnace.

It was Sewanee who broke the silence. "Who *is* this guy?"

Adaku pushed her knee. "Right!? You ever heard anyone like–"

"No. No. No, he's . . . no."

Adaku cackled and Sewanee could tell she liked seeing her thrown. "See? Lean in, Swan, I'm telling you, this is some hot shit!"

At that moment, Sewanee's phone dinged.

She deflated slightly and picked it up. "Sorry, but I'm waiting for an e-mail from Seasons' billing depar–"

Her gasp had Adaku spinning toward her. "What? Is it Blah-Blah?"

"No." Sewanee looked up. "It's Brock McNight."

 **PART 3**

We work in the dark. We do what we can. We give what we have. Our doubt is our passion. Our passion is our task. The rest is the madness of art.

—Henry James

I don't know where my ideas come from, but you know where they come to? My desk. And if I'm not there to greet them, they leave. Ass in the chair. Ass in the chair. That's art.

—June French in *Cosmopolitan*

CHAPTER NINE

"Epistolary"

From: Brock McNight
To: Westholme, Sarah
Date: December 6, 5:24 PM
Subject: CASANOVA, LLC—and hello!

Hi Sarah,

Brock McNight here. Got your email address from Jason. Thought I'd give you a shout before we give this thing legs.

I don't believe we've had the pleasure of working together before (thousand apologies if I'm wrong!), but I'm a big fan of your work in June's Shadow Walkers series.

Feel free to reach out once you've read the first few episodes. Any pronunciations/character voices to discuss, let me know.

This'll be fun,
Brock

From: Westholme, Sarah
To: Brock McNight
Date: December 7, 8:41 AM
Subject: RE: CASANOVA, LLC—and hello!

Thank you so much, Brock. I'm a fan of yours, as well.

I'll dig in to the first few episodes and will definitely reach out with questions. Warning: I tend to have a lot of questions!

Looking forward to doing this.

Best,
Sarah

From: Westholme, Sarah
To: Brock McNight
Date: December 13, 3:16 PM
Subject: RE: CASANOVA, LLC—and hello!

Hi again,

Okay, finished reading the first three episodes. Enjoyed it! But, as I warned you, I have a significant number of questions (attached). Also sending along a sample of what I'm thinking of doing with the voices. Let me know if these work for you.

Best,
Sarah

From: Brock McNight
To: Westholme, Sarah
Date: December 14, 10:27 AM
Subject: RE: CASANOVA, LLC—and hello!

Good questions. Made notes in the attachment. Character samples sound PERFECT.

Brock

SEWANEE WAS LOADING the dishwasher with the usual lunchtime detritus when she saw Mark come out of his office and hit the button for the house's ancient intercom system.

"May I have your attention, please. The e-mail . . ." He gave his best dramatic pause. ". . . has arrived." Sewanee stopped loading, retrieved a stack of clear plastic cups from a cabinet, and unstacked them on the island. Mark went to the garage and returned with two bottles of Kirkland brand sparkling wine.

Normally, the house was library-silent during the day. The rotating narrators and engineers were ensconced in the four bedrooms and the editors were sitting at desks in the living room listening to raw audio files. If conversation happened, it was murmured lowly in the kitchen or more volubly in the garage; on the deck you could laugh without being heard. But now, the floorboards above Sewanee's head creaked, doors opened, and footsteps made their way down the thickly-carpeted stairs. The editors pulled off their headphones.

The herd gathered in the kitchen, Alice among them. She rarely came to the studio anymore, but her home booth was currently out of commission. Most full-time narrators had home studios, so Mark's place usually hosted new narrators, old hold-outs, actors who only did audiobooks occasionally, and celebrity or author readers. It was nice to see a familiar face.

Alice slipped her arm around Sewanee's waist, giving her a kiss on the cheek. Sewanee moved to throw her right arm across Alice's shoulders, but she'd never regained full range of motion. She substituted a snuggle into Alice's side. "How you?" Alice whispered.

"Good," Sewanee murmured back. "You? What are you re-cording?"

"They're unicorns. Except when they're humans. Then they screw a lot."

"Hear ye, hear ye!" Mark cried, pulling a folded raft of pa-pers out of the back pocket of his Dockers. He liked to preserve tradition whenever possible and he particularly enjoyed this one. He'd be damned if he read this off a screen. "I have in my hand the sacred scroll! The communique from on high! The fates of every living being! Gather 'round to hear your fortu-ity!"

Alice and Sewanee snorted.

"For the uninitiated, the Audies are the Oscars of the audio-book world. And we have among us, here, in this very kitchen, gods of the realm. Your Meryl Streep of Romance"—he looked to Alice here—"your Daniel Day-Lewis of Sci-Fi"—a nod to Brian, a narrator who insisted on wearing a tie in the booth because it made him feel like he was at work—"your promising-newcomer, the, shall we say, Adaku Obi of Faith-Based and Inspirational . . ." Sewanee laughed as Mark gestured to a baby-faced woman she thought might have been named Carly. "And, of course, your Cate Blanchett of Fiction and winner of last year's Best Female Narrator award, Sewanee Chester." A tip of an invisible hat.

"Don't forget yourself," she called out. "The Katharine Hepburn of History and Biography."

Mark curtsied amid the hoots, but continued, "Now, the Academy Awards might have a celebrity-strewn televised announcement of the nominees, but we aren't nearly as fussy, are we? Nay! We are humble artistes, who prefer our accolades to arrive via electronic mail, on an awkward mid-week afternoon right before the holidays." More chuckles. "This year's ceremony will take place on . . ." He scanned the paper. ". . . Wednesday, March 10th. Now, the ceremony. Ahhh, the ceremony. First and foremost, arrange transportation because each ticket includes not one, but two drink coupons!"

Mark said louder, over the laughter, "The event is black tie, so leave your sweatpants at home, *mon amis*. Shave all the parts no one usually sees. Decide which footwear you'll spend the evening complaining about!" He looked back to the paper. "And what is this? Do mine eyes deceive me? Hark! This year, the event shall take place here, in the City of Angels!" At this, a victorious cry went up. "Los Angeles, rejoice! New York, pack your sunblock!" The entire group applauded and whistled. "And so, without further ado, while I read the categories and nominees, *une petite* Blanchett over here will distribute the bubbly."

At that, Sewanee moved away from Alice and to her task. Mark began to read. She knew if she checked her phone, she'd probably see texts and e-mails from friends and colleagues who had already scanned the nominees and reached out to her. But she preferred it this way.

In the end, Mark was nominated for a Jefferson biography, Alice was nominated twice in the Romance category (one a co-narration with Brock McNight, who had an additional nomination of his own, prompting a pointed raised eyebrow in Swan's direction from Mark), and she herself was nominated in general Fiction for *Them Hills*. No one in the room would have sensed her disappointment at not being nominated in the big kahuna Best Female Narrator category she'd won the previous year. She was too good an actress to let any suggestion of a sting show. But when she saw the shocked joy on Carly's face at having been nominated, for the first time, in Young Adult, she was reminded that all of it was an honor. More than the awards, she had a steady job in an industry she loved.

As everyone chatted and sipped their meager ration of spar-kles, Sewanee found Alice in a corner of the kitchen. One of the engineers, Petra, came up to them and they congratulated her, too—she'd engineered one of the nominated books—and Alice smiled at her, setting her plastic glass in the sink. "Let's finish out the chapter and call it a night. Let Swan get in studio 3." Alice knew Sewanee recorded whenever there was a free booth— that's how she made the bartering work with Mark—and today there wasn't one.

They hugged once more and Alice and Petra moved to leave, but Alice turned back. "Oh, Mark told me about the June French series. Fantastic!"

"Thank you."

"You'll love working with Brock."

"Yeah?"

"Sweet kid. Communicative, thoughtful, respectful." Sewanee opened her mouth and Alice held up a hand, smiling. "No, I don't know who he really is. But he's one of the good ones."

Interesting.

Sewanee finished her congratulatory rounds and then, when everyone had gone back to their work, she started the dishwasher and leaned on the counter. She took out her phone and composed an e-mail:

From: Westholme, Sarah
To: Brock McNight
Date: December 17, 3:11 PM
Subject: RE: CASANOVA, LLC—and hello!

Congrats on your Audie nomination(s)! May you somehow win them both!

From: Brock McNight
To: Westholme, Sarah
Date: December 18, 5:27 AM
Subject: RE: CASANOVA, LLC—and hello!

Thank you! I'm honored. Though being nominated twice in the same category means even if I win, I lose.

From: Westholme, Sarah
To: Brock McNight
Date: December 18, 1:36 PM
Subject: RE: CASANOVA, LLC—and hello!

Lol.

I'm planning to record the first episode after the holidays. If we don't speak (type? Correspond?) before then, I hope you and yours have a good rest of the year. Looking forward to getting into this with you in the new one.

From: Brock McNight
To: Westholme, Sarah

Date: December 18, 1:37 PM
Subject: Automatic Reply: CASANOVA, LLC—and hello!

Hello,

I won't be checking email until January 7. I humbly implore you to join me.

Peace and love and New Year's countdown kisses,
B

From: Brock McNight
To: Westholme, Sarah
Date: January 7, 6:14 AM
Subject: RE: CASANOVA, LLC—and hello!

Happy New Year! Hope you and yours had a good holiday. Have you looked at the next two episodes Jason sent? You'll be doing the voice of Claire's late husband in a flashback section. Can you send me a sample of how you're doing it? I have one dialogue exchange where he's condescending to me at the rehearsal dinner and I want to make sure we are in sync.

From: Westholme, Sarah
To: Brock McNight
Date: January 7, 9:57 AM
Subject: RE: CASANOVA, LLC—and hello!

Happy New Year to you and yours! Hope it was merry and bright.

I'm thinking high and reedy, slightly sniveling. To contrast with your Alessandro, The Ultimate Man™.

Question: Jason had mentioned you'd never done a June French book before. So, I admit, I looked you up and surprisingly it's true. 400 audiobooks and none June's? Curious how this project found its way to you.

From: Brock McNight
To: Westholme, Sarah
Date: January 7, 4:35 PM
Subject: RE: CASANOVA, LLC—and hello!

You Googled me, huh? Thought I felt something.

You know, it's interesting. Before June died, she reached out and told me about the project and said I was the only voice she wanted reading it. So, I promised her. And honestly, I wanted to do it. To honor her. Her legacy, I guess.

One more thing you should know: she was equally insistent about you. It had to be both of us or she didn't want it done. Jason and I decided not to tell you that in the beginning. We didn't want you asking for a bigger cut. ☺

From: Westholme, Sarah
To: Brock McNight
Date: January 7, 5:15 PM
Subject: RE: CASANOVA, LLC—and hello!

I would definitely have asked for a bigger cut. ☺

That's actually very heartwarming. I appreciate you telling me. She was very good to me when I was first starting out. I loved doing her books, even if they were in a category I later pulled back from. I'm sad she's gone. But we will do right by her!

From: Brock McNight
To: Westholme, Sarah
Date: January 7, 5:33 PM
Subject: RE: CASANOVA, LLC—and hello!

Agreed.

Question: I Googled you, too (feel anything?), and 75 Romance novels but nothing in the last five years. Curious. Why did you stop and, more importantly, how can I?

From: Westholme, Sarah
To: Brock McNight
Date: January 7, 7:48 PM
Subject: RE: CASANOVA, LLC—and hello!

Haha. Well, I started in Romance, used it as a training ground. Full disclosure: I never enjoyed the genre. Other than June and a few other authors who <u>were wonderful</u> writers, I just don't like Romance. It's not my . . . thing? Speed? Taste? I think I'm too cynical. For what it's worth, I don't do Faith-Based and Inspirational either.

Bah humbug.

From: Brock McNight
To: Westholme, Sarah

Date: January 8, 10:22 AM
Subject: RE: CASANOVA, LLC—and hello!

I get it, Scrooge. Trust me. I ONLY do Romance. And some days you're just not in the mood for happily ever after.

From: Westholme, Sarah
To: Brock McNight
Date: January 8, 5:21 PM
Subject: RE: CASANOVA, LLC—and hello!

Most days.

(But also I did some terribly written omegaverse/wolf erotica and that put me over the edge. Here lies Sarah Westholme, slain by her own prudery.)

Also FYI, Sarah Westholme is a pseudonym, that's why there are only 75 titles under that name. I record other books under my real name.

From: Brock McNight
To: Westholme, Sarah
Date: January 9, 7:13 AM
Subject: RE: CASANOVA, LLC—and hello!

At least Sarah Westholme sounds like an actual person. Brock McNight sounds like a porn star.

From: Westholme, Sarah
To: Brock McNight

Date: January 9, 7:15 AM
Subject: RE: CASANOVA, LLC—and hello!

Well, congrats. Nailed it.

From: Brock McNight
To: Westholme, Sarah
Date: January 9, 7:24 AM
Subject: RE: CASANOVA, LLC—and hello!

I almost went with ROCK McNight but might as well be Stiff McStufferson at that point.

Anywaaaaaay, have you recorded the first episode yet? If so, can you send? I want to hear your tone/pacing before I start.

From: Westholme, Sarah
To: Brock McNight
Date: January 9, 7:35 AM
Subject: RE: CASANOVA, LLC—and hello!

It's attached, Stiffy. Have a great weekend!

From: Brock McNight
To: Westholme, Sarah
Date: January 12, 2:15 PM
Subject: RE: CASANOVA, LLC—and hello!

Hope your weekend was good.

Listened to the first episode. I have to tell you—maybe I

shouldn't tell you—no, I'm going to tell you: you're ridiculously good. Shadow Walkers was a while ago and that impressed me. But this is exceptional.

You should read books out loud. Has anyone ever told you that? People might even pay you! Something to look into.

From: Westholme, Sarah
To: Brock McNight
Date: January 12, 9:26 PM
Subject: RE: CASANOVA, LLC—and hello!

Thank you! That means a lot, coming from you.

I was a bit concerned I was out of practice. Any tips or tricks you have for narrating Romance these days would be welcomed.

From: Brock McNight
To: Westholme, Sarah
Date: January 13, 11:43 AM
Subject: RE: CASANOVA, LLC—and hello!

I wouldn't worry about performance. People listen at 3X speed.

Kidding.

Kind of.

From: Brock McNight
To: Westholme, Sarah
Date: January 13, 11:47 AM
Subject: RE: CASANOVA, LLC—and hello!

Sorry, that was glib. Of course you should care about performance.

One of us should. *cymbal crash*

From: Westholme, Sarah
To: Brock McNight
Date: January 14, 6:12 PM
Subject: RE: CASANOVA, LLC—and hello!

Why do you only record Romance (if I may ask, obvs)?

From: Brock McNight
To: Westholme, Sarah
Date: January 14, 7:31 PM
Subject: RE: CASANOVA, LLC—and hello!

Money aside (LOLZ obviously it's the money):

It's a crash course in learning about women. A subject I have repeatedly flunked.

From: Westholme, Sarah
To: Brock McNight
Date: January 14, 7:38 PM
Subject: RE: CASANOVA, LLC—and hello!

That would be like me learning about men from narrating Sci-Fi. Ten pages on the inner-workings of the spaceship's command center A.I.? That can't be the extent of what goes on in their heads.

From: Brock McNight
To: Westholme, Sarah
Date: January 14, 7:41 PM
Subject: RE: CASANOVA, LLC—and hello!

No, that's entirely accurate. But please husk your voice when you read, "The main shaft drives the dual condenser into lockdown."

From: Westholme, Sarah
To: Brock McNight
Date: January 14, 7:44 PM
Subject: RE: CASANOVA, LLC—and hello!

Like this? [voice memo attached]

From: Brock McNight
To: Westholme, Sarah
Date: January 14, 7:46 PM
Subject: RE: CASANOVA, LLC—and hello!

Oh. My. God. 😆

    I'm so glad we're doing this project together. I know this is about the money for both of us, but I can't help feeling like maybe June knew something about the two of us individually that

From: Brock McNight
To: Westholme, Sarah

Date: January 14, 7:49 PM
Subject: RE: CASANOVA, LLC—and hello!

DID NOT MEAN TO SEND THAT MY STUPID FAT FINGER SLIPPED I
WAS TRYING TO ERASE ALL THAT DRIVEL UGHHHHHHH

(I have had a few drinks. Sorry. Ignore me. Going to bed now.)

From: Westholme, Sarah
To: Brock McNight
Date: January 14, 7:56 PM
Subject: RE: CASANOVA, LLC—and hello!

Stiffy? No apology necessary.

Quick business question: How are we saying Claire's company,
Visage? VIZ-idge (like the actual word) or vi-ZAWzh?

Be nice if we could ask June.

From: Brock McNight
To: Westholme, Sarah
Date: January 15, 8:17 AM
Subject: RE: CASANOVA, LLC—and hello!

You're a gem, Westholme. Truly. You're not only the right voice,
you're the right person for this. (He wrote, completely sober this
time)

And good question. But I defer to you, Claire's your domain.

From: Westholme, Sarah
To: Brock McNight

Date: January 15, 12:51 PM
Subject: RE: CASANOVA, LLC—and hello!

So much pressure! I think vi-ZAWzh sounds more like a fake cosmetics company.

And thank you. That's kind of you to say. I was thinking, but only if you're completely comfortable with this, that we should exchange phone numbers. Just for texting. Just for that. Just in case another pronunciation question comes up. I don't check emails when I'm in the booth. But only if you are COMPLETELY COMFORTABLE with this. Please know I would never abuse the privilege. I would of course keep your number confidential.

From: Brock McNight
To: Westholme, Sarah
Date: January 15, 12:51 PM
Subject: RE: CASANOVA, LLC—and hello!

Hey, here's my phone number, can I have yours? I don't have email set up in the booth or I'd never get any recording done, but I do respond to texts. Just in case we have questions that require an immediate response. But only if you're COMFORTABLE with this. Please keep my number confidential and I will, of course, do the same.

From: Westholme, Sarah
To: Brock McNight
Date: January 15, 12:52 PM
Subject: RE: CASANOVA, LLC—and hello!

LOL! Great minds!

From: Brock McNight
To: Westholme, Sarah
Date: January 15, 12:52 PM
Subject: RE: CASANOVA, LLC—and hello!

Whoa did we send those at the exact same time???

From: Westholme, Sarah
To: Brock McNight
Date: January 15, 12:53 PM
Subject: RE: CASANOVA, LLC—and hello!

YES AND NOW THESE LAST ONES, TOO! ACK! STOP! GOODBYE!

* * *

January 19

SEWANEE:
Hi, it's Sarah. I have questions. Many questions.

BROCK:
Hi Sarah, it's Brock. I have many answers.

I also happen to have a question.

SEWANEE:
You first.

BROCK:
Are you doing Italian pronunciations for all people/places/things, with R trills, etc?

SEWANEE:

of courrrrrrrrrsuh. We should keep it authentic, no?

BROCK:

Rrrrright, we should, si.

Your turn.

SEWANEE:

So. Speaking of pronunciations, we both have clitoris coming up and we should make sure we give it the same emphasis.

BROCK:

Please. Continue.

SEWANEE:

Well. MW has two acceptable pronunciations: 1st is KLIT-ur-us, 2nd is kli-TOR-us.

BROCK:

Door #1. Number 2 sounds like a dinosaur.

SEWANEE:

Agreed.

Can't you just see ol' Merriam and Webster debating this one?

BROCK:

The men who wrote the DICK-shun-airy? Absolutely.

Or is it dick-SHUNNERY?

SEWANEE:

That's just the tip of the iceberg. What about areole?

BROCK:

Not sure that's the tip of an *iceberg*.

SEWANEE:

Haha. Are we going with the technically correct pronunciation, even though I've never heard it said like that? Ever? Aw-REE-oh-luh?

BROCK:

You've obviously been out of the Romance game for a while. MW recently added air-ee-OH-luh as an official alt pronunciation.

SEWANEE:

NO!

BROCK:

Yes.

SEWANEE:

They must be turning over in their graves!

BROCK:

Hope they don't bruise their air-ee-OH-luhs.

air-ee-OH-ly?

It's complicated when there's two of them.

SEWANEE:

I have another question.

BROCK:

Is it above the neck?

SEWANEE:
Way above. Why is the sky blue?

BROCK:
ha.

Seriously?

SEWANEE:
Yeah, I've always wondered.

BROCK:
Simple: reflection.

WAIT NO. Refraction.

SEWANEE:
Wrong. Particles. *sends link to NASA website*

BROCK:
That article is incorrect.

SEWANEE:
Oh, NASA's incorrect?

BROCK:
Sarah. These people staged the
moon landing, for Pete's sake.

Hey here's a question: who's Pete?

SEWANEE:
?

BROCK:
Pete! Pete's sake. For the love of Pete. Sneaky
Pete. Honest to Pete. Who tf is Pete??

SEWANEE:
. . . God?

BROCK:
Oh my Pete! 🫢

* * *

January 21

BROCK:
Why is the OCEAN blue?

SEWANEE:
Well, Brock, it's not always blue. It can also be green, or gray, or other colors depending on how the light bounces. It only appears blue because water absorbs colors in the red part of the light spectrum which acts like a filter, leaving behind colors in the blue part of the spectrum.

BROCK:
Brando's Godfather voice you come into my house on the day my daughter is to be married and give me SCIENCE.

SEWANEE:
Forgive me, Don Corleone. There is no science anymore. FAKE NEWS.

BROCK:
ALTERNATIVE FACTS

SEWANEE:

WITCH HUNT

Grazie, Godfather.

BROCK:

Prego.

From: Jason Ruiz
To: Brock McNight; Westholme, Sarah
Date: January 23, 10:27 AM
Subject: Casanova—ep 1

Hey you two,

Just wanted to let you know the first ep is locked and it is DOPE. SO good. It's all set to drop on Valentine's Day. Fans are stoked. The preorders are through the roof. As I'd said, I'll send out payment at the beginning of each month, so your March 1 deposit will reflect two weeks of sales for episode 1 and one week of sales for episode 2.

Sarah, I'll have pickups to you for episode 3 tomorrow.

Thanks!
JR

AS SEWANEE PLACED eight used mugs in the studio sink, Damian, an engineer with dreads down to his ass, entered the kitchen. "Hey D," she said.

"Hey," he sighed, smiling wearily, and opened the fridge. He retrieved a mason jar of his homemade kombucha. He took a pull on it as if it were a cold beer.

She inclined her head at him. "Tough day?"

He shook his back at her tightly: later.

Just as, into the kitchen, walked Doug Carrey.

Jolted, Sewanee spun back to the sink.

Not once in the last eight years and now twice in the last two months? Why? How? Help.

"So, brothah, we all good?" Doug asked Damian.

"All good, my man, you're free to go," Damian replied. Doug pulled him into a bro-y handshake/back pat combo and Damian said, "Great job," but Sewanee knew him well enough to know he didn't mean it.

"Who woulda thunk reading a book out loud could be so wicked hahd, huh? Even a kids' book!" Damian took another swallow of kombucha as Doug floated his head around the kitchen and living room. "This house is sick. Who owns it?"

"Mark Clark."

Doug snorted. "That practically rhymes." It *did* rhyme. "He ever think of selling?"

Sewanee kept her hands in the sink, her gaze down, doing her best to disappear.

"No," Damian answered. "I mean, I don't think so. Not with the studio and all. Right, Swan?"

Shit.

Doug angled his head toward the disappearing act at the sink. "Waaaaitaminute, what a pissah! Swan?!"

She wiped her hands, turned around, faced Doug fully. "Of all the gin joints," she drawled.

"God *damn*!" Doug enthused. "How'd I miss that backside this time?" He laughed, of course, and Sewanee wished they could go another eight years without this happening again.

"So, uh, yeah, no," she said, steering him back to the topic of the house, "Mark will never sell."

"Well, minds are meant to be changed. Tell him to give me a bell. I been lookin' fah one of these old places in the hills fah years."

Damian took one more chug and returned the mason jar to the fridge. "I gotta go export the files. Nice working with you," he lied, and Sewanee wanted to tell him *she'd* export the files and could he please stay, please? But Damian was already gone and then there were two.

Doug smiled with all his teeth and Sewanee smiled back with pressed lips. Now what?

Doug pointed to his eye. "Still rockin' the patch, huh? Damn, how long you gotta keep it on?"

"Uh. Forever," she said, and, off his head tilt, added, "It was a bad accident."

"Oh." His grin wavered. "That's brutal. I thought it was something temporary . . ." The grin officially went out. "Shit. And you were so good. I mean, I'm sure you still are. Fuck. I'm so sorry."

Doug's sincerity, while perhaps fleeting, reminded Sewanee why she had felt some little something for him way back when. Even if that something had been just as fleeting. "Thanks."

"When'd it happen?"

"Seven years ago."

His silence got to her and she found herself reaching for words. Any words. "Did you enjoy recording—"

"Don't give up," he said suddenly. "The business has changed. You know what I'm sayin'? People are more open to . . . you know." He waved a hand. "Diversity."

She knew he meant disability, but either way he wasn't wrong. She had considered it herself. She still wanted to act, sometimes so desperately she had to go lie down until the yearning passed. But she knew that doing so would force her to face the truth, or at least her truth: she couldn't reclaim who she once was when who she once was no longer existed.

After a moment of gazing at her, he closed the distance between them and pulled her into a hug. It wasn't sexual, fortunately. It was delicate. A bit careful. The way you might hug someone you felt sorry for, but who also might be contagious, you weren't sure. Better safe than sorry. Still, it was Doug's version of trying. Of being a good guy.

She pulled back first, anything that could give her the illusion of having the upper hand, and glanced at the sink, hoping he'd sense she had to get back to work.

He did. He stepped fully back, but said, "Hey. Didn't you used to hang with Adaku Obi?"

She smiled. "Still do."

His smile came back, too. "Man, say hi fah me. We keep missing each other at awards shit. Tell her I'd like to connect."

Sewanee said, "Will do." But Sewanee thought, Will not.

He backed away, out of the kitchen. "And tell Mark—Mark?—I want this house. Serious. Gimme a bell." He winked. "Here's looking at you, Kid." Again, with the terrible Bogart impression.

An hour later, when the house chores were done and Damian had finished exporting, Sewanee let herself into studio 1 to start recording for the day. It still smelled like cologne. His cologne. A cologne he hadn't changed in eight years.

She stepped out, turned up the fan in the booth, and went down the hall to studio 4. She sat down inside and tried recording, but she was tripping over every other sentence. This only happened when she was tired, PMS-ing, or . . . just plain bothered.

She wanted a hug. A real one.

Instead, she picked up her phone.

SEWANEE:
Question: what happens after we die?

He responded immediately:

We don't have to record Romance anymore.

She smiled.
Another text appeared:

Unless we go to hell. Which is pretty likely tbh. Then that's all we do.

SEWANEE:
You really don't like doing Brock McNight, do you?

BROCK:
Would YOU like doing Brock McNight??

SEWANEE:
How DARE you ask me that?!

BROCK:
Walked right into that one.

Sewanee paused, considering how to respond. Her decision was made easier when her phone lit up again.

BROCK:
You know, the problem with sexual innuendo is . . .

you can't keep it up.

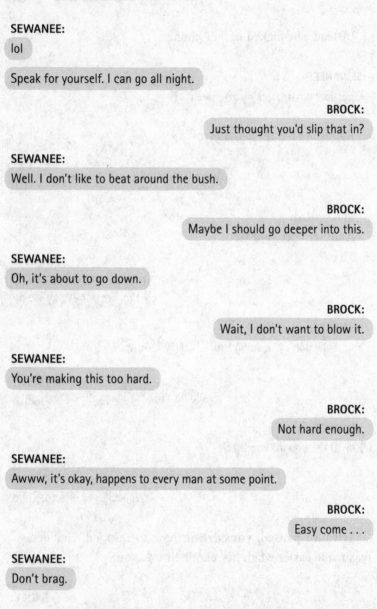

SEWANEE:
lol

Speak for yourself. I can go all night.

BROCK:
Just thought you'd slip that in?

SEWANEE:
Well. I don't like to beat around the bush.

BROCK:
Maybe I should go deeper into this.

SEWANEE:
Oh, it's about to go down.

BROCK:
Wait, I don't want to blow it.

SEWANEE:
You're making this too hard.

BROCK:
Not hard enough.

SEWANEE:
Awww, it's okay, happens to every man at some point.

BROCK:
Easy come . . .

SEWANEE:
Don't brag.

Sewanee's cheeks ached from the smile on her face. If someone walked in, she knew she'd appear absolutely deranged. A picture appeared in the chat. A meme of a Golden Retriever holding a giant femur in its mouth. The caption read: WANNA BONE? She blurted a laugh, then, realizing how loud it had been, closed the booth door.

SEWANEE:
No thanks. I should get off.

BROCK:
And scene!

SEWANEE:
Oh, are you done?

BROCK:
Almost. Just finishing.

She debated for half a second.

SEWANEE:
Need a hand?

She watched bubbles appear . . . then stop. More bubbles . . . another stop. What was he typing?
Then:

Okay, okay, I'm out, you win. Service ace.

SEWANEE:
And match.

BROCK:
Good volley.

Can I have my balls back?

SEWANEE:
bahahahahaahaha

BROCK:
You.

SEWANEE:
What?

BROCK:
Just. You.

SEWANEE WAS IN an epic line at Costco when her phone dinged.

BROCK:
Question. Got a sec?

SEWANEE:
No, I don't know where babies come from.

BROCK:
Dammit.

Before pulling out of her parking space, Sewanee texted:

Still waiting for your question.

BROCK:
Still waiting to ask it.

Leaning against the replenished shelves in Mark's garage, Sewanee texted:

Seriously?

BROCK:
You know what? Never mind.

SEWANEE:
oh COME ON!

BROCK:
It doesn't matter.

SEWANEE:
I am never letting this go, you know that, right?

BROCK:
Ughhhh

SEWANEE:
Waiting . . .

BROCK:
Forget it.

SEWANEE:
tick tock

BROCK:
It's just, I thought it mattered,
but now I think it doesn't.

SEWANEE:
Cool. Now tell me.

She went inside. Checked the apple supply. Put the kettle on. Refreshed the pretzels.

SEWANEE:
SERIOUSLY??

BROCK:

ok ok give me a second!!!

Please take this in the spirit with which I mean it.

I want to make sure nobody's getting hurt.

Or confused.

I don't want anything weird.

Between us.

In the end.

SEWANEE:

Nice haiku. Question please.

BROCK:

Blargh.

SEWANEE:

STIFFY!!!!!

The bubbles started, so Sewanee put the phone on the counter, grabbed a mug, a tea bag, promised herself she wouldn't look at her phone until she heard it ding. Betrayed that promise thirty seconds later, felt like an idiot, had just set the phone back down on the counter when it dinged again.

BROCK:

It's just this: since we began texting, I have gotten concerned—albeit irrationally (can't believe I used the word 'albeit')—that maybe I/you/we were possibly, potentially (probably?), crossing a line.

SEWANEE:

And?

BROCK:

And . . .

I was thinking that I should ask

You

If you're single.

(I feel like I'm in middle school for christsake.)

SEWANEE:

*pete's sake

BROCK:

This would be easier if Pete could pass a note with check boxes to one of your friends in study hall.

SEWANEE:

So you want to know if I'm single because . . . ?

BROCK:

bcuz someone else could be looking at your phone!! You never know who's looking at your phone!!

Not that there's anything inappropriate.

Too inappropriate.

(for the record this is going just as badly as I predicted)

What I mean to say is THIS:

> I would never want somebody to think
> I was coming on to his woman.

> (Or her woman???)

Again with the smiling she couldn't seem to contain. His adorable awkwardness prompted her to answer him amusingly, but sincerely. Why was her hand shaking?

SEWANEE:
You're safe. I'm single.

His next text appeared simultaneously:

> I know I can be jokey and flirty. And it might
> be confusing to tell what's real and what's
> not. Am I making any sense at all?

Followed instantly by:

> FML Don't read my last text PLEASE

Sewanee's full-body laugh sloshed some tea out of her cup and onto the counter. She wiped it up with her sleeve and quickly typed:

lol you kidding I'm gonna frame it.

BROCK:
> sigh

> So . . .

> we're good?

SEWANEE:
We're good.

BROCK:
Thank Pete.

SEWANEE:
Thank YOU.

* * *

February 14
(On WhatsApp)

MOM:
Good luck today, Swanling! Today's the day, right? We're so happy for you!

SEWANEE:
Thanks! Yes, first episode releases in about an hour.

MOM:
Oh good we didn't miss it. Stu wants to say something.

I mean type something.

SEWANEE:
Okay.

Go ahead, Stu.

I can see that you stopped typing. Did you press send?

Stu?

MOM:
These buttons are too damn small.

SEWANEE:
Agreed.

MOM:
But that was not what I wanted to say.

SEWANEE:
Okay.

MOM:
Wait your mother wants to know if you are going to send us the episode.

SEWANEE:
No.

MOM:
Yes! Please send. This is Mom again.

SEWANEE:
NO I am not sending.

MOM:
Can we download it?

SEWANEE:
NO no downloading.

MOM:
But we want to hear it!

SEWANEE:
NO you do not. Trust me.

MOM:

We are happy to pay for it. This is Stu.

SEWANEE:

You are not allowed to listen to it. Okay?
I record 50 books a year you could
listen to that aren't Romance.

Mom tell me you understand you
are not allowed to listen to it.

MOM:

We'll see. Love, Mom.

This is what I wanted to say. We saw
dolphins. We were docked. Came right up
to us. Did the EE-EE-EE right to us.

Oh this is me.

Stu.

SEWANEE:

Wow! How cool!

MOM:

It was talking just to us.

SEWANEE:

I'm sure it was. ☺

MOM:

Wish you were here with us Swanling, from Mom.

SEWANEE:

One of these days.

MOM:
You better young lady. Do not make me come get you. I would put a smiley face here but I do not know how to. This is Stu. Bye now. LOL. Stu.

SEWANEE:
Bye!

MOM:
It's Mom. He thinks LOL means lots of love.

SEWANEE:
Well, LOL back.

MOM:
Miss you, darlingest of daughters.

SEWANEE:
Miss you. So much. 🖤

From: Alice Dunlop
To: Sewanee Chester
Date: February 15, 10:27 AM
Subject: Audies presenting?

Hey hon,

Helping to organize presenters for the Audies and wondering if you'd have any desire to present the Lifetime Achievement Award (posthumously ☹) to June French? The public doesn't have to know your connection, but I think it would be a nice wink wink nod nod for the industry. What do ya think?

Hugs,
Alice

P.S. Have you seen the Facebook groups? Everyone is losing their minds over *Casanova, LLC.* I've never seen anything like it. Brava!

From: Sewanee Chester
To: Alice Dunlop
Date: February 15, 11:06 AM
Subject: RE: Audies presenting?

I would LOVE to. Thank you so much for asking.
    And no, haven't dipped into FB. Will do so now.

From: Sewanee Chester
To: Alice Dunlop
Date: February 15, 11:38 AM
Subject: RE: Audies presenting?

OH. MY. GODDDDDDDD.

SEWANEE:
Hey are you on Facebook?

BROCK:
Hell no.

Why?

SEWANEE:

Fans are loving the first episode. Like, a lot.

BROCK:

Nice.

SEWANEE:

Like, a lot a lot.

I think this might end up being huge.

BROCK:

👍

SEWANEE:

That's it?

BROCK:

Did you know the real Casanova was a terrible
human? Horrible. Actual criminal. Did time.
Rapist. Even knocked up his own daughter.

SEWANEE:

"And now, Children, Story Time with Brock McNight"

BROCK:

heh. Sorry. I'm happy for us, I am.

SEWANEE:

You just don't care?

BROCK:

No, I do, I'm just . . .

IDK.

SEWANEE:

You're checked out.

Of audio.

Of Romance.

BROCK:
I guess so?

I'm sorry. You deserve a better partner.

SEWANEE:
It's okay. Really. Like a trophy wife, I will console myself with the piles of money you brought to the marriage.

BROCK:
deal.

* * *

February 22

SEWANEE:
Question.

BROCK:
Sorry, wrong number, this isn't Question.

SEWANEE:
groaaaaaaaan

BROCK:
Deepest apologies, that was truly horrid Dad humor.

SEWANEE:
So, not judging, but what do we think of this hero?

BROCK:
...?

SEWANEE:
I'm having trouble deciding if Alessandro's complicated. Or just an asshole.

BROCK:
He's an alpha.

SEWANEE:
riiiiight but

BROCK:
He only cares about his art. Relationships are transactional for him.

SEWANEE:
Yes, most. With all the others, but not with her. When she gets what she came for (no pun intended) she's prepared to honor their agreement. He then treats her terribly (which, okay, typical Romance Hero having his Feels), but why?

BROCK:
IDK

SEWANEE:
Well, how are you going to play it?

BROCK:
What do you mean?

SEWANEE:
Is he really that oblivious to what he wants or is he protecting himself from going after what he wants in case he can't have it?

BROCK:
What do you mean?

SEWANEE:
I meeeaaan, why is he?

BROCK:
*who?

SEWANEE:
No, why. You can't just look at who someone is. You have to look at WHY someone is. Surface versus substance. That's the difference between caricature and character.

BROCK:
I just figured out why you're a better narrator than me. You're an actress, aren't you?

SEWANEE:
Was.

BROCK:
Why'd you stop?

SEWANEE:
Mmmmm story for another time.

BROCK:
I'll hold you to that.

What do YOU think Alessandro's "why" is?

SEWANEE:
off the top of my head . . .

I think he's tired of being seen as this sex god. I think he's desperate to end the performance, but who is he without it? Who would want him, the real Alessandro, when all the women he has ever known only seem to want the fantasy? All except her. She wanted something no one else saw in him: the person, not the commodity (represented by how she falls in love with his art, i.e. his soul, i.e. his truth).

So I err on the side of he's not oblivious, he's scared. Because he's falling in love with her. So: attraction = fear = self-protection = assholery.

BROCK:

Yeah that's totally what I was going to say.

That's good.

That's Really Good.

Mind if I steal it?

SEWANEE:

It's you.

*yours

SEWANEE WAS NAMED after her grandmother's hometown. Everyone who'd been involved in the decision had liked it. It was possibly the only thing they agreed on, if for completely different reasons. Elegant, her grandmother had said. Magical, her mother had said. Allegorical, her father had said.

Sewanee had wanted to live up to all of it.

But her name did not endear her to her grandmother. Not at first.

It wasn't personal. Barbara Chester had never shown much interest in children, and she'd had no use for Sewanee until she was old enough to have a conversation and not run mindlessly back to Henry and repeat it. But by the time Sewanee was eight or nine, they'd discovered what was missing from both of their lives: each other.

On school holidays or weekends or summer workdays, Marilyn would drive up Beverly Glen and pull over on Mulholland, where Sewanee would get into Blah's waiting car and they'd drive down the other side of the hill to Bitsy's house. They'd watch old movies in the shagged living room and Sewanee soaked it all up, knew every line from *The Philadelphia Story*, every step of "Make 'Em Laugh" from *Singin' in the Rain*, every head tilt from Lauren Bacall.

At the height of the day, they'd go out to the green-tinged pool and Blah would teach her how to swim, telling her the combination of swimming and dancing would give her everything she'd need to maintain her yet-to-appear figure. At some point, Blah would say, "I suppose your parents expect me to feed you," and they'd glide into the kitchen and Blah would forage for something, anything, that constituted food. Usually Ritz crackers or apple slices. Always Mallomars. Sometimes Bitsy would stop by between her lunch and dinner shift at Du-pars and bring them pancakes, which Sewanee loved, but her real appetite was elsewhere.

One more dance step; rewatch a Hepburn/Tracy film and talk about "chemistry"; go through Bette Davis's entire oeuvre.

By the time Sewanee was in middle school, they would drive around the Valley in Blah's Oldsmobile convertible and go consignment shopping on Ventura Boulevard. They'd sweep down the racks, pulling anything remotely intriguing. When Sewanee would say, "I like this, what do you think?" Blah would respond, "I think you're a knockout, Doll."

This was when Sewanee began sensing what it might be like to be Sewanee. She would show up at school in jeans, T-shirts, flip-flops, and ponytails, but every Homecoming or Snow Ball or Prom she was decked out in impeccably tailored vintage and makeup, looking about a decade older than she was.

It was at one of these dances her junior year when a class-mate's father, a television producer, asked if she had any interest in acting. She said it was all she wanted to do. What she didn't tell him was that her parents had told her she couldn't until she was eighteen. They lived in Los Angeles, after all, they knew the horror stories. So when the producer asked her to audition for his new show, she did so without telling her parents. Because she was sure she wouldn't get it. She just wanted to test herself out. Like a first date.

So when she inevitably got the role and was forced to tell them, they said no, of course she couldn't take the part, hadn't they discussed this?

But, but, but!

They fought, their first real teenager knock-down drag-out, and Sewanee slammed the front door, got into her rattletrap Jetta, and steamed over the hill to Bitsy's.

She and Blah had sat out by the pool in the warm October evening while Sewanee sobbed, hurling invectives at her par-ents. Blah calmly sipped her martini and waited for Sewanee to breathe. Then she handed her the last gulp of her drink, which Sewanee immediately threw back and just as immediately nearly threw up, making a face only a lemon could love. They both laughed; Blah's aim all along.

She reached into the pocket of her quilted dressing gown, pulled out a lighter and the silver cigarette case her agent had given her in '58. It was inscribed on the back, "To: A great pair of get-away sticks. May they take you where you want to go." She tapped out a cigarette, lit it, smoke dancing in the pool lights.

Sewanee had heard the story of how Blah had been discovered many times over the years, but like all of Blah's stories, new layers were added as Sewanee got older.

"Bitsy and I had moved to Nashville for work. We were cocktail waitresses at a dive in Printer's Alley. And one day, a man walked in." Most of Blah's stories included the line: a man walked in.

"They were location scouting for a honky-tonk in Nashville. Big deal at the time, going on location instead of making a soundstage in Hollywood look like a honky-tonk. So, I sauntered up, talked him into staying for a drink and into using our bar to shoot in. He came back two months later to film, and I went from being a waitress-in-life to a waitress-in-a-movie. I saved my tips, got on a bus, and when I got to Hollywood, I telephoned him. He got me a room at a good boardinghouse. He got me a coat check job at Musso and Frank. He got me my first agent. And all he got was my virginity."

Sewanee's mouth dropped open, but Blah waved off her shock. "He was a looker. And it was time to get rid of it anyway."

"But . . ." Sewanee sputtered. "He used you!"

Blah raised an eyebrow. "Did he? Two people can use each other, you know."

She barely dared ask. "Grandpa?"

Blah shook her head. "He was later. He was love. He was a playwright out of New York and he thought *I* was interesting. Imagine that.

"What I'm saying, Dollface, is I never slept with anyone I didn't want to sleep with. I always had a reason. Was it right? Was it wrong? Who the hell knows. You've seen movies about that time. People write their little tell-alls now. Casting couches, randy directors, lifted skirts against a dressing room door." She scoffed, took a drag. "I'm not saying that's not how it was for some gals. And I'm sorry if that's how it was. But for me, it was three-martini lunches and bonfires in Malibu that lasted until the sun came up and 'my wife is visiting her sister for the weekend, you ever been to Catalina?' Reciprocal, you understand?"

"But you wanted to be an actress and they exploited that."

Blah cackled and ashed her cigarette. "I didn't want to be an actress. I wanted to be famous."

"But you worked?"

"But I wasn't good! Shit's sake, I couldn't act my way out of a wet paper bag. My choice was, I could be in it the way I was, or out of it because of what I wasn't." She pointed her cigarette at Sewanee. "And Doll, I can see on your face that won't work for you."

She took a final drag and snuffed it. "You want me to take your side and rail at your parents but—much as it pains me, and Lord knows it does—they're right. This? Who you are now and what you're being offered? Is how things end badly."

Sewanee stamped her foot, every inch the child she didn't think she was. "So what am I supposed to do?"

Blah leaned back, wrapped her hands around the frame of the lounger, crossed her legs. "What I never did. Get good. So goddamn good they can't tell you shit."

Blah's lack of talent had never prevented her from understanding how it manifested in others. She helped Sewanee develop emotional accessibility, a command of words and language, a body that moved freely, effortlessly, sensually through space. She set about making her granddaughter her, but better. And when Sewanee applied to Julliard and got in? It was the greatest accomplishment of Barbara Chester's life.

And by the time Sewanee graduated, she had Blah's star quality, Marilyn's innate goodness, Henry's analytical skills, Julliard training, and four years of New York spit shine on her. She was unstoppable.

Until she wasn't.

* * *

February 25

BROCK:

Been thinking about our convo the other night. I want you to know: I'm not an actor. Everything you said about Alessandro made so much sense. I never think about stuff like that.

SEWANEE:

How did you get into audiobooks if you're not an actor?

BROCK:

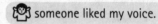 someone liked my voice.

SEWANEE:

It is a good voice.

BROCK:

I once called the DMV and the representative said, "I loved the way you said your VIN number. Would you mind doing it again a little slower?"

SEWANEE:

Haha appreciate what you have, my friend.

BROCK:

I do. I'd be lost without it.

Hey AM I your friend?

SEWANEE:
Figure of speech.

BROCK:
Ouch.

SEWANEE:
JK it's not that we're not not friends.

Ooof, too many nots.

We. Are. Friends. No nots.

I hate texting.

BROCK:
I heard they're testing a new invention. Calling it a tellingphone or something like that. They're saying we'll actually be able to talk to each other through this here typing box! Science!

SEWANEE:
FAKE NEWS

Eleven minutes later:

SEWANEE:
What did you do before you were a narrator?

BROCK:
Mmmmmm story for another time.

Sewanee made herself wait until she was done for the day, still dripping from the rain that had been lashing during her climb back up to the casita, to text:

OKAY IT'S ANOTHER TIME!

> **BROCK:**
> Is this MY Another Time or YOUR Another Time?

SEWANEE:
Nice try. You're up.

> **BROCK:**
> K just let me wrap up this chapter.
>
> Maybe make myself a drink first.

SEWANEE:
Ooh I'll join you!

> **BROCK:**
> You a wine-spritzer lady or a
> whisky-neat woman?

SEWANEE:
Depends. What kind of story am I settling in for?

> **BROCK:**
> A tale of enduring friendship in
> the face of dashed dreams.

SEWANEE:
I'm breaking out the tequila.

> **BROCK:**
> Olé

57 minutes later:

> **BROCK:**
> Tequila ready?

SEWANEE:

Turns out I only have a little cheap vodka in the back of my freezer.

BROCK:

Only a little?

SEWANEE:

It's a little freezer.

What are you drinking?

BROCK:

Beer.

SEWANEE:

LOSER

BROCK:

And you don't even know the story yet.

SEWANEE:

I'll get my little vodka while you type.

BROCK:

Ok, here goes.

I was in a band. We were killing it. We had a record deal. We were on tour. We were young and fearless and had nothing to lose. Long story short, the lead singer, my best friend, flamed out. Drugs.

SEWANEE:

Wow. I'm sorry.

BROCK:

So typical it's embarrassing in hindsight.

SEWANEE:
Did you try a solo career?

BROCK:
No. He was the musical genius. I just write a little, play a little guitar, and sing a little.

That's my M.O.: do a lot of things a little.

SEWANEE:
You and my freezer.

How's your friend now? Or shouldn't I ask?

BROCK:
That's the silver lining. He's sober. Has been for five years.

SEWANEE:
That's great!

BROCK:
It is. Few months ago we started playing together again. To see if there was anything left.

SEWANEE:
Was there?

BROCK:
He wants to take another shot.

SEWANEE:
And you?

BROCK:
IDK

SEWANEE:

Are you afraid he'll relapse?

BROCK:

He's not the problem.

SEWANEE:

?

BROCK:

I'm not afraid for him specifically. I'm just afraid.

SEWANEE:

Of what?

BROCK:

Sigh. How much time ya got?

SEWANEE:

About a finger's worth of vodka.

BROCK:

I was a fearless boy who became a fearful man.

There. Nostrovia.

SEWANEE:

Ennnhhh I don't shoot vodka. If you
want me to finish this, I'm going to
need a little more than that.

BROCK:

K. I'll skip to the end.

When the world's your oyster? And you gobble it up?
There's nothing worse than getting food poisoning.
Just the sight of one after that makes you sick.

> (I promise I'm a better songwriter than
> this analogy would suggest)

SEWANEE:

But if you never open another
oyster, you'll miss the pearls.

> **BROCK:**
> Yeah. Well.

> For the record, I hate talking about this.

SEWANEE:

Brb gonna go post on Facebook that Brock
McNight is afraid of eating oysters.

> **BROCK:**
> I will completely understand if you
> never want to talk to me again.

SEWANEE:

R U kidding? I'm making popcorn.

> **BROCK:**
> Okay, enough about me. What's your Another Time?

Sewanee sat back and sipped her vodka. How would she even begin? Was she ready to tell her story? To open herself up like that?

Maybe she could at least address the fear. Tell him she knew something about life getting pulled out from under you. Maybe use the awful oyster metaphor. At least let him know how much she understood his struggle. Talk straight, one ruination to another.

But she didn't want to.

She wanted to talk about songwriting and vodka and sexual innuendos.

And where he lived.

And how old he was.

And what he did for fun.

And did he have hair?

Was he tall? He sounded large, but not necessarily tall. Which was fine. She didn't care. Why would she? Who was she to care about such things?

It was novel, having this strong a connection with someone she'd never seen. Who'd never seen her. Then again, maybe that's what made it possible. Would seeing each other, meeting each other face to face, fracture the relationship they'd built? He would probably say *a little* relationship was safer and he'd be right.

Which was why, she realized, she could identify with Brock much more than with someone like Nick.

Nick.

The man who always went 'round the bend, who would look into the well even if it meant crushing disappointment. Nick was who she wished she were; Brock was much closer to who she actually was.

It was as if she had been staring at a painting and foreground-Nick and background-Brock had switched. When had that happened?

Her phone lit up.

BROCK:

You're not literally making popcorn?

SEWANEE:

Ha no, sorry. Thinking about a worthy answer.

BROCK:
Take your time. I took mine.

Actually, no. I totally forgot. I have rehearsal.

SEWANEE:
Oh!

BROCK:
I'm so sorry.

SEWANEE:
No, no it's okay! Trust me.

BROCK:
God my brain these days!

SEWANEE:
No listen I dodged a bullet here.

BROCK:
Grrr. I don't want to leave this. It's important.

SEWANEE:
No, your rehearsal is important. It's not like you wanted to know why grass is green. My story can wait.

BROCK:
I know that one! Chlorophyll! TBC!

FRIDAY. HAPPY HOUR. Seasons.

Sewanee signed in at the front desk, as she did almost every Friday. But this time, Adaku joined her.

Adaku was in self-imposed lockdown as she trained for the Lysistrata-in-the-jungle movie (which was titled *The Originator*, for reasons Sewanee did not understand), and when she'd texted last night I NEED TO GET OUT OF MY HOUSE, Sewanee had suggested she join her at Seasons and they could have dinner after.

They headed to Blah's room to rouse her. "Ten bucks says she'll be on the left side of the couch, two pillows behind her, headphones on her head, an audiobook playing, fast asleep." They were chuckling as they entered Blah's room and found her exactly as Sewanee had predicted.

She opened her eyes, instinctively sensing their presence. "Dollface! What are you doing here? And who is this?"

"Blah, I'm Adaku. I don't know if you remember me, but I–"

"Of course I remember you! Who could forget that smile?"

Adaku bent over to give Blah a hug. "It's so great to see you again."

Sewanee couldn't be sure whether Blah recognized Adaku or not, but she supposed it didn't matter. "It's Friday!" She fingercombed the hair on the back of Blah's head. "What do you say we get ourselves together and head down to happy hour?"

"What are we waiting for? Hand me my lipstick, Doll." She did and Blah applied it—flawlessly, without a mirror—while telling Adaku, "Don't go anywhere without your lips. You never know who you'll run into. Or kiss, for that matter."

When they went downstairs, Adaku moved toward a corner table in the half-filled lounge, but Blah said, "The bar, hon. Stools. Shows off the gams." So they commandeered three of the four stools and ordered martinis, Adaku unhappily abstaining for the sake of her regimen. Blah crossed her legs and ran an elegant hand along her thigh as if straightening a gown's high slit instead of smoothing the beige polyester of her elastic-waisted pants.

"Two martinis, one dirty with extra olives, just the way you like it, Blah," the orderly-cum-bartender said, pushing their glasses toward them.

"Thanks, Dan," Sewanee replied, sliding the special one to her grandmother. "Blah, Dan gave you three olives. It's normally two. Something you want to tell me?"

"That's between me and Dan," Blah simpered. She saucily slid one off the toothpick, then winked. "That's why the extra one." She turned to Adaku. "I hope you're taking notes."

Adaku laughed. "Always."

Sewanee took the opportunity, while Blah was sipping her drink to, once again, reinforce the impending move to memory care. "So, I was thinking, when it comes time to move to your new room, I'll bring over some roller suitcases and make it easy." She'd been repeating this every time they talked for the last two months, but she wasn't sure it had stuck. Or, if it had, if Blah completely understood the implications.

Blah merely nodded and sipped her martini. "Whatever you want, Doll." She jerked her chin at Dan. "Let's get Popeye here to help. He looks more than capable."

Dan smiled. "Where are you moving to, Blah?"

Blah's smile froze. She glanced at Sewanee. "Where am I moving?"

"Just to another wing," Sewanee answered, smiling at Dan, infusing her voice with calm for Blah's sake. "She'll still be here every Friday so keep those olives stocked."

This seemed to mollify Blah, who raised her glass to her lips and looked out into the room, casing the door, as if this were the bar at the Roosevelt Hotel and Gregory Peck might walk in.

He didn't, but Mitzi did.

When Mitzi entered a room, orange preceded her. Orange lipstick, orange fright-wig-looking hair, even the tennis balls on the feet of her walker were electric orange. All gracefully wrapped in a leopard-print stole. None of it, however, was meant to outshine the enthusiastically applied blue eye shadow that went all the way up to her drawn-on eyebrows. It was about balance, you see.

"Look who came to visit!" Mitzi's voice was a handsaw cutting a 2x4.

"Mitzi. So good to see you." Sewanee leaned into Adaku and murmured, "I apologize in advance."

"Ooh, noted," Adaku whispered back, grinning.

Mitzi did her best to climb onto the bar stool next to her. "Why are these goddamn things so tall? And who are you?" she groused. Loudly.

Blah winced, rolled her eyes at the girls, and said, "Mitzi. Turn your hearing aids down. You're shouting."

"What?" she shouted.

"Your hearing aids! You're shouting!"

"You don't have to shout!"

Mitzi adjusted her hearing aids as Dan said, "What can I get ya, Mitzi?"

"Two cents plain, I'm off the sauce." Her volume decreased to an acceptable level. She turned to Adaku. "So, mystery woman. Nu?"

"I'm Sewanee's friend, Adaku."

"AdaWho? What is that?"

"Nigerian. Igbo."

"IgWhat?"

Sewanee caught Adaku's eye, mouthed: "Apologizing."

Adaku waved her off and answered, gamely, "It's an ethnic group in—"

But Mitzi's attention—short-lived at best—diverted to the glass Dan put in front of her. "What's with the fruit? Two cents plain is two cents plain. You should bartend in jail." She lifted the lime wedge from her glass and put it to those Day-Glo lips.

Blah leaned over to look at Mitzi as though they were two old miners down the pub after a long day in the shafts. "You usually get a 7 and 7."

"You remember her drink?" Sewanee exclaimed.

Blah shrugged. "I don't know what to tell you." Back to Mitzi. "Why the change?"

Mitzi set her glass down. "What, I should publish it in a newspaper?"

Sewanee felt Adaku's fingers claw into her forearm, her breath hot in her ear, the giggle in her voice. "I'm never leaving."

"Just wait," Sewanee whispered back, then fed the fire: "Hey, Mitzi! How's the hip?"

"Terrible. This one gets better, this one gets worse." She slapped her left thigh and then her right. "The only good thing about getting old is nothing. But I don't complain." She went to take another sip, found it empty. "Goddamm it."

Dan smiled. "'Nother?"

"What am I, a camel?"

"Hellooooo!"

All four women turned to see Birdie, a Midwestern Mrs. Claus-looking woman in a Champion sweatshirt with Westie appliques on it. "Are we having a party?"

"Oh, Christ," Blah and Mitzi said in unison, turning back to the bar.

Birdie stepped up to them. "If I'd known we were having a party, I would have brought dip."

"Not the dip!" Mitzi barked.

Birdie leaned in to Adaku. "I don't think we've had the pleasure. I'm Bertha, but everyone calls me Birdie."

Sewanee cut her off at the pass. "This is my best friend, Adaku, but everyone calls her A."

"You couldn't have told *me* that?" Mitzi, again, barked.

"How lovely!" Birdie chirped. "We both have nicknames!"

"Yes, lovely," Adaku concurred.

Birdie turned her attention to Sewanee. "And how's my dear Swan?"

"You always remember my name, Birdie."

"Well! As the saying goes, 'birds of a feather' . . . do something."

Blah was gazing down at the bar. "Dan, we need a refill." Sewanee clocked her half-drunk martini. "And please remember the olives this time."

"Sure thing, Blah." Dan took the glass without comment. "Birdie? What can I get you?"

"Oh, you know me, I'm a teetotaler. But since we're having a party! Vodka, rocks, twist."

"Coming right up."

Birdie tapped the bar. "Dagburnit, I wish I'd brought my dip."

"Birdie, why don't you tell A about your dip?" Sewanee suggested, to which Blah and Mitzi cried, "Oh, Christ!"

Birdie had blue eyes that were wide and dim, though—if Sewanee were being cruelly honest—perhaps no dimmer than they'd been her entire life. She looked at Adaku now with those fathomless-lake eyes and said, "Would you like that?" and Adaku was toast.

"Please!"

"Well. You'll need sour cream. A good-sized tub of it."

"Okay."

"You might want to write this down, honey. You wouldn't want to forget something."

"Of course, good idea." Adaku smiled, pulling out her phone and going to her notes app. "Ready!"

"Where was I?"

"A good-sized tub of sour cream."

"Yes! Now, you don't want one of the huge tubs, mind you, because then the ratio gets thrown off. Just a good, normal tub. Next comes the taco seasoning. You can find that in the Mexican aisle. I don't mean to offend you."

Adaku came up from her phone. "Why would I be offended?"

"I don't think I'm supposed to say Mexican anymore. My daughter is trying to help me be more appropriate. But what's wrong with being a Mexican anything? Even seasoning?"

Adaku patted Birdie's hand. "Nothing."

Birdie raised her other hand to her chest and exhaled. "Phew." Then she paused. "Where was I?"

"Taco seasoning."

"Yes! The Mexico aisle. You're going to want to look for a small package about this big and it's going to say: Taco. Seasoning." She watched Adaku type this while Dan delivered the fresh drinks.

He pointed at Mitzi's empty glass. "You sure?"

Mitzi talked right over Birdie's lecture. "Jack and Coke."

Blah said, "I thought you weren't drinking?"

Mitzi gave an eye-rolling nod in Birdie's direction. "That was before the dip showed up."

Birdie heard Mitzi and stopped her recital. "Do you want the recipe, Mitzi?"

"Oh, Christ."

"Now, the package tells you to put it in ground beef, but don't. No . . . ground . . . beef."

"No . . . ground . . . beef," Adaku parroted.

"You'll take the sour cream and put it into a bowl. Then you take the packet of Mexican seasoning and you open it. Then you sprinkle it into the sour cream and you stir. Sprinkle it! If you pour it all in at once, you'll get those garsh dang lumps. Believe you me!" She laughed. "Sprinkle. Stir. Sprinkle. Stir."

"Do you mix it clockwise?" Sewanee asked.

Mitzi shouted, "Shoot me!" then pointed at her glass and said, again, to Dan, "You should bartend in jail. More rum."

"You mean Jack?"

"What am I, your manager? I don't care how you make it."

Birdie was looking down at the bar, engaged with an imaginary bowl. She placed her hand above it and moved first clockwise, then counterclockwise. She paused. Did it again. Then she looked up at Sewanee, satisfied. "Yes!"

"And what else do you put in it, Birdie?" Adaku asked.

"Oh, nothing," Birdie said, eyes bugging. "Well, I suppose you could add a touch of salt, but I wouldn't risk it. My husband, Jerry, loves it. And the boys can't get enough. They won't watch a game without it." Sewanee was pretty sure Birdie's husband had passed away, that that's how she ended up at Seasons. Her daughter was an executive at one of the studios and she brought her out here to be closer. Plucked out of Michigan, condemned to spend the rest of her days with Hollywood barracudas like Mitzi and Blah.

A silence fell over them.

Sewanee watched Adaku feel the silence. A different kind of silence than they were used to with their friends. With their friends, a group silence felt as if they were all busy paddling a canoe to an agreed-upon destination. Here, it was more like being set adrift.

Birdie broke in, picking up a paddle. "Mitzi, what's your husband's name?"

Mitzi hacked. "Which one?" She took a slug of her Jack and Coke then looked at Dan. "What the hell is in this?"

Birdie now looked to Blah, who was staring at the bar. "Do you have a husband?"

Blah lifted her eyes. And her new glass. "No."

"Oh. You lost your husband, or did you never have one?"

Blah froze mid-sip. She paused. "I don't know. I don't remember."

Mitzi scoffed, "I wish I could forget."

Blah didn't look to Sewanee for an answer, so Sewanee didn't provide one. She watched Blah stare at her drink and wondered, not for the first time, if forgetting all the things that had made one's life worth living before one's life came to an end was a cruelty or a mercy.

"Well, maybe you didn't have one!" Birdie suggested, cheerfully. "Maybe you were just sleazy!"

A knife-cutting silence as Blah thought about this. "God, I hope so," she said and drank.

ADAKU AND SEWANEE tucked into a curved red vinyl booth at the back of Smoke House, joining the other early-birders. Adaku ordered a steak salad with oil and vinegar on the side and Sewanee, wanting to be supportive, did the same.

"How's the training going?" she asked.

"I feel like Mitzi," Adaku answered. "Everything hurts."

"Well, you look great. You are officially a badass."

Adaku grimaced. "I better be if I'm gonna make it through this film."

"Please tell me you're not doing your own stunts?"

"God, no! But it's still gonna be a bitch. Running through the jungle and all the fight choreography. I—" She stopped herself, seeming embarrassed to be heard complaining about starring in a film anyone else would have killed for. That "anyone else" being her best friend sitting across from her. She smiled and chippered up. "I should shut up is what I should do."

"No, A, you shouldn't shut up. You have every right to feel the way you do."

But Adaku shook her head. "Uhn-uhn. I'm not gonna become

one of those actresses we both hate listening to." She mindlessly reached for the basket of garlic bread and snapped her hand back. "I don't want to talk about me anyway. I want a Brock McNight update!"

Sewanee flushed. "Oh! There's nothing to report."

Adaku's eyes flared with intrigue and she waved her whole hand around Sewanee's face. "That is *not* what I'm seeing."

"I just mean, nothing's, you know, *happened*."

"But you like him."

"Sure. He seems . . . nice. We have a good . . . working relationship."

Adaku shook her head slowly back and forth, back and forth, digging a trough with her chin. "Nope. Nope, nope, nope."

Sewanee threw her head back. "Ugh, fine! He's great. He's funny. He's a hundred times more interesting than I thought he'd be. He writes in complete sentences. Correctly capitalizes proper nouns."

"Wow, where are you guys registered?"

Sewanee snorted. "You know, more than anything? It's just been nice collaborating with someone. Makes me feel . . ."

"What?" Adaku again reached for the bread then flagged a passing waiter. "Excuse me?" She pointed at the basket. "Can you disappear this, please? Thank you." She turned her attention back to Sewanee. "Feel what?"

Sewanee took a moment to sip her water. To make a decision. Voicing what she was about to, especially to Adaku, felt final. Irrevocable. Once it was out, her friend would have something to hold her to. Adaku was a cat waiting to pounce. "Like I'm acting again. Really acting. And it's made me realize . . . that I miss it."

Adaku dropped her chin, gazed solidly at Sewanee through the tops of her eyes. "This is new. What are we going to do about this?"

Sewanee flicked her hand. "Nothing. It'll pass."

"It is not nothing. I will not let it pass."

They looked at each other.

Sewanee prepared to say something, but she wasn't sure what. Adaku didn't give her the chance. "You know I think you threw in the towel too soon."

Grateful to be spared a moment of her own reckoning, Sewanee nodded. "Yeah, I know. You're wrong, but I know."

"You were the only one who told you it was over. Even your agent said—"

"He's an agent. He thought he could capitalize on it. If I'd been more established before the accident, *maybe*. But I wasn't."

She'd wondered: Had she done that show back in high school, had her parents let her, would she have been famous enough to overcome what happened to her? If she'd had fans, and they'd lived through it with her? If the industry felt it owed her something? It would have been a story, at least. She could have—and God, she hated this word—*leveraged* it. But how could she have a comeback without a place to come back to? As it was, she was simply another actress who disappeared as quickly as she had been discovered. Not a star; a shooting star.

And then Doug Carrey of all people had said, "Don't give up." That maybe there was a place for her. And then Brock had talked about his fear of trying to reclaim what he'd had before and she hadn't been able to sleep that night for thinking.

Adaku still peered at her. "It's a simple question. Do you want to act?"

"It's not a simple question. I can't—"

"Yes or no."

"I miss it, but I don't know if I'm just being—"

"Yes! Or! No!"

"I don't know!"

"You don't know? Try saying it. Try saying it and see how the truth feels."

There was an interminable lacuna. "Yes."

Adaku banged the table so forcefully Sewanee lunged for her water glass and the whole restaurant turned. Adaku was unperturbed. "Then what are we waiting for?! Here's what we do!"

"A, please. Everyone's looking," Sewanee murmured.

"Yes, they are! At two co-stars of *The Originator*!"

"What, no, A, no—"

"You don't get to talk right now, you get to listen." Adaku leaned over the table. "There's a role in this film and when I read it? All I could think was, I swear to God, I thought: this is Swan. This is Sewanee Chester as I live and breathe. But you're so stubborn about never acting again—"

"I'm not stubborn, I'm realistic."

Adaku ignored her. "It's the best role in the film! Not big. Maybe six scenes. But pivotal and memorable and just"—Adaku groaned loudly, fiercely, garnering more looks—"delicious."

Sewanee quirked her head. "In *this* film? Isn't it chicks in hot pants with machine guns in the jungle—"

Adaku waved her finger at Sewanee's mouth. "You got to close this up and hear me out, okay?"

Sewanee could have been blinded by the light in her friend's eyes. She sighed with internal excitement and external caution and said, "Okay."

Adaku brought her hands together, as if in prayer. "She's the leader of this resistance group that's been living in the trees—"

Sewanee snorted. It was involuntary.

Adaku glared at her. "And when I stumble upon them with my tribe, she almost kills me. Bowie knife to the throat. But then we ally—"

"Let me guess: She dies in the final battle?"

Adaku's hands turned into fists, taking the reins on her patience. "Swan. There's so much meat on this bone. It's such a good death. They hang her!"

"They *hang* her? Jesus—"

"She goes out like the true warrior she is." Adaku leaned in. "And as they're raising her up real slow, real torturously, because they're dickwads, she and my character? They make eye contact. And there's this beautiful camaraderie, this, like, *witnessing*. This, 'I will make this right if it's the last thing I do, you *will not* die in vain' thing. And I'd have tears streaming down my face and you'd have one tear rolling down your cheek—'cause you have that freakish ability to time your tears—combined with this steely go-ahead-you-shitheads-kill-me defiance on your face. And then your life force . . . just . . . fades out. I mean, come on!" Adaku spread her hands over the table, at this imagined spread of opportunity. "It's your role. I can do this."

"What do you mean you can do this?"

"Star power, babe! It's what we've been fighting for since our Tony's pizza days and now I've got it."

Sewanee tried to squash the jolt of excitement that shot through her. "Okay. Okay. What's her backstory?"

"She was kidnapped and forced to work in a brothel. And she refused to do what they told her to. A queen from the jump."

Sewanee paused. "So, they punished her."

Adaku paused, too. "Right. But because she was so—"

"She's disfigured."

Adaku took another pause. "Yes, but that's not the point."

"No, my ability to time my tears is the point." She balled up her napkin, tossed it gently onto the table. "Come on, A, at least be honest."

Adaku huffed. "You know what?" Sat back, huffed again.

"*Honestly?* Sometimes you really piss me off. You want to think the only thing anybody sees is that scar, go for it. But meanwhile, there's a chance for us to do something together. To make something happen *together*. And you are perfect for the part because of everything you are, and everything you've survived, and sorry, but yes, that has a lot to do with that scar."

Adaku stopped there as the food arrived. She dug into her salad with leashed frustration. Sewanee picked at hers for a few moments before saying, "I'm sorry. You're right. I just wish—"

"And I just wish you'd deal with it already," Adaku rushed out, in loving exasperation. "Because it's holding you back and it kills me to watch you—"

Sewanee held up a hand. "I know." She encircled Adaku's wrist. "I'm sorry." She widened her eye for emphasis.

Adaku sighed and lifted her wrist to her lips, kissed the top of Sewanee's lingering hand. "Me too. I'm hangry all the time now. This training's turned me into a roided-out gym dick."

Sewanee chuckled and Adaku dug back into her salad. Sewanee took a bite and a sip of water. "So. How real is this? Me doing this?"

Adaku swallowed. "First thing tomorrow, I'll check in with the studio. I know they haven't found anyone yet. I can't guarantee they'd make a straight offer. Even I had to audition. But it'll be a formality. They're going to fall in love with you."

* * *

February 27

BROCK:

Heads up: in one of my sections, Claire asks what Alessandro wants out of their lovemaking and he says, "I want to change your voice." And then at the end, he references that he did at some point and how it was the hottest accomplishment of his life or some such. So maybe find a place to change your voice in one of your sections?

SEWANEE:

You want me to change my voice?

BROCK:

IDK. Maybe just something that gives a little heat to Claire's typical cool/calm/collected thing.

SEWANEE:

You really want that?

BROCK:

No. Not necessarily. I'm just spit-balling.

SEWANEE:

Well, is there a specific spit-ball you have in mind?

BROCK:

You know, whatever. Something a little wild. Maybe.

SEWANEE:

Wild? Really.

BROCK:

Ok, not wild.

Maybe just wanton.

SEWANEE:

Wanton?!

BROCK:

Forget it. I shouldn't have brought it up.

SEWANEE:

BROCK:

Are you . . . laughing at me?

SEWANEE:

Wantonly.

Hey, uhhhhh, heads up: In one of my sections it says, "I'd never heard my own voice sound like that, I didn't sound like myself. Or maybe I sounded exactly like myself. My true self." So maybe if you could, like, IDK, do something worthy of that response...

BROCK:

 you already knew all this.

SEWANEE:

But rest assured I thoroughly enjoyed you trying to talk about it.

BROCK:

It wasn't easy.

SEWANEE:

I could hear your voice change.

BROCK:

☺

Twenty-eight minutes later, as Sewanee was standing in a towel in her bathroom, combing out her hair, her phone dinged.

BROCK:
It's a good line, isn't it? I want to change your voice.

SEWANEE:
It is.

BROCK:
It is.

SEWANEE:
June knew what she was doing.

BROCK:
I would vaporize if a woman said that to me.

SEWANEE:
I would vaporize if a man achieved it.

She watched the bubbles appear. Watched them stop.
Start again.
Stop.
Start.
Stop.
Start.
Stop.

* * *

February 28

SEWANEE:
Question. Any interest in doing something other than Romance? A friend is casting a Clancy-esque book and needs an alpha assassin sound.

BROCK:
It's gratifying to know I sound that masculine to you.

SEWANEE:
Sounds can be deceiving?

BROCK:
Let's just say the voice is the only thing I have going for me in that department.

SEWANEE:
Don't forget you're a musician. Lots of women dig that.

BROCK:
Not you tho?

SEWANEE:
I live in LA. Every guy is a musician.

BROCK:
Anyone ever written a song about you?

SEWANEE:
mmm . . .

I don't think so?

BROCK:
You wouldn't remember?

SEWANEE:
I've listened to a lot of bad boyfriends' bad songs. I just don't think any of them were written about me. At least I hope they weren't.

BROCK:
Fair.

SEWANEE:
So should I put your hat in the ring?

BROCK:
I appreciate it, really, but honestly?
Even the thought of it . . .

it makes me tired.

you want to know how unsuited
I actually am to this job?

SEWANEE:
PLEASE

BROCK:
Here it is:

I'm not a reader.

I don't like reading!

There! I said it!

SEWANEE:
The first step is admitting you have a problem.

BROCK:
I feel so much better!

Freeeeeeedom!

I want to dance! I want to sing!

SEWANEE:
lol

BROCK:
I want to grab you up and kiss you!

Got carried away.

Sorry.

SEWANEE:
Don't be.

BROCK:
ok.

(I wasn't anyway)

From: Jason Ruiz
To: Brock McNight; Westholme, Sarah
Date: March 1, 4:56 PM
Subject: Casanova, LLC payment

Hi,

Just made the first deposit, let me know if you don't see it hit
your accounts in the next few days. Receipt attached. ☺
JR

From: Brock McNight
To: Jason Ruiz; Westholme, Sarah
Date: March 1, 4:58 PM
Subject: RE: Casanova, LLC payment

HOLY SHIT!!

From: Westholme, Sarah
To: Brock McNight; Jason Ruiz
Date: March 1, 4:58 PM
Subject: RE: Casanova, LLC payment

HOLY SHIT!!

BROCK:
did we send that email at
the same time?

SEWANEE:
did we reply at the same time again?

BROCK:
lol

SEWANEE:
LOL

BROCK:
STOP IT

SEWANEE:
omg stop

k you go, I'll wait.

BROCK:
I REPEAT: HOLY SHIT

SEWANEE:
SERIOUSLY. Congrats!

BROCK:
You too! See, now I care! Now I feel like the trophy wife!

SEWANEE:
I wish we could go celebrate.

BROCK:
I wish we could go celebrate.

SEWANEE:
AGAIN?!

BROCK:
AGAIN?!

SEWANEE:
This is ridiculous!

BROCK:
This is ridiculous!

SEWANEE:
LOL!

BROCK:
LOL!

SEWANEE:
Four score and seven years ago

BROCK:
You got out! Well done.

SEWANEE:
Thank you.

Now go buy yourself something pretty.

BROCK:

Will do, Daddy.

Ew.

SEWANEE:

Ew.

SEWANEE WAS STANDING over her kitchen sink, eating a salad, running lines—for her upcoming audition—in her head, Golf Channel on in the background, when her phone vibrated.

ADAKU:

Hey, what day did you say you wanted to go over the scenes?

SEWANEE:

The 4th. Day before the audition.

ADAKU:

Sweet, then can I ask a favor?

SEWANEE:

Course

ADAKU:

Can you help put me on tape for the Angela Davis thing? I wore him down! He said he'd at least watch a self-tape.

SEWANEE:

OMG YES! Exciting.

ADAKU:

She'd just set her phone down when it vibrated again.

> **BROCK:**
> Can I be honest? I don't know how much longer I can keep this up.

SEWANEE:
Are we doing innuendos again?

> **BROCK:**
> No. Seriously.

SEWANEE:
What?

> **BROCK:**
> Narrating.

SEWANEE:
oh. Phew.

> **BROCK:**
> phew what?
>
> what did you think I meant?

SEWANEE:
Uhhhhh this. The texting thing.

> **BROCK:**
> Why would I want to stop this?!
>
> And do we have a THING?

SEWANEE:
I don't know! Lol

BROCK:

Actually, maybe we should stop this.

Remember that telewhatever invention
I was telling you about? I hear it's up
and running. Wanna give it a try?

Sewanee froze, forkful of lettuce halfway to her mouth. She set it back in the bowl and stared at her phone. She wrote Okay, sent it, and typed When do you want to set up a time to

The phone vibrated with an incoming call.

She threw it on the counter as if she'd been electrocuted. It kept vibrating, pulsing away from her in bursts, the words "BROCK MCNIGHT" taunting.

She didn't move again until it stopped moving.

Don't panic, don't panic, she thought. Why are you panicking? There's nothing to panic about.

The phone vibrated once.

BROCK:

?

She spun in a circle, blew out some Lamaze-style breaths, and made herself pick up her phone. She quickly typed:

I wasn't ready. I mean I'm not ready. I don't
know why I'm not, but I'm not. I'm being weird.
Sorry. I'll get back to you. Double sorry.

She pressed send before she could second-guess it.

She watched his bubbles appear.

Then:

> No worries. Take your time.

* * *

March 2

> **BROCK:**
> Question. Weren't you gonna get back to me?

SEWANEE:
Sorry. Yes. Just got tied up.

> **BROCK:**
> kinky.

SEWANEE:
Fifty Shades of Deadline. In the middle of a book intent on killing me. World War Two. Every accent on earth. Screaming men. Gonna need a couple of days.

> **BROCK:**
> Should I apologize for last night?

SEWANEE:
No!

> **BROCK:**
> Be honest.

SEWANEE:
NO. I am. I will. I want to talk. And I will.

I think this is what a crazy person sounds like. ☺

BROCK:

It's ok. We really don't have to talk.

SEWANEE:

I pinky-swear promise I'll get back to you. Maybe an email. Or a letter! Or a carrier pigeon? Regardless: soon.

BROCK:

Good.

THE NEXT DAY, Sewanee sat in Adaku's living room running the scenes. Adaku assured—and reassured—her that everyone was already convinced she was perfect for the role. The studio was insisting they see a few token actresses, which they both knew was industry standard, but—Adaku adamantly repeated—they were *so* excited to see her.

Adaku read with her and kept trying to boost her up (you're brilliant! Love that line reading! They're going to die, you're perfect!), but it wasn't necessary. Sewanee was genuinely fired up to get back in an audition room. Besides, nothing was more daunting than performing a book. It felt luxurious, actually, building just one character instead of an entire world.

Then they filmed the Angela Davis self-tape. After a few takes, Adaku said, "Any notes?"

Sewanee glanced down at the pages, assessing them the way she might a particularly opaque novel. "Try it distracted. Harried. You don't have time to be having this conversation."

"Hmm," Adaku grunted, and they ran the scene once more. "Yeah," she said after, nodding. "That's better. Makes room for the ambiguity."

"Let's try one more and that last line? Don't look at her when you say it. You're already on your way out. Leave her to interpret it."

Adaku tried it and, after Sewanee had cut, tossed back her head. "Yes! So much better!" She thanked Sewanee with a hug. "You've always been my best director. And I miss acting with you!" She fluttered her hands by her face. "Ahh, I can't wait!" She spun away and took a drag on her super-duper protein shake Sewanee thought smelled like moldy spinach. "This will move fast, Swan. Get all your recording done because we're gonna be in Australia for three months."

Sewanee smiled. "I only have six scenes, remember?"

"Yeah, well, the last time we were on location together it was only supposed to be a week and look how that turned out."

Sewanee watched Adaku realize what she was saying as she was saying it. Saw the flare of panic in her eyes, the last-minute decision to add a cheeky grin at the end, the way she went back to her smoothie in an effort to look casual. As she'd said, Sewanee was her best director; she knew all the tics in Adaku's performances.

To put her at ease, Sewanee changed the subject. "You know, I should go with you to the gym, see what routine they've got you doing."

Adaku shook her head and did some hamstring stretches. "You're on your own for that. I'm heading to London tomorrow for the *Girl in the Middle* premiere and press. I'll be there for . . ." She stared at the floor, calculating. "Three? Four days? Then back here, but just for an overnight, because *The Originator* is sending me to Georgia for some off-grid team-building thing with the other girls in my 'tribe.' And then there's two weeks of weapons training, which I'm sure you'll be a part of. Then Australia." Adaku took an intense slurp and said through her cringe, "I can't believe I'll be trudging through backcountry Georgia swampland this time next week."

Sewanee peered at her. Adaku's usual go-go-go attitude seemed to be limping a bit. She always approached the world like one big improv setup: yes, and! Right now, though, Sewanee was seeing more yes, but. "You taking care of yourself?"

"Yeah! Just tired is all."

"Can I do anything to help?"

"Be brilliant in this film so we can do more of this."

Sewanee stood to go. She had a lot of recording to burn through if she was going to Australia. She quickly calculated when she might next see Adaku, given her schedule, and the answer was bleak. So she said, "Hey, why don't I take you to the airport for the Georgia trip next week?"

Adaku shook her head. "It's the morning after the Audies, you don't love me that much."

"Wanna bet?"

Adaku smiled. "Okay, but I'll meet you at your place. No need for you to come all the way East only to take me all the way West. Plus"—she winked—"give you more time to get Brock out of your bed."

Sewanee scoffed as she walked to the front door. "I doubt he'll be at the Audies."

"Why not?"

"He's all smoke and mirrors. The whole pseudonym thing. No one knows who he is!"

They said goodbye, Adaku taking her empty shaker into the kitchen, Sewanee closing the door behind her.

As she walked to her car, she rolled the audition pages into a telescope, tapping them against her leg in a jittery beat.

The thought of acting again, of putting herself fully out there after having hidden away in a 4x4 sound booth for all these years, was making her heady. Was she really ready to do this?

Yes.

Hell, yes.

It shocked her that whatever trepidatious fear she'd carried for so long could be so instantly, so thoroughly, overruled by excitement. By being given the opportunity to make it right. Like being given a second chance. Like Claire and Alessandro. And all of it, somehow, kept her circling back to thinking about Brock.

If she were Adaku, she might say everything happened for a reason or the universe was harmonizing or some shit, but she . . . well, that wasn't her.

Still. Something was cohering. Maybe it was one of those seven-year cycles people talked about. Maybe she was finally coming around the dark side of the moon.

She'd text him later: Question. Why does the moon go dark?

But right now, in this moment, she had a question for herself:

Why was she so afraid to talk to him?

It made no sense.

Everything was coming together for her, and he was a part of that. Why couldn't she bring herself to tell him the story she'd put off telling him? Twice now. Her "Why."

What was the worst that could happen? She would discover it wasn't—*he* wasn't—the fantasy she hoped he would be? No. Was it that *she* would no longer be the fantasy she wanted to be? Yes. And how pathetic was that?

The time had come. She would act again and she would stop acting with Brock. She'd be honest. And worst case? They'd stay friends. Colleagues. They'd continue to make a ton of money voice-banging, as the Facebook fans called it. The idea that he would, for some reason, cut her off entirely was as absurd as the idea that the fantasy was real. Both imagined outcomes so equally ludicrous they essentially canceled each other out.

The shit she could convince herself of, to keep her from being herself. Remarkable. Ridiculous. Really.

That was as far as her thinking had gotten by the time she parked in front of Mark's house.

As she climbed sixty-four stairs, she decided Adaku had been right at dinner: she had to deal with herself. She had to get over it. By hiding, she wasn't doing herself any favors, never mind him. And wasn't he the right person to open up to? Wouldn't he understand? Someone who shared the same fears, a similar past? Who knew what it was like to have the world spread out at your feet, only to trip over it?

From: Westholme, Sarah
To: Brock McNight
Date: March 4, 7:12 PM
Subject: RE: CASANOVA, LLC—and hello!

Hey,

To start, I want to apologize. I know I made it seem like I don't want to talk to you on the telethingy, but that's not true. I would love to talk to you. But you want to know my "Why," my Another Time . . . and the problem is I'm not prepared to talk about it. I am prepared to *tell* you about it, though. I hope you can understand the difference.

So.

I was 24, about two years out of Julliard. I was getting some work, episodic TV, failed series, micro-budget indie film stuff. I was considered a "hottie" (their opinion, but okay also mine) who could actually act. I was getting close on a lot of stuff. My almost-resume was amazing. It felt like it was just a matter of time. Something was gonna hit.

And then it did.

I booked the lead in a film. To be more precise, the co-lead of a major film. It was a DEA thing, kind of like *Training Day*, but with cartels and a female newbie. Overnight, I went from obscurity to relevance. That's our business. Nobody to somebody instantly. Like one of those dried up sponges that kids put in water and voila it's a dinosaur or a cow or . . . never mind.

Sidebar: You ever heard that joke about actors in Hollywood? It's the five stages of an actor's life:

Who is Sarah Westholme?

Get me Sarah Westholme!

Get me a Sarah Westholme type!

Get me a younger Sarah Westholme!

Who is Sarah Westholme?

Anyway, we were filming in Mexico. There was a small role for my character's best friend and I got my real best friend cast in it. (And now I think she's trying to repay me for this, but that's a whole other story.)

I'd been there for about three weeks. Two weeks of rehearsals, one week of filming. My best friend's scenes were scheduled early in the shoot, first few days, and they went great. They wrapped her on Friday and I made her stay the weekend because I wanted to celebrate. This was our big break, right, so we looked for something memorable to do. Exciting! Fun! A little crazy! (read: stupid. Well, maybe not stupid under normal circumstances, but the kind of thing you probably shouldn't do at the beginning of a job in a foreign country known for its dubious safety regulations.)

We went skydiving. The kind where you're strapped to an

experienced jumper. So we get into a plane and up we go. The higher up, the more significant the panicking. I was flip-flopping back and forth in my head: am I scared or am I excited? I wasn't sure. (This is, like, a theme of my life, btw, and prob explains what happened the other night when you called.)

Anyway, we level off and suddenly my friend is strapped to her guide and they're standing at the open door. She smiles big, gives me a double thumbs-up, and they're gone. My jumping companion walks me forward and I look out, look down, feel the grab of the wind. I don't jump so much as fall and then there's nothing under my feet and that wind is slamming against me. I hear a voice. No, not God. The guy on my back is counting down. He's telling me to pull the cord. But I can't move. So he reaches for it, grabs it, and yanks.

And yanks.

And yanks.

At that moment, I had a weird acceptance of dying. Truly. I dissociated. An unexplainable letting go. I was finished. And I was okay with that.

But then: the parachute opened. Some reserve something-or-other. Simple as that. And we landed. Albeit (as you would say) harder than normal, but we were fine. We were alive.

My jump buddy unbuckled me and we hugged like we had survived a war together. My friend came running over and we grabbed each other, screaming adrenaline-fueled nonsense. I can't describe how alive I felt having come so close to death. I was high like I've never been high, and lemme tell you I've been hiiiiiiiigh. In the van, on the way back to the airstrip, I couldn't shut up. I went over every little detail. I remembered everything, every single piece of the puzzle.

And the irony? I don't remember it now. Not one piece.

Everything I've told you is what my friend told me I'd said.

Apparently, I jumped out of the van at the airstrip before it had fully stopped. Did a cartwheel, supposedly, though I don't think I'd ever done a cartwheel in my life. Ran over to the plane we'd jumped out of, which had just landed, and attempted to wrap my arms around the front of the fuselage in an awkward hug. Kissed it. And then I whipped around and stepped right into the plane's prop, which was invisible because it hadn't stopped spinning. It carved into me.

I guess I could have started the story here. Sorry. But I wanted you to know all of it. I wanted you to be there. For the whole thing. The whole thing I can't remember.

What I do remember is waking up on December 4th, two days after the accident, in a hospital room with my parents, my grandmother, and my best friend around me.

What I wish I could forget is the feeling in my gut, in the very coil of my intestines, that I'd lost everything and that it was my fault.

The propeller had sliced diagonally down my face, taken my right eye, and separated my clavicle from my shoulder. I was so lucky. It could have been so, so, so much worse. If it had been going any faster, if I'd run into it at a different angle . . .

Exponential ifs.

The one bright side: when I came out of my first surgery, I spoke to the film's director and I convinced him to test my friend for my role. They were obviously up a creek thanks to me so they agreed and she killed it, of course, and they hired her. They only had to reshoot a week of scenes to make her the lead, recast her role, and that was that. It kickstarted her career. I'm happy for her. I know it might not seem that way, but I am. Really.

Sooooo now you know what you're dealing with. Exactly what you imagined, I'm sure. Such a common story.

To preemptively answer your questions: I've learned to live with my disfigurement and to compensate for having one eye (are the violins playing yet?). The human body is a marvel. My shoulder is mostly fine (though I'm not competing in Olympic weight-lifting anytime soon). I wear an eye patch, which has become as second nature as lipstick or nail polish. Most people aren't intentionally rude assholes. I try to avoid drunks and children. But to be fair I did that before the accident, too.

And now you have my "Why." Finally!

There. Sewanee sat back, basking in the satisfaction of having told the story, all of it, hiding nothing. She placed the cursor over the send icon and then, just as she was about to click, lifted her finger. She realized she should give it a read, to make sure autocorrect hadn't sabotaged her words, to make sure the story, and her thoughts, were as clear as she felt they were.

So she did.

And whatever courage she'd acquired prior to sitting down leaked away with every sentence.

She couldn't send this.

She wasn't ready.

His story had given her a peek into his personality; her story was a naked reveal of all her rawest parts. It was not an equal exchange of insight.

How could she hand over her soul when she didn't even know his real name?

She deleted everything but the first paragraph and added what she hoped was a distillation of her truth. Enough of it, anyway:

Hey,

To start, I want to apologize. I know I made it seem like I don't want to talk to you on the telethingy, but that's not true. I would love to talk to you. But you want to know my "Why," my Another Time . . . and the problem is I'm not prepared to talk about it. I am prepared to *tell* you about it, though. I hope you can understand the difference.

So that's how I started writing this email to you. The email in which I was going to lay it all out there, bare myself in the harsh light of a computer screen. Problem is, "I'm not prepared to talk about it" is true. "I am prepared to tell you about it" is apparently not. I'm sorry. There's a lot to this. To me. And I thought I was ready, but I'm not.

In what I wouldn't classify as a happy coincidence, but a coincidence nonetheless, I do want to tell you we share something in common: loss. Loss of what we once had and who we once were. Fear of having to go through anything like that ever again. And just telling you *that* feels good. Like you must have felt when you told me? So that's something, I guess.

I feel better having put this out there, even this sorry, abbreviated version. I hope we can continue. With all of it. The work, the play, the banter, and of course the sexual innuendos when they . . . come.

Onward, friend.

She began to write Sewanee, changed it to Sarah, and then, simply, truthfully:

S

She pressed send.

SEWANEE LEFT EXTRA early, to be safe. The audition was only three miles directly down the hill, but one never knew.

She'd left her face bare, not a speck of makeup, and the hair she'd refrained from washing for three days hung straight down. She wore cargo pants and a tank top, then realized her arms didn't look like Adaku's looked these days, like she'd been carrying the dead weight of her comrades through underbrush for a year. So she found a loose-weave boatneck sweater and threw it over the tank. Combat boots. Eye patch.

Without any traffic, she was at Sunset Gower Studios in ten minutes.

She gave herself another ten in the car to run the scenes.

She had it.

She left the pages; she didn't need them. Besides, it was empowering to walk in the room without a script. She left her phone, too. She walked to the pedestrian gate. The guard checked her ID and gave her a map of the lot, but she knew where she was going. It was like visiting her elementary school.

Walking through the lot, she remembered past auditions. Some better than others, most unfruitful, but all exciting because they represented possibility. She'd even shot a few guest spots and an independent film on this lot. Blah had worked here, too, it had been around that long.

She found the right office and knew she'd been here before, but it belonged to a different casting director now. Everyone was new. Seven years was an eon in Hollywood.

She rounded the corner into the waiting room. Normally, it would have been overcrowded with wall-to-wall actors, having the feel of a commercial poultry farm. But today, Sewanee was one of a select few. She signed in and took a seat. The actress sitting next to her leaned over. "Eye patch. Nice touch. Wish I would have thought of that." Sewanee nodded in thanks.

The casting director entered the waiting room, tailed by the actress who had just auditioned, and checked the sign-in sheet.

She turned around, eyes searching, and they landed on Sewanee. She smiled. "Sewanee Chester. Thank you for coming in."

"Thank you for having me." Sewanee returned her smile.

The other hopefuls watched this exchange like five baby birds whose mother had returned to the nest with a worm for only one of them.

The casting director turned back to the sign-in sheet. "Kristin? Ready?"

The woman who'd complimented Sewanee's eye patch stood up.

Silence fell over the room for a moment, which was fine with Sewanee. She'd never liked talking before an audition. But two of the women on the other side of the room resumed a conversation.

"He's doing good, he booked a pilot, thank God," one whispered. "Just a guest star, but if it goes he'll be recurring. Then maybe we can afford a wedding. The Jake Meadows one for ABC?"

"Oh I loved that one. Didn't Jenna get the lead on that?"

"She was let go."

"Noooo."

"Right after the table read."

"Nooooooooo."

"Humiliating. And get this. Her film—the radioactive hummingbird one—had its release date pushed back."

"Well, I'd heard the editor—"

"Editor. More like predator. They had to bring in the DC Comics guy, whatshisname."

"The one Mattie sued?"

"Wait, that was the same guy?!"

"Yeah, the valet lurker!"

"Who"—she made a jerkoff gesture—"on her tires?"

"Yes. Men: you can't live with them and you can't live with them."

"Right? So, have they recast Jenna's role yet?"

"Unfortunately."

"Shit. Who?"

"Some YouTuber. Brandon tried to get me in for it, but they must have had this chick in the wings. Jenna hadn't even taken out her extensions yet and, bam, it was on Deadline."

There were certain things about this business Sewanee did not miss.

An hour later, she was the last one left. A redhead came out of the audition room, amid a chorus of Thank Yous and That Was Greats. On her way out, she said under her breath to Sewanee, "Tough room. Good luck."

Sewanee knew this tactic. Put the fear of God into the competition right before they go in. It didn't faze her.

The casting director reappeared and beckoned her inside.

One, two, three, four, five, six, seven, eight people. Eight people in a clamshell, a camera in the middle pointed at the door. At her.

She turned on like a floodlight. Prom photo beam, marionette wave, game show host "Hello!"

Even the ones absorbed with their phones looked up long enough to smile at her. A man in the center stood, held out his hand. "I'm Colin." A Brit. "The director. Thank you so much for coming in. Sorry for the wait."

"No problem!" Sewanee chirped, feeling, instantly, seven years younger. She stepped forward and took his hand briefly. "Sorry I don't have a photo and résumé for you. It's been a while since I–"

He looked surprised. "Oh, the internet's made all that a thing of the past. I would say the bigger challenge is living up to Adaku's glowing review."

Sewanee held out her arms, smiled. "Well, I'll try."

"Excuse me," one of the women spoke up. "I love audiobooks. Are you that Sewanee Chester?"

Sewanee smiled bigger. "That would be me."

"You are amazing. Big fan."

"Thank you so much."

The woman addressed the room. "She won the Audie for Best Female Narrator of the Year."

"What is that?" another person asked.

"It's the Oscar of Audiobooks."

The whole room *ahhhhhd.*

"For what book?" a man who Sewanee guessed was a producer asked.

The woman looked to Sewanee. "*Wasted Space,*" Sewanee answered.

There was silence.

"Reese optioned it," the woman said.

The room *ahhhhhd* again.

She turned her attention back to Sewanee. "I repeat, amazing."

"And I am more than happy to repeat, thank you so much." She'd never been in a room this friendly before.

"You attended Julliard with Adaku, correct?" Colin asked.

"Yes. That's how we met."

"And you've been wasting away in audiobooks. Shame."

Sewanee paused. "Well—"

"Well. Let's see if we can change that, eh?" Colin smiled. "Are you ready?"

Was she. "Absolutely."

"Off you go."

"Who will I be reading with?" Sewanee asked.

A younger woman next to Colin raised her hand. Sewanee nodded at her. The man running the camera said he was rolling.

The room took on the hollow silence of a church. Cell phones were put aside, a few throats cleared, and every pair of eyes fixed on her. It was the moment before the music started for an ice skater. The moment before a diver took the first step toward a triple twisting two and a half somersault. The moment before the starter pistol fired and a sprinter ran the 100-meter dash.

Sewanee stilled, took a meaningful breath. Then she stepped into the role and onto the field.

She felt like the person she once was. She felt whole. She felt unstoppable.

It was a gold medal performance.

From: Brock McNight
To: Westholme, Sarah
Date: March 5, 4:23 PM
Subject: RE: CASANOVA, LLC—and hello!

I understand. I do. Onward, absolutely. If and when you want to tell me about it, I'm here. (Please note the word "tell" not "talk.")

So, after reading your email, I went for a run, came back, took a beer up to my roof, and read it again. Here's what I think:

We both believed in something, in ourselves, and we lost it. And we want it back. Can we have it back? And what happens if we get it back? Can't we lose it again? And then what?

We're both scarred. (SCARRED, not scared, though both are probably true. God, I ALWAYS misread those two words. SO many pickups.)

Anyway. That's what I've been thinking about. Obviously not getting anywhere.

Other than it reconfirms why I want out of Romance. HEA is too much of a setup. It makes you believe we just need to get back what we lost and life will be rainbows forevermore. But it doesn't address what happens if you try to get it back and fail, does it?

There's also the possibility it's not a problem with Romance, it's a problem with us?

IDK. Maybe I should have taken a longer run.

AFTER THE AUDITION, Sewanee realized she'd never told Mark about Doug's interest in the house. So she told him now in passing, bringing paper towels in from the garage, while he was adding more ink to his printer. It was only when she got to the kitchen that she metabolized what he'd replied and walked directly back into his office. "Did you say you'll give him a call?"

Mark looked up from the disemboweled printer, brow furrowed. "Huh?"

"Are you seriously considering selling?"

Mark jerked his head toward the office door. She closed it and came over to his desk. He was back to fiddling with the printer. "I've been thinking about it for a while. Now might be as good a time as any."

"But . . . *now* now?"

He shrugged.

"You've been saying no for years."

"That's before I got old."

"Stop it."

"I can't even change an ink cartridge anymore."

Sewanee snorted and stepped forward, taking over the printer. Mark dropped into his chair and sighed. "I'm tired, Swan."

"You know you never sleep well this time of year." His partner, Julio, had died on Leap Day fifteen years ago after losing a brutal battle with esophageal cancer. Early March was never good for Mark.

He sighed again. "This is different."

Sewanee stole a glance at him. "You want to retire?"

He didn't look at her. "Doug Carrey would pay a lot for this house."

Sewanee took longer to change the cartridge than necessary, buying herself a moment to think. "And what about the studio?"

Mark sat in thoughtful silence, then abruptly leaned forward and began typing. "I want to show you something." He hunted around, clicking the mouse, scrutinizing the screen the way he always did, as if it were the first time he'd seen a computer.

Sewanee snapped the printer back into place, put the old cartridge in a bag for recycling, and came around the desk to peer over his shoulder.

Eventually, he found what he was hunting for. A web page featuring the cover of a book. Under the image, he clicked a play button and a strong male voice came through the speakers. Sewanee listened for about a minute until Mark stopped it. "What do you think?"

She straightened. "He's good. A bit generic, maybe. But good tone, good cadence. It's a pretty straight nonfiction read. The end of his phrasing needs some work, but sure." Mark was staring at her. "What?"

"Kid. There is no him." He pointed at the text below the book cover. "That's a real book, a real publisher. And a bot narrating."

Sewanee stared at the screen.

This was the monster under the bed.

"Is he . . ." she corrected herself, "*it* . . . manufactured from a real voice, or a combination of voices, or . . . is it entirely synthesized, or—"

"Does it matter?"

No. No, it didn't. Except:

"Well, they can't just copy our voices, right? Without our consent. That would be illegal."

"Would it?"

Sewanee flung a hand at the monitor. "To create AI that sounded exactly like you or me? Of course! It has to be illegal."

Mark scoffed. "You better be saving that June French money, because that's an expensive lawsuit, getting a court to determine what defines a voice. Whether it's even proprietary. People do impressions." Sewanee pushed away from the desk, feeling trapped. "And then once a court does decide," Mark continued, blithely, "from that point forward they'll just toe right up to whatever line was decided and be forever in the clear."

Sewanee held up a hand. "It can't act, though." She hesitated. "Can it?"

"Give it time."

"Accents? Characters?"

"What's stopping it? Look, it's coming for *me* first. Nonfiction will be the first to go."

She was shaking her head, barely listening. "People won't want this. People want people, the human connection, authentic storytelling."

"Do they? I think we do, because we care about the difference. Hell, we *know* the difference. But the five-year-old who already lives in their iPad or Game Boy or whatnot?" He waved a hand. "What the hell do I know about this? I felt old back when this industry moved from tape to digital. All I know for sure is I'm officially a dinosaur now and this is my meteor. So"—he leaned back and crossed his hands over his stomach—"I'm gonna go buy me a swimsuit, a very small one, and I'm gonna find a beach where the only decision I have to make is what my next cocktail's gonna be. You get to figure out this problem. But I'll save you a lounger."

Sewanee's breaths were growing shallow. Mark studied her. "Hon. It's not like we didn't know this was coming. It was just more philosophical than practical. Not anymore."

When she'd first met Mark, first started in this business, they'd talked all the time about Sewanee taking it over when he was ready to retire. That's why she'd moved into the guesthouse, started working for him. It was an apprenticeship. But in the last year or two, talk of the future had drifted out of their conversations. While it was true the handwriting had been on the wall, as she cleaned everything else in the studio, she'd kept cleaning that off, too.

She mumbled something and Mark cocked his ear toward her. "What?"

She swallowed and repeated, as evenly as she could, "I can't lose this, too. I can't."

Mark sighed sadly, sweetly, softly. He stood and held out a wrinkled hand. "Come here, kid."

She went right to his open arms, pressing her cheek into his narrow chest. He kissed her forehead, then rested his chin on top of her hair and said, "Everyone talks about coal miners, farmers, steel workers. The horror of automation and what we owe them. No one talks about artists."

They stood quietly like that for a minute, the hush of the house beyond, the particular quiet of their particular work getting done around them. The stories being told, the entertainment being created, the humans making it happen. Mark lifted his head. "Do you know how much your mom's condo on that cruise ship costs?"

Sewanee chuckled. "A lot."

"1928 Spanish Revival in the Hollywood Hills a lot?"

"Possibly."

"Doug Carrey a lot?"

"Probably." She looked up at him, letting him see in her eyes just how unpalatable she found this idea. "What a pissah."

"What does that mean?"

"No idea."

He squinted at her. "Didn't you two . . . ?"

Sewanee groaned and stepped back.

Mark lifted an eyebrow. "Dare I ask?"

"Porny. He jackhammered me off the bed." Mark belted a laugh as Sewanee turned for the door. "The bruise on my hip outlasted the relationship."

"Well, maybe I'll let you give him a private tour of the house. Show him where he can hang his Red Sox banner." He quirked a brow. "Where he can put his lobstah roll."

She chortled and emphatically shook her head. "Pass." Then she took a breath. "I'm gonna go slip into studio 3, get some recording done."

While she could.

From: Westholme, Sarah
To: Brock McNight
Date: March 5, 7:07 PM
Subject: RE: CASANOVA, LLC—and hello!

So, after reading your email, I decided to go for a run, and then I came back and took a glass of wine out to my porch and I read it again. Here's what I think:

You're right.

From: Brock McNight
To: Westholme, Sarah

Date: March 5, 7:34 PM
Subject: RE: CASANOVA, LLC—and hello!

You should have taken a longer run.

HER PHONE VIBRATED, skittering across the nightstand. Sewanee lifted her bleary head and grabbed at it. There was only one number she'd programmed to be able to call during her pre-set Do Not Disturb hours. "Hello?" she croaked.

"Help me."

She came awake instantly. "Are you okay?"

"No." Blah's voice was adamantly edgy. "Marv is late. I've been waiting for hours. He's terribly late and I don't know where he is! Where is he?"

Sewanee bolted upright, sheets twisted around her legs. "Okay, take a deep breath. I'll find Marv. Everything's fine."

"Everything isn't fine, Bitsy! Stop it, just stop it!"

"BlahBlah, it's Sewanee. Listen to me, it's—"

"No, you listen! Marv left me here and I have to be in Westwood and it's already too late! Marilyn's gonna kill me." Each fragment of thought was another log hurled onto a fire.

Sewanee didn't know what to do. She looked at her bedside clock. 2:14 A.M. "Blah—"

"You're no good to me! You're no fucking help, Bitsy! I'll handle it!"

"I'll come get you, stay there."

"No!"

The line went dead.

Through the blood pounding in her ears, Sewanee called Seasons and spoke with the night nurse, asked him to please, immediately, check on Blah, and then waited while he did. Each second felt like an hour. She couldn't sit still. She fought her way out of bed, started pulling clothes on, then stopped, not knowing what was coming next.

Five minutes later, the nurse's voice was back, informing her Blah had been standing in front of the window in her room, holding the entire phone—cradle and all—no longer agitated, just confused. So he'd helped her back into bed. He said he'd check on her throughout the night. Sewanee thanked him profusely and hung up.

Shaken, she went to the kitchen and put the kettle on, pulled out her Tea-For-One set, and had a good two-minute cry. Then she sat, drank her chamomile, and thought. And thought. And thought.

The Tea-For-One usually grounded her. Reassured her she was fine alone. But tonight, in this living room that might soon no longer be hers, after talking to a grandmother who was slipping further away, this kind of alone was not fine.

She pulled out her phone, and though she knew he wouldn't see it until morning, texted:

> Then there are the things we lose and can't get back. I don't know what to do about that one.

She sent it, re-read it, and added:

> Good morning.

She set her phone down and sipped.

In the dimness of the guesthouse, lit only by the faraway lights of a sleeping city beyond the sliding glass door, the face of her phone illuminated.

BROCK:

Took a little midnight run?

SEWANEE:

Nooooo your phone is on?! I'm so sorry!! You're awake? Why are you awake? Are you awake?

BROCK:

No I'm sleep-texting.

SEWANEE:

I'm so so sorry.

BROCK:

It's okay, really.

What are you doing up?

SEWANEE:

Couldn't sleep.

BROCK:

You know what's good for that?

SEWANEE:

Ugh I don't have innuendo in me right now.

BROCK:

No wonder you can't sleep. Tell Innuendo to get busy.

SEWANEE:

Good one. But I can't. Seriously.

BROCK:

Okay, seriously? I was going to say audiobooks.

I have fans who listen to my voice in bed to fall asleep.

SEWANEE:

That is . . . not what they're doing.

BROCK:

Still. I could try reading you a story? See if it helps?

SEWANEE:

I don't think your kind of story will help.

BROCK:

K Goodnight then.

SEWANEE:

Night. Thanks for the chat. Truly.

Sewanee found that she was smiling. The tears were gone. The tea was gone. She slipped off the sofa and went into her bedroom. She set her phone on the nightstand, crawled back into bed, and hoped Blah would be okay, would go to sleep, would let *her* sleep. She took a restful breath. She wanted to be able to close her eyes and think of Brock, not her grandmother. But before she could, her phone illuminated again, dropping that oh-no feeling back into her stomach. She snatched it up.

A voice memo.

From Brock.

She pressed play.

His voice sounded like early morning. It was soft-edged, as if he were close enough to warrant a whisper. There was no preamble. He just read.

She recognized it instantly. It was *Goodnight Moon*.

In the great green room
There was a telephone . . .

Now she closed her eyes. She rested her head on her pillow and her phone rested itself on her chest.

She listened.

After he spoke the final refrain, there was a moment of lingering silence. She waited for him to say something else. She wanted him to say something else. To sign off, perhaps. To chuckle, maybe. She wanted more.

But there was nothing else. The recording stopped. In a moment of greediness, she thought about playing it again. But she didn't move. There was no need. She was satisfied. Beyond satisfied. Beyond *Goodnight Moon*.

She texted:

You.

He replied:

Again. You.

* * *

March 6

SEWANEE:
For future reference, what time zone are you in?

BROCK:
EST.

?

SEWANEE:
So next time I have an existential insomnious crisis I can time my texts better.

BROCK:

Insomnious: the Roman god of late night thought.

I'm an acolyte myself.

SEWANEE:

And from whence in the EST doth the acolyte hail?

BROCK:

Newest of York.

And whence . . . yourth . . . hailest?

SEWANEE:

Lol still live in L.A.

BROCK:

So close!

SEWANEE:

Only if Los Angeles is still just above 96th street.

(Jokes aside for the moment: I really appreciated the bedtime story last night.)

BROCK:

(Jokes aside, my pleasure)

L.A., huh? Interesting.

SEWANEE:

The first time in recorded history a New Yorker has ever said that.

BROCK:

Gotta make nice, I'll be there in a few days.

SEWANEE:

Oh! Wait, for the Audies???

BROCK:

PETE NO.

SEWANEE:

Hmmm

BROCK:

Hmmm?

SEWANEE:

Just hmmm

BROCK:

Well hmmmm back.

From: Brock McNight
To: Westholme, Sarah
Date: March 7, 1:57 AM
Subject: RE: CASANOVA, LLC—and hello!

Hello!

So, my acolytic self has been thinking. I know how you feel about talking on the telewhatever. Understood! New thought: we don't talk.

We meet.

Our options, as I see them:

1. Meet face to face. We then:
   a. Keep walking.

    b. Stand there.
    c. Speak and screw it all up.

And then we:

2. Decide to never see each other again and:
    a. Go back to texting OR
    b. Touch each other to make sure we're real, then never see each other again

3. Decide to see each other again:
    a. Right then and there
    b. Another time

If the answer is 3.a then we:

    i. Add in the talking, or
    ii. Keep staring at each other for a while.

What's the worst that could happen? Things stay as they are. We finish the project, of course, be professional, of course, be courteous, more than of course, and etc, etc, etc, of course.

We have tons of questions. Don't you want answers?

We have the chance to put this to bed. Whatever bed that is. Maybe it's a friend bed. That's fine. It'll be a bunk bed. You can have the top.

OK. Insomnious hath spoken.

Me

SEWANEE WAS IN a booth, long after all the other studios had emptied of people, attempting to get ahead on her recording and trying not to think about Brock's latest e-mail—succeeding at neither—when her phone lit up with a call.

She immediately, if cautiously, picked up. "Blah?"

"Dollface!"

"Everything all right?"

"Right as rain! What are you up to today?"

"Just recording." Sewanee readjusted herself in the booth, removing her headphones and cracking the door for some air. "How are you feeling?"

"Oh, fit as a fiddle!"

Right as rain. Fit as a fiddle. Suspicious, Sewanee tried again, "You sure everything's okay?"

"Can't an old lady call her granddaughter? That a crime now?" Definitely something in her voice, right there beneath the teasing. Tentativeness like an undertow. Sewanee sensed the pull of an impending conversation. There was a pause as each waited for the other to start it.

Blah finally said, "Read any good books lately?"

"That supposed to be funny?"

"I didn't hear you laugh, so no."

Which made Sewanee genuinely laugh, which made Blah laugh. But when it subsided, the undertow remained. So Sewanee asked, "Do you remember calling me last night?"

Blah sighed. "No. Well, sort of. Goddamn it. I'm sorry, Doll."

"There's nothing to be sorry for."

"Tell me what happened. I want to know." Though she sounded as if she didn't, not really.

Sewanee left the booth. She needed space to breathe, to think, to talk. "You were upset. And frustrated. You said you were late for something. You thought I was Bitsy."

"Well, shit," BlahBlah said thinly.

Sewanee sat on the floor, back against the outside wall of

the booth, and tucked her knees into her chest. "Are you aware of . . . do you know when it's happening?"

"Not a clue. There's some kind of before and after, but the middle? Black as night." She exhaled. "I hate it, Doll. I need a prescription for Dumb Pills."

Sewanee snorted. "I don't think that's what they're called."

"Well, that's the generic."

They both chuckled at that. Then, there was such an extensive pause Sewanee was sure she'd lost her. That the next thing Blah would say was, "Did you see Mitzi's face-lift?"

"Betty Lou McCarthy lived in the hollers."

Dammit. Sewanee hated being right. "Who's that?"

"School friend. And if I was out there when the fog rolled in . . . I wasn't going nowhere. Happened in an instant. Like God poured gravy over everything."

Maybe she was wrong. Maybe Blah hadn't veered as far off track as she'd thought.

"You could barely see your hand in front of your face. And shapes you knew were out there—the old oak, the mailbox, her daddy's truck—all those comforts would get . . . sinister. They moved around. Weren't where they were supposed to be."

Sewanee didn't dare interject.

"It feels something like that when it starts. Then people are born out of that fog. Some I recognize, some I don't. Everything . . . shifts."

"I can't imagine."

"It's kinda like being on a soundstage, doing a big dance number. Stagehands take up a backdrop and lower another. A desk flies in on wheels, a soda fountain disappears, and now there's a door, and in comes Gene and we're tapping away in an office building instead of a diner."

"God," Sewanee murmured quietly, not wanting to break this spell of clarity.

"And then . . . well, uh . . . what the hell was I . . . dancing, wasn't I?"

Sewanee swallowed. "You were talking about everything shifting around you, what it feels like in your mind? Did you want to say something else about it?"

"Oh, I'm just rambling." Blah cleared her throat and her voice was crisper when she said, "Anyway, this is all to say, Doll . . ." Sewanee heard the rustling of paper on the other end. "I think I'm going to need more help. That it might be time to take the next step. Before I don't know where the step is."

Sewanee hadn't known it was possible to feel relief and shock at the same time. She sat forward. "You don't have to worry about any of that. Soon you're going to have another place. *At Seasons.* You'll be just down the hall, in memory care, okay? More help when you need it, but you'll still have Mitzi and Birdie and Amanda and, of course, me. You'll have me, whether you like it or not," she joked.

A charged kind of silence fell, like the expectant moment right after the power goes out, waiting for it to come back on. Sewanee heard paper rustling again.

"Listen to me, Doll. I appreciate you more than you'll ever know. And I love you so much. And I want you to do something for me."

"Anything."

"Promise me."

"I promise. Anything."

"Good. When the next step comes, you are not to visit me anymore. You—"

Sewanee jerked. "What are you—"

"Let me finish. No visits. No phone calls. You are not to be any part of this."

"Of what?"

"My end."

All of Sewanee's blood rushed to her head. "I'm coming over. You're going to say this to my face—"

"No! No, you're not! I've thought this through, thought it all out. I wrote it down so I wouldn't forget." The paper shook near the phone. "I've decided. It's done. Now, enough of all that. I want to tell you about Birdie."

"I don't want to fucking hear about Birdie, what are you—"

"We are not discussing this." Blah's voice cracked and Sewanee's eye filled with tears as if they shared a body. "Endings are messy and I'll be damned if you remember me as a mess."

Sewanee was on her feet. "That is *not* how I'll remember you! I'll remember you at the pool and cruising around in the Olds and trying on clothes and smoking and drinking and swearing and laughing and rolling your eyes at Mitzi."

"No, trust me. You'll remember the end."

"Stop saying the end!" Sewanee was shouting. "Shut up about the end!"

"Don't tell your grandmother to shut up!" Blah sputtered.

"Shut up! Shut up! Shut up!"

After a silence in which Sewanee felt like all her nerve endings had been thrown into a blender, Blah laughed. And kept laughing. Sewanee couldn't make her face smile the way she wanted to.

Then Blah started to cry. To hear that and not be able to touch her could barely be endured. Eventually, Blah spoke. "It's just so sad, Doll. Don't make us say goodbye. I can't bear it. I need you to understand that. Leave 'em laughing, remember? Please."

The tears fell fatly down Sewanee's cheek. "You could ask anything of me. Literally anything but this."

"Dollface. Please."

Three distinct thoughts came to Sewanee simultaneously:

Tell her what she wants to hear.

Argue until she forgets what she's asking.

And Henry saying, she would see. That she could take her turn caring for Blah, if she wanted, but, trust him, she'd see.

Sewanee had to gather all the pieces of herself that had splintered off before she could speak again. "I can't do it," she said. "But I will."

As much as Sewanee didn't want to admit it, Blah had a point. Didn't a person have the right to decide how they wanted to be remembered? And didn't she owe it to her grandmother to honor that? In the end, what the hell else was there to leave behind, really, but memories?

She decided she would keep her promise as long as Blah remembered to hold her to it. She knew, at a certain point, that would no longer be the case, and then Sewanee would do whatever she believed was right for herself. This was fair. To both of them.

Blah exhaled. She said, "I love you, Doll," which echoed through Sewanee as if it had been shouted from a mountaintop.

"I want to see you," Sewanee murmured.

"Who's stopping you?"

Sewanee dropped back down to the floor, a strangled laugh escaping her. "I swear to God." She shook her exhausted head. "One of these days, Alice, bang, zoom, you're going to the moon."

"Did I ever tell you my Jackie Gleason story?"

Sewanee smiled. She loved that story. "No."

Blah told it. Then asked, "Are you coming to happy hour this week?"

"Not sure yet. But we'd already decided I'd get ready for the Audies at your place. Does that still work? The venue is around the corner."

"Ooh, when is it?"

"Wednesday night."

"What's today?"

"Sunday."

"And when's the event?"

"In three days. Wednesday night."

"Bet you've told me that."

"A few hundred times."

"Is that all? Maybe I'm getting better. Talk tomorrow. Love you."

"Love you to death."

"Hey, don't rush me."

They both laughed and Sewanee remembered something. "Wait, what did you want to tell me about Birdie?"

"Huh?"

"You'd said you wanted to talk about Birdie."

Blah clucked her tongue. "Oh, right. She died."

"What?!"

"Bless her heart."

Sewanee didn't want to doubt her, but, "Are you sure?"

"My mind brings dead people back to life, Dollface, not the other way around."

"*Birdie*, not Mitzi?"

"Mitzi? Mitzi will outlive the earth."

"When?"

"Oh, Christ, what's today? Yesterday maybe."

"How?"

"Went in her sleep, apparently. Lucky lady."

"Oh my God."

"Well, she was old."

"She wasn't *that* old!"

"Don't be fooled, she'd had a lot of work done. Doll, that new girl is here, I've got to go to dinner."

"Okay, okay, go, I love you."

"Love you." She made kissing noises into the receiver and hung up.

Sewanee continued to sit there, on the floor, leaning against the booth.

Then she began crying again. Crying for herself, sure, for Blah, of course, but mostly, it seemed, for a woman whose greatest accomplishment was a two-ingredient dip her boys liked forty years ago. Why had this sunk its claws so deeply into Sewanee? The utter callousness of an unremarkable life unceremoniously ended.

She had to stop. She made herself stop. She couldn't cry; she had to record. If she continued crying, she'd have to wait an hour for her voice to clear. She didn't have an hour. She didn't have any time to waste.

She stood shakily and took up her phone. She went to her messages, scrolled down to Brock, second only to Adaku, because Adaku had texted while she'd been on the phone:

ADAKU:

OK update: they're focused on wrapping up the deal with the male lead. Surprise surprise. But then they'll get to your role and hopefully send an offer early next week. Okay to let Manse handle it for you?

Sewanee gave the message a thumbs-up and went to her chain with Brock.

SEWANEE:

So . . . I got your menu. Sorry, email.

When exactly are you going to be in LA?

BROCK:

Ah, yes, would've been good info to include.

Arrive early morning on the 10th,
leave late morning of the 11th

SEWANEE:

???

BROCK:

I know. Wish I could stick around, but my
recording schedule back here is punishing.
I have two priorities in L.A.: Meetings
on the 10th (sadly including dinner) and
meeting you any time after that.

Oops. Also have a breakfast meeting on the 11th.

SEWANEE:

????

So what, we're meeting at midnight?
Who am I, Cinderella?

BROCK:

Let's make it 11. Don't want any
Prince Charming expectations.

For real, I'm SO sorry.

SEWANEE:

It's okay. It was a last minute idea. Meet me at
Miguel's in Burbank at 11 pm on the 10th.

BROCK:

Lemme check my schedule.

SEWANEE:

I swear to Pete.

BROCK:

Jk jk I'll be there.

SEWANEE:

I'll be coming from the Audies
so might be a little late.

BROCK:

Bring all my awards with you.

SEWANEE:

Sorry, I'll have my hands full with my own.

I'll be the one in the ballgown.

BROCK:

That makes two of us.

Forty-seven minutes later:

SEWANEE:

Are we really doing this?

BROCK:

We're really doing this.

SHE WAS RUNNING late. The dishwasher in the studio had inevitably decided to stop working that afternoon and traffic had been unusually bad. Her intention had been to have an early dinner with Blah before getting ready for the event, but she'd missed dinner and arrived with less than an hour to make herself presentable. She was frazzled, rushed, and could not stop thinking about the fact that, in five hours, she was going to meet Brock.

She stood in front of Blah's sink, leaning into the mirror, trying to catch the light properly. Blah stood behind her, propped against the sliding door of the small closet, where Sewanee's ballgown hung.

"Damn fluorescents," Blah muttered. "The good lord didn't intend for makeup to be applied under fluorescents."

"I can manage. Doesn't have to be camera-ready."

"What lipstick do you have?"

Sewanee dug in her bag and handed it to her. She inspected it and nodded. They said, in unison, "It'll bring out the purple in the dress."

When she was a kid, Sewanee would watch BlahBlah put on her makeup, sitting at her vanity in her room at Bitsy's house. Marilyn had been a mascara and ChapStick kind of mom. The slightest hint of some plum eye shadow for special occasions. Blah, on the other hand, never left the house without a full face on. She had learned makeup as a craft, from the studio makeup artists, and she'd passed it all down to Sewanee the way some grandmothers passed down recipes.

She fell into a memory of her grandmother's smiling face beside hers in the mirror. The smell of nicotine fingers on her chin and the peppermint Altoid in Blah's mouth to cover it. Blah boinking her on the nose with a blush brush and saying, "Dollface." Like an anointing. A coronation. A curse?

Blah grunted as she moved away. "Want a Mallomar?"

"I'm good, thanks."

As Sewanee applied the lipstick, she heard Blah murmur, "What in the world . . ." and Sewanee poked her head around the corner. Blah was standing next to her bed, staring down at the nightstand.

"What?"

"They're gone."

"You probably ate them."

"Luckily, it's not summer. I can still stock up."

Sewanee went back to the mirror. "I never understood that."

"They don't ship in the summer months. Nestlé was afraid the chocolate would melt. No refrigeration trucks."

"But that was a long time ago."

"Over a hundred years. Can you believe it? That cookie's been around longer than me. You still can't get them during the summer, though. Now I think it's a marketing ploy. Supply and demand. Extortionist sons of bitches. Do you know they make it in Canada, but you can't get it in Canada? They have this other thing called a Whippet. Supposed to be the same, but I don't believe it. I think they even put some kind of jam in them. The bastards."

Sewanee came out to where Blah was standing. "You know, for someone who's losing it, it's ridiculous what you remember."

"No, it's Mallomars. The one true love of my life. Besides you." Blah turned to her. "Now, you are a sight! Perfection." That said, she rubbed a crooked finger under Swan's eye, right at the lash line. "You always forget to blend."

"With one eye I only have half the practice now."

Blah pshawed. "You're gorgeous, Dollface. The most gorgeous girl I know."

Sewanee groaned theatrically as she walked back to the closet. She took the dress off the hanger and slipped into it. She secured her eye patch over her updo and gave herself a good once-over in the mirror. Not bad. In truth, the awards were not what she was dressing for tonight. Sewanee tried to breathe through her anxiety. And Spanx.

"Where are my Mallomars?" she heard from the other side of the wall.

"You ate them," Sewanee repeated, coming around. "We'll get some more tomorrow. Remember, it's still cold out, so—"

Blah shook her head. "They were right here!" She pointed at the nightstand. Her voice had grown anxious. "Someone stole them! I don't like the new nurse here. She comes in whenever she feels like it and watches me. I bet she stole the Mallomars."

"She didn't steal—"

"I want to go home."

Sewanee took her grandmother's hands and tried to catch her eye. "Blah, you are home. This is your home. And you have a wonderful home. Everyone here cares about you. You're just forgetting you finished your cookies, that's all."

Blah calmed, but pointed at the nightstand. "I keep them right there."

"I know, but . . ." Sewanee looked where she was pointing.

There was a glossy 8x10 folder covered in stock photos of elderly people laughing. At the top, the words: SUNNYSIDE–A BETTER CARE SOLUTION. She stilled. "Where did that come from?"

But Blah was walking toward the kitchenette, muttering, "Where are they?"

Sewanee picked up the folder and opened it. Inside, there were pages of information and stats, marketing materials for—what was now obvious—an alternate living facility. She closed the folder, confused, a foreboding sense of anger rising up inside her. And then her eye landed on the dark bold print at the bottom right of the idyllic front cover: MEDICAID ACCEPTED.

Sewanee's mouth tightened. "Was Dad here?" Blah didn't answer. She'd sat down in her rocker and gone silent.

There was a knock on the open door. "Hello? It's me again. I forgot something, but I also got you—"

Henry stepped into the room just as Sewanee turned around to face him. He stopped in his tracks. "Oh. Hi." He held up a familiar yellow box. "I ate her last Mallomar, so I bought her more."

Sewanee held up the folder. "Oh. Hi. You want to explain this?" Her voice was admirably calm.

Henry saw what she held. Shifted his weight. Took a breath. "Options."

"Options!?" Her voice was not admirably calm.

He exhaled and shook his head. "May I have it back? Please?"

"No, you may not have it back. Please, thank you, or anything else."

"Sewanee, you have no right—"

"*I* have no right? What are you talking about? I have every right. I'm paying for this!"

Henry inclined his head at his mother. "She wants to move."

"She wants—*what*?!"

"We discussed it. She's happy to move."

Sewanee scoffed. "I thought it was the Mallomars. Now I know why she's really upset!"

He rolled his eyes, actually rolled his eyes at her. "I'm simply doing what's best for all concerned, including you. Even if you're too damn stubborn to see it."

While he was talking, Sewanee turned her attention to Blah and said, over him, "What did he say to you? What did he tell you?"

Her grandmother stared blankly back and shook her head, little shakes, close to shivering. She pointed to the box Henry was holding. "There they are!"

Sewanee walked over to the window. There were extra safety latches on it, which normally made it challenging to open. But rage has a propulsive quality and within moments Sewanee had managed it and the Sunnyside folder had taken flight.

Henry huffed something that sounded like a chuckle. "Your flair for the dramatic doesn't change anything, you know that, right?"

She marched over to him. In her high heels they were eye to eye. "Stay out of this. I told you I'm taking care of it." She said this in the lowest part of her voice.

"You also told me I should visit her." The smugness. The smugness!

"You're not helping anyone but yourself. All you've managed to do is confuse her. Hurt her. Hurt me," she hissed. "Don't you get that? Don't you care?!" She yelled the last part.

Henry replied in his patient professor voice, "My problem is I care too much. And I won't watch you do this to yourself. Or to her."

"Do what? Take care of her? Protect her? Love her?"

"At the expense of your own future! This is a waste of your money and for what? For my mother, who I care about more than you know, but who is not going to know the difference between Sunnyside and Seasons. She'll think they're the same thing because they both begin with an S."

Sewanee took a moment to regroup. To be more adult. To tamp down the urge to hit him. "You think that's funny? She is sitting right there, she can hear you. God—" She groaned. "This is precisely why I'm making this decision without you."

"And we all know how well things turn out when you make decisions with no regard for your future."

The snap inside her was instantaneous, as if he had stepped on a twig. "IT WAS AN ACCIDENT! AND I BLAME MYSELF FOR IT EVERY FUCKING DAY! FEEL BETTER?" she screamed, a part of her voice she hadn't used in years. She couldn't even be sure he meant *that* decision; he seemed to hate every decision she'd ever made, every one that had excluded him. All the regrets that lived dormant inside her, cumulatively coiled at the base of her heart, he had the power to awaken with the slightest provocation.

Henry visibly stepped back. "That's not what I—"

She stalked forward, got right in his face. "When you decided to fuck your student, who did *you* consult? How much were you thinking about the future? About anyone other than your selfish, self-absorbed"—she sputtered—"self? That decision turn out well for you, Dad? I scarred myself. How many people did you scar?"

He was silent.

She knew he'd never been hit this hard, certainly not by her. And it enraged her further that the hurt blooming on his face only made her want to reach out and grab him, hold him, cry with him. Jesus Christ, what *was* it with the two of them?

She didn't have time for this. She had to get to the Audies. She had to get to Brock. She left Henry standing there while she gathered her purse, her phone, her control, all while saying, "If you keep at this, I will never let you near me ever again. *Ever again.*" She went back to him, grabbed the Mallomars out of his hands. "And don't eat her fucking Mallomars!" She walked over to Blah and handed them to her.

Blah smiled as though seeing a photo of a long-lost friend. "I knew they were around here somewhere."

"I love you, Blah, see you tomorrow." She walked past her father without acknowledging him. As she reached the door, he said her name and his voice cracked. She stopped. She wanted to face him once more, but was afraid if she did, she would lose it. So she said, to the hallway, "This isn't one of the bad decisions, Dad."

As she left the room, she heard BlahBlah say shakily, in the strongest Tennessee twang she'd ever heard from her, "Well. Ain't we just blue-ribbon people?"

THE AUDIES CEREMONY was being held at a five-hundred-seat theater less than a mile from Seasons and yet Henry had deactivated Sewanee's sense of direction. Fuming, muttering to herself, she fast-walked to the event only to look up twenty minutes later and find herself in a neighborhood. She dug her phone out of the ballgown's pocket and brought up a map. After one more misdirection, landing her in a grocery store parking lot, she arrived at the theater.

She had missed cocktail hour. She really hadn't wanted to miss cocktail hour. A double vodka soda would have definitely helped numb the throb of her feet in her heels and the Henry-sized pain in her ass. But people were already being ushered into the auditorium and she was swept into the current of hugs, cheek-kisses, and hand-squeezes. Once inside, she was plucked out of the crowd and ushered to the front row where the other presenters were sitting.

She couldn't focus on the ceremony. No idea what was going on, who was speaking, who was winning, nothing. She heard her name being read as a nominee in her category and numbly clapped when someone else won. About halfway through the ceremony (as far as she could tell, anyway), Alice, who was sitting next to her, leaned over and whispered, "I think you're up," and inclined her head toward an event coordinator standing in the wings waving at Sewanee.

"Thanks," Sewanee muttered, but continued to sit there for a few more seconds. Then, as the coordinator's waving grew more frantic, it registered, and Sewanee was instantly up, tripping on the front hem of her gown. Alice reached out a steadying hand, but Sewanee stabilized and bombed backstage.

Once there, her training kicked in. She took a few quick huffs of breath. Watched the coordinator give her the five-finger countdown.

She walked to the podium like a beauty pageant contestant, held momentarily for applause, and read with graceful authority from the clear teleprompter to her left, making sure to address the right side of the room whenever possible. A total professional.

"Every year, this body recognizes one person's contribution to the world of audio storytelling. This year, I am deeply honored—bittersweet though it may be—to present the lifetime achievement award, posthumously, to June French." The audience applauded and Sewanee joined in at the podium.

"June was a *USA Today* bestselling author and RITA winner many times over. She sold her first novel to Harlequin at twenty-seven. Last year, sadly, she passed away at the too-young age of sixty-six. During those years she was one of our most prolific writers, having penned seventy-eight novels and sold over fifty-six million copies worldwide in twenty-three languages. In the last seven years of her life, June became a pioneer in the audiobook industry. She was a producer, an entrepreneur, and a creative force who broke down barriers of genre, production, and, yes, sales. Many of the people in this room have benefitted from her work in our industry.

"In a now canonical interview with *Cosmopolitan* magazine, when asked about her work in audio, June said, 'The human voice is the thread that connects one soul to another. It's as innate as the murmur of your mother's voice as you nursed at her breast and as potent as your father's words of approval. It is the conduit of all human expression. It is as elemental as life itself because it helps us love and be loved.' She loved audiobooks, she loved us, and tonight we honor her. Accepting this award on her behalf is the person who knew her best, her nephew. So, let's welcome him here tonight, into our community, with the same love June showed us."

Sewanee stepped back from the podium and clapped along with the audience, scanning the room. She didn't see anyone approaching the stage. The applause faded and there was a slight titter in the room as the audience began searching for him. Someone shouted something from the back of the auditorium. "What?" Sewanee called out.

"He's in the bathroom," came the muted reply.

The crowd laughed. Sewanee chuckled and shrugged. "Well, in the meantime," she braced an elbow on the podium and leaned down into the mic, "will the owner of a white Toyota Corolla please come to the security desk? Your audiobook is still playing." The crowd chuckled. She continued to vamp. "Hey, how many narrators does it take to screw in a lightbulb?" She cupped a hand around her ear and the audience called out, "How many!"

"Two. One to do it and one to tell you they narrated a seventy-hour book on the history of the lightbulb once and did you know that Thomas Edison—" Sewanee dropped her head to her chest and snored. The audience laughingly groaned. "One to do it and everyone else to say we should be getting royalties for it." This made the audience clap. She adopted a theatrical grimace. "Okay, now *I* have to go to the bathroom!" Big laugh. "No, I really do!" Bigger laugh. "Power of suggestion—"

"Here he comes!" someone shouted from the back.

"Oh thank God." She tented a hand above her eye to see past the lights bearing down on her.

A sleek shadow dashed down the steps of the auditorium, practically jogging. The crowd cheered and Sewanee joined in, watching him reach the stage, head bowed, bounding up the stairs. He turned to the crowd and made a show of looking down at his fly in horror, mimed quickly zipping it. The crowd hooted and he took a small, mocking, self-deprecating bow. He turned, heading directly for the podium, for her, and the spotlight caught his face. Their eyes met.

And they were in a car crash.

Glass shattered, steel crunched, they were spun around, and around, and around. Like a roulette ball.

His pace slowed and her heart surged. He approached her as he had in the Las Vegas suite.

Deliberate.

Powerful.

Inevitable.

PART 4

It is time for writers to admit that nothing in this world makes sense.

—Anton Chekhov, letter to Maria
Kiselyova, January 14, 1887

Just make sure there's some kind of sex by the mid-point. A reader will only trust you for so long.

—June French in *Cosmopolitan*

CHAPTER TEN

"Snowed In"

NICK AND SEWANEE DIDN'T STAY IN THE SUITE.

She was content at first, enjoying their conversation in their little snow globe. Then she'd decided to give him a tour, Nick following her so closely she could hear his breathing. But when they'd entered her bedroom and he'd placed both of his palms on the bed and pushed deeply into it, as if testing its buoyancy, she turned heel and beelined back to the safety of the living room.

When he rejoined her, hands thrust casually in his pockets, not a care in the world, she announced that she wanted to go down to the club, which was news to her.

She did her best to package her butterflies in the festive wrapping of a good idea. There was a table, with bottle service, waiting for them. She hadn't been to a club in years. She was, you know, dressed for it. Why waste the opportunity? After some confusion about whether Nick was invited to join her (of course he was; oh, because it had sounded like she'd wanted to go by herself; oh, had it, she hadn't meant it that way), they silently left the suite, silently waited for the elevator, got on the elevator silently, got off on the wrong floor, got back on the elevator, laughed to break the silence, got off on the right floor, found the club's nondescript entrance, spoke with the host, and were led through the three-story warehouse-style venue to a low-slung silver velvet horseshoe banquette with a bottle of vodka in an ice bucket on the glass table surrounded by various mixers.

They sat on opposite sides of the U.

The condensation rolling down the ice bucket mirrored the sweat she felt rolling down her lower back. The lights were low and vaguely purple. The occasional strobe. It was still early by club standards and the dance floor beyond the table was only half-full. Sewanee wouldn't call what was booming through the room music so much as a succession of beats with some occasional screeching. But it entered her body and pounded inside her chest cavity.

She realized she hadn't looked at Nick once since they sat down. She glanced up and he was looking at her. He smiled and raised an eyebrow, like, *well?* She couldn't help it; she chuckled a little and shrugged, butterflies still fluttering.

He gestured at the vodka bottle and she enthusiastically nodded. He got to work, filling one of the glasses with ice, splashing vodka in, and pointing to the different mixers. He seemed relieved to have something to do. Sewanee gestured at the club soda. He obliged and squeezed a wedge of lime for good measure. He handed it to her and she mouthed "thanks." He made himself the same drink and then slung his arm over the back of the banquet, crossed an ankle over the opposite knee, and gazed out into the crowd.

What. The hell. Are we doing here? she thought.

She took a significant gulp, was about to set it down, caught his eye, smiled tightly, brought the drink back to her mouth, and finished it. Then she set it down. He'd looked back out into the crowd so she matched him. Whatever he wasn't looking at, she could not look at, too.

A server appeared next to Nick. She put her hand on his shoulder and leaned down to his ear, her corset overflowing.

Sewanee clocked this, thinking, really? I am literally right here. But then she took stock of just how much space was between them, even though they were directly opposite each other. She was as far away from him as the banquette would physically allow.

Nick pulled his head back and looked at Sewanee. He held up a hand, beckoned her toward him.

God, that hand. Those fingers.

She began scootching around the U, but her dress twisted around her thighs. She changed tactics, making small hops, an inelegant frog attempting to move laterally between lily pads. Eventually, she arrived.

He dipped his head so close to her ear she couldn't tell if it was his breath or his lips that touched it. Either way, a shiver ran through her. "She's saying we can have a bottle of champagne, if we want. That it's included."

They pulled back and she looked into his eyes. His focus racked to her mouth. All she said was, "oooh," because it was a word that pushed her lips into a pout. He turned back to the now-standing server and nodded. She left and they were alone. Glued to each other's side. He pivoted back to her ear. "I think I'm too old for this."

She laughed and yelled back, "Same."

His eyes were bright. She watched him take her in, her mouth, her chin and cheeks and neck and chest. Like he was memorizing her. Mapping her for future exploration. He sat forward, picked up his drink and took a sip, never taking his eyes off her. Then he was back at her ear. "You going to dance?"

She shook her head and brought her lips to *his* ear, enjoying the rush of gratification she felt when she saw goosebumps appear on the side of his neck. "Are you asking me to?"

"Yes."

"Are you joining me?"

"No."

"Oh, I'm supposed to dance alone?"

"Well, if you insist."

"I would take you up on that generous offer, but I can't dance to this noise. Are these actual songs?"

As if the DJ had heard her, the music morphed into a clubby remix of Phil Collins's "In the Air Tonight." Nick cocked his head: *You were saying?*

The gauntlet had been thrown. He tucked his knees to the side, giving her room to pass, and extended his hand. Taking it, she levered herself to standing. She didn't immediately move past, but paused before him. At her stillness, his head came up and she looked down to meet his eyes, hand still in his. A timeless configuration, a Lady and her knight-errant. A timeless connection, clear and comfortable and right. An understanding of their respective place in this eternal dance, instinctively knowing when to lead and when to follow.

She moved to the dance floor and his eyes never left hers, not for a second.

She started dancing.

It should have been awkward. She was so out of practice. A well-preserved vintage car garaged for too long, its battery drained. But the music was a key slipped into the ignition and, to her surprise, the engine turned over. She began to move. The avidity in Nick's eyes burned off whatever insecurity remained and the butterflies finally settled. She had no idea why he was so into her, but he was, and it was freeing. Freeing from something. For something.

She moved deeper into herself, her moves becoming small, intimate, private. In these matters, while other women might be overt, she'd always found that covert operations yielded the best results. Give him just enough to guess the rest. Make a man use his imagination and he couldn't help but be curious. They didn't need the explicit version. What they wanted was Pictionary. And she knew how to draw.

When the server returned with an ice bucket of champagne and placed it on the table in front of Nick, he shifted to see around her, to keep watching Sewanee, and had she ever felt more powerful? Had she?

The cast of his eyes shifted. From watching to thinking. A secret tugged at his lips. With the thumb of his right hand, he spun the ring on his middle finger.

The song didn't end so much as become something else, back to unrecognizable noise.

She stopped moving. She stood there, people stepping around her as if she were a spilled drink.

Nick's silent grin reeled her to him. As she drifted off the dance floor a strobe light began throbbing. She watched it fracture him. He grew larger in pulses as she came closer. She could only imagine what she looked like, coming toward him in fits, skipping ahead. Instead of swinging his knees to the side, this time he simply parted them. So she slipped between them, the outside of her legs kissing the inside of his. His hands stayed on his thighs. She saw them clench the fabric.

Once again, they looked at each other.

He had the sweetest look on his face when he said something she couldn't hear over the music.

So she yelled, "What?"

He laughed. Shook his head. Yelled back, chagrined, "I said I miss talking to you!"

She laughed, bowing her head, dropping her hands to his shoulders to steady herself. Chuckling, he reached up, cupped the back of her neck. His fingers slid through the fine hair there and his cheek slid along hers until his mouth was back at her ear. "Would you like some champagne?"

Her cheek still touching his, she turned to his ear and said, simply, "No." Then she took his lobe into her mouth.

In response, he gathered her hair and squeezed.

She stepped back, took his hands as she straightened, and pulled him up. As she led him away from the table, she noticed a group of young women loitering at the periphery of the dance floor. They looked unmoored. Dinghies left to bob in a rising tide. Their dresses too short, heels too high, hair too glossy. One kept shifting her weight, already regretting her choice of footwear; another, with the shortest dress of all, kept tugging it down, drawing more attention to the very things she was trying to hide. The sharks were beginning to circle.

She dropped Nick's hand and stepped over to them. She pointed at their table, at the nearly full bottle of vodka, at the unopened champagne. She caught the server's eye and gestured at the girls, then back at the table. She nodded. The girls' mouths dropped open. One pulled her into a hug. Another jumped up and down, hands to her chest, nearly collapsing when her ankle buckled.

They exited the club, but on their way to the elevator, Nick suddenly took her hand and guided her into a vestibule, through double glass doors, and outside. The blast of cold, snow-scented air hit Sewanee like an adrenaline shot and she gasped, but it was instantly muffled by Nick's hands taking her face, his mouth taking hers, his body backing her up until her ass hit an icy wall. She melted into it as his body melted into hers.

She remembered they were on a public walkway when she

heard the unmistakable hoots of a pack of boys. Nick broke the kiss, his hands moving from her face to the wall behind her, fencing her in. She dropped her head into his chest as he located the offenders, growled good-naturedly, "Feck off, yeah?"

The cackling faded and Sewanee chuckled into his shirt. She looked back up and past his shoulder. Billowy clouds of breath carried her words: "You have to see this."

He turned his head. "My God." He rolled off her, leaned back against the wall so they were side by side, facing the Strip, right above the small lake where the gondolas were kept. There was a bridge and the replica of St. Mark's tower, the campanile. The lights of the Mirage and Treasure Island on the other side of Las Vegas Boulevard. Snow continued to fall over it all, though more gently than before.

She shivered and Nick snaked an arm behind her back, dragging her over to settle against his front. He swept her hair off her neck and, softly as snow, kissed her exposed skin. His fingers brushed her collarbone and the crevice below it. The sound she made was entirely new to her. "I don't understand," he murmured. "I don't understand how this happened. How everything with you is magic."

"I. Don't. Know," Sewanee huffed out. He took her chin and tipped her lips back to his and kissed her in ways she had either long ago forgotten or never experienced in the first place.

At some point, she managed to turn thought to speech. "We need to go."

"Yeah."

"Now."

"Agreed."

They didn't move.

"Any time."

"I'm going to need a minute."

Sensing her confusion, he pressed ever-so-gently into her. She grinned and gave him a meaningful press back. Did it again.

"Not helping." He grinned back. She did it once more. He pushed her away, slightly. "All right. Here's what we need to do. Because I can't be trusted to stop touching you. You go upstairs. I'll be up in a minute."

"Methinks you're already up—"

"Jaysus, no mercy with you, is it? No quarter given?"

In confirmation, she pushed back against him one more time.

"Witch," he hissed, jumping to the side, laughing. "Go."

She stepped away, turned back. "3524."

"I know."

As she opened the door she glanced back one more time and said, "You've got your key?"

"Worried I might not show?"

Honestly? Yes. She was worried she'd somehow imagined him. That she would go back inside and it would all disappear as magically as it had appeared. Her disappointment poised like a guillotine about to drop. But Nick said, "I'm the 'round-the-bend guy, remember? See you in five."

SEWANEE WAS STANDING in front of the window in the living room when she heard the key card turn the lock. She spun around, and the moment Nick came through the door with that energy he possessed that calmed the very air, she took off her eye patch.

That he had no reaction only affirmed her decision.

She clasped her hands behind her back and leaned against the window, saucily crossing one ankle over the other. The epitome of casual.

He smirked at her, fully aware of what she was doing. "Comfortable?"

She smirked right back at him. As he walked into the living

room, he took off his jacket, draped it on the back of the couch. He loosened his tie, took it off altogether, threw it on the jacket. Unbuttoned the first three buttons of his shirt. The lights in the room were low, but the neon seeping through the windows highlighted the leisurely striptease. He began to roll up his sleeves. Slowly, with all the hurry of a sadist. He shook his head slightly. Looked down at his task. "What am I going to do with you?"

His voice had taken on a grit she found she didn't mind at all.

"What do you like?" he asked, his eyes finding hers.

"Everything?"

"Sounds good to me." His smile nearly ran off his face. "Where to start, then?" He finished with his sleeves and put his hands on his hips. "You know what I want? To be James Bond right now. Not have to think about the next move. It's just right there." He snapped his fingers. Sewanee smiled. "Don't worry, once we get going, I'll be fine. It's merely that first . . . you know. Move."

She laughed. As far as she was concerned, he could start anywhere. She was a buffet. Take a little bit of everything! Start with dessert! Who cared? She needed to say that, to say something, he was waiting. But she wasn't sure what.

And then she was.

"I have a question."

"Oh, no worries," he said, "I'm tested and clean."

God, she hadn't thought of that. What was wrong with her? She felt like the buffet had closed right as she'd gotten to it.

"And I have a condom. A few."

The doors opened again, just for her. She took a breath. "Not what I was going to ask, but good to know."

"Ask your question. I love your questions."

She swallowed. "When I was dancing. You were watching me. And I think you were thinking something. Were you?"

The slight awkwardness of the past few moments evaporated.

The room got warm. He stared at her. His gaze went molten, as it had in the club. "Yes."

"About me?"

"Yes."

"About something you wanted to do to me?"

He hesitated for the space of a breath. "Yes." He clearly interpreted her silence as embarrassment, because he prompted her with, "Would you like to know what I was thinking?"

"No." He deflated slightly. "No, I don't want to know. I want you to do it."

Nick stilled. "Alice." *Alice?* She had to remember who she was. "Wouldn't you like to know—"

"No."

"You don't want to know—"

"Do. It. To. Me." With each word her voice walked down a flight of sultry steps.

He took a long inhale. A longer exhale. "Feck me." He assessed her. "Say stop at any point and I stop."

"I trust you." Lord knew why, but she did.

He ran his tongue over his bottom lip, thoughtfully. He jerked his chin at the lower half of her dress. "Are you wearing anything under there?"

A coquettish smile crept across her face. "What do you take me for?"

He matched her smile. "I'm not judging. I just need to get . . . the lay of the land."

"The lay of the land? Yes, I'm wearing something under here."

His eyes heated again. "What?"

Sewanee paused. She wasn't sure she remembered. "Uh. A thong."

"What kind?"

"Black. Lace."

"Grand."

"Not really."

"Take them off."

She paused again. "Just like that?"

He tilted his head again. "Unless you want to stop?"

In reply, she let her fingers slowly slide up the side of her thighs, hiking her dress enough to reach the sides of her thong, but not enough to reveal anything beyond the joining of her legs. She watched him watch her slowly, methodically slide it down, sure she'd never forget the image of him, tall, strong, fully dressed, in his rolled-up shirtsleeves, standing on the white marble floor, lit by filtered neon.

"Can I assume your . . . state of affairs . . . still resembles our bottle of wine?"

She got the thong to her knees and let it drop the rest of the way to the floor. "Lay of the land. State of affairs." She didn't move. She waited for instruction.

"Not the kind of euphemisms you find in your books? Kick them to me."

One moment of hesitation, but she did. "I told you, we don't use euphemisms anymore."

"Right, sorry, I forgot." He picked up the thong. Fisted it. "Wet."

She couldn't speak. Words had left her.

He put it in his front pocket. Then, as if his sole intention were to torture her, he lifted his right hand to his mouth and licked the top ridge of the ring on his middle finger. Eyes never leaving hers, he eased the ring off and put it in the pocket with her panties. "I would ask you to open your legs."

She did, happily.

He moved toward her. She pressed further into the window.

When he was standing in front of her, she tipped her head

back to see him. He stepped closer. His right leg found a perfect stall between her open ones.

His now-ringless right hand slipped between them, under her dress, knuckles sliding up her left inner thigh, and continued upward until, without pause, his middle finger slid effortlessly inside her.

She inhaled.

He exhaled.

She bore down.

He crooked his finger.

She mewled.

He banged his left hand flat against the window beside her head.

She pulled him to her.

He pressed his chest to hers.

She pressed her lips to his neck.

He ground against her hip. Once.

She grabbed his ass.

He pulled back.

She wouldn't let him.

He cursed.

She writhed.

He jackknifed his wrist, brought the heel of his palm right where she needed it.

And she shattered.

Under normal circumstances, this would be too fast, too foreign, too inappropriate, too embarrassing, not the way it was "supposed to be." Yet, somehow, far beyond her ability to comprehend exactly how, something seemingly so much less became so much more. All the ways this was wrong were exactly what made it so right.

But there was no sense to be made of this now. Now, she

was beyond herself. Beyond consciousness. Beyond the ability to register all that was happening.

The siren wailing thirty-five floors below. The blue light pulsing on his shirt. His cologne. The grain of his slacks under her palms as she mindlessly kneaded, urging him on. His inner thighs clenching around her leg. The heat in the suite redundantly kicking on. Gasping his name against his neck. The feel of him thick at her hip. His head dropping to her shoulder as he gave in. That groan. Her heaving. His trembling. How they slowly slalomed back to earth like leaves.

Consciousness returned the way a sunrise returned light to the earth. A moan, a sigh, a shudder, a laugh, an apology, an *are you kidding*, a promise to go slow next time, a *so long as next time is right the fuck now*, a chuckle, a disentangling, an unhitching, a *Jaysus, you regressed me*, a strangled *right back atcha*.

A step away.

A good stare.

A swallow.

Another.

A step forward.

A kiss.

More.

CHAPTER ELEVEN

"The Reveal"

SEWANEE HELD THE GLASS AWARD OUT TO NICK AND HE ARRIVED JUST in time to keep it from dropping to the floor. His hand cupped her elbow and he leaned in to give her an industry-standard kiss on her cheek. His jaw against hers nearly took her out at the knees. He pulled back, took one full moment to gaze into her eye, and everything passed between them in that second of infinity: confusion, shock, awe, happiness, betrayal—every god-damn thing—and then he, Nick, Nick, Nick turned to the podium and she, Sewanee, stayed rooted to the spot, afraid if she moved an inch she would go down. She stared at him. Under normal circumstances, this would be the appropriate thing to do. Give the honoree one's full attention. In this circumstance, it wasn't a choice.

As the applause faded, he spoke. "Apologies, apologies," he murmured into the microphone, that all-too-familiar Irish lilt on full display. "My aunt would have appreciated my absolute mortification here." He laughed, and the room laughed with him, and he cleared his throat. "First, I must thank you for honoring her . . ." He abruptly stopped . . . swallowed . . . took a breath. The audience surely thought it was owing to the emotions of the moment. They were more accurate than they knew.

". . . With this award. She would have so appreciated this night, being feted by those of you who brought such beautiful voice to her words." He gazed down at the award. "She would have been well chuffed by this, I can tell you that. She loved audio. She loved the melding of writing and performance. And she was in awe of all of you. Especially those who brought her characters, their struggles, their well-earned happily ever afters to life. You have her eternal gratitude." He assessed the crowd. "And mine as well. Cheers."

He raised the award once more and grinned, that Harrison Ford grin, that battering ram grin. He turned to take Sewanee's arm, as was customary, but she was already moving off, head down.

He trailed her into the wings as he'd trailed her through the suite and the MC brushed past them on his way back to the stage. A few people murmured their congratulations, their condolences, and Nick murmured his thanks. Mark was there, waiting to go on. He squeezed Sewanee's arm and said, "Good save, Swan." She smiled reflexively and kept walking and then felt a different hand on her arm and finally conceded there was no escaping this.

So she stopped, took a courageous breath, and turned to face him.

His bewildered eyes drank her in. He opened his mouth, repeatedly, a gaping fish on a dock.

She was aware of two things: they had about a million things to say to each other and they were in the wings of a theater. What to say? Where to start?

"Hi," was all she came up with. But at least she said it quietly.

He barked a laugh. "Hi?!"

It was too loud for backstage. Someone shushed them.

She said, "How are you?" Utterly inane, but at least it, too, was quiet.

"How the hell—" Nick began, but the stage manager hissed at them. Nick rolled his eyes in frustration, took her arm again, and led her to the nearest exit. They burst, missile-like, into a hallway, and he steered her—as he'd once steered her outside into the falling snow—into the empty lobby. They stopped in front of the bar.

After a moment of nothing but staring, Sewanee had to say something. Anything. What came out was, "Surprise." And then she laughed.

He laughed, too. "I missed that dry wit, Alice."

A voice behind them: "Swan?" Her eye squeezed shut. "You okay?" Mark entered the lobby. She met his worried, harried eyes. He was supposed to be going onstage any second, but she *had* been bodily removed from the wings by a man Mark didn't know.

"Yup!" she bleated. "Everything's fine. Thank you. Get back in there before you miss your cue." She sounded mostly normal, if perhaps overbright, so after one more wary stare at Nick, Mark retreated down the hallway.

"What's with the Swan thing?" Nick asked, brow furrowing in a way Sewanee didn't like. "Pet name?"

Sewanee swallowed. "No. That's my name."

"What is?"

"Swan."

"Like . . . the bird?"

"Sewanee, actually."

"Well, who's Alice?"

"There is no Alice. Well, there *is* an Alice, but I'm Sewanee Chester."

"Are you—but you're a Romance editor?"

"No."

"Is Alice the—wait. You don't have an accent. Why don't you have an accent?"

"Because I don't have an accent."

This was happening too fast. She didn't know how else it could happen, but her mouth was answering before her ears were hearing and she was only just catching up with the conversation.

He stepped back and quirked his head at her. "Are you a sociopath?"

"No."

"Pathological liar?"

"No!" Sewanee groaned. "I'm an actor."

"Can't say I see the difference." He grinned indulgently, a bit pityingly, a touch ruefully.

Sewanee took a deep breath, trying to regroup. She was keenly aware of the bartenders packing up, pretending they weren't riveted by this.

"Well," he continued, blowing out a breath. "I have to give it to you . . . Sewanee, was it? Wonderfully convincing."

She closed her eye. "Okay, please—you have to let me explain." She opened her eye. "Please."

Nick dropped an elbow onto the bar, crossed his feet at the ankles. "I'm all yours."

Given an opening, Sewanee froze. She didn't know where to begin. How to begin.

Nick watched her expectantly. "Why all the lying?" He twirled a finger. "Annnnd action."

She stomped her foot in frustration, threw her head back, and said, a bit too loudly, to the ceiling, "Because I'd had a bad day!" She took a get-control-of-yourself breath and continued. "Because some random guy approached me in a bar. Because it was only supposed to be one drink." Now that she had started, she gushed. "I felt terrible about it, Nick. As soon as we got to dinner, I thought, tell him the truth, but—again—you were leaving after that and, and . . ." She sighed. "I was protecting myself. Maybe. I don't know, but it doesn't really matter why I did it, I just shouldn't have done it and I'm sorry." She looked into his eyes, really looked. "So, so, so sorry, but please believe me when I say that what started as a lie did not end as one."

He just stared at her.

Unable to hold his gaze, she looked at her shoes. "Go ahead. Say it. I deserve it."

"How could you . . ." He drifted off and, stomach in her throat, Sewanee glanced up. "Keep all of that going the whole time?" There was a genuine note of reverence in his voice. "I mean . . ." He lowered his gaze at her. "The *whole* time."

She opened her mouth to explain further, but he started clapping. "An editor from Texas named Alice. Brilliant!" Then he shrugged. "And, yeah, I get it. Vegas." He pointed at the bar. "Wanna drink?"

"Are you . . . you're not upset?"

"Upset? I want to take lessons from you."

"That's—that's it?"

"Well, that and . . ." His eyes roved down her body. "That's a beautiful dress." He turned to the bar, pitched his voice. "Mate! Before you pack it all up, could I bother you for—" He turned back to Sewanee with a collusive smile. "Vodka soda, was it?" At her open-mouthed blank stare, he said to the bartender, "Two vodka sodas, please." He came back to her once again, leaned an elbow on the bar once again. "So how you been?"

"Can we . . . I have a few hundred questions for *you*, June French's *nephew*, that I'd like to—"

"Ah, sure, yes, shoot."

She began vibrating. A pulsing vibration. Before she could ponder how he had this effect on her, she realized the vibration was real and coming from her ballgown's right pocket. She dug her phone out to dismiss the call, assuming it was Mark check-ing in on her, only to see on the screen: SEASONS.

"I-I actually have to—"

"No worries. I'll be here. Admiring that dress."

Flustered, still looking at him, she brought the phone to her ear. "Hello? What?" She pivoted away, her attention going fully to the call. "When? I was just there! I'll be right over. No, I'm com-ing right now, don't do anything else." She dropped the phone from her ear, but instead of moving, she simply stood there, let it dangle at her hip.

Nick straightened. "Everything all right?"

"It's my grandmother." Sewanee raised her eye to his. Heard herself say, "She tried to kill herself." Once the words were said, she jolted into movement. "I have to go. Oh my God." But she stopped again.

"What can I do?" Nick's voice helped spur her to movement once more.

"I don't know. Nothing. I'm sorry, I . . . I have to go." She went out the main doors, Nick right behind her. There was a taxi parked in a waiting zone. Then Nick was opening the door and she was plunging through it. He jumped in after her, she told the driver where to go, that it was an emergency, and minutes later, Sewanee was jumping out before the car had fully stopped. Nick threw cash at the driver and charged after her.

She was already through the front doors when Nick called out, "I'll wait in the lobby!"

She heard the words, but made no acknowledgment. She was already navigating the hallways leading to Blah.

SEWANEE ROUNDED THE corner into her grandmother's room. There were three people huddled around the bed. "Where is she?" Sewanee demanded.

All three turned to her and stepped away, revealing Blah's frail form slumping upright, nightgown twisted around her thin, veiny thighs. "Blah." Sewanee went right over to her. "It's okay, I'm here." She tried to catch her grandmother's gaze, but her eyes were unfocused and glassy, wide with residual terror, darting loopily around the room. "What happened?" Sewanee asked, trying to sound steady.

"She'd been—" a young female nurse started, cleared her throat. "She was agitated. Telling people to get away from her, but no one was there. Then she wanted to go see the movie. And that seemed to calm her down. But when it was over—"

"Before it was over," an older woman chimed in.

The nurse—who, Sewanee glimpsed from her name tag, was Gina—nodded. "Before it was over, she started up conversations with imaginary people—"

"What was she saying?" Sewanee asked.

"Things like, 'You're always like this' and 'leave me alone.' So I brought her back to her room, got her into bed, and then I went to talk to Carlos about meds—"

Carlos interjected, professionally, "I suggested her usual dose of Ativan."

"And?"

"I got the Ativan," Gina continued, "came back into her room and . . ." She pointed at the window. "She was halfway out."

"How the hell did—" But Sewanee stopped.

The window had been open.

Because she'd opened it.

And not closed it.

This was her fault.

"I yelled for Carlos. We pulled her back inside and that's when the screaming started." Sewanee noticed Gina was holding her right forearm with her left hand. There was gauze underneath her fingers. At Sewanee's questioning look, Gina said, "She scratched me. Just a little. I'm fine."

Reeling, Sewanee turned back to Blah. She appeared completely disoriented. Her mouth had gone slack, her hair was standing up as if she'd been in a pillow fight.

"Blah?" Sewanee reached for her hand. "Everything's fine. I'm here."

Her grandmother's eyes settled on Sewanee's face and went wide. Sewanee smiled, trying to provide a hint of familiarity, of normalcy. But then Blah said, "Who are you?"

Sewanee squeezed her hand. "Sewanee."

Blah pulled her hand back. "Get away from me."

Sewanee took it again. "Blah, please, it's Dollface—"

Blah yanked it back. "No!" Her voice was raw. "Don't you touch me!" Frantic, too. Sewanee leaned in closer, which only made Blah retreat further, which made Sewanee say, desperately, "I'm Henry's daughter, your granddaughter—"

"Help!" Blah screeched. "Somebody help me!"

Sewanee felt Carlos's hand on her shoulder, urging her back. She threw it off. "BlahBlah!" Sewanee barked.

Blah thrashed, trying to get away, get up, get out. Gina grabbed her shoulder.

The older aide said, "We may have to call an ambulance."

Sewanee changed tactics. She made shushing noises, and in her gentlest voice said, "You're my grandmother and I love you and you're safe and everything's fine."

"AAAHHHHHHHH!" She'd reached banshee hysteria.

"Okay, Barbara, okay, easy," Carlos murmured, grabbing her other shoulder.

Sewanee made one final attempt. She couldn't help it. She took Blah's face in her hands, looked in her eyes, trying to connect through force of will alone. "BlahBlah, listen to—"

Blah spit in her face.

Sewanee was so shocked, so utterly dumbfounded, that all she could do was nothing. She was paralyzed.

"You're not my granddaughter! My granddaughter is beautiful!"

"Blah—" Sewanee choked.

"MONSTER!!!"

Sewanee didn't remember leaving the room. She didn't know how she ended up downstairs and outside, on her knees in the grass in the garden sobbing so hard she couldn't breathe. She felt faint and nauseous and inflamed all at once. She felt as though she were on fire. The sounds coming from her were the primal keens of the mortally wounded. Her forehead dug into the muddy grass, she pulled clumps of it up by the handful. She cradled her head and burrowed the mud into her scalp. Her throat burned like a crematorium. Eventually the sounds subsided and what was left were residual heaves. And the hand on her back.

The hand. On her back. Not moving, not soothing, not petting. Resting. The full span of it nested between her shoulder blades.

WHEN SHE RESURFACED, she was surprised to find herself curled in Nick's lap. That they were sitting on a bench in the garden, the one she'd sat on with Amanda. She opened her eye and, through the blur, could see that the chest of his tuxedo shirt was a mess. Wet and smeared with the remnants of her mascara, lipstick, and foundation. It looked like a crime scene. She couldn't fathom what she must look like. She also couldn't meet his gaze. "I'm so sorry," she choked out.

"Shhhh." He brought his hand to the side of her head, guiding it to his shoulder, his jacket soft and dry.

"This was—" Then, to herself, "Oh God." Back to Nick: "You don't have to stay, I'm fine now—"

"Don't be an arse," he murmured, his tone soothing despite the playful admonishment, "I'm not going anywhere."

So she let herself be cradled by him. In fact, she brought her arm up across his chest and around his other shoulder, snuggling closer. She let his fingers play at her hairline, took comfort in the steady beating of his heart.

After an epoch, when she felt she had returned to some reasonable baseline, she was left with the heady, slightly-stoned feeling extreme sobbing generates. She wanted to talk, but wasn't sure she was capable of coherent speech. She took a breath and gave it a try, rhetorically murmuring, "June's nephew. No wonder you were so good at the Romance version."

She felt his chuckle like thunder in his chest. "I could have been a wee bit more honest, too."

Sewanee paused. "Your name is Nick, right?"

"Yes, you see, I didn't know we were making up names." She heard the teasing in his voice. "But I shouldn't have played it dumb."

"Why did you? You didn't have to. You had an opening. 'I'm a Romance editor.' 'Oh, what a coincidence, my aunt basically built the entire category, perhaps you've heard of her?'"

"Right. That would have been a thing to say." He paused. "What would you have said to that?"

Sewanee thought for a moment. "I don't know. Maybe . . . maybe I would have taken the opportunity to come clean. You wouldn't have been some random guy in a bar anymore."

"But I was a random guy in a bar."

She dared to look up. He made a pouting smile, probably at the absolute disaster of her face. She started to go back into hiding, into the safety of his jacket. But he stopped her. Put his hand on her chin and kept her head up. He gazed at her. "I think we both wanted random," he murmured. "That was the fantasy, no?"

The word "fantasy" sparked a dormant ember inside her.

Brock McNight.

She sat up. "What time is it?" She fumbled in her pocket.

"Probably ten or so," Nick answered, but Sewanee already had her phone out. 10:30. 10:30! She'd been crying for, what, an hour? She stood up, shakily, her hand clinging to Nick's shoulder. "I have to make a call."

"Of course." He probably thought she needed to call family, and she did. She did. But first, this.

She moved away from him then, about twenty feet. She pulled up her text chain with Brock and started typing. I'm so sorry. You won't believe this, but a family 911 . . . She paused. Deleted. Started again. I had an emergency and I'm so sorry for the super late notice but I won't be able to

Everything felt inadequate. She owed him more than a text. He'd have questions and she wanted to be able to answer them. She wanted to hear his voice and, more importantly, she wanted him to hear hers. To hear how sorry she was. That she wasn't getting cold feet. That it was a matter of timing, nothing else. After all these months, she finally *wanted* to talk to him.

So, she took a steadying breath, tapped his name, and pressed the phone icon. She brought it to her ear.

First ring.

Second ring.

There was a ring in the garden, too.

Third ring.

Again, in the garden. Annoying.

She put a finger in her ear and looked around. She saw Nick stand up, turn away from her, and answer *his* phone.

In her phone, Brock finally picked up. "Sarah?" That familiar richness, that burned caramel, of eighty thousand downloads and counting.

Relieved, Sewanee said, "Yes, hi."

"Well, hello." His voice came through her phone.

And, also, simultaneously, across the night air.

He continued, "I'm glad you called. I might be a bit late."

His voice was in stereo.

"Something unexpected came up. I'll explain when I see you."

Again, stereo.

Her eye stayed glued to Nick's back. "Did you hear me?"

A word finally dropped from her mouth. "Brock?"

Again. Stereo: "Yes?"

Immediately, she said, into the phone, "Nick?"

Automatically, he answered, into the phone, "Yes?"

Silence. Deafening silence.

Then she shouted, finally, across the courtyard, "What the *fuck*?"

CHAPTER TWELVE

"The Reckoning"

NICK SPUN AROUND.

They stared at each other.

They lowered their phones. Or, more accurately, their phones lowered themselves.

Nick was the first to speak. What he said was, "Holy mother of shite."

Sewanee had a whole dump truck of things to say, but the hydraulics were broken.

So Nick said, again, "Holy mother of shite!"

Then he grinned. He grinned and then he threw back his head and he hooted. He clasped his hands in front of his chest and laughed. He grabbed his head and spun around and did a little jig.

Then he moved toward her, his eyes twinkling like Christmas morning. Like the gift of his dreams lay unwrapped at his feet.

She stepped back.

Way back.

He froze.

She looked at him from the corner of her eye, a dog guarding a bone.

Nick's smile faded slightly. "What?"

"What?" she said, incredulously. "What?!" she said, more incredulously. "Who *are* you?"

Sewanee watched him attempt to banish the smile, to give the circumstance the sobriety she needed. It only made him look like he'd licked a sour ball. "I'm me. Nick!" He couldn't do it. The smile came back with a vengeance. And a laugh for good measure. "Don't you see how incredible—"

Her finger shot up. "Wait. Stop. Questions."

His arms went out. "I'm all yours."

Sewanee took a breath. "June French's nephew?"

"Yes!"

"And?"

He nodded. Once. "Yes. I am also Brock McNight." He said it in Brock's voice.

"What."

He said it again, and again in Brock's voice. "I am also Brock Mc—"

"No, no, no, no, no, no don't do that."

"All right." His arms lifted, reaching toward her. "And you're Sewanee Chester. And Sarah Westholme." It wasn't a question. "Fantastic. Nice to meet both of you." He gestured at the bench, stiffly, like his arm didn't belong to him. "Shall we sit?"

She didn't move.

"Or we could stand. Standing is good." He watched her, waiting for a signal.

She sat.

Nick placed himself carefully at the other end. He pointed at the large space between them. "Now there's room for all four of us." At her silence, he said, "Right, too soon."

"Could have been 'a wee bit' more honest, too?" she said, tightly.

He shook his head lightly. "Yes, let's clear everything up. One:

I don't work for a venture capital firm. That's my dad, my bio-
logical dad, he does that."

"And the accent?"

"Well." He spoke the next words with a stronger burr. "I do
tend to thicken it up a bit when I'm looking to meet someone.
Women do love a good accent, you know."

She dropped her head into her hands. "Oh my God."

He dropped the excessive lilt. "Sorry, just being honest."

She inhaled sharply. "Okay. Okay." She breathed. "I know why
I lied." She looked at him. "Why did you?"

He spread his arms wide, as if to show her he held no weapons.
"I'm not you. I don't have a career under my own name. I'm just
a pseudonym. A ghost. So, when—if—I say what I do for a living?
People—women—they want to know what I've recorded and what
do I tell them? Out myself as a vocal porn star?"

Sewanee kept trying to clear a path through the mounds of
mental clutter. "So the Brock McNight voice is—"

"Fake. It's entirely put on." He sighed. "It's a long story."

"Give me the short version."

"When the band fell apart, I started narrating. One of June's
friends gave me a shot—"

"The band's real?"

He blinked at her. Seemed to finally understand the gravity
of her confusion, her reticence, her suspicion. She was doubting
everything, not only Vegas, but also their correspondence. He
inched over to her on the bench, carefully. Cautiously. She didn't
move away, but she stiffened and folded her arms across her
chest. He paused his advance. "Everything—every single thing I
wrote to you—that was real. That was me. Just a different name,
that's all. In fact, the band mate, my best friend? That's Jason.
Casanova's producer."

Sewanee threw up her hands. "Sure, why not? And the cocktail waitress in Vegas was your sister." She looked at the ground, but could feel him peering at her.

If everything was real, then why did she feel duped?

The night had already been too much. This officially put her over the edge she could have sworn she'd already fallen off.

Nick was talking. "This is good, you realize that, right? It's amazing. Have a laugh, darling, it's funny." The last few words were infused with a gentle chuckle. He reached out to lay a comforting hand on her knee.

But she wasn't ready for that. It actually angered her. The fact that he found this funny seemed to prove he wasn't nearly as invested in either version of her as she'd been in both versions of him.

Plus, she was covered in spit and mud and makeup and tears while he looked like James Bond.

She stood. "This is stupid. I'm done. Enough. I have real concerns, real problems. My grandmother's in there trying to kill herself, my father's an asshole, and . . ." Something boomeranged back around. "I lost tonight! I was nominated in *one* category and I lost, and that hasn't happened since I started doing audiobooks, so I don't know what that means, if anything, but it's probably not good, and I just . . . goodnight."

"Oh, come on!" Nick called to her retreating back, his voice still filled with mirth. "Don't storm off! Sewanee!"

She disappeared into Seasons.

"YOU SMOKE?"

It was not what she'd intended to say, but the sight of Nick lying on his back on the bench, bringing a cigarette lazily to his mouth, made everything else she'd planned to say leave her.

He startled at her reappearance and quickly sat upright, snuffing the cigarette. He'd undone his bow tie and unbuttoned his collar. He had no right looking so good. "Not since high school," he said, sheepishly, "but I— It's been . . . a rough few months." In all of this confusion, she'd forgotten his aunt—who he had clearly been close with—had died. She walked back to the bench, but didn't sit.

Puppy dog eyes gazed up at her. "You came back."

She swallowed. "I'm so . . . spun out and I don't know how much I can handle right now, but I do know I don't want to walk away like that."

"That's commendable. Quite grown-up."

Sewanee shook that off. "I tend to catastrophize. My father would tell you I have a flair for the dramatic."

Nick shrugged. "You're passionate."

Her face heated at that, at the casual knowingness of his statement. Also, the erroneousness of it. She wasn't passionate, not really. She'd only been so with him.

She gathered her wits. "I want to know why you think this is good. Why you think it's amazing."

He slapped his knees. "Gladly!" He stood, which had the effect of putting them entirely too close, but Sewanee wouldn't embarrass herself by stepping back. She boldly met his gaze instead. "Because in what world could you imagine this happening to you?"

"None! This belongs in one of June's books."

"Right! But this is real!"

"Is it?"

"Yes!"

"What is?"

"This! The whole this." He waved his arms, encompassing the entire universe. "We're so lucky."

"How?"

"Because I've been a mess for weeks." The excitement in his

voice accelerated his pace. "I, Nick, couldn't stop thinking about the woman from Vegas. You. Alice You. But I was all discombobulated. Why? Because I, Brock, was having these feelings, *real* feelings, for you. Sarah You. So I Nick and I Brock were at, like, odds with each other because we're having these feelings for two different women, but they're both you! Sewanee You! Don't you see? This is . . ."

As he ran out of steam, she quirked her head at him. *What? This is what?* She sure as shit didn't know. She didn't even know what he had just said. But she was able to cherry-pick from it . . . how much he liked her. All of the hers.

He sighed and stuck out his hand. They were so close he had to keep his elbow tucked into his side to do it. "Hi. My name is Nick. Nick Sullivan. I'm a narrator of Romance. Nice to meet you. And you are?"

She looked at his hand, that hand that had been places. She swallowed and took the bait. "Sewanee Chester."

He gently shook her hand. He didn't let go. "I'm sure the answer's no, but I'd be remiss if I didn't at least offer to make good on our date tonight. Would you like some food? A Last Word?"

She chuckled softly. "As wonderful as that sounds . . ."

He patted her hand with his other one. "I get it. It's been . . . a night."

She nodded. "I need some time."

Nick let go and held his hand up. "Absolutely. Text me when you're ready to talk."

There was no *if* in his statement. As far as Nick was concerned, this was a humorous bump in the road.

So what was her problem? Yes, she was hollow and spent and completely flummoxed, but why did she feel like she was missing something key? She had the feeling of being confused without knowing the source of her confusion. Like trying to find her car in a parking garage and cycling through the possible scenarios: Was it stolen? Was it towed? Was she on the wrong floor? Did she even drive that night?

She tentatively smiled and stepped back. She gave him a little wave, which he reciprocated, and she turned around, walking back into Seasons.

"WHY WERE YOU in Las Vegas?"

She hadn't been gone as long this time, so she caught Nick as he was leaving the garden, scrolling the phone in his hand.

He startled and then laughed. "Is this a bit? Are you doing a bit?" But he must have seen the suspicion on her face because he sobered. "For the convention."

"Why?"

"June had been scheduled to be there and when she . . . when she died, her publisher—of her backlist—they wanted to turn it into a memorial, of sorts. It seemed like the right thing to do for her fans. They could stop by, pay their respects, get a limited-edition postcard of her original covers." He added, "She was like a mum to me."

"But out of all the hotels, why were you staying at the Venetian?"

"June had booked the room. Because of *Casanova*. A poor man's research trip."

It was almost too plausible. Why didn't she trust this? Any of this?

"Were you at the convention as Brock McNight?"

He looked horrified. "Christ, no! I don't do anything as Brock McNight."

"So, you didn't know I was there?"

He blinked at her. "I didn't know who you were, how could I know you were there?"

"I mean," Sewanee said, starting to gather a full head of steam, but not understanding precisely *why*, "you didn't see me hosting a panel on audiobooks, manning an audiobook booth?"

He looked more bewildered. "No! Emphatically no. I couldn't care less about audiobooks! Sewanee . . . I don't know you. I don't even know how to spell your gorgeous name."

"You've never heard of the narrator with the eye patch?"

"For feck's sake, no!" She could see he was trying to figure her out. Like maybe if he looked at her hard enough her head might crack open and he could take a peek inside. "Why are you doubting that I didn't know who you were?"

She shook her head. "You expect me to believe, you honestly, that you randomly . . ." She took a ragged sigh. She didn't want to start crying again.

"What?" He reached for her, but she decisively pulled away from him.

She found her voice. Steeled it. "Why'd you come up to me in that bar?"

"Why that bar?"

"No. Why me?"

She watched his face change. It went slack. For the first time tonight, he finally looked as gutted as she felt. "Oh. Yes, okay. It's not . . . it's so daft."

"You thought I'd be easy?"

"What? No—"

"That the girl with the eye patch would be grateful?"

Nick's eyes shuddered closed and his hand clutched his chest. "No. You're breaking my heart right now. How can you think that about yourself?"

Sewanee answered, simply, "Because I've had pity pickups before."

"That is *not* what it was. Not at *all*. My *God*."

"Then what?" He didn't have a quick comeback. "Nick?"

"My darling girl—"

"Stop." She was doing her best to give him an opportunity to surprise her, but she was bracing for the truth. "It's okay, just admit it was a pity—"

Nick threw his arms out and walked a few steps away. He spun back. "You really want to—fine." He huffed a sigh. "You'd been sitting with Adaku Obi. Okay? So I came over." He shrugged. "Thought I'd get in good with the friend. I figured you were the wingman so . . ." He took a breath, widened his eyes, shook his head. "Simple as that."

Simple as that.

Sewanee turned and walked away.

"I'm sorry," he said and from the nearness of his voice, she could tell he was following her. "You asked me and I told you the truth. I don't want— I *can't* lie to you anymore about anything. Whatever the consequences."

She said nothing.

He continued, "But while, yes, that's how it started, that's obviously not how it ended."

Sewanee fired back, "Right. She didn't come back to the table, did she?" She felt like such an idiot. Such a pathetic idiot. She'd been wondering what this guy saw in her and it had been *so* obvious, and she'd been *so* blind. Willfully blind. God.

They left the walled garden and reentered the building. They walked through the empty main room, the lobby, Sewanee's eye on the double doors in front of her. She had to get out of here.

"Before you leave, what is it now, for the tenth time . . . ?" Nick tried to poke a hole in the tension, but she saw no humorous light come through it. "Please think about this: how it began doesn't matter. It doesn't! Because remember when you got the text from your friend who couldn't make it to dinner?" Sewanee held up her hand, willing him to stop. That text had been yet another of her lies.

Nick ignored her hand. "Did I leave you then? Did I walk away? No! I asked for the check and I went with you to dinner, because I wanted to, because I wanted to be with *you* at that point!"

"Because I was what was left!"

Sewanee breached the front doors and noticed a taxi pulling up and all rational thought fled. She wanted to escape and this was the fastest way. "I can't do this. I need some time to—it's too much, it's, it's . . ." As she got to the cab, the door opened.

"Swan!" Mitzi croaked, heaving herself out. "You look like leftovers. Like something someone scraped off a plate. Nice dress, though."

"Thanks," she mumbled.

As the driver brought her walker around the cab, Mitzi leaned on Sewanee and her eyes landed on Nick. "Hoo hah, what's this?"

Sewanee caught the driver's eye. "Are you free?"

"Sure, climb in."

"Sewanee—" Nick began, but Sewanee cut him a look that could shatter glass. She turned back to Mitzi, who was now settled on her walker.

"See you Friday, Mitzi."

Mitzi gave Nick an elevator glance. "Bring whatever this is."

Sewanee ducked into the cab and slammed the door. Nick scrabbled to the window, said, through it, "Did I plan to have anything other than a drink? Did I plan anything beyond dinner? I was leaving! Did I plan the snow?!"

Sewanee told the driver where to go and the cab started to pull away. Nick slapped the top of it. "Sewanee! Come on!" But Sewanee shooed the cabbie onward.

She turned around, as if she actually had something to yell back at him, and watched his hands find his hips as he called out, "What do I need to do?" Then his attention turned to Mitzi, who was tugging on his jacket.

"So. You single?"

CHAPTER THIRTEEN

"The Break"

IT WAS 3:15 A.M. AND SEWANEE LOOKED AT THE CLOCK ONCE AGAIN. She was sure it had been at least forty-five minutes since the last time she'd looked.

It had been twelve.

Thoughts moved in and out of her mind like hummingbirds at a feeder.

He didn't pity her. Did he? No, he didn't. The way he had been with her, his touch, his care, his determination. None of it had felt like pity. She knew the difference.

But she hadn't been his first choice. He'd wanted Adaku. She'd been a consolation prize.

And what about their goodbye in Vegas? Why didn't he give her his number? Why didn't he ask for hers?

She flipped over. Pulled her pillow tight. Closed her eye.

Images of the two of them, together, rushed in.

Sitting opposite him in the soaking tub, afterward.

The texture of his skin made slick by the water.

Her fingers tracing the hollow of his throat.

She flopped over, hoping to leave her mind on the other side. But the words they'd exchanged came through like taunting ghosts.

He'd said, *I'd love to continue this, but . . .*

She'd said, *no of course.*

He'd said, *it's probably better to leave it.*

She, crushed under the weight of her lies, could only agree.

Then he'd touched her scar. Simple, unencumbered, natural.

Then Blah screamed, Monster.

She opened her eye. 3:18 A.M. Unbelievable.

She flipped once more, reached compulsively for her phone, but there was no message since the one Carlos had sent hours ago: Blah had stabilized, she hadn't needed to go to the hospital. But they'd keep the Ativan in her for a few more days. Probably best if Sewanee gave her some space.

No message from "Brock," either.

How would she get over being someone's—God, she'd hated the term since the first time she'd heard it from some walking jockstrap in junior high—sloppy seconds?

But that wasn't it. That wasn't even the right terminology. What was she trying to . . .

She'd been used. That was it, that's what had happened. Plain and simple. She'd been used by a man who knew exactly what he was doing. He was Brock McFuckingNight. He'd appeared to her like a hero out of a Romance novel because that was precisely what he was. That's all he was. But she? She was all too real.

Except for the lying.

"You have got to get some sleep," she groaned out loud, parenting herself. She flipped one more time, squeezed her eye shut, and refused to open it.

3:19 A.M.

Dammit.

WHEN SEWANEE FIRST heard the knocking, it presented as church bells in the dream she was having. A foreign city, springtime sun, the vague sense of unease, as if she were late for something she couldn't remember. But church bells shouldn't sound so deadened, so inelegant.

She opened her eye into silence. Waited. The knocking came again. This time more of a banging.

Adaku! The ride to the airport!

She sprang out of bed, tripping over her purse from the night before, and flung herself toward the door.

The sun was full behind Adaku's new military-short afro. "Morning!"

Sewanee brought a hand up to shield her eye. "What's going on?" she croaked.

Adaku misinterpreted her unwelcoming tone. She grinned and stage-whispered, "Am I interrupting?"

"What?" The night rushed through her like an express train through a station stop. "Oh. No. Not at all."

Adaku deflated. "Boo. Why?"

Sewanee tried to form words, but she couldn't. She just stood there. Speechless. Motionless.

"Oh, babe," Adaku murmured. "Okay, okay! Inside!"

Adaku set her on the couch, buzzed around the kitchen for a minute, and then there was a glass of water in front of Swan and a command to drink it. She did and another minute later there was a cup of coffee in front of her and her feet were in Adaku's lap on the love seat and Adaku said, "What happened?" and Sewanee told her. Everything.

They were on their second cup of coffee by the time she was done. It was sad, and still surreal, but not quite so dire as it had seemed when Adaku arrived.

"I'm so sorry about BlahBlah," Adaku said.

"At least she won't remember it."

Adaku huffed a bittersweet chuckle. "True. Now Brock on the other hand, or should I say Nick—"

Sewanee held up a hand. "I don't want to talk about him. Them."

Adaku persisted. "Okay, but, I mean, from where I'm sitting, it seems . . . insane." The last word came out in a giddy laugh. "One night stand turns to unwitting correspondence! That's Fated Mates stuff—"

"More like bad Fantasy," Sewanee interrupted, stood, and wandered into the kitchen. "Don't romanticize it. It's awful. Humiliating. It's—" She saw a white paper bag on the counter. "Did you bring me a breakfast burrito from Beachwood?"

"I did," Adaku responded from the living room.

"Aww, thank you." She tore into the bag. "Where's yours?"

"No can do. The only part of a burrito I can eat right now is the paper it's wrapped in."

Sewanee put the burrito in the microwave, shook her head, and continued talking from the kitchen. "I probably shouldn't eat this, either, huh? Oh, you'd be proud of me, I started doing push-ups last week. I mean, I figure they'll give me a trainer, but thank God I'm not doing the boot camp with you right now, I would not survive—" She gasped, covered her mouth. "Oh my God, A, I'm such an idiot. I left my car at Seasons last night. Shit! I'll order us a ride, I'm so sorry—"

She spun around and Adaku, who'd come to stand at the entrance of the kitchen, said, "You didn't get the part."

The microwave beeped, but Sewanee didn't move. As if she had been shot but the surprise of the impact preceded the pain of the bullet.

"I'm so sorry, Swan. I still can't believe it." Adaku looked wretched, as if she had pulled the trigger.

Sewanee turned back to the microwave. Opened the door. Removed the burrito. Took a huge bite. She continued to eat until Adaku said, "Talk to me."

Sewanee swallowed, preemptively steadied her voice. "When did you—"

"Yesterday. I didn't want to tell you before your big night. But I'm leaving and I wanted to tell you face to face and . . ." She drifted off.

After one more suspended moment, Sewanee took another bite. "It's fine. Thanks for letting me know. I'll go get ready."

"No, Swan, you're not riding with me to the airport, that's ridiculous."

"Yes, I am!" She took an aggressive bite. "I told you I'd take you and I will." She brought the rest of the burrito with her when she left the kitchen.

Adaku followed her into the living room. "I saw your audition. It was so good, Swan! It was more than good." Sewanee chuckled. "It was. They just decided to—"

"Go a different way?" Sewanee did not try to hide the sarcastic bitterness in her voice. The classic *it's not you, it's me* brush-off of Hollywood.

"Colin wanted you," Adaku soothed, "but the studio—everyone thought you were incredible. Truly brilliant, they said."

She searched for her phone, took another bite, and asked, "Who got it?"

"Swan."

"What? Someone famous who they'll ugly-up instead of someone unknown who already is?"

"Sewanee—"

"I can see the Oscar campaign for best makeup already—"

"It had nothing to do with—"

"Who got the part, A?"

Adaku sighed. "They found this, this girl, Amber Something. She's a YouTube celebrity, influencer, TikTok personality, whatever. When she was seventeen, her arm was bitten off by a shark."

Sewanee choked down the last of the burrito. "Missing arm beats out missing eye." She snapped her fingers sardonically. "Every time."

Adaku shook her head. "You gotta stop. It's about followers. She has like forty million followers. You think talent *used* to take a backseat? Now it's in the trunk. She has a meditation app and cookbooks and shit. But they wanted you!"

Sewanee couldn't contain it anymore. "So what happened to 'I can do this'? What happened to 'star power, babe'?"

Adaku put her hand out, like a crossing guard trying to slow Sewanee down. "I tried, I really did. I was as pissed as you, believe me. But their loss! We'll find something else. Something better! You're back in the saddle now! It was just one audition. This happened for a reason, okay? Everything's meant to be! You'll see."

There was a moment in every argument where it could end. Nothing irreparable had been said, no major boundary had been crossed. There was a natural point of no return.

Sewanee blew past that moment.

She flailed her arms like one of those inflatable tube-men outside a car dealership. "Stop it! Just shut up! Everything happens for a reason?! You know the last time I thought everything happened for a reason? When I had two fucking eyes! Everything's meant to be?! Was *this* meant to be?" She jabbed her finger at her eye so fast, so hard, she didn't have time to recall that she wasn't wearing her eye patch. She hit her scarred eye socket and the wave of pain bent her in half, raised her gorge.

"Swan!"

She felt Adaku race toward her, and she pushed her back, one solid shot to what she thought must have been her hip. "Back off!" She touched her face gently. Saw blood on her fingertip.

"You're bleeding," Adaku gasped.

It wasn't gushing. The scar was long-healed, it wouldn't have opened. She must have caught her fingernail on it. There was a rational part of her brain still working, that could process all of this logically. But the other part kept looping through the unfairness of all the shitty things that had happened and her inability to accept them because they never should have happened in the first place. Not to her. She had never thought, not once, poor me; but she could never escape thinking, why me?

She lunged back into the kitchen, to the freezer, whipped the door open, grabbed a handful of ice, and slapped it to her face, muttering the whole time, "This is all on you. *You* want me to act again. *You* need me to be whole again. *You* need me to win. Because for you, if it doesn't all work out in the end, then you'd have to admit that everything doesn't happen for a fucking reason."

"Swan . . ."

Great, Adaku was crying. Well, so was Sewanee. It took her a moment to realize it with the ice starting to drip down her cheek, but that tightness in her chest, Adaku's blurriness, her inability to draw a full breath? That was tears. And they made her furious.

"You can't fix this. You will not make this better. No matter how much positive-thinking horseshit you sling at me."

Adaku stepped toward her. "Tell me what to do."

Sewanee met her toe-to-toe and screamed, "Let me hate the world and what it's done to me!" At Adaku's stricken face, she spun away and sobbed, "And leave! Please!"

She was crying too hard to hear Adaku's own sobs, her footsteps walking away. All she knew was within a minute, she heard the front door close softly. She made it to the sink just in time to throw up.

SHE DIDN'T KNOW how long she stood there at the counter, looking out at the view of the city, slowly coming back to herself. She just knew she had no idea what to do next.

She turned on the faucet and washed her torment down the drain. It nearly made her throw up again.

Tea. She should hydrate. A manageable first step.

She opened a cabinet and reached for the Tea-For-One gift from her mom.

The moment it slipped from her hands and onto the tile floor, shattering into, conservatively, a billion pieces she knew she would be finding months later, felt, in hindsight, preordained.

She continued to stand there.

What do you want to do, Swan? she thought. Should she pick up the larger pieces, at least? Should she get a broom? Should she try crying again? Should she scream her throat bloody?

In the end, she did none of those things. Instead, she left. She walked out of the kitchen. She stepped on a few pieces, their crunch having no noticeable effect. She walked into her bedroom, grabbed a duffel bag out of the closet, snatched up arbitrary pieces of clothing, and threw them inside, zipped it up, walked back into the living room, picked up her phone, ordered a ride, took one last look at the shattered pieces, and said, aloud, "I want my mom."

AS THE CAR made its way to LAX, Sewanee sat in the back gazing out the window. She felt good about her spontaneous decision. There was even a sense of righteous relief. She wasn't exactly sure from what, but it convinced her she was doing the right thing. This was necessary.

It was also exciting. She'd never done something like this, just gone on her phone and booked the cheapest seat on the next flight out while in the backseat of a car already heading to the airport. The destination hadn't mattered, but when she'd texted her mom to find out where she would be for the next few days and her mother had replied, "Venice" . . . well. Maybe some things *were* meant to be.

Her phone dinged but she didn't want to deal with it. "Brock" had texted now, a few times, but she hadn't read them. What difference did it make? She was going to Italy now. But, she'd also texted Amanda to tell her she'd be unreachable for a while, to call Henry if Blah needed anything. What if this was her reply?

Sewanee looked at her phone.

Shit. Jason.

She scanned the e-mail:

Hey Sarah! Two more episodes to go, scripts attached! As these are the consummation scenes, I think they should be performed in duet, sharing lines back and forth. So I'd like to schedule a time to have you and Brock patch in to record together.

Absofuckinglutely not.

The driver had pulled up to the curb and was getting out to retrieve her bag. She quickly typed:

Not available. Ask Nick.

She sent it, turned off her phone, got out, thanked the driver, grabbed her bag, and walked into the terminal.

Next stop, Venice. For real this time.

PART 5

Character is destiny.

—Heraclitus

Pick a flaw, any flaw. Clock it at the beginning. Let it stalk the character in the middle. Then it pounces. The ensuing moment of fight or flight. You've done your job. Don't overcomplicate this.

—June French in *Cosmopolitan*

CHAPTER FOURTEEN

"The Retreat"

THE FIRST THING SEWANEE SAW WHEN SHE WALKED INTO THE PEN-sione her mother had arranged for her was Marilyn and Stu sitting in two overstuffed club chairs in the lobby. In unison, they beamed and raised their hands in the air as if she'd scored a touchdown.

"There she is!" her mother exclaimed, standing.

"Nice of you to stop by. Come to borrow a cup of sugar?" Stu joked, groaning as he, too, stood.

Sewanee felt the back of her eye tighten with tears. Marilyn looked so good. So happy. Her silver-streaked brown curls fell just below her chin, her face was bronzed, and her blue eyes bright. She'd always been a trim woman, but now she was fit. Strong from walking over cobblestones, hiking through castle ruins, and scaling mountains to get to breathtaking views. She was sixty-five and she'd never been more beautiful.

As they hugged, Marilyn asked in Sewanee's ear, "To what do we owe the pleasure?" She pushed back, looked deep into her daughter's eye. "Working too hard again?"

Sewanee shrugged away from her mother, mumbling, "Always," and reached for Stu. She'd only met him twice before, but within five minutes of the first meeting she'd loved him.

She stepped back and saw that Marilyn was peering at her. "But there's something else?"

"There are a few somethings else."

Her mother raised an eyebrow.

Sewanee took a breath. "Dad."

"Well, when is he not—"

"And Adaku."

"*Ada?* Why—"

"And Blah."

"Oh, no."

"And acting. And robots. And Mark is selling his place. And there's a boy. Who's two boys, actually. Who're the same boy." Sewanee took another deep breath.

Marilyn handed Stu one of the key cards to Sewanee's room. "My love, would you—"

"Yup," Stu said, took Sewanee's duffel bag, and smilingly walked away. Easygoing, uncomplicated, generous Stu.

Marilyn tucked her hand into the crook of her daughter's elbow, leading her onto the hotel's patio. She ordered them two Aperol Spritzes in half-decent tourist Italian and thanked the server for the bowl of olives and basket of breadsticks he placed on the table.

"Let's start with the boy," she said, decisively, placing a palm flat on the wooden table. As Sewanee told her the whole sordid tale, Marilyn's face progressed from slight surprise to damp-eyed sweetness to shock to, finally—much to Sewanee's consternation— uncontrollable laughter.

Sewanee paused the retelling and glared. "Mom."

Marilyn waved her napkin in front of her face, a surrender. She tried, valiantly, to say, "I'm sorry," but the words tumbled around in her laughter like sneakers in a dryer.

"Why does everyone find this so funny?" Sewanee groused, reaching for her drink, waiting for her mom to get it all out.

"Because it's like a movie!" Marilyn cried, wiping her face, pushing her glasses up to the crown of her head. "It's just so . . ." and she lost it again, bent at the waist.

"All right, you know what . . ." But there was nothing to say, no empty threat to level. Her mother's reaction—so like Nick's, so like Adaku's—simultaneously annoyed and humbled her. It forced her to consider everything anew. It still stung. But. There was another side to it. Marilyn saw it. Nick saw it. Adaku saw it. And maybe, if you looked at it from a certain direction, maybe, in certain ways, it was, maybe, a little bit funny. Maybe.

Marilyn regained control of herself, patted her eyes with her napkin. "I'm sorry, Swanling. Truly." They sat in silence for a moment, each taking a sip of their Spritz. Then Marilyn continued with a gentle voice, "And what's going on with your grandmother?"

Sewanee explained all of it. Blah's current state, the necessary move, the exorbitant amount of money she was prepared to spend, and why Sewanee felt it was important to keep Blah in a familiar place with familiar people, whatever it cost.

"Of course," Marilyn interjected quickly at the end, like it was an obvious conclusion, which validated something inside Sewanee she hadn't known needed validation. "Surely, Henry's on the same page?"

Sewanee leaned across the table. "He's not even in the same book, Mom. He resents Blah for going to Seasons in the first place. Resents her for using up her savings to stay there. Resents her for never listening to him, about anything. And worst of all, I thought he would be thrilled when I told him I was paying for it! That it would relieve him of any burden he felt, free him from all the resentments, give him the opportunity to appreciate his daughter, maybe even, I don't know, *love* his daughter?!"

Marilyn chuckled sadly. "Oh, honey. That was never going to work." She took a sip of Spritz and fished the orange slice out, eating it with relish.

"I don't understand him. I try, but . . . It's like he's jealous of me or something. Which is crazy, but that's how it feels."

"Well. They say jealousy is nothing more than admiration turned inside out."

"Mom . . ."

"He probably is jealous. He's definitely resentful. But it has nothing to do with you being his daughter, or me being his wife, or Blah being his mother, or even little Coed Kelly being whatever." The orange rind was poised like a cynical cigarette between her fingers. "We are all one big ball of women. And sorry to say, but that's your father's real problem."

"How so?"

Marilyn sat forward, dropped the rind on her plate. She put her chin in her hands and paused, thinking. "Your father did love something once. Not someone, something: New York City. And when his father died, he left his 'love' to be with his mother, to help his mother. To be loved by his mother? To do the right thing? I don't know. He just wanted to feel useful and ended up feeling useless. Not on purpose, but . . . Barbara was Barbara." Marilyn shrugged. "Henry felt rejected, unappreciated for everything he had given up to help her. He was hurt. He's *still* hurt."

Marilyn was quiet for a while. Sewanee could see her tongue working at her teeth inside her closed mouth, trying to dislodge orange pith. "It all boils down to this, I think: Your father has never felt *appreciated*. The male code word for feeling loved. And sadly, Henry is a man who always found love to be a question, never an answer. It started with Barbara and metastasized in every woman who ever crossed his path. So unhealthy. Not that he would ever *say* that, not that he would ever *ask* for that, God forbid. As far as your father is concerned, women are supposed to intuit this."

Marilyn leaned back, sighed. "So you take all of that hurt and resentment, suffered in silence, and you let it simmer for decades and it distills down into anger." She looked out at the canal next to them, the water close enough to throw late-afternoon ripples onto her face. "That's what I found so hard, Swan. I didn't know how to love an angry man who pretended to be fine." To stave off Sewanee's response, Marilyn held up a hand, her left one, ringless. "We had a good life together. Life is never one thing. But I think I was his consolation prize. And if there's one thing I've learned, Swanling: never be a consolation prize."

How could Sewanee not think of Nick when Marilyn said this? Didn't this justify her feelings? And then Marilyn added, "Especially your own," which spun Sewanee's head around.

A heavy silence fell over them, and she took an olive, washed it down with a sip of Spritz. The salt and oil and the alcohol and the bitterness and the prosecco's fizz hit her and seemed to immediately restore her equilibrium. The Italians have it all figured out, she thought abstractly. She considered her words as she chewed. "Everything feels fake, Mom. Like this is not my life. Like I'm *acting* my life. Like I'm playing out someone else's, waiting to get mine back." She swallowed. "And then I tried to get it back because"—she rolled her eye—"Adaku thought I could and it turns out I can't."

Marilyn squinted, trying to put this puzzle together. "What did Ada do—"

"She just . . . she *pushes*. She's so relentlessly optimistic and she doesn't . . . she doesn't understand why I haven't—" She snapped her fingers. "—gotten over everything. Moved on. For-gotten about it. But I have! In my own way."

The last came out more defensively than she'd intended. Se-wanee waited to hear that her mother agreed with her, while Marilyn took another sip of her Spritz and said, "Well, these things do take time."

"Exactly." Relieved, Sewanee picked up her drink again.

"But is it possible," Marilyn began, and Sewanee set the glass back down, "that you may have *gotten* in your own way and mistaken that for *doing* it your own way?"

"Are you agreeing with A?"

"I don't think so. I'm just saying to check in with yourself."

"You don't think I have? I do?"

Seeing her mother's unvoiced answer, the desire not to hurt warring with Marilyn's compulsive need to tell the truth, in-stantly brought tears. Sewanee surreptitiously wiped her cheek, pivoting away from the rest of the crowd on the patio. "I wanted my life and it wanted me. And now it doesn't and I still do."

Marilyn leaned forward, took her hand. "Of course you do. And your best friend wants it for you. And so do I. And so does anyone who cares about you. But if I'm being honest, I think we all want that only because you haven't given us an alternative. I think everyone around you is waiting for you to accept yourself as you are now, so we can as well. And the bitch of it is you're waiting for everyone to accept you as you are now so you can accept yourself and, sorry, but love, it's your move. You've gotta go first."

Sewanee's head bowed, as if physically unable to stay upright under the weight of her mother's words. She knew it was her turn to say something. But she was saved by Marilyn leaning toward her daughter's head and repositioning her glasses on the bridge of her nose. "You have a gray hair!"

Sewanee's head popped up. "What? Where?!"

"Right in the part."

"Well, yank it out!"

Marilyn chortled and pulled away. "Ohhhh, no! Nope." She stood. "You're going to leave it be. You're a tiger and you earned that stripe." She bent over, kissed the top of Sewanee's head, right where that stripe had sprouted. "I think you should rest. Take a few hours, we'll come back at seven to take you to dinner." Marilyn's eyes flicked toward the lobby and Sewanee now saw Stu had stationed himself in a chair there, reading a book. "A delightful little trattoria. And tomorrow night, there's a place Stu is trying to get us a reservation at but it's one of those six-month-out situations." She shrugged. "If he can't, well, we'll be forced to wander the canals eating gelato."

"*Quelle horreur*," Sewanee murmured.

Her mother affected a perfect Italian hand, fingertips up and together, a garlic bulb. "*Che orrore*," she enunciated. She winked and settled her pashmina more securely over her shoulders. "*Ciao, bella!*"

AT SEVEN O'CLOCK, after a nap as solid as if she'd been anesthetized for surgery, Sewanee met her mother and Stu in the lobby and they left the pensione, the night air warm for March. They walked to a picture-perfect restaurant and slipped into a tight corner table. The scent of garlic and wine cork captured her, the feel of white linen under her fingertips comforted her, the taste of Barolo calmed her. She leaned her shoulder against the wood plank wall and watched the candlelight play in her mother's eyes and over Stu's capable hand as he dished up side-plates of the house's special fish risotto. The pleasures of other patrons wafted through the restaurant and combined with the ambient hum of conversation. When their plates had been cleared and they'd shared an affogato, they squeezed themselves past the other diners and slipped back out into the now-chilly night.

Marilyn and Stu insisted on walking her back to the pensione. Getting lost in Venice wasn't difficult, it was a given. She had no idea where they were, might as well have been in a maze. They turned left, made a sharp right, walked down a street that was narrower than a hallway, down a flight of tiny steps, under some arbitrary and beautiful wood beams, and there they were: back at the pensione's garden gate.

She was even more surprised by the figure standing in the shadows about ten feet in front of them.

She stopped walking. Stared. "What are you doing here?"

Nick's hands went out to his sides. "This is the grovel."

He looked wrecked. He carried a single backpack, his hair stuck up in a few different directions, and he clearly hadn't shaved in days. He wore black sweatpants, a gray Trinity College Dublin hoodie, and glasses. She didn't know he wore glasses. He'd never looked worse and she couldn't believe how attracted she was to him. This is how he would be on a Sunday morning when he was long past trying to impress a woman. He was alluring in a suit, he was devastating in a tux, but he was dangerous like this.

"How did you find me?"

"Mark. After you e-mailed Jason, he called me and said, 'what did you do?' You weren't answering your texts, so Jason told me to try Mark. I drove to the studio and, once I explained who I was, Mark, too, said, 'what did you do?' He grilled me for an hour before telling me where you were."

She pulled her sweater tighter around her body.

"Can we talk?"

Sewanee turned slightly and his eyes darted to the two people standing behind her. She was about to introduce them, but her mom jumped ahead of her. "Hi, I'm Marilyn, the mother." She looked entirely too pleased for Sewanee's taste. "And this is my partner, Stu Hart."

Nick straightened up, quickly took Stu's outstretched hand. "Pleasure." He then took Marilyn's hand and said, "Ma'am, I'm Nicholas Sullivan and I had a wee misunderstanding with your daughter so I'm here to get it sorted."

Marilyn held on. "Well! Welcome to Venice, Nick. Or should I say, Brock?"

"Mom."

"She told me everything. I've never laughed so hard—"

"Mom!"

"Where are you staying?" She didn't look at her daughter when she said, "Swanling, why don't you see if they have availability here?"

"I actually found a place over there." Nick waved a hand to the right, considered, and waved again to the left. "Or possibly there. Thank you, though."

"We're staying on the ship, but I wanted Swan to be able to immerse herself in the city, so we put her up here. Her first time in Venice and all."

Nick's eyes turned to Sewanee. "First time in Venice?"

She met his eyes. "The real one."

"You've been here before, Nick?" Stu asked.

"Not since I was a lad. We'd holiday in Lombardy occasionally and my aunt had a thing for Vivaldi."

"Oh," Marilyn breathed and Sewanee watched it happen, watched the Nick Spell settle itself over her mother. Dammit. "Nick, you should join us for dinner tomorrow night. Stu, can we make the reservation for four?"

"Mom!" Sewanee's voice was overloud in the quiet garden. She course-corrected. "That's very thoughtful, but Nick just got here and I'm sure Stu—"

"Leave it to me, Swanners." Stu turned to Nick. "Rest up, buddy boy, this isn't a dinner, it's an experience. We went there the last time the ship came through Venice and—"

"Let them go in blind, Stu," Marilyn interrupted, "the way we did the first time."

"You're right, you're right." Stu nodded, but had to add, "I'll just say this: wunderkind chef, twenty-eight. Michelin star. On an island. And the entire place . . . at a Marriott. A Marriott! Can you believe it?" He turned to Marilyn. "Okay, I'm done."

Nick glanced sheepishly at Sewanee. "That's so kind, really, thank you so much, but I'm not sure—"

Marilyn patted his hand. "The boat leaves at seven from the St. Mark's dock. We'll meet you there." She brooked no argument. She turned to her daughter and kissed her cheek. "It'll be fun! Ciao!" And she and Stu hurried away down the path.

Nick and Sewanee stood in silence for a moment. When she finally opened her mouth, Nick handed her his phone. "Press record."

"What?"

"Frame me up." He stepped away, turned back around, faced her. "Is it recording?"

No idea what was happening, Sewanee pressed the big red button on his phone's screen and said, "Uh, yeah?"

Nick dropped to his knees and, after a moment, bent over. He laid fully out, arms forward, in child's pose.

"What the hell—"

"I'm not worthy!" he yelled into the pavers. "Have mercy!"

"Oh my God, Nick!"

He began crawling forward. "I will kiss your feet now!"

Sewanee jumped backward. "You most certainly will not, what the fuck is wrong with you?"

"I'm sorry!" Still yelling. "Do you accept my apology?!"

"Get. Up."

He explained, at normal volume, "I can't get up until you accept my apology."

"What?"

"I promised Mark," he mumbled into the ground. "He needs video proof."

In spite of herself, Sewanee laughed. She flipped the phone around and said into the camera, "I forgive him. Okay? You sadist. Jesus." She turned the camera off. "He's such an asshole. Please, just get up."

Nick sat back on his knees, but he didn't stand. He gazed up at her. "I am sorry. I should have seen how upset you were. I should have seen that side of it. But in the moment, I found it funny as all hell, and now I see it's not funny, not funny at all, you were right—"

"No, you were right," Sewanee shrugged, "it is funny as all hell."

Nick dropped his head back, closed his eyes, groaned, "Oh, thank Jaysus, I haven't been able to stop laughing." He met her gaze again. "Still. Please understand, I never meant to—"

She held up a hand. "Can we just . . . this is such an unnecessarily elaborate way to get me to finish the series."

Nick's voice was strong, tight, all joking gone. "Feck the series. I'm not here because of the series. You'll finish it or you won't. I couldn't care less."

She would finish the series. She was a professional. That was never in question, even if she'd given Jason the opposite impression. She'd only needed time. But the fact he hadn't come for business softened her a bit and compelled her to say, "Of course I'll finish the series."

"Well. I guess I'll be going, then." But he didn't move.

She huffed a small laugh. "What are you doing here? And will you please get up?"

He stood, brushed off his knees. "We never had our date."

"You flew to Italy for a date?"

He grinned. "Well, I'm the 'round-the-bend guy."

"Are you?"

His grin wavered. "No, not really. I used to be. I want to be again." He swallowed. "I don't want to be afraid of oysters anymore, so I got on a plane."

At his honesty, Sewanee looked at her feet. "I'm sorry, too. I'm sorry I left. The other night, but also the country. I was just . . . you know." She brought a flat hand up parallel to her jaw. At capacity.

"Yeah, well, it was a lot. For all four of us." His attempt at levity made her smile and he matched it. "So you're not angry?" He sounded hopeful.

She had to think about that. Was she? She was a lot of things, but was she mad? "No. Not at you. Not anymore."

The Italian moon was full in his eyes when his tone shifted and he said, "You're so beautiful."

"Nick—"

He cringed. "Sorry. Right, we have to talk first. I'll throw myself at your feet later."

She held up a hand again. "No. No feet-throwing. Please." She wrapped her arms around herself. "Let's go sit in the lobby, it's chilly."

"You sure? I don't want to pressure you—"

"Oh, now you're worried about boundaries? Go." It felt so good to tease him, to remember that, all the confusion and convolution aside, they actually enjoyed each other. They always had, each iteration, each interaction.

They commandeered a table in the empty lobby and the bored desk manager was more than happy to set them up with a pot of peppermint tea and some biscotti. Nick excused himself to the bathroom and arrived back just as the tea did, looking like he'd splashed water on his face and run his hands through his hair.

She poured them both a cup and they sipped in silence while Sewanee embedded herself in the moment. The buttercup glow from the deco floor lamps, streaks of moonlight limning the ripples of the canal out the window behind Nick's chair, the occasional creak of a floorboard from a hallway above them. Eventually, Sewanee felt warm enough, inside and out, to ask, "So, what would you like to talk about?"

Nick took a sip of tea. "My aunt."

Not what she'd expected. She'd thought they'd immediately start exhuming their relationship, sorting what was truth from what was fiction. To go back to the beginning and dig themselves out. But, really, what was more formative than family?

NICK'S MOTHER HAD been pregnant at twenty-one and dead from an overdose at twenty-five. He had no memory of her. Which he knew sounded sadder than it actually was. He hadn't known who his father was until a 23andMe test five years ago, which led him to a middle-aged finance guy living in New Jersey with two kids in college and no honest-to-God memory of Nick's mother, either. But he'd been nice and apologetic and had wanted to hear Nick's story and this is what Nick had told him:

His aunt, Deborah June Sullivan, had been older than his mother by about a decade. She'd been a radical feminist (at least by Prescott, Arizona, circa 1994 standards) doing graduate work in Ireland. She hadn't wanted a toddler; she was, after all, intentionally husband- and child-less. But Nick was the only family she had left and June could be sentimental when she wasn't being contrarian. They lived in Dublin for twelve years, but when June broke up with Tom, the closest thing Nick had to a father, she moved them back to the place she swore she'd never return: Prescott. Why? Nick didn't know. Except that June liked a good fight.

Once he'd covered high school in Arizona, summers in Dublin at Tom's pub hanging around musicians, best-friending Jason sophomore year, and the teasing he endured because of his funny accent and the fact his aunt wrote "smut," he summed it all up by saying, "You know, typical dysfunctional family when you get down to it."

He told Sewanee his aunt had issues, generally, with men, present company included. He never felt he could live up to her expectations. She wrote fantasy men and measured real ones against them. He wasn't academically motivated, he didn't care about his appearance, he answered her questions with monosyllabic answers, he would rather play guitar than spend time with her . . . in short, he was a typical teenage boy. But to June, he was becoming just another poor excuse for a man.

He went back to Dublin for university, but only lasted a year. He came home, a college dropout who wanted to play music. A whole lot of nothing looking for something. One thing he was sure of: he would never become one of those men June lionized.

The night manager, alone in the hotel with nothing to do, brought them two small glasses of grappa, just because, and Sewanee and Nick thanked him. As they sipped, Nick said, "Do you think people sometimes know they're dying, the way elephants do? Because June had started working on this project based on what she wished had happened between her and the guy she'd loved before she went to Ireland and met Tom. Of course, in her fictional version, Tom died a horrible death and the one-that-got-away was a legendary lover."

Sewanee smiled. "Of course."

Nick smiled back. But it quickly faded. "She called last October and said we had to talk. In person. I went. Her premonition or intuition or elephant-sense or whatever was spot-on. She attempted to make everything right between us. The struggles, the past, the conflicts . . . you know, as one tends to do at death's door. Then, she laid out the *Casanova* project she was writing and made me promise to do it and that I would also promise to have you do it. She was adamant. To the degree that it was not to be done unless we did it together. She had to have things her way right up until the end. I actually admired that about her." He stared off. "Three weeks later the writing was done and so was she."

Sewanee winced. "When was this?"

"Right before Thanksgiving."

"So, in Las Vegas . . ."

He nodded. "I was very much in it." He gazed at his shoes. "I'm still in it." He slunk down in his seat, stretched his legs out, crossed the ankles, rested the teacup on his chest. Sighed. "And when I plunked down next to you in the bar, I'd just come from sitting at a signing table for six hours. And being completely honest? I was livid at her then. Livid she waited too long to go to a doctor. That it took her dying to tell me how she felt. She left me with everything we could have had if only . . . it was a lot." He fell quiet.

Then he finished the grappa and stood. "You look as knackered as I feel. I'm going to go."

Sewanee stood, too, glancing at the clock above the reception desk and startled to see it was 2:15. "I'm a little insulted you didn't try to pull off Just One Room. You could have run out the clock here and then been like, 'oh, wow, look at the time, wherever shall I lay my weary head tonight?'"

"I considered it. But I thought it was a wee repetitive so I went with The Perfect Gentleman Who Knows He Should Give a Woman Space."

"Ah, that old chestnut."

Nick considered her. The way he looked at her: Would she ever tire of it?

"Do you have plans tomorrow?"

She shook her head. "Mom and Stu aren't going to come into the city until dinner, so I'm on my own. Just walking around, alone. Exploring Venice. Alone." She couldn't help smiling after the last one.

Nick smiled back. "Well, since you'll be alone and all, how about I meet your alone self at the train station. Ten o'clock?"

Sewanee blinked. "The train station? Are we going somewhere?"

"Depends if they have trains at the train station."

They were both tired enough that this made them laugh.

"Where?" she asked.

He quirked an eyebrow. "Trust me?"

She did. God help her, she did. She didn't know why, exactly, but if he was even a fraction of the man she'd corresponded with, a fragment of the man she'd spent a glorious night in Las Vegas with, then the sum of those parts was enough. She nodded. He flashed her a grin, picked up his knapsack, and left her standing in the lobby.

CHAPTER FIFTEEN

"Getting to Know You"

A TABLE AND TWO TO-GO CUPS OF COFFEE BETWEEN THEM, SEWANEE heard the doors close and felt the cabin lurch gently beneath her and it occurred to her she was on a train, about to roll over the Italian countryside, with Nick, and how the hell had that happened? She'd always wanted to travel through Italy and now she was. She was beginning to glimpse how difficult she could make things. How she tended to see obstacles instead of answers. Why did she overcomplicate everything?

It was too early—both in the hour and her own introspection—to be asking herself this, so she gazed at the outskirts of industrial Venezia, and said, "Forty-eight hours ago, I was in L.A."

"And seventy-two hours ago, we were fighting in the garden of an assisted living home in Burbank."

Sewanee turned to him. "And three months ago, we were in Las Vegas."

"I still dream about that steak."

"The steak?"

"It *was* Wagyu." He grinned. "And that wine."

"The wine."

"The wine."

At the heat in his eyes, she lost her courage, looked back out the window. "Where are we going?"

"It's a surprise. Don't you like surprises?"

"Sure. Long as I know what they are."

"Where's the fun in that, eh?"

Sewanee assessed him, the very fact of him, sitting there across from her, on a train in Italy. She felt like she knew so much about him, but it seemed backward, as if she had watched a film from the end to the beginning. "Well, if it's going to be a while, entertain me. Tell me the story of Brock McNight."

Nick dropped his chin to his chest. "Jaysus. All right." He took a breath. "After the band broke up and Jason got out of treatment, we moved back to Prescott to get on our feet. We started seeing old friends and one of them mentioned this kid we all knew in high school, this defensive lineman, Brad. She says, you won't believe what Brad's doing now. And she pulls out her phone, brings up a . . ." He lowered his voice to the point where he was almost mouthing the words: "porn site. And Brad had a whole channel. His name was upandcoming69—I know—and he would . . ." Nick shifted in his seat and Sewanee peered at him, already feeling herself start to redden. "He wanks into the camera and—*buongiorno!*" Nick bleated at the man who'd materialized to check their tickets in the slots by their headrests. He only grunted in reply and moved on.

Sewanee stifled a laugh. Nick leaned in and lowered his voice once again. "And he'd dirty-talk. In this caveman voice. And look: I'm no expert and Brad having a hand shandy is definitely not my, er, kink? But even I could tell it was hot."

Sewanee wasn't sure her grin could be any bigger, that the laws of physics would allow it.

"So, me being me, I ran with it. I started messing with Jason, doing the voice around the house. Like, he'd be on the phone with his ma and I'd get right up next to him and say, 'you like seeing Daddy hard, do ya? Give that tight little ass to Daddy.'"

Sewanee covered her mouth, but too late to smother the laugh that blasted through the train.

Nick helicoptered a hand and Sewanee noticed a little pink tinge appear on his cheeks. "You get the picture. And then one day, I lost a bet to Jason, and the penalty was I had to talk in the Brad voice the whole day. And then whenever I lost a bet—we bet a lot because we're overgrown children—he'd make me use the voice. Go talk to that girl. Ask for directions. Order takeout. And it started . . . working. People responded to it. And then June was casting one of her books—this is after you stopped doing 'em— and I thought, well, I could do that. Not one of hers, obviously, that would just be—"

"Right."

"But I sent one of her friends a sample of the Brad voice . . ."

"And the rest is history."

"Yes. And now it needs to *really* be history."

"So, you do want to stop? What you said in the e-mails wasn't bullshit?"

Nick heaved a sigh. "Sewanee, I'll say it again. I'll say it as many times as you want, but nothing in the e-mails—or the texts— was bullshit. That was me. That was real. All of it. Every bit."

Sewanee believed him. Or certainly wanted to. "But you have such a good thing going. You could maybe pull back a little to focus on the band, but why do you want to stop completely?"

"Because it's been four hundred books and five draining years and because . . ." He chewed on his lip. "Because I've lost track of who I am when I'm not pretending to be stupid Brad."

Before they knew it, the train was pulling to a stop in Padua and Nick popped up and shuttled Sewanee out of the train and, as she said, "Padua? Why Padua?" Nick led her to a bus. With an eyebrow raise from Sewanee and an answering smirk from Nick, they climbed aboard.

After settling into two small seats, Nick's knees tucked up hard against the seatback in front of them, he turned to her and said, "So. L.A. Really?"

She pointed a finger at him. "There's the New York snobbery! I knew it was only a matter of time."

"It's just so . . ." He moved his head around, the namby-pamby, ineffectual gesture more accurately descriptive than any word could be.

"Hey, that's my hometown you're *not* talking about."

"Is it?" Nick looked surprised. "I figured you were there because of acting."

Sewanee shook her head. "Born and raised. I went to college in New York, though."

"Where?"

"Julliard."

Nick whistled. Then he looked at his lap. "You ever think you'd consider going back? To New York?"

Not too long ago she would have said absolutely not. The weather, alone. The expense. Her family and friends in L.A. But now? "Anything's possible, I guess. Given everything that's changed over the past few years, I don't *have* to be in L.A. Other than for my grandmother." She paused. Swallowed. Waited. She found she couldn't use her voice just then.

Her phone hadn't rung once since she'd arrived in Italy. Sewanee had wondered: that last call they'd had, where Blah had talked about what losing her grip on reality was like . . . had she rallied just long enough to say goodbye?

At her obvious vulnerability, Nick stayed silent. He simply reached over and took her hand in her lap.

"That's why I'm doing the series to begin with, you know," she forced out. "To pay for her care."

"And here I thought you'd just wanted to meet me." Sewanee chuckled gratefully and Nick asked, "I am curious, though, what would you do with the money if you didn't have your gran to care for?"

Sewanee didn't have a quick response. She couldn't honestly say she'd never thought about it. Of course she had. But she had never given it voice. "I suppose I'd pay off debt. School and medical. I'm going to have to start thinking about moving, so maybe a down payment for a place somewhere more affordable than Hollywood?" She made an idle gesture at her eye patch. "Maybe get another surgery."

"You need another surgery?"

"No."

"Then why would you be getting another?"

She shifted uncomfortably. "I'm not saying I would, I . . . I mean, it's never going to look normal. But they can do a lot now, so." She did her best to make that last bit sound offhanded.

"Does it make it harder to do your job? With how much you have to read?"

She shook her head. "Not anymore. In the beginning, it was exhausting, getting used to reading with one eye. Doing anything with one eye. Left to my own devices, I could sleep fourteen, sixteen hours easily."

"I can do that easily and I've got both of mine."

Sewanee bumped his shoulder appreciatively. Her head found its way there, and his arm came around her, resting itself effortlessly against her side. He gave her a light squeeze when he said, lowly, "I'm truly sorry that happened to you." There was a silence. He took a breath. "And I've been thinking about what I said to you the other night, about why I came up to you at the bar, and your friend, and that whole palaver, and it didn't come out the way I . . . I didn't get a chance to say everything I wanted to say."

Sewanee lifted her head and met Nick eye to eye. "If Adaku hadn't been sitting with me, if she never existed. If all you saw in that bar was this woman"—Sewanee pointed directly at her eye patch—"would you have come over—"

"Yes. And that's the exact hypothetical scenario I was going to give you. The answer is yes, I would have come over."

"Truth?"

"Yes, absolutely. But—"

"*But.*"

Nick forged ahead. "But! Ultimately, I don't think it matters what I say, does it? Will you ever truly believe, deep down, that anything other than pity brought me over to you? Nothing I say can make that scar disappear *for you*. I can tell you I don't see it and you will always see it. I can tell you you're everything that keeps me up at night and everything I daydream about and how that makes you feel might last a day or a week or an hour. Feelings are temporary. They stick around as long as you believe in them and then they're gone, waiting to be believed in again. If they were permanent, then we'd only have to say I love you once and be done with it for the rest of our lives."

Sewanee stared at him. "Did you practice that?"

Nick smiled. "It was a long flight." He squeezed her hand.

The bus began to slow and Nick leaned over her to look out the window and stood, pulling his hand away. She glanced outside and saw a two-lane country road lined with coastal pines. Though as far as she could tell they were nowhere near the water. Nick pulled her up. They disembarked.

The air was crisp, fresh, a slight note of citrus blossom, but there were no citrus trees. There was an open field. A warehouse at the far end of it. A house painted a Tuscan orange. A squat redbrick apartment building.

Nick began walking. She followed. She felt him watching her. "What?"

"I think I'm a bit in shock that I can just . . . look at you. That I can think about you and then just . . . look at you."

Sewanee smiled. "If you'd rather text, I'll understand."

Nick hooted a laugh. "Not when the reality is so much better than whatever I'd cooked up in my head."

"Yeah, yeah."

He shrugged. "It's the truth."

She stopped walking. She had to. "Nick. I heard what you said on the bus and I understand it, I do." He stopped walking, too, but that made it feel like too much of a *discussion*, so she started walking again. "But it's hard for me. You met *this* me, but there was another me once. And for the record I found it as difficult to believe men and what they saw when they looked at me then as it is to believe you and what you see when you look at me now."

"Is that supposed to help us?"

"I don't know," she sighed. "What I'm saying is, I want to move forward. I just don't think we can realistically forget how this whole thing started."

"But how it started is not how it ended."

"But it did end."

He laughed. "Then for Pete's sake, what are we doing here?"

She stopped again. He had a point. But it still didn't feel settled. So she threw out her arms. "Where is *here*, anyway? Where the hell are we?"

Nick only smiled and reached for her hand and she let him take it. And they walked like that down a sidewalk somewhere in Italy.

When the silence got to her, she looked over at him and found he was watching her again. "What?!"

He looked down. "Just thinking this time."

She smiled. "About?"

"Honestly?" He looked up. Then back at her. At her hairline. At her mouth. At her eye. Taking stock. "Right now? In this moment? About moving to L.A. and taking you down to City Hall and figuring everything else out later."

"Nick," she breathed.

He shook his head, squeezed his eyes closed. "Sorry. You know I don't have a filter." He took a breath. "Ignore me, I'm jet-lagged."

But what if I wanted that, too? she thought. It was appealing, the prospect of it. Of giving up on figuring anything else out right now. To have someone instead of herself to focus on. To just be happy for as long as possible. To ignore the future.

She realized she'd been silent for too long when Nick asked, nervously, "Now, what are you thinking?"

She looked wistfully up at a tree. "That we should finish the series. Here."

A beat. "What?"

She smiled at him. "We're together, the scripts are ready. Jason wanted to do Duet Narration for the sex scenes. Why not?"

Nick dropped her hand and skipped out in front of her, turning around to walk backward. "Recorded on location in Venice, Italy!"

Sewanee chuckled. "Ready-made promotion!"

"*Ka-ching!*" Energized, Nick whipped his phone out of his pocket. "Let me text Jason, see if he can find a studio for later today." He quickly typed while Sewanee gazed about. Eventually, Nick stopped walking and she figured he needed to concentrate on his phone, but when she looked at him, he was looking up at her, his hand wrapped around one pole in a large, open iron gate. A sign proclaimed:

LUXARDO—MARASCHINO.

Sewanee blinked at it. Then she blinked at Nick. "As in . . . the cherries? The liqueur?"

He smiled. "Fancy a Last Word?"

CHAPTER SIXTEEN

"The Consummation"

BY THE TIME THEY ARRIVED BACK IN VENICE, JASON HAD SECURED A studio and e-mailed the scripts there. They would lay down one episode that afternoon and the other the next morning and then the series would be done.

They found the studio on a quiet backstreet in the Jewish Ghetto, rang the buzzer, and climbed to the top floor, where they were greeted by a small man with a rock 'n' roll face and chin-length hair. He introduced himself as Cosmo and gestured them into the space.

It was comfy, built more for music than voiceover, with a large control room boasting a full soundboard and couches, and a live room with oriental rugs, amps, a drum kit, and half a dozen mics spread about. In broken English, Cosmo explained he'd set up two mics face to face, given Jason's specs, and stood panels behind them to cage the sound.

Sewanee peeled off her coat and did some vocal warm-ups. Trills, buzzes, scales, lip flaps. She noticed Nick watching her. "What?"

"Do you always do those?"

"Not always, but I had a little milk in my coffee this morn-ing and then we had the liqueur sampler and there was a lot of cheese in that pasta on the train . . ." They'd carbo-loaded as if preparing for a marathon instead of just trying to prevent stomach grumbles while recording. At the bafflement on his face, she said, "You don't, I take it?"

"No. But now I'm thinking I should."

"Yeah, maybe you'd work more," she deadpanned, and Nick chuckled. She pushed her hair back from her face, banded it into a high pony.

Nick rolled up his sleeves. "Okay, so, I think I'm up first. To remind ourselves: it's after the gondola ride—"

"Ah yes, the heavy petting—"

"And Alessandro opened up a little, told her about his uncle, the Casanova line, the responsibility—"

"And then Claire said she was ready. Finally. And they were heading back to his palazzo."

Nick nodded once, put his hands on his hips. "Right."

Sewanee mirrored him. "Right."

They stared at each other, the reality of what they were about to record inserting itself between them. Now that they would be reading with the other person present, watching, it was awkward, and clearly not only for her.

"So," Nick said, "Alessandro's point of view."

"Alessandro's point of view." She inclined her head at Cosmo, waiting at the open studio door. "In you go."

Nick looked at her for one more beat then walked into the room.

Cosmo stood Nick behind one of the microphones, began adjusting the height of the mic, the angle, the distance from the music stand and Nick's distance, in turn, from that.

Sewanee settled in behind the control panel on one end, leaving most of the area clear for Cosmo, who, he'd told them, would be engineering the session. There was a tablet waiting for her and the episode's text was already queued up. She scrolled through.

Cosmo came back in, closing the double doors to the studio behind him. Sewanee liked the air-locking sound of closing studio doors. There was something safe about it. As if she were being sealed off, protected from the punishments of the outside world. Cosmo smiled sweetly at her and she smiled serenely back thinking, you have no idea what you're about to hear, do you? He hurriedly sat himself in front of the board, nudged the mouse, brought his monitors to life, and went from a tiny Italian man to Captain Kirk navigating the *Starship Enterprise.* He caught her eye and pointed at a large red button on the desk. The God Mic. He pressed it and spoke. "Signore, you can hear?"

"I can," Nick replied, voice booming through the entire studio, shooting right through Sewanee's ribs like an electrified cow prod. Cosmo cut her an apologetic glance and made adjustments. In a moment, he nodded toward the set of headphones next to her and she put them on. "*Scusate*," he said, "once more."

"Test, test. This is only a test to test my voice. This is me, me testing the test of me . . ."

The nonsensical ramble was spoken as Brock, and Cosmo jerked his head up as if expecting to see someone else had snuck in front of the microphone. Sewanee stifled a laugh, going back to her tablet, scrolling the text, plotting, charting, quick-gaming her performance the way an architect might scan blueprints.

Eventually, Cosmo said, "*Bene*, is good."

Sewanee pressed the button to talk to Nick. "So let's get your flashback section done and then I'll come in for their dialogue."

She watched Nick nod through the glass, never taking his eyes from the text. "Yes, ma'am."

Cosmo hit his keyboard, and said, "Rolling," trilling the R delightfully.

Nick launched in.

Sewanee read along while she listened to him set the scene:

Claire and Alessandro walk back to the palazzo, tension buzzing away between them; he pours her a glass of wine, which she refuses at first, then gulps down; he finds himself nervous, which never happens, this is his job, where has his professionalism gone, why was this woman affecting him unlike any other? Then he began the flashback: what, exactly, had happened that had blown them apart five years ago.

She lifted her head from the tablet and watched Nick through the glass.

He stood straight, shoulders stiff, one hand on one side of the headphones, as if he were getting ready to sing instead of talk. Which made sense, she supposed. He played nicely into the mic, straight on, never moving his head lest the movement change the sound. His Brock voice was hypnotic. That hushed whisper, fog trawling over a rocky riverbed, whiskey tumbling over ice, velvet-draped steel . . . however it was his fans described his voice.

But that wasn't what held her attention. She was watching his eyes as they moved over the tablet in front of him.

Nothing.

Vacant.

It was the simple act of taking in information and sending it back out.

He could get away with it because That Voice, but she couldn't help thinking how much better it would be if there were more . . . Nick in it. How the superficial would become substantial.

Twenty minutes later, he stepped back from the mic. "You want to come in now?"

Sewanee held down the button. "Sure." Cosmo jumped up to open the soundproofed doors. She grabbed her tablet and walked into the room, stopping at the music stand across from Nick's. While Cosmo flitted around her, she stayed in the text. Then he left them, closing the double doors again.

She read a paragraph while Cosmo made his adjustments at the board and then said, into her headphones, "Is good."

"Great, thanks," Sewanee murmured.

"*Si*. Rolling." He trilled the R again and she smiled.

She glanced up, hoping to catch Nick's eye before he began, hoping for a moment of connection. But he started reading.

"Aren't you going to say something?"

Sewanee read her line. *"I think we've done enough talking."*

Nick continued, *"The tightness in her voice stopped me. I went down to my knees in front of her. I plucked her fingers up, which had been nervously toying with the bedspread, and held them. 'This is safe. This is us.' I clenched my jaw. 'This is my job,' I said, though I wasn't sure who I was reminding, her or myself. 'When you filled out the preference sheet, you had to think about what you wanted. Now, I want you to voice your wants.' She swallowed and I watched the ivory column of her throat bob. I had an irrational desire to bite it. I ran a finger lightly over her hand."*

Sewanee said, *"'I want you to touch me,' she finally said."*

Nick, in his own voice, said, "Hang on, I need to say the dialogue tags."

"Right, sorry," Sewanee said. "Gotta get used to this. Cosmo, can we punch in right before my line, 'I want you to touch me'?"

"*Si*, rolling."

They heard "I ran a finger lightly over her hand," in their headphones and then Sewanee said, *"I want you to touch me . . ."*

And then Nick said, *"She finally said. 'Where?' I asked,"* and they were back on track.

"Wherever you want."

"I tsked at her." Nick paused again. "Should I tsk?"

Sewanee considered this, glad he was engaging her. "Have you ever done it and made it sound good?"

"No! Never! It pops on mic."

"Yeah! Or sounds like static."

"Right? So weird. I'll keep it the way it is." Audio nerd moment over, Nick signaled Cosmo and asked him to come in after "I tsked at her."

"*Si*, rolling."

Nick picked up his cue: "*'Where would you like me to start?' I asked. 'Here?' I tapped her knee with the hand that wasn't already engaged with her fingers. She shook her head.*"

"*Maybe higher.*"

"*I removed my hand from her knee and placed it on her cheek. I slid my fingers under her chin and gently raised her head, so we looked each other in the eye. 'High enough?' I said with a whisper of a smile.*"

Sewanee murmured back with the faintest sensual giggle, "*Maybe lower,*"

"*She murmured with a sensual giggle. I freed her chin and ran the backs of my fingers down that throat, let the knuckles pass down over her collarbone. Lower. Her breath hitched. I flipped my hand over and gently squeezed her breath. So perfect, so—*"

"Ooh, kinky."

"Huh?"

"Squeezing her breath."

"What?"

"Who knew June French was into erotic asphyxiation?"

"What in the world are you—"

Sewanee finally let out her laugh. "Breath! You said breath!"

"I said breast, Sewanee, breast."

"You said breath, Nick, breath."

"I did not! I said—"

Cosmo punched in. "*Scusa*, but you say breath. No breast. In Italy, we know the difference." His laugh was cut short when he released the button.

Nick threw up his hands. "Well, maybe we should change it! I never liked the word breast anyway. I don't even like saying breast. It makes me think of chickens."

Sewanee guffawed and Nick chuckled. He tried to take a sip of water, but they weren't done laughing yet and he almost spat it out, which made Sewanee laugh harder and she felt like they were back in the Venetian casino pushing each other into the chairs in front of the slot machines.

Cosmo came over the God Mic. "I think maybe I record this, eehh?"

"No, no, sorry, Cosmo," she said. "We'll get it together." She caught Nick's damp eyes and they smiled at each other.

He cleared his throat. Sniffed. Cleared again. "Okay, Cosmo. I'm ready."

"Rrrrrolling."

"*I flipped my hand over and gently squeezed her breast.*" Sewanee saw his jaw tick, the only tell that he'd almost lost it. But he carried valiantly on. "*So perfect. Perfection matched only by the soft moan that escaped her. 'There?' I asked.*"

"*I want,*"

"*She panted,*"

"*I want . . . you to undress me. Just my blouse. And bra. I want my skirt on when you take me the first time.*"

"*My erection was immediate.*"

Sewanee's laugh was so loud and so directly on-mic that Nick jumped back as if it were a physical thing he could dodge, a bee or a shoe or a fist. He was still whipping the headphones off his head when she bleated, "Sorry!" and covered her mouth.

Nick glared playfully at her. "What are you, twelve? It's just a word! Erection!"

She dropped to the floor in hysterics.

"Oh, come on," Nick groaned.

"Signore," Cosmo interjected.

"I'm sorry, Cosmo, I'm gonna need a minute. I'm dealing with a toddler here. She—"

"*Si*, but the last thing you say, erection? Eh *scusate*, but I think I read something different."

Before Nick could respond, Sewanee weakly reached a hand straight up and tapped the tablet on her music stand.

Nick looked down at his. "Ah. 'Reaction.'"

Sewanee fell back into a pile of laughter.

With all the mature dignity of a tuxedoed man-of-distinction fixing his bow tie before a night at the opera, Nick settled the headphones back on his ears. He stared down at the laugh-puddle in mocking reprimand, the imperious duke of a thousand Romance novels. "Would you care to take a break, Ms. Chester?"

"No," Sewanee wheezed.

"You sure?"

"Yes."

"You don't sound sure."

"Just give me a . . ." She stood up unsteadily, a newborn foal in an uneven pile of hay. She reached over to the table between them and cracked a fresh water bottle. Drank. Breathed. Blew her nose. Had more to drink. Pulled some lip balm out of her pocket, applied it. Cleared her throat. Inhaled. Exhaled.

She didn't dare look at Nick during her recovery. Only when she was sure she was ready did she glance over at him. He was staring at her, a mien of pleasure and puzzlement on his face. She simply nodded and said, calmly, "I'm good."

"Good." Grinning, Nick centered himself back at the mic. He pointed to Cosmo, and they heard "rrrrrolling," and then the pre-roll, and then Nick said, *"My reaction was immediate."* And Sewanee pressed her lips together so tightly, they retreated into her mouth. *"I could envision it all and I wanted it. I ached for it. And she'd said, 'when you take me the first time.' Implying . . . well. My fingers went to the buttons on her blouse as I said, 'There's nothing more attractive than a woman who knows what she wants.'"*

This was the sort of section where Brock McNight shone, all by his lonesome, setting the scene. The undressing, the worship, the interiority of a hero's desire. Sewanee kept her interjected dialogue as unobtrusive as possible ("yes," "there," "just like that") within his ruminations about the perfection of her body, her response, how wild she was driving him.

He performed well. As Alessandro performed well, she supposed. It worked for him here, in these sections. But when the character required connection, struggle, relationship, that's when she saw his limitations. When she got past that smoke screen of a voice, there was nothing behind it. Like the buildings on a movie set: a beautiful facade, but in reality, nothing but 2x4s propping it up. Was he holding something back on purpose?

When his section was over, right at the moment Alessandro entered Claire, and Sewanee was about to take over the narration, Nick drank some water and flicked a finger at the tablet.

"Why'd she change point of view here? It was just getting good."

Sewanee saw an opportunity and decided to take it, hoping it might connect him more to the text. "Because June knew how to take formula and elevate it."

"In what way?"

"She knew the point of view should belong to the person—the character—who has the most to lose. The foreplay is from his perspective because he wants this so badly and she may not give it to him and, worse, she may not come apart in his hands, may prove him a fraud. But once he enters her, once he is inside her, he's won. The rest is from her perspective because this is her moment of transformation. From this point on, she will never be the same."

Nick stared at her. "Oh."

Sewanee went back to her tablet. Took a breath. And began. *"I was so full. I'd been so empty, for so long, even before my husband died, and now?"*

She read, as she often did, without a mistake, entering the near fugue state that happened when she was fully invested. This scene—these scenes—were entire books in miniature: rising action, climax, denouement. As such, she let her voice rise, crescendo, fall.

Slowly, she brought it home, the aftermath:

"He braced himself on his elbows over me, so as not to crush me. He kissed the side of my neck, gave me one last, long stroke, and pulled out. He stood and walked, like David *come to life, into the bathroom. Shut the door. I floated nicely for a few minutes, waiting for him to come back. When he did, when I heard the bathroom door open, I expected him to crawl back into bed with me. He didn't. His footsteps stopped and I opened my eyes. He was fully dressed. Collecting our wineglasses. Moving to the bar. Turning on the faucet. I came up on an elbow."*

Nick murmured, *"It's later than I thought. I have a meeting."*

"I looked at the ornate rococo clock above the mantel. 'It's ten,' I said."

"Time got away from me."

"You have a meeting at ten o'clock at night?"

"It's the only time she had."

"She? I said it aloud: 'She?' He dried the glasses now."

"Prospective client."

"You have a client right here."

"Clients pay."

"My anger flared. 'Fine. How much to not be an asshole?' He set the wineglasses down and walked over to the bed. Stood above it. Stood above me."

"*Trust me, this is what you need right now: distance. I'll be back by midnight. You're welcome to stay until then.*"

"*With that, he turned heel, picked up his jacket, walked to the door. And left. He left. Left. I couldn't stay here a moment longer. Shaking, I clambered out of the bed, got dressed, tried to gather my wits so I didn't leave anything—dear God, please don't let me leave anything—hastily ran my fingers through my hair, fumbled with the straps of my shoes, and staggered to the door. I turned back once more, looking at the bed. The site of my humiliation. I knew what I had to do. I opened my purse and pulled out my wallet. Seven hundred fifty euro. A fraction of his value, an insulting amount. And yet: all I had to my name. I walked back to the bed and left it there, right in the middle, in the divot my shoulders had created, still warm. He would never be able to say he did me a favor. This was a transaction. Services paid, services rendered. Quality product, timely delivery. Five stars. Choking back sobs, I left the palazzo, leaving the door unlocked behind me.*"

Sewanee stared at the tablet in front of her, the absence of more text, of more story. The white space. She was still reverberating, still coming back into herself. She was so overtaken by where she'd gone, she needed time to come back to where she was. It wasn't like sex, but it wasn't unlike it, either.

Nick huffed a laugh. "He's such a dick. Oh, sorry, cut it, Cosmo."

"*Si*, we cut." She heard the sound of Cosmo slapping the table. "*Belissima*. This last thing, you make me cry. We continue, yes?"

"No, the next episode is the last episode so we're gonna do it tomorrow."

"But how do I sleep, eh?"

Nick chuckled and took off his headphones. "If we hooked Cosmo, we can hook anybody. I'm so glad you suggested this. How grand was that, eh?"

Sewanee had no desire to burst Nick's bubble, so she replied, in an exaggerated leprechaun voice, "Grand it twas!"

He moved for the door. "Let's go get a coffee. Get a breast of fresh air."

THEY STOOD AT an espresso bar, waiting for their shots, while Nick prattled on about how good the read had been. "I'll say it again, you suggesting we record together, here? Brilliant."

Sewanee smiled tightly. "Thanks." She took her little cup from the woman behind the counter and blew on it. Something had occurred to her on the walk over, a possible explanation for his disconnection from the material. "So, considering you never wanted to do one of your aunt's books, was it awkward for you to read the sex scene?"

"Surprisingly, no." Nick threw back his shot, tossed the paper cup away. "Maybe I'm just inured to Romance at this point. Like, if you kill people for a living does it matter who gives the orders?"

Sewanee chuckled, added a small spoonful of raw sugar to her cup, and stirred slowly. She wanted to take this further, but also wanted to tread carefully. Then again, they didn't *need* to talk about it. It was just a job. A job he didn't want to do anymore, anyway. Who was she to tell him how to do something he'd had enormous success doing?

She noticed they were being crowded out of the small shop, so she downed her espresso and they wandered out to the piazza, taking a seat on some granite steps at the feet of a bronze gryphon.

At her silence, he bumped her knee with his. "Euro for your thoughts?"

"Oh, it's nothing."

He studied her. "You're not feeling insecure about your work, are you? Because if I haven't said it enough, I'm sorry. You're remarkable, you really are."

She could barely contain her surprise. "Oh! No, God, no. That's so . . . thoughtful of you. No, I'm just trying to figure something out."

He reached over, tucked a wind-blown ribbon of hair behind her ear. "What?"

"I was just wondering . . ." Abort, abort, abort. "You know what, never mind."

"Sewanee, come on. We can be honest with each other. Whatever it is, we'll deal with it. Talk to me."

She looked into the welcome mat of his gaze, dusted off just for her. "Okay. I wasn't . . . I couldn't tell if you were invested in what we did today."

"Me?" Nick's grin hung in place. "Invested how?"

Sewanee shrugged. "In your performance."

The grin flickered like neon about to go out. "I mean. That's how I do it."

"Right, and it's great," she assured him, touching his thigh. "All I'm saying is . . . when you're Brock? You seem detached."

Nick pulled his knee out from under her hand. He busied himself with removing his jacket. "Detached?"

"Yeah. I mean, did you feel connected to me at all? As we read together?" He seemed confused by the question, so she tried another way in. "Why did you want to do Duet?"

He pulled a pack of cigarettes out of the jacket now slung onto the steps. "Jason suggested we do the last two episodes as Duet Narration because listeners like Duet. They think it's hotter."

"But it's only hotter when the two people actually work off of each other. What was the point of reading it together if it sounds as if we didn't?"

Nick scoffed. "What are you, a director now? I thought it

would be cool to read it together, that's all. Why are you making this such a big deal?"

"Why are you being a smart-ass?"

"Why are we fighting—are we fighting?" The grin was back, but it was forced and he looked bewildered. He lit his cigarette.

"We're not fighting, okay?" She touched his thigh again. "You don't need to get defensive—"

"I'm not getting defensive," he said, once again dodging her hand, this time standing. "I just don't know what you think I should have done differently." He sounded exasperated as he blew out his first puff.

"Invest more of yourself."

Now he spoke slowly, as if explaining something to a child for the umpteenth time. "I don't want to invest more. I want out."

Her hackles went up at his tone. "And I think if you invested more of yourself you might not want out. I think—"

"More of what self?"

"Nick!"

He threw back his head, answering his name. "What?!"

"No." Sewanee huffed out a frustrated laugh. "Nick! Yourself. Your real self." She paused. "You've put a firewall between Nick and Brock. Why? Together, they're something special."

He shook his head. "It's either/or. You can't have both together. They are fundamentally incompatible."

She shook her head. "You're wrong."

He threw out the hand holding the cigarette. "Are you disagreeing just to disagree? I'm pretty sure I know more about me than you do."

"When you read *Goodnight Moon*. It was Brock's voice, but Nick's heart."

This stopped him. He stared at her. Then he looked down, took a long drag. "Swan," he exhaled. "This ain't *Goodnight Moon*."

"No, it isn't. But you are."

He kept looking down. Had she gotten through to him?

But then he muttered, "Right. You wish I were something I'm not. And I think not just in my read, but in life."

Sewanee snapped her head back. "Are you—what universe are you currently transmitting from?"

"Yours, lovie."

"Don't put words in my mouth, that's not what I—"

"Trust me, that is exactly what this is." He nodded rapidly, having convinced himself, if not her. "*You* want both. You want me to be, to be . . . uh . . . Brock McNick! That's what you want!" He victoriously kicked away someone else's cigarette butt.

"That's who you already *are*, you, you . . . you fart-head!"

Nick had to laugh. "Fart-head?"

Sewanee had to join him. "It's the best I could come up with, *Brock McNick!*"

"Well, that's the best *I* could come up with!"

They both took a measured breath. Nick flicked ash from his cigarette and Sewanee attempted a gentler tone. "All I'm trying to say is, when you're working, you're Brock. And when you're not, you're Nick. And I don't understand why one has to get sacrificed for the other. It's all you, Nick."

He took another drag. He was the picture of composure. Almost performatively unruffled. "Yeahhhh," he exhaled. "I get it now."

"Good."

"This is about you, not me."

Her eyebrows snapped together. "What? What are you—this has nothing to do with me."

"It has everything to do with you. You're projecting."

"Projecting?!"

He attempted a casual shrug. "You said it yourself. You're trying to reconcile who you once were and who you are now."

Her mouth fell open. "You are so off-base here. This conversation started because I was talking about *the work*!"

"And I'm calling bullshit. I don't think it is about the work. I think we're talking about something much bigger than the work and—news flash—I don't give an ever-loving feck about the work anyway." He came closer, pointed the cigarette at her. "That's you! That's you the actor! That's not me."

She sliced her hand through the smoke and her voice sharpened. "Can you not wave that in my face? I *do* give an ever-loving feck about the work so I don't like secondhand smoke, okay?"

He stepped instantly back. "Sorry." He muttered a curse, threw the cigarette down, and stamped it out. He said, mostly to himself, "I'm quitting again soon."

Sewanee gestured at the butt. "You drop something?"

"Huh?"

She rolled her eye and stood and picked it up. "I will never understand why people don't think this is littering."

He held out a hand. "Give it here."

"No." But now she was walking around trying to figure out what to do with it.

He made a grabby motion. "Seriously."

"I'll take care of it." Sewanee searched for a trash can.

Nick took out his hard pack of cigarettes, flipped it open. Shook it. "*I'll* take care of it."

"I just need to find a—"

"There's not a one in sight. Just give it here."

She looked around. He was right.

She stomped over and dropped it in, as if depositing a bag of dog crap on his doorstep.

They retreated from each other, to opposite sides of the stairs. He leaned against one stone banister, she did the same on the opposing one.

A moment of reprieve.

Sewanee watched Nick from the corner of her eye, waiting to see if he had more to say. Because she did. She had something else she desperately wanted to say, but the last time she decided to say what was on her mind—all of five minutes ago—it had ended like this. She didn't want to hurt him further. She didn't want to hurt *them*. But she'd come to realize something from this tiff that felt more relevant than how it began. More relevant than them, even.

She said, in the most caring, nonconfrontational voice she could muster, "Have you thought about why June insisted you do this project?"

He sighed, battle-weary. "What are you on about now?"

"I don't think she was just giving you a way to make some money. Is it possible she was giving you a road map?"

Now he looked at her.

"You said this series was a revisionist take on her own story. And maybe that's true, I didn't know her that well. But she wrote it *for you*. Did you ever ask yourself why? Why she might write about a *sex god* who sacrifices himself for his profession and ultimately finds a way to integrate the performer with the person?"

He took out the cigarette pack again. Opened it. Glanced at his watch. Closed it and put it back. "Right." He moved off the stone banister, and Sewanee's impulse was to move, too, to reach for him. She straightened expectantly, but he didn't go to her. He went to his jacket on the steps between them and said, while putting it on, "I might say the same to you. She did insist that you play the heroine, after all. The woman who needs to get over her past and get on with her life."

He turned and started down the steps.

"Don't just walk away, Nick." She was mortified to hear the need in her voice.

Nick rolled his eyes and came back toward her. "I'm not walking away, fart-head." Then, gently, "*We're* walking away." He looked at her and she saw that though he'd been worn thin, there was a tenderness there. Some residual hurt and lingering frustration, but mostly tenderness. He was a bruise still sensitive to touch, but healing. Which relieved her.

And in her relief, she reheard what he had just said about her. About June.

This fight had begun because she'd pointed out a separation in him, and he retaliated by pointing out a similar divide in her. But the defensive heat went out of the argument when they had—as Henry might have said—brought in textual evidence to support their claims. By highlighting what June had done, they were now looking at themselves instead of each other.

She was still mulling this over when Nick said, "We have dinner with your mum and Stu, remember?"

She'd forgotten. She went toward him on the stairs, pulled out her phone, and looked at the time. "We still have forty-five minutes."

He shook his head. "It's best we get going." So they walked side by side across the piazza as he murmured, "We should clean up. And change."

CHAPTER SEVENTEEN

"The Proposal"

THEY DOCKED AT THE ISLAND FIFTEEN MINUTES AFTER LEAVING ST. Mark's, disembarked, and walked toward an outbuilding to the right of the sprawling hotel. Stu led their small group like a puppy that may have been trained to heel, but was incapable of obeying when excited. "I promised Marilyn I wouldn't spoil this by telling you anything about it. But, come on, can you believe this is a Marriott? Okay, I'm shutting up now, here comes the hostess."

As if conjured by Stu, an elegant woman appeared in the warm glow of the pathway's lights. She called them forward and Sewanee let Marilyn and Stu take the lead, hanging back with Nick.

They had wordlessly gone to their separate hotels to get ready and by the time they'd each arrived at the pier, Stu and Marilyn were waiting. They'd all climbed aboard the boat and Stu had sequestered Nick at the bow to talk about dolphins, so she hadn't been able to check in with him.

"Are you okay?" she whispered.

He nodded, but said, "I wish we'd had a few moments at the dock before—"

"Me too. But can we put everything aside for tonight and—"

"Of course." He gave her a small grin. "We can fight later." Sewanee matched his grin and felt her shoulders loosen.

Stu teasingly yelled, "You two coming or do we have to get you a room?"

"I only stay at Hiltons," Nick yelled back and they picked up their pace, joining a laughing Stu at the open door of a terra-cotta brick structure that might have once been a barn. It had floor-to-ceiling windows banded with black iron every six feet or so. Once inside, the soft illumination of candlelight and chandeliers off to the right beckoned them into the dining room.

But the hostess instead ushered them to the left, bringing them into a lushly understated bar. "Ooh, a cocktail, yes please," Sewanee murmured.

"Oh, Swanners," Stu enthused, "you're about to—"

"Stuuuu," Marilyn warned.

He zipped his lips, but turned to Nick and side-mouthed, "Just you wait." The hostess offered them a tray with four reddish-brown golf ball–sized orbs on it, each sitting in its own delicate cup. She instructed them to put the entire ball into their mouths and be prepared for a surprise. They clinked the cups together and did as told. Sewanee felt the hard shea butter exterior instantly collapse and a gush of sweet, tart, perfectly balanced liqueur burst to life, coating her tongue. She was stupefied. The splash of flavor had cleared her mind and awakened all her senses at once, like jumping into a cold lake.

"What'd I tell you, huh? Well, I didn't tell you, but when have you ever had *that* happen in your mouth?" Stu held up a hand. "Don't answer that." Nick and Sewanee laughed as Marilyn slapped his arm.

The hostess led them through the bar, out a door, and into the garden behind the restaurant. As they strolled the meandering path, she pointed to specific produce they would be consuming that night. Every so often, there was a tree stump and on it was a little taste of something. A mushroom puff pastry. A caramelized turnip in a single leaf of arugula. An aperitif glass containing an anise liqueur with a cherry at the bottom.

By the time the hostess took them into the restaurant and relieved them of their coats, Sewanee's senses were strung tighter than a bowstring. There was the faint smell of woodsmoke and garlic, but also an undernote of something floral. Everything was intentional.

They were handed off to someone else and swept to a table by the windows. The tabletop was glass. The ceiling, thirty feet above, was mirrored. The windows offered a view of the garden they'd just toured. Beyond the sparse landscaping lights, the Venetian night was a black void.

Stu directed Sewanee and Nick to sit on the side that allowed them a view of the entire restaurant, the entire show. Marilyn and Stu sat across from them and Stu could not stop smiling, though it did vary; from gentle to impish to full-on clown.

Three more people appeared, one bringing a glass bottle of water, a waiter who confirmed they were doing the tasting menu, and a sommelier who confirmed they were doing pairings with the tasting menu. Stu didn't let anyone answer before saying, "Absolute-mente!"

"*Fantastico.*" The sommelier smiled politely. He pulled a bottle from behind his back and said it was off the menu, but he had it open and wanted them to try it. He poured a splash into each of their glasses and departed. They raised them, clinked, and took a sip.

"What do you think?" Stu solicited, before they'd set down their glasses.

"Yummy," Marilyn enthused.

"Wow," Sewanee and Nick said and then, under his breath,

Nick murmured, "It's tight, it needs to open," and Sewanee's cheeks had never heated faster and Stu said, "Sorry, what?" and Nick answered, "Just right, doesn't need to open."

"Oh! Do you enjoy wine, Nick?"

"I've been known to diddle. Sorry, dabble. Diddle's the Irish."

Sewanee bit her lip.

Stu snapped his fingers. "I thought that accent was Irish!" Which prompted Sewanee to playfully explain how it was much more pronounced when he hit on women in bars and no true Dubliner had that accent anyway. Which prompted Nick to oh-so-innocently ask Sewanee which part of Texas she was from again, and—short of kicking each other under the table—they moved on.

Nick quickly lifted his glass. "Can't thank you enough for letting me join in tonight."

"I'm glad you're here, Nick! And so happy you're here, Swanners! What a night. Special night."

Stu's spirited embrace had Sewanee relaxing further and she could feel the same thing happening to Nick. An uncomplicated, pleasure-seeking father figure seemed a foreign, but welcome, concept to them both. Their fight faded into the recesses of their better selves and Sewanee had the urge to take his hand under the table. But she didn't.

A flurry of servers presented the first artwork of a course and the sommelier poured a white. Nick was about to dig in, but Stu clucked his tongue. "Whoa there, cowboy, everything comes with an explanation." The head waiter launched into a detailed description of what sat before them. This was immediately followed by the sommelier telling them why he chose this specific wine to "not only complement the dish, but to create a relationship with it." Sewanee thought, if this were Los Angeles, it would be pretentious, artificial, chi-chi. But here, in Venice, on an island, it was earned.

They took a sumptuous bite and chased it with a healthy sip of wine. All four sat in a moment of silence. The kind of reverence reserved for prayer, as though they had never eaten before this moment.

"That is . . . this is . . ." Nick murmured, the first to attempt articulation. "What the hell *is* this?"

Stu banged the table. "And it's a goddamn Marriott!"

Each subsequent course somehow surpassed the last. Number seven arrived and was served with a beautiful orange wine which, until tonight, Sewanee hadn't known was a color of wine that existed. The conversation partnered with the food and drink as if it had asked the meal for a dance.

Currently, they were discussing the June French project, and Nick's relationship to his aunt, and what it was like being raised by a writer, which had Marilyn asking, "Have you ever wanted to write?"

"No. Well, I guess if you count songwriting then sure."

"Hold everything." Stu quickly swiped his napkin across his mouth. "You're a songwriter?"

"Sort of."

"And does that mean you're a musician?" Stu smiled wide.

"I was in a band, in another lifetime."

Stu beat his chest. "I used to have a band." Marilyn chortled. "What? So it was in high school and a year or two in college, it's still a band!"

Nick grinned. "What do you play?"

Stu twinkled all ten fingers. "Keys. You?"

"A little guitar. Sing a bit."

"And you wrote your own songs? That's huge. We never got that far."

Nick nodded. "A few of the songs. My best friend was the lead singer and did a lot of the writing. He's the real talent, I . . . I do what I can."

"Did you have any success?" Stu asked, popping the last piece of perfection on his plate into his mouth.

"We had a record deal. A hit song. We were touring."

"Oh, what I would've given. Living the dream! What happened?"

"Well. My best friend drove that dream faster than he could handle it. Crashed and burned." Nick looked at his plate and Sewanee could feel him warming to the topic, could sense him wanting to tell this story. "'Course we had our 'people' saying, keep going, this is what makes it great. But I watched him almost die one night and that was the end for me. Got him to the hospital in time—pure luck—and as soon as they released him, took him straight to rehab. Burned a lot of bridges, broke a lot of contracts."

"Did he make it out?"

"He did."

"You still friends? You still play together?" Stu demanded, fully invested.

"Thanks for asking, yeah. He followed me into audiobooks, actually. Became my proofer then June scooped him up as her producer. He has one of those magic ears, you know? Perfect pitch and such. Gearhead, too, on the tech side. A total sound wizard."

"That's one hell of an impressive friend you got there. You saved more than a life, chief. You ever pick it up again?"

"Not for about five years. We'd noodle around when we were in the same city and send each other licks, random stuff, but we weren't in it. Then, end of last year, after June . . . passed, he started talking about wanting to try again. I was thinking it might be worth a go. So we found a drummer. New keyboard-ist." Nick tipped his head across the table. "Wish I'd have known, Stu."

"You better watch yourself, Nickster, or you might have some old geezer show up sometime."

"Anytime." They shared a nod of musicians' camaraderie, even if only one of them was a professional musician.

The next course arrived. Stu held up his hands. "Question: Anyone happen to notice the *bread*?"

Marilyn tried to, yet again, pull up his reins. "Stuuuu."

"What? We're on number eight and nobody's said anything. I've been patient." Stu turned back to the kids. "So, the breads. Anything?"

Sewanee entered in. "Well, I did notice them changing the bread a few times over the course of the dinner."

"A few times? Every time! Every course comes with its own bread. You get what I'm saying? It's like with the wine. They pair it! And again I have to say—"

And all together, they said, "It's a Marriott!"

When he'd stopped laughing, Stu continued, "Okay, back to the band. You got a name?"

Nick took a bite. "We have a temporary name. It's a joke mostly, an inside thing, a reference to spending the last five years doing Romance novels."

Sewanee raised an eyebrow. "What is it?"

Nick paused. "The Bodice Rippers."

Sewanee laughed into her napkin.

"Ooh!" Marilyn exclaimed. "How about this? How about The Notorious Rakes?"

"Or just The Rakes," Sewanee put in.

Nick looked at her. "The Rakes. Aye, that could work."

"What kind of music do you play?" Marilyn asked.

"Americana, roots. But a bit indie. Singer-songwritery. Kind of." He looked at Sewanee. "Jaysus, I'm terrible at this."

Stu asked, "You got anything we can listen to?"

"Oh, no. We're just getting going again, it's not ready—"

"You gotta start putting stuff out there."

"Ha, yeah, no. I'm not even sure I'm good enough to make this kind of music yet. But if something does come of it, I'll definitely pass it along."

"What do you mean, not good enough?" Stu went back to his plate.

"Just . . . it's new for us. For me. It's a sound that demands much more of myself than I'm used to and it's, uh . . . got a high level of risk, you know?"

"So?" Stu asked, focused entirely on getting the right combination of flavors on his fork.

"So . . . I don't really do risk."

Sewanee could feel Nick choosing not to look at her.

"Why?"

"Because I'm not too keen on losing everything again."

"How are you gonna manage that, chief?"

Nick chuckled. He took a self-deprecating breath. "Can't fail if I don't try."

Now Stu was looking back up, smiling. "That's a neat trick."

"Ta, I think so." He picked up his wine, grinning. "You're dying to sort me out, aren't you?"

"Who, me? No way. I got enough to deal with right here." Stu brought a knuckle to his head, tapped it. "But you did say something that struck a chord with me—musician to musician!" He burst out laughing. "I didn't even see that one coming!"

Nick joined in. "I think you see everything, Stu. What's the chord?"

This had taken on the air of a friendly ping-pong match, as

if each man had picked up a paddle after a few drinks and said, let's see what you got. Sewanee and Marilyn watched avidly, spectators in the stands, enjoying every volley.

"You're ass backwards."

Nick threw his head back on a laugh. "Am I now?"

Stu chuckled. "Sorry to be the bearer of bad news, buddy boy."

Nick stuck out his hand, welcoming Stu's response. "Hit me."

Stu sucked a tooth, took a moment. "You're absolutely right. You'd regret trying and failing. But I'll do you one better. If you don't try, give it all you've got, you'll regret the hell out of never knowing if you would have succeeded."

Nick smiled. "Helluva chord, mate. Look, you're right, I give you that. But it's still scary."

"So what? So it's scary, why's that such a big deal?" Nick was silent. "I'm not trying to put you on the spot, Nickster, I—"

"No, man, I know. I just can't think of a good—"

"Because regret haunts you for the rest of your life," Sewanee chimed in from the cheap seats. She hadn't intended to say anything, but as soon as she felt the answer it was out of her mouth. She caught Marilyn's eye. Her mother smiled sadly at her. "It's like a ghost that refuses to leave your house."

Stu bugged his eyes. "Why's it gotta leave? What, you think you can get through life avoiding regret? Avoiding failure?" He laughed. "Spoiler alert: life is regret, life is failure. But like that ghost, you learn to live with it. Because failure makes success matter."

Stu threw his hands up, out, encompassing the whole restaurant. "This kid, this twenty-eight-year-old chef with a Michelin star. You think someone just stuck it on him, like they used to do in grade school?" He gestured at his now-empty plate. "You think he made this, whatever-it-is, foam-cloud-thing, perfectly the first time? The tenth time? This is a plate of failure. Now, I'm not saying we'll all get a Michelin star if we just persevere, rah-rah-rah. More often than not, things don't work out. Speaking for myself, I flat-out failed way more than I succeeded."

"But you were successful."

"At times."

"Overall," Nick argued.

Stu shook his head. "But life's not a straight line, senator. You go up, you get smacked down, you get up, you get knocked down. I put in forty-seven years with Nike, went from shoemaker to senior VP of yaddayaddayadda. And truthfully I was almost fired as many times as I was promoted." Stu took a moment to think and drink before leaning into Nick. "I'm gonna be the old guy here and give you some blunt advice you didn't ask for: Take the risk. Fail." Stu turned to Sewanee. "And let regret come along for the ride." He held up a finger. "A passenger, not the driver." He sat back. "I've seen too many people get into midlife crisis territory wondering where the time went and why they didn't do anything with it. You two are still young enough to avoid all this crap. The world is your oyster!"

"Oh, Nick hates oysters," Sewanee said, side-eyeing him, smirking.

Nick bit back a laugh and said to Stu, "You have regrets, then?"

"You kidding? My backseat's full. And the trunk! Look, I loved my job, but I loved it so much my real life passed me by. Never had a woman sitting next to me for the long haul." He flung a hand. "Never had a Sewanee sitting across the table. Never had this magnificent creature, this beautiful timepiece that I got to nurture and watch grow and who now calls me just to see how I'm doing. I mean"—he reached over and tweaked her chin—"how could a stupid job making shoes compare to one of these?" He and Sewanee smiled at each other and he mused, "It can't. I'll never see myself in anything other than a mirror. And now all I see is this." He pointed to his balding head and Nick chuckled.

He took Stu in and then he looked down at the table, contemplating. "Wouldn't it be grand if we could have multiple lives to live? Do it a few different ways and then pick the best one?"

"Oh, Nicky." Stu gave him a fatherly smile. "All I know is—" He broke off and looked past Nick's shoulder, into the back of the restaurant. He sat up a bit straighter. "Ah," he mumbled. "Here we go."

The waiter placed a gorgeous mirror-top chocolate cake in the center of their table. It had white piped writing on it. Sewanee craned her neck, looking at it upside down. "What does that say?" She glanced at the waiter, who was worrying his fingers and, for the first time that night, wasn't forthcoming with an explanation.

"Your mother's gotten quite good with her Italian," Stu said, and Sewanee's eye went to Marilyn, whose hand had gone to her mouth.

"Stu," she exhaled.

"What does it say?" Silence. "Mom?"

"*Sposami.*" Marilyn barely got the word out.

Sewanee was about to say "what" once more, but then Stu slipped off his chair, got down on one knee, and pivoted toward Marilyn, bringing a small velvet box out of his jacket pocket.

"Holy shit!" Sewanee shouted and the entire restaurant hushed. She slapped a hand over her mouth, the mirror image of her mother. One of Marilyn's hands reached for her daughter's. Sewanee clutched her mother's trembling hand and watched her life change.

"Marilyn," Stu said, then his voice softened: "Love." And Sewanee heard the sob that came from her mouth before she felt it. "You are the surprise of my life. I never imagined this old sneaker-maker would—Jesus." He chuckled and glanced at Sewanee and Nick. "That sounds like a slur." They all laughed through their blossoming tears and Stu turned back to Marilyn. "That I could end up having what I'd given up on. Someone who makes me happier each day than I was the day before. And I want that someone to be my wife." He opened the box.

Marilyn stared at him. They waited. She uncovered her mouth, put her hands on her hips. "Well, other than a slice of that cake, I can't say I've ever wanted anything more." They both smiled tearfully. "Yes. I would love to be your wife."

She stood, gave Stu a helping hand up, and he gently worked the ring onto her finger. Then they kissed, and held each other, and kissed and held each other as Nick hooted and Sewanee batted away the joyful tears streaming down her cheek. The entire restaurant applauded and Stu's hand found its way onto Marilyn's ass and she gave it a playful slap and everyone laughed.

A silver tray appeared next to the table, hosting four glasses of champagne. They took them up. Stu paused, steadying his voice. "It took me a lifetime to find my place in this world, but it was worth it, because it's with you."

They all drank and the whole restaurant cheered again, offering congratulations in many languages.

Caught up in the collective vibration of the room, Sewanee looked around and saw the waitstaff clustered in the door to the kitchen, watching, their hands up at their chests, their smiles wide as the Grand Canal.

ON THE TRIP back across the lagoon, Sewanee and her mom chose the warmth of the small cabin and Nick and Stu braved the late-evening chill, planting themselves once again next to the captain at the bow. As Marilyn told her about their next port of call, Bari, Sewanee watched Nick and Stu converse. When they docked, Sewanee saw the two men hug, a sight that felt like an extra bite of dessert.

They stood on the St. Mark's dock, waving, as the boat took Stu and Marilyn back to the cruise ship.

Nick turned to Sewanee as she turned to him, an expectant look in her eye. She didn't know what to say first. She wanted to apologize for everything she'd said earlier. She wanted to relive every taste of the night. She wanted to cry over how happy her mother was. She wanted to thank him for being a perfect date tonight. She wanted to kiss him, Lord, did she want to kiss him. But before she could broach any of it, Nick deadpanned, "Well, thank God that's over."

She burst out laughing. "Insufferable. Have you ever met anyone more boring?"

"I was this close to pushing him over the side of the boat."

"Ugh, and that food? It just kept coming and coming and coming."

"And being forced to sit through some lame proposal? It was like we weren't even there."

"We should do something to celebrate it being over."

"Amen." Nick smiled down at her and her stomach flipped. "What should we do?"

"What do you want to do?"

"We could fight again?"

She chortled. "Pass."

"Well, what then?"

She lifted a slinky shoulder. "I'm open."

He cocked his jaw. "And I'm not touching that."

"Yet."

Nick chuckled softly, reached out and took her fingers, looked down at them. She felt herself being pulled closer to him, but couldn't be sure the sensation was entirely physical. "Sewanee," he sighed, looking up. "I so want to . . ." His eyes went dark. "You know exactly what I want."

She thrilled at that. "Do I?" She hoped the coquettish tone covered any insecurity that might reside in the question. "You haven't tried to make a move once."

He entwined their fingers. "We've been a wee busy, haven't we?" His face puckered. "Besides, what are you talking about—I proposed to you this morning!"

Sewanee raised a teasing brow. "*Maybe* I'll take you down to City Hall, *maybe*, who knows, oh never mind, don't listen to me, I'm *jet-lagged*? I'm positively aflutter. Downright twitterpated."

"Fine, I could have polished it up a bit. But, in my defense, I didn't know Stu was gonna upstage me!" They laughed and pulled closer together. "Rest assured," he murmured, "I want a reprise of everything we had in Vegas. I want to push you up against a Venetian wall, a real one this time."

"Is that a threat or a promise?"

Nick took a deep breath. "But."

"Not another but," Sewanee groaned.

He squeezed her hand. "But! Not tonight. Tonight, I'm going to make sure you get back safely to your place. Might even go so far as to get you ready for bed—"

"I'm already ready for bed," she husked.

"Christ, this was already going to be hard and you're determined to make it harder."

"You mean your *reaction*?"

"Cute."

She pushed into him, bringing them flush.

Nick bowed his body away from her, like a child trying to wriggle out of a car seat. "Buuut," he huffed on a laugh. "I will be leaving you alone tonight. I have something to do."

She leveled him a look. "No you're not and yes, you do."

"Yes I am and no, it's not you."

They stared at each other, eyes twinkling with challenge and mischief and longing. It occurred to her that, for the first time, she felt truly comfortable with him, even though her body was a live wire of need. How could he have this effect on her? How could he so thoroughly wind her up and simultaneously put her completely at ease? A dangerous combination, she thought.

"Well," she said haughtily, "we'll see what happens when we get to my hotel."

"That we will."

Sewanee took Nick's hand and they began walking, the sound of their footsteps on the wooden pier filling the midnight mist.

CHAPTER EIGHTEEN

"The Resolve"

SEWANEE STOOD IN FRONT OF THE ENTRANCE TO COSMO'S STUDIO gearing herself up to ring the buzzer.

She had a lot on her mind.

The dinner and conversation. Marilyn and Stu's engagement. Her talk with her mom. The things she needed to change in herself if she wanted anything else to change. But all of that was overshadowed by the way the night had ended with Nick.

How? How had he walked her all the way to her pensione, and up to her room, and watched her undress—especially given *how* she'd undressed—and tucked her into bed, and then . . . *left*? Every step of their walk home she'd been thinking it was cute, how far he was taking this whole will-they-or-won't-they thing. But then he did it. He . . . *left*! And still, she'd been sure she'd hear a knock on the door any minute later. Any couple of minutes. Any five minutes, ten, twenty minutes later.

She did not.

She knew he wanted her. He had made that clear on the dock. And yet, there was that gnawing feeling creeping around inside her. That stalking insecurity.

She took a deep breath of crisp morning air and pressed the buzzer.

She was immediately admitted, walked up the stairs, and found Nick's scruffy face waiting for her at the top of the landing. "Morning," he said, barely above a whisper. He was smiling, so Sewanee followed his lead, smiling back.

"Morning. You got here early, too."

His smile broadened. "Come on through," he whispered. He held a finger to his lips as he stood aside to let her pass.

She entered the studio's control room and found Cosmo sleeping on the couch. That explained the volume. Nick waved her into the small breakroom, went to a tiny Formica table, picked up a to-go coffee and a white paper pastry bag. "First: caffeine and carbs." He held the items out to her.

She smiled appreciatively and took a much-needed gulp of coffee and a bite of roll, and asked, with affected innocence, "So. How was your night?"

"Good."

"Get done what you needed to get done?"

"Absolute-mente," he answered, in a remarkably spot-on Stu impression.

"Looks like you didn't get much sleep. Who was she?" Took another bite.

Nick chuckled. "Don't even."

Cosmo shuffled into the breakroom in leopard-print slippers, hair mussed, eyes two watery slits, mouth a crooked smile, mumbling "*Buongiorno*" and "*Scusami*" and something entirely lost on Sewanee other than the word "*Caffe*." Nick moved out of his way and said, "Take your time, we'll go into the studio."

"*Grazie mille.*" His voice sounded like a bullfrog with laryngitis, but he turned around, remembering something, and continued, "Oh Nick. I tell you, last night . . . you surprise me. You so good."

"Cheers, mate."

Cosmo turned back to the coffee machine. Nick and Sewanee left the breakroom and Sewanee murmured, "So it was a he?"

"What?"

"Nick-uh," she breathed near his ear, "you so good-uh."

Nick groaned and crossed to the soundboard, picking up a set of headphones. "Take a seat."

She held up a hand. "I'm not judging! He *is* adorable."

He took her by the shoulders and sat her down in the chair. "Headphones. On head."

She grinned. "What am I listening to?"

"Listen to as much as you can stand, then you can yell at me, hit me, do whatever you want to me."

"Promises, promises." She put on the headphones and crossed her arms.

Nick walked away, pressing a button on the control panel.

The sound of Brock McNight's voice filled her ears.

It was the scene they'd recorded yesterday.

She opened her mouth to tell him he'd put on the wrong thing, but then she heard it.

The difference.

This was not yesterday's performance. The words were the same, but the vocalization was new. It was connected. It was the voice she had heard when he'd read *Goodnight Moon*. It was Brock McNick.

She was drawn into the story as an aroma draws one to a meal. She uncrossed her arms, put her forehead down on the desk, and just *listened*. When it got to the steamy portion, she couldn't help but look up at Nick. He'd sat down in Cosmo's chair and was leaning back in it, his boots propped on the edge of the low coffee table. He cradled a guitar.

She'd never seen him in his element. He made so much sense this way. As she listened to Brock describe what he was doing with his hands, she watched Nick's hands glide up and down the guitar's neck and expertly pluck its strings. The sound was not breaching her headphones. He was playing quietly, head tipped back, lips moving only slightly. She didn't think he was singing; was he writing something in his head?

In her ear, his voice cracked with lust. With emotion. The vulnerability was unnerving. Arousing.

When his section was over and hers began, she slowly took off the headphones.

At her movement, Nick stopped playing and turned the chair slightly to face her. She wasn't sure what to say, but she knew him well enough already to know he wasn't one to let a silence linger. Unless there was touching involved.

"Okay," he muttered. "Go ahead, take your best shot." He put his elbows on his knees and jutted out his chin as if he were putting his head on a chopping block. He closed his eyes.

Sewanee placed a kiss on his cheek, letting her lips linger there.

Nick opened his eyes.

She pulled back just enough so they could look at each other. He smiled. She smiled. Then she brought her lips to his with the tenderest touch. They suspended there, never breaking eye contact. It wasn't a taking, like Vegas; it was a giving. An exchange. Of respect, of admiration. The gift of being seen through a kiss.

They eventually parted and leaned back in their chairs.

"Nick." Despite her smile, her throat tightened slightly. "That was incredible."

He nodded once. "And I loved doing it. Go figure." He took her hand. "And I'm sorry for what I said yesterday. You *are* a director. A damn good one. So between you being you and Stu being Stu, all I can say is, thanks. I needed that."

"How long did it take you? How many takes?"

"One."

"Seriously?"

He shrugged. "I imagined you standing there across from me, and I spoke to you."

Sewanee grinned. "You acted."

He shook his head. "I was being real."

She grinned wider. "Exactly."

Cosmo walked in with his coffee. "He show you what he do last night?"

"Yes he did."

"Is good, no?"

"Is good, yes."

Cosmo beamed. "I go set up the room." He shook his finger at them. "I going to miss you, the both of you." He went into the live room and started rearranging mics.

Sewanee turned back to Nick. Her hand went to her heart. "Can we keep him?"

Nick chuckled. "I wish we could."

She gestured at the soundboard. "He is an amazing engineer."

"And you should hear him on bass." Off Sewanee's confused look, Nick said, "We jammed a bit."

"Last night? It was midnight when you left me."

Nick scoffed. "It's a music studio, I knew he'd be here. He happened to be rehearsing with Enzo and Mario and . . . some other O. So I hung out and when they took a break around two, I asked him if he'd let me do another take."

"And then you went back to your hotel?" she asked rhetorically.

"Well." Nick rubbed a hand over his scruffy jaw. "The other O had to go home and they needed a guitarist, so—"

"So let me guess." Sewanee smiled.

So did Nick. "Then, around four or so, the other guys left and

Cos opens some vino and then he starts telling me about this American actress he's had a crush on for years."

Sewanee laughed. "And he's like, *you're* from America, do you know her?"

Nick laughed, too. "Right? But he didn't know her name, just knew the show she was on. Very popular here, apparently."

"What was the show, maybe I know her?"

"It was called *Get Chelsea*, and when we looked up—"

"Nick!" Sewanee's eye bugged. "I did a season on that show."

"And when we looked up the cast, guess who the actress was?"

She blinked at him. Late to the party. "Me."

"It was driving him mad yesterday." Nick chuckled. "Swore he recognized you. But he was too embarrassed to ask."

Sewanee peeked through the glass and caught Cosmo's eye. He smiled sheepishly and waved. She waved back while saying, through clenched teeth, "This is oddly mortifying."

"Why? You were great."

Her head whipped back to Nick. "What?"

"You were. We were able to watch—"

"You watched the show?"

"No."

She exhaled in relief.

"We found your old demo reel online and watched that."

Her face heated. Her throat tightened. "Tell me you didn't."

Nick shrugged. "Okay, we didn't."

"You didn't?"

Nick laughed. "Of course we did! Why wouldn't we watch it?" His smile softened. He took a beat. "Why wouldn't you want us to watch it?"

The answer sat silently between them. Sewanee's ever-stalking insecurity unable to be spoken aloud. At a loss, she looked down again.

"You were brilliant," Nick murmured. "Just like you're brilliant in *Casanova*. You're something else, Swan."

"No," she mumbled, "I'm someone else."

Nick's lips separated. He reached out and tipped her chin up. "Eventually, don't know when, but eventually? You're gonna have to stop thinking you're nothing more than the damaged version of yourself."

Before Sewanee could respond, Cosmo came back into the control room and said their mics were set up and they could start whenever they were ready.

Nick stood.

He held his hand out to her.

"I may have missed my opportunity last night, but how about we put this to bed?"

THEY EXITED THE studio into the bright light of day, giddy. There'd been a grovel, an admission of love, mind-blowing makeup sex, and then, but of course, a proposal and ensuing HEA. And throughout it all, they'd been connected. Real.

They paused on the sidewalk and Nick clapped his hands together. "Right! Should we go to yours or mine?"

Sewanee made a show of considering this, batted her lashes. "Well, gosh, Nick. I'm not sure."

He smirked and took her hand, then her wrist, then her forearm, reeling her into him like a rope. "I can make right here work."

Sewanee unspooled herself, stepped back, put her hands on her hips. "Oh golly! Gee, I simply couldn't." And then she bounced away. Nick had no choice but to give chase.

He raised a suspicious brow. "Why do I feel like I'm in a scene from *Grease*?"

Sewanee giggled coyly. "Let's get a celebration drink first, mister, and see where that takes us."

"Tell me you mean booze and not a milk shake."

"Why, of course, you silly!"

He sidled up close to her, his fingers finding their way to the back pocket of her jeans. "Is it weird this whole retro thing is turning me on?"

She slapped his hand away. "You behave yourself, Nicholas Sullivan."

Nick groaned. "Is this payback for last night, Sandra Dee?"

Sewanee stopped, turned around, all wide doll eyes, and placed her hand on her chest. "Why, whatever do you mean?" Never breaking eye contact, she slowly slid her hand downward, and then around both breasts, and then out for him to take. Daintily. Like a lady. "Shall we?"

Just as he was about to take it, she turned and kept walking.

"Oh, we are going to 'shall we' all right," Nick promised, trotting after her.

They crossed a piazza, the open door of a taverna on the other side beckoning. There were a few tables set up outside, folded wooden chairs leaning against them. They sat and waited for the server to come and take their order. Normally Sewanee would have ventured inside to get someone's attention, but not today, not now. Every extra minute she played Nick was an hour in Nick time. Besides, she was more than content to be sitting in a somewhat rickety chair, at a somewhat rickety table, with a very solid Nick. A solid if somewhat frustrated, somewhat derailed, somewhat put-out Nick.

Before the waiter even landed at the table, Nick held up two fingers and called out to him, "Prosecco, *grazie*."

The waiter spun right around and went back inside.

Nick was silent, looking out at the piazza. He drummed his fingers on the table between them.

"What are you thinking?" she asked in her normal voice.

"What I want to do to you first," he answered without hesitation.

Would his honest directness ever not catch her off guard? It was so disarmingly sexy.

She looked down at his hand. At the ring on his middle finger. She reached over and touched it. "Does this have a story?"

He interlaced their fingers. "It was Tom's. June's ex-partner? She refused to marry him. And she didn't believe in rings. But he did, so he wore one."

"That's sweet."

"No, it's not. It was a fight. Everything with them was a fight. You don't want to marry me? Fine! I'll wear a ring anyway, how do you like *that*?" Nick had to chuckle. "Maniacs." His focus went back to it. "I found it in her stuff after she died. I never knew she'd taken it with her when she moved us back to the States."

"Is he still around?"

"He is. I'm actually going to stop over in Dublin on the way home. Check on him." He looked into her eye. "He took it hard. Even though it's been, what, twenty years since they split. I think he always believed she'd come back to him."

The waiter dropped off two glasses of bubbly and Nick gave him cash, told him to keep the change. When he was gone, they raised their glasses.

"To . . ." Nick said, an echo of their Vegas toast. He waited for Sewanee to join in, but she took a moment and then said instead:

"To June."

"Of course," he murmured, "to Junie." Then, "For bringing you to me."

"And you to me."

They both sipped.

"I decided last night I'm officially done," Nick said, setting down his glass. "*Casanova*'s gonna be Brock's last project."

"Really?"

Nick waved a hand. "I'm ready. And I couldn't have a higher note to go out on." He smiled. "Besides, Sarah Westholme's spoiled me for any other co-narrator and she's retreating back into the mists of retirement."

Sewanee watched the bubbles rise up in her glass. "I actually don't know about that." Nick quirked his head at her and she met his gaze. "I liked it. I liked doing Romance."

Nick put his hand over the top of her glass. "Don't drink any more of this, I think they put something in it."

Sewanee chuckled, shrugged. "I'm serious."

"But you hate the HEA bullshit."

At his skeptical look, she took back her glass. "I mean, yes. I hated the premise that all we have to do is endure the twists and trope-y turns of life and then, *bam*, we get rewarded. Ridiculous."

"Indeed."

"But recently I've been thinking . . ." She looked out at the piazza. "I haven't got this totally figured out, but I think my problem was that it promised something unattainable. We can now rest assured these people will go forth and live happily ever after. But, really, HEA comes from fairy tales and fairy tales end with: and they lived happily ever after. Lived. Not live. Past tense, not present. And that works for me."

Nick's brow crinkled. He leaned forward. "Sorry, the *tense* change made it work for you?"

"Granted, I'm a word nerd, but yeah." He still looked confused so she leaned forward, too. "To *live* HEA is to say, from today onward life will be happy. I mean, how can you know that? Shit happens. Over and over. It's what Stu was saying at dinner, that's what got me thinking about this. That life isn't linear. About that incredible dish being a plate of failure." Sewanee took a sip. "I don't think you can know if you lived happily ever after until your life's over." She set down her glass. "Maybe that's why your whole life flashes before your eyes when you die. So you can see the movie from beginning to end and know."

Nick dropped his chin in his hand and gazed at her. He tapped his temple. "Is it always like this in there? Does your neck get sore from holding that big brain up all day long?"

She snorted. "Anyway, it's not ridiculous. It's not bullshit. It is possible. It's not fantasy *or* reality. A happily ever after is built by both, together, over a lifetime."

Nick took a moment. "Yeah, I've been thinking the exact same thing." Sewanee laughed, but he said, "No, seriously, it's almost exactly what I was talking to Stu about on the boat ride back to St. Mark's."

"No."

"Yes."

"What were you talking about?"

"Emerson and dolphins."

Sewanee chuckled.

"After a thrilling dissertation on the striped dolphin's migratory patterns and mating irregularities he brought up that Emerson quote: it's not the destination; it's the journey. And he said Emerson was ass backwards like me. That it *is* the destination and not the journey. Because only after you've arrived can you judge the merit of the journey. But then he said"—and here, Nick dropped into his dead-on Stu impression—"it probably wasn't Emerson anyway, it was probably some bumper sticker writer and no one should take advice from a bumper sticker, *or* a has-been sneaker-maker for that matter, and did I happen to notice how each wine came in a different-shaped glass at dinner?"

Sewanee laughed, then, imitating her mom, said, "Stuuuuu."

Nick laughed as well. "I think those two have a shot at HEA."

He sat back, took another sip, and assessed her. "So more Romance, eh?"

Sewanee sipped, too. "Maybe. Not necessarily narrate. Maybe direct some Duets. Maybe find the next Brock McNight."

Nick had a particular look on his face.

She reached over, patted his forearm. "Aww, don't worry. You'll always be my first."

He caught her hand as she pulled it back. He brought it to his mouth. Ran his lips from her wrist up along the side of her pinky. Kissed the tip of her finger. Then the center of her palm. Breathed in. "Done playing games?"

Her face opened like a flower. "Yes."

With her other hand, she lifted her glass. He pulled back and lifted his. She quietly sang, "You're the one that I want, you are the one I want."

He grinned and returned, "Ooh-ooh-ooh."

They finished the prosecco, stood, and left the table hand in hand.

AS THEY WOUND through the Ghetto and back to the center of town, the distant sound of a cello drew them into another piazza. In the middle, a lone cellist sat on a stool, hat at her feet brimming with coins, playing a sonata. After watching for a moment, Nick tugged Sewanee into his arms and began dancing.

As much as she wanted to get back to the hotel, this rhythmic swaying felt like the pinnacle of intimacy and she melted into him. "Can we stay like this forever?"

She felt his chuckle in her chest. "Yes. At least until we have to go back to the real world. Or get hungry."

They continued dancing. Sewanee knew that beyond Nick's humor, there was a sobering truth. She knew what she could expect from him in a hotel room; she didn't know what lay beyond that. She felt safe enough in his arms to ask:

"What happens then?"

"Are you asking what my intentions are?" She heard the smile in his voice.

"Kind of. Yeah."

"Simple. I want to be with you." At her silence, he pushed her away, coaxing her out into a lazy spin. "What do you want?"

Sewanee smiled back, but exhaled. Long and slow.

Nick reeled her back to him. "Remember, now: there's nothing more attractive than a woman who knows what she wants."

His tone was light, all unaffected nonchalance. But she also felt the slightest hint of discomfort.

"I want to know this is real," she said. "But how can . . . is that even possible?"

"You want the Romance version or the Women's Fiction version?"

She looked up at him. "Neither. I want the real-life version."

He spun her back out, thinking. "We do long distance for a while. Until we can organize our lives in such a way that we can be together." He pulled her back in.

"How?"

"We'll figure it out."

"But how?"

"We just will."

"How can you be so confident?"

"Because I believe in us." He peered down at her. "Don't you?"

"Of course." She used the opportunity of ducking under his arm to break eye contact. "But there's so much going on. So much up in the air. For both of us. Something could happen and then what?"

"Something will happen. Probably many things. We'll get frustrated. Angry. We'll disappoint each other. We'll say things we don't mean but deep down kinda mean a little."

"Or worse."

His feet slowed. "What's going on?"

She tugged his shoulder toward her, willing him to recommit to the dance, even as she kept her gaze averted. "I think I'm scared."

"Of?"

"You. You're . . . you're like some . . ."

"Yes?"

"Some super-stealth sex weapon that could go rogue at any moment," she blurted.

Nick belted out a laugh. "What?"

"You're like the Jason Bourne of Romance. You know things no man should know. A military-grade weapon just walking around in broad daylight." She widened her eye, leaned into how absurd her fears were, especially as she was now saying them aloud. "How can I know you won't use your powers for ill?"

Nick answered honestly. "You can't."

In for a penny, in for a pound, she supposed. "How can I know you'll always want me?"

"You can't." Again, with a tone of sincerity. His refusal to engage in false reassurances or empty flattery tugged a disconcerted chuckle out of her. "I'm serious. How can you know you'll always want *me*? What if I gain a hundred pounds? Lose my hair? My mind. What if, what if, what if?"

"I'd still want you," she answered seriously.

They stopped dancing, but remained close. He shook his head. "You don't know that."

"I do."

"Feelings aren't constant, they're transient. Sometimes for the better, sometimes not. You can believe in them, but you can't know them. How can you know what something is before it becomes it? It's like . . ." His voice faded. "Like a caterpillar and a butterfly."

"What?"

Nick shook his head. "Nothing. Riffing." He reached up, pushed her hair off her face. "You just got done telling me you can't know an HEA until it's been lived, but now you want a guarantee of getting there?"

"Not a guarantee, no, but some assurance that—"

"I can assure you I won't cheat on you, because that is in my control. I can only control my actions, I can't control . . . life." Nick started dancing again. "Why do you automatically assume the worst?"

His tone was remarkably void of judgment. He was curious. She sighed. Her accident? Her father? Her insecurity? Pick one. "Because . . . because . . ." Ah-ha. "Because we don't feel real to me. It feels like we fell out of a Romance tree and hit every trope on the way down."

He laughed. "Snowed In."

"Just One Night."

"Epistolary."

"Mistaken Identity."

"Love Triangle."

She chuckled. "For a minute."

"I think that means we're on to Second Chance, no?" She didn't answer. His hand widened, fingers spanning more of her waist, her back. The hand holding hers interlaced their fingers and he brought it to his chest. "This isn't real enough for you? What do you need? Some deus ex machina? Some contrived fight over a pointless misunderstanding to make you realize what you had and almost lost?"

Sewanee shook her head. This wasn't a June French novel. They didn't need to dramatically blow apart in order to come back together. They were just two people doing their best to not step on the other's toes while figuring out how to dance.

The cellist had ended the song. They parted for a moment and clapped appreciatively. She began playing again.

Before reengaging, though, Sewanee said, "I want to know we aren't mistaking this for some Romance novel."

"We're not. We can write our own book. Day by day, page by page."

She saw the slightest flicker of doubt in his eyes. Not doubt in what he believed to be true, but in whether she could believe it, too. In her capacity to believe something that couldn't be known. Sure, she could accept the concept of HEA in the philosophical abstract, but here, in the practicality of an intimate moment, in having to make a choice and live with its consequences . . . he wasn't sure she could do that.

She saw him fully, then. The pieces of himself that he'd disparately shared with her and which she'd diligently collected, but couldn't assemble: a child who grew up never having the security of believing he'd been wanted; a man who'd lost his dream and was learning how to believe in it again. She saw failure and success, weakness and strength, and most of all, the longing for someone to love all of it. To love him.

"Ask me again what I want," she murmured.

"What do you want, love?"

"I don't want to be in any book with you anymore. I want to be in real life with you."

"However it may end?"

"Yes."

"Happily or not?"

She was surprised to find the answer so easy to say. "Yes." Then, "Absolute-mente."

The kiss they shared this time was not chaste.

She heard clapping, a couple of catcalls, and was transported back in time to a Las Vegas blizzard, Nick pushing her against a wall, a roving pack of unchaperoned boys hooting. The difference this time was she had nothing holding her upright, they were unmoored in the middle of a cobblestone piazza, and she felt her head swim and her knees liquify. She clung to him tighter until he muttered, "We need to go."

"Please," she panted.

"I'm legitimately terrified something's going to ruin this."

She guffawed. "We're tempting fate."

He grabbed her waist. "Did you feel that?!" He met her eye. "That wasn't an earthquake, was it?" Then he tickled her.

"Oh, no!" she screeched, squirming away.

He grabbed her from behind. "I'll save you!" He picked her up and walked, the way a slightly larger child carries a slightly smaller one. They were laughing giddily, tripping over themselves, utter embarrassments. "Anything could happen! At any moment—"

Her phone rang.

They froze.

"No," Nick whispered as if it could hear him. He dropped her. She spun around. His finger came to her lips. "Don't answer it."

"Nick, I-I have to. It hasn't rung once in three days, what if—"

"No, right, of course." He stepped back, raked a hand over his face, took a shaky breath, all while she fished her phone out of her jacket pocket.

An unfamiliar number, but an L.A. area code. Her heart stuttered. She answered. "Hello?"

"Hi, is this Sewanee Chester?"

"Yes?"

"Hiya, this is Adaku Obi's manager, Manse Rollins, how ya doin'?"

"Uh. Fine."

"Good, good, glad to hear it. So, listen, we have an issue."

An issue? An issue a talent manager would be calling *her* about? Did they want her for the role, after all? The thought made her stomach flip. But, interestingly, not in joy or excitement. In something uncomfortably close to dread.

And in that instantaneous gut check, her relationship to acting became clear: she didn't want it anymore.

"What's going on?" she asked.

"Well, Adaku's in the hospital."

CHAPTER NINETEEN

"The Reconciliation"

SEWANEE LANDED AT LAX AND MADE ONE STOP BEFORE GOING TO THE hospital, where she showed her ID at three different desks, and was admitted to Adaku's private room. When she tentatively stepped inside, her breath caught at the sight of Adaku sitting up in bed, alone, looking out the window. It was as if she'd booked a tragic role in some medical drama. But the room, the smell, the monitors, the gauze patch on her right eyebrow, the IV drip taped to her hand made it all too real.

Sewanee wasn't sure what to do. Approach her silently? Announce herself? She swallowed and, with a voice that sounded like placing a hand gently on her friend's back, said, "Adaku?"

Her head turned slowly to the door. She blinked. "Swan. What are you doing here?"

Sewanee held up the small, white cardboard box. "Just thought you might want some In-N-Out."

The smile was not Adaku's usual blindingly bright one. It was more a bleed of sunlight in an overcast day. "You always could make an entrance." Sewanee crossed to her and handed over the box. "How did you—"

She wanted so badly to talk, she answered before the question was finished. "Manse called me. I'm your emergency contact, remember? I would have been here sooner, but I was in Venice."

"Traffic is terrible on the West side," Adaku said automatically.

Sewanee chuckled. "Not Venice Beach. Italy. I was in Venice, Italy."

"What? What are you—how long have I been here?"

Sewanee took in Adaku's bloodshot, watery eyes and understood this was worse than she'd been told. On the first call, Manse had said they didn't know what was wrong, just that she'd been admitted. That was enough. Sewanee had thrown her things together and rushed to the airport, Nick in tow, doing his best to calm her. He offered to go, too, but she thought it better he stick to his plan to see Tom in Dublin and he agreed. By the time she'd landed at her layover, Manse had left a voicemail: actually, Adaku was only a little dehydrated, and anything Swan could do to get her back to Georgia as quickly as possible would be super appreciated.

She sat down on the edge of the bed. "It's been about eighteen hours. The nurse said you've been asleep for most of it." She opened the box. "Double-Double, fries extra crispy."

Adaku slid her hand under the paper-wrapped burger and lifted it from the box like an Oscar. She took a bite, closed her eyes, and moaned. She grabbed some fries and stuffed them into her burger-filled mouth. Sewanee enjoyed watching this as much as Adaku enjoyed doing it. She rested her hand by Adaku's hip, purposefully not touching her even though she wanted nothing more than to do just that.

"Oh my God, cheese. Grease. Bread. So good." At least Sewanee thought that's what she said. "And the way the burger mixes with the fries in your mouth?" She swallowed and opened her eyes. "Thank you." The pleasure that had lit her face a minute before slid away. "Swan, I don't know what to say—"

Sewanee interrupted again. "I'll talk, you eat."

Adaku smiled weakly but wryly. "You know how to shut me up." She picked the burger back up and took another eager bite.

Sewanee breathed. "First the easy part. I'm so sorry, A. And those words don't come close to describing how badly I feel about everything I said. I was in a horrible place. For a much longer time than I even knew. And when that role came along, I . . . it was like throwing a drowning person a life preserver. It was going to save me. Save us. We could be us again."

"I want that so bad." Adaku swallowed. "When I watched that propeller . . . I couldn't do anything to stop it. This was how I could finally do something. Go back in time and make it go away," Adaku whispered and Sewanee's heart broke.

She moved her hand from its careful position on the bed and gently settled it on Adaku's thigh. "But that's not possible. And I made you feel terrible for failing to do the impossible." Sewanee smiled sadly. "As much as your relentless optimism drives me nuts, I wanted it. And you certainly have enough to go around. So I pretended to have it, too. But it wasn't what I needed."

Adaku nudged the box toward Sewanee. "What you need is some of these fries."

Sewanee put a few in her mouth, chewed. "When I saw Mom, she said—"

"When did you see your mom?"

"In Venice. That's why I went. We talked and there was one thing she said that I so wish you could have been there for. She said that you've all been waiting for me to be okay with what happened, to accept myself as I am now, so *you* could be okay with it. But I've been waiting for all of you to tell me it's okay, that . . ." Her throat squeezed. "That *I'm* okay. And it was so unfair of me to put that on everyone else. I wanted you to throw me a life preserver because I didn't want to save myself. I didn't want to learn how to swim."

Adaku chewed thoughtfully, silent.

"And then Nick said—"

Her eyes bugged. "You're talking to Nick?"

"Yeah, he was there, too."

"What?" She swallowed her food. "When did you call this summit and why wasn't I invited?"

"He said I need to stop thinking I'm nothing more than the damaged version of myself. That who I was *is* who I am." She looked down at the blanket. "And it made me think: we break, in many different ways. But it doesn't mean we're broken. Do you get what I mean?"

Adaku waved a weak hand around the hospital room, her gown, her busted head. "Not in the slightest." She tossed the now empty box aside, and held up her arms, begging Sewanee into a hug. "Can you put all that into my drip and directly into my vein?"

They fell into each other and held on as if they were floating. Neither needing the other for saving, both able to swim, but resting on each other for a moment, catching their breath.

When they separated, Sewanee pointed at her eye patch, then at her friend's bandage. "Twinsies!"

Adaku blurted a laugh.

Sewanee took a moment. "So, what happened?"

Adaku sighed, looked down, picked the salt from under her nails. "It's so embarrassing. When I left your place—I wasn't a hundred percent from the London trip. Tired, nauseous, muscle aches, running on adrenaline. Got to Georgia and they immediately took us to the woods. Camping, hunting . . . bonding." She rolled her eyes. "But two days in a storm hit and we went back to civilization. Where I got an e-mail. The Angela Davis people wanted to have a meeting—"

"No."

"Yes. So I got on a red-eye back to L.A." Adaku continued, sarcastically, "Because it was meant to be! And I can handle it. I handle everything. No sleep, no problem. Train six hours a day, seven days a week, sure. Years without a single day to myself, bring it. All this time busting my ass and I still feel like we're back in Washington Heights, me with one audition for every ten of yours. Twice as hard to go half as far, right? That shit never ends. So of course I'll kill myself to make that meeting happen. Kill myself to be the unimpeachable picture of the strong Black woman manifesting her success, and—" She abruptly sobbed. Tears poured from her eyes and she turned toward the window, as if she could grab oxygen from it. Sewanee clutched her hand and stroked her leg through the blanket, swallowing back her own tears. Adaku wrested control and continued, in a strained voice, "I didn't make the meeting."

"What happened?"

"I guess a panic attack? But I pushed through it. Then I got off the plane and stepped out to the arrivals curb, and . . . splat. On the sidewalk." She pointed at the gauze. "Crack."

Sewanee winced. "God, A."

"Exhaustion," Adaku mumbled. "What a cliché."

Sewanee picked up a cup of water on the tray table next to the bed and gave it to Adaku. "Drink."

She took a sip, handed it back to Sewanee. Took a moment. "This is a fucked business, Swan. Nobody cares. It's about nothing but money, power, the special treatment. We didn't get it at the time, but remember our big goal? Make a million before we're thirty-five? It wasn't about art, or talent, or being someone in this world. It was about being something. A commodity. Something that would one day be worth a million dollars." She closed her eyes, tipped her head back. "You don't know how lucky you are. This never stops being hard. Every time I win, I don't dare think about what that win cost me. I'm just on to the next one." She opened her eyes, gestured harshly at the bed. "I mean, what does it take for us to wake the fuck up?"

Sewanee squeezed her hand. "I don't know."

"This better be it." She sighed roughly. "I don't even know what I'm doing this for anymore. Serving a system that doesn't serve me? Forgoing happiness to maybe be happy eventually?" She shook her head, bewildered.

Sewanee wasn't prepared to help her through this the way she wanted to be able to. All she could do right now was give her water and hold her hand and be there, finally be there, for *her*. When Adaku had calmed a bit, Sewanee said, "Do you think we could find a two-for-one deal on a therapist?"

Adaku chuckled. "You and I would break a Groupon shrink. We need the Cadillac package."

"I'm in if you are."

Adaku held up a pinky. "Deal."

Sewanee hooked hers into Adaku's and then Adaku took a deep breath and closed her eyes. "How about some Nick details for your girl?"

"Later. You should sleep."

"No, I'm good." But she sounded like she was already half-gone.

Sewanee stood. "I'm gonna go take care of some stuff. I'll be back in a bit."

"Can you . . ." She really was almost out.

Sewanee smiled. "What?"

"Bring me a black and white . . . you know. The milk shake . . . with the . . . ?"

And then she was asleep.

SEWANEE EXITED THE hospital, stepped over to a sitting area, took out her phone, and called BlahBlah. She'd been told to give it time and she had. Surely it had been long enough.

Instead of her grandmother's voice, she got a recording. The number had been disconnected.

Her panic was instantaneous. She called Seasons' general number and attempted to calmly ask the right questions in the right order. She got as far as "Barbara Chester" and the harried receptionist told her to please hold.

The next thing she heard was, "Hellooo?"

Sewanee let out a ragged sigh, dropped onto a bench. "Blah-Blah. It's Sewanee."

"Who?"

She'd expected this. "Dollface?"

Three full seconds and then: "Dollface! How's my favorite girl?"

That refrain had never sounded better. The best refrain in the history of refrains. "I'm fine," she said shakily, "but how are you? Is everything okay?"

"Oh, heavens yes! Everyone is so nice here. This lovely young man is reading to me." Blah lowered her voice. "I think he's a bit of a flirt, if you ask me. You should say hello to him."

"No, BlahBlah, that's okay. I just wanted to—"

"Hi, Swan."

The unmistakable voice of her father. "Dad." She tightened right back up. "What are you doing there? What's going on? Is she okay?"

"Relax, Sewanee. The world is still turning on its axis."

"Dad, please, tell me what's happening."

"I'm getting her settled in her new room."

"What?"

He adopted a more serious tone. "Amanda called. The time had come, there was an opening. So I moved her into memory care."

Sewanee's mouth opened. "Oh. Wow. Okay. How is it?"

"It's nice. Very nice. She's very happy here." There was the slightest pause before he said, "I'm glad you listened to me."

Sewanee's mouth opened wider. But then he chuckled. Rueful. Conciliatory. She decided to play along. "Well, you do know best."

"Sometimes." That was as close as Henry would get to an apology.

She'd take it.

She paused. "Are you really reading to her?"

"I'm a sorry substitute for the professional in the family, but she doesn't seem to mind."

"What are you reading?"

"Hemingway."

"Trying to put her to sleep?"

"Funny."

"Thank you."

They ran out of banter. She couldn't remember the last time she'd felt comfortable during a silence with her father. She wasn't thinking of something smart or sarcastic to say. She wasn't thinking three steps ahead. Instead, she repeated the two words, this time with a different tone. "Thank you."

Now Henry paused. "You shouldn't be thanking me."

"I disagree." Sewanee chose her next words carefully. "You're so hard to listen to because you don't listen. But this time you did. And you changed your mind. So, thank you. I appreciate that, Dad. Appreciate you for doing that."

"That's not necessary, you don't have to . . ." but he went quiet and his breath hitched. After a moment, he broke through. "Thank you. Here's your grandmother."

Sewanee heard him tell Blah her granddaughter was on the phone. Then she heard Blah tell him she didn't have a granddaughter. Then Henry said, "Swan, Mom, Sewanee."

And Blah said, "Who?"

And Henry tried once more. "Dollface?"

She was about to tell her dad to forget it. She would call Blah another time. But before she could, a sweetly lyrical voice on the other end of the line said, "Dollface! How's my favorite girl?"

By the end of the call, Sewanee felt—it astounded her—content. She leaned her head back, closed her eye, and took a restorative breath. As she basked in the new state of things, her phone rang.

"What!" she shouted to the world, but it wasn't listening. She looked at the number. Of course. She grudgingly picked it up. "Hello?"

"Manse here. How is she?"

"Resting."

"Excellent! So listen, I've been trying to get an update from the doctor but that's been a nonstarter. And her phone keeps going to voicemail."

"Yeah, I don't think she's taking calls, Manse."

"Totally, totally. But production's getting antsy. Any ballpark on when she'll be able to get back to Georgia, sweetie?"

Sewanee took a moment before responding. She thought about herself. About her passion for acting. About how it had always been challenged by the realities of the business. About the vagaries and rejections and frustrations. About how most of her prodigious talent went not to the actual work, but to acting as if she liked people like Manse. About what Adaku had said: how lucky Sewanee was.

"Sweetie, you there?"

She'd wanted to keep the anger out of her voice but decided now that, actually, she didn't. Her voice, after all, was her superpower. "First, it's Sewanee, not sweetie. I know, easy mistake. Second, do you know why this happened?"

There was a small beat. "Because she's a gladiator! She's a—"

"You. You and the clown car of assholes around her who pretend to care. She'll call you when—"

"Hey, easy, k? Just because Adaku—"

"Don't interrupt me or I'll hang up. She'll call you when she's ready. Meanwhile, if production is antsy, so be it. It's a movie. It doesn't matter. Adaku matters. And if *you're* antsy, I suggest you take some time to reflect on how your actions contributed to this situation. For instance: You keep pronouncing her name AH-duh-koo. It's ah-DAH-koo. You're her manager, all these other people take their cues from you, and if you can't even—"

"Whoa, don't spin this like I don't care, you don't know me—"

"Manse, you interrupted. Bye."

She hung up. And felt like a million dollars *before* taxes and commissions. She stood, stretched, and decided she'd get herself a milk shake, too.

SEWANEE WALKED THROUGH her front door around midnight, after having been kicked out at the end of visiting hours, stopping by Seasons to retrieve her abandoned car, and attempting to sneak into Mark's to appropriate some snacks for the next morning only to have the man himself bar her exit until she told him absolutely everything.

She turned on the light and was greeted by the shattered Tea-For-One service still scattered across the kitchen counter and floor.

Ah, yes.

She swept up all the pieces, then took a shower and was falling into bed when her phone rang. Her exhaustion took a backseat to her happiness at the name that appeared on her screen.

"Look at me picking up when Brock McNight calls."

She heard his husky chuckle. "How far we've come."

"Good . . . morning?" She was beyond the ability to do time zone math.

"It is. Good evening to you?" He sounded equally unsure.

"It's dark, so maybe? I exist outside of time now. I've transcended . . . the . . . thing."

He laughed. "How's it going there?"

She caught him up briefly, promised to tell him more tomorrow, and sighed. "I'm so sorry we didn't get to . . . you know."

"That'll teach you to play games, Sandy."

"Lesson learned. That is not how I wanted our trip to end."

"Well, if you want to *you know*—and here I thought you didn't like euphemisms—I'm currently looking at flights to L.A. in a couple weeks' time."

They locked in a date and it made Sewanee so happy, that date, so anticipatory, that she wasn't sure how she would get through all the other dates before it. "How's Dublin? How's Tom?" she asked.

"Good. Better. And his pub's doing fantastic. The lads and I jammed last night."

"That's great."

"So, listen. I found something here."

"Okay?" Her tone took a sharp left into tentative.

He chuckled. "Why do you always expect the worst?"

She huffed. "Have you met me?"

He chuckled again. "So, this is . . . well, you'll decide what it is. It's yours."

"Again, okay?"

"Tom had a box of June's old books. Early ones, out of print now. No idea if any of them hold up, but I was thinking . . . you said the other day you might want to do more Romance and, well, none of these books have audio versions."

"Oh my God."

"So, the box is yours."

"Oh, Nick, no—"

"Tom's got a lawyer here, so I'll get something drawn up that gives you the copyrights." The silence was too long. "You still there?"

"Nick. That's . . . you can't."

"I can. I am."

"But it's—it's too much. A whole box of June French IP, that's a gold mine for you. I can't—"

"You can and you will. I want you to. Please. She'd want you to."

Sewanee flopped back on the bed. What she could do with this. The projects she could make, the people she could employ, the possibilities—

"They might be good for nothing but kindling. According to the flap copy, one of them is about a video store clerk and a pager salesman. But you'll read them and decide. Do with them as you will."

She swallowed. "Nick?"

"Yeah?"

"I'm happy. Right now. In this moment. In this very real life of ours."

He sighed. She heard his smile. "Me too."

She was so happy that even after they hung up she couldn't stop smiling. She had been exhausted thirty minutes ago and now she was wired. She wanted to do something. Put on some music and dance? Watch an old movie? And then it came to her.

She knew exactly what she wanted to do. She had been thinking about doing it ever since Nick had mentioned it.

She went online and found her demo reel.

Just seeing the thumbnail of her old face . . . could she really do this?

She took a breath and pressed play. Once she was looking, she couldn't stop. It was weird. It was sad. It hurt. It was great.

Glued to the screen, she could not recall a time when so many emotions colored her, as if she had all 120 Crayola crayons at her disposal. She had thought watching this would make her feel so much less of herself, but the opposite was true.

She had been good. She belonged there. She was captivating. She had thought it would be like watching someone else. Except it wasn't. It was, undeniably, her. A part of her that had come home. Was welcomed home. A part of her that would live with her now. A part of her to be proud of.

The reel ended and the feeling that lingered when all the other colors faded was contentment. Similar to how she'd felt sweeping up the Tea-For-One: regretful but accepting.

It was a past she no longer wanted back. It was simply a part of her present and she was free to pursue her future. Heart full, Sewanee pressed play and watched it again.

She loved it.

THREE DAYS LATER, she picked Adaku up from the hospital in a garage under the back alley most people didn't know existed. The "High Roller Exit," Adaku snarked. They'd waited until 1 A.M., but it hadn't made any difference. Adaku sat in the passenger seat looking at her phone. "My neighbor says there's five or six of them camped out in front of my house."

"Well," Sewanee sighed. "You feeling strong enough to tackle sixty-four steps?"

"I thought you'd never ask."

So they went back to Sewanee's. And they spent the next few days reading, watching movies, and sitting outside talking and talking and talking. Adaku eventually called Manse back—he'd never called Sewanee again—and told him she wasn't returning to Georgia. And then she told him that she was done jumping through hoops for the Angela Davis project but that he should feel free to do his job and get her an offer for it and, oh, she wanted a producer credit on the film, too. When she hung up, they high-fived.

The night before Adaku had decided to go home, Sewanee went to the store and bought sour cream and taco seasoning. It was comically delicious.

They sat out on the porch dipping carrots, celery, chips, and anything else they found in Sewanee's cabinets. They game-planned their next steps as the sun went down. Adaku asked her what she might do with the June French books and Sewanee told her some initial thoughts she'd had. "You know what Nick said to me after we recorded together in Venice? He said, 'You're a director.'"

"Really. Who would've thunk? I've only been saying that for a *decade*."

"You have not," Sewanee said like a third grader.

Adaku gave it right back. "Have, too! Have, too!" She dipped a carrot into the bowl of Birdie's Delight and tossed it into her mouth. "I even said it a couple weeks ago! When we did that self-tape."

"Nuh-unh!"

"Yeah-hunh!" She held a celery stalk up to Sewanee. "All seriousness: Can we sell this shit? Clooney has tequila; I could have dip."

"Do you still have the recipe?"

They laughed and Sewanee's phone dinged. The way her mouth went all smiley when she checked it prompted Adaku to say, "Let me guess."

"He sent a cut of the final episode."

"Ohh!" Adaku clapped. "Play it!"

"You're not the boss of me."

The absolute *face* Adaku threw her had Sewanee raising her hands in laughing surrender. She went inside, retrieved her Bluetooth speaker, and connected her phone. She sat back down next to Adaku, right where, three months ago, she'd listened to Brock's voice for the first time.

"–THIS HAS BEEN *Casanova, LLC*, episode eight. Written by June French. Performed by Sarah Westholme and Brock McNight. Thank you for listening."

Adaku jumped to her feet and applauded.

Sewanee's face lit up. "Yeah?"

"Oh my *God*! Babe, that was—what did you *do* to him?! Send it to me immediately, I gotta listen again." Sewanee laughed. "At home, by myself, in the—"

"And now," Brock's voice said from the speaker, "an original song written and performed by Nick Sullivan." Adaku and Sewanee's mirthful eyes collided. "It's called 'Swan Song.'"

Sewanee grabbed the phone and pressed pause. Startled, all playfulness gone, she looked back up at Adaku. "You heard that, too, right?"

"Oh, I heard it." Adaku crossed her arms. "You gonna press play, or do I have to?"

Sewanee stilled. She'd known Nick was writing, but she hadn't expected anything so soon. And she especially hadn't expected to *be* the song.

At the look on her friend's face, Adaku uncrossed her arms

and stepped gently over to her. "Actually. I'm going to put the kettle on, make us some more tea." She dropped a hand on Sewanee's shoulder. Squeezed. "You go ahead." She went inside and closed the sliding door firmly behind her.

Sewanee sat back, took a breath, and looked out over the railing at the last beads of light being washed from the sky. She pressed play.

A lone guitar. Slow. Rhythmic. Lulling. Like the silky drift of a gondola. An effortless chord progression, masterfully played.

Then a voice. Rich. Caramelized. The pace and cadence of a sensual lullaby. Lyrics, poetic yet plain. A stealth hit to the heart.

For all its simplicity, it was deceptively deep, as if she'd stepped boldly into shallows and found herself over her head.

Even as it beckoned her forward, she missed where she'd been. It was far from over, but it took every ounce of willpower to not stop it and start over.

It felt soulfully Irish and yearningly American. It felt like Nick.

And his voice. What did he mean he only sang "a bit"? Good God.

Then it changed. A build began. A driving, forceful purpose accelerating toward some ethereal summit.

The tingle began in her scalp. It traveled down to her jaw. To her throat. Another tingle began in her toes and rose to her hips, her stomach. They met deep in the hollow of her chest. They mingled and vibrated together as he sang the song's final note and his voice, to Sewanee, felt like a call to God. A prayer. An offering. A promise.

It felt like something to believe in.

CODA

Resolution doesn't mean a happy ending—which I've been accused of. I don't think I write happy endings. . . . I try never to end the play with two people in each other's arms—unless it's a musical.

—Neil Simon in *The Paris Review*

Of course there should be an HEA. I'm so sick of this question. It's a Romance! That's the deal we make with our readers. It's misogyny, plain and simple. You don't see anyone telling Mystery readers they're silly and unserious for wanting to know by the end of the book who the murderer was. Fuck off.

—June French in *Cosmopolitan*

"A Stranger Comes to Town"

BLAHBLAH WOULD HAVE APPROVED OF THE SERVICE. IT HAD BEEN elegant and cheeky and a touch theatrical. Just like her.

They interred her ashes at Hollywood Forever Cemetery, six weeks after she died, and were currently having a garden-party reception at Seasons. Sewanee knew Blah would have wanted to wait that long to be put to rest if it meant more people were able to attend, social butterfly that she'd been.

It had worked.

Marilyn and Stu flew in from the Panama Canal and were chatting with Dan, who was helping Sewanee bartend the event and had just brought them two martinis; Mark was over by the food, telling Alice about the condo he'd found in Costa Rica; Adaku had wrapped the Angela Davis project the previous week and was talking with Mitzi—well, listening to Mitzi—who was still going strong and loud; Henry was on the bench Sewanee had sat on with Nick all those months ago, conversing with Amanda.

Adaku left Mitzi (not that she seemed to notice), took a Mallomar off the massive platter, and came sidling up to Sewanee. She followed her friend's gaze over to Amanda and Henry and whispered, "Is he making a move?"

Sewanee swatted her.

"What, at least she's age-appropriate! Progress!"

Sewanee reluctantly laughed as Dan came back, dropped off his tray, and left again to get more ice. The two women quietly assessed the crowd. Adaku hooked her arm into Sewanee's and murmured, "She would have liked this."

Sewanee nodded softly.

Adaku gave her a knowing squeeze. It had been a rough six months even before the last two, which had been horrible. But it had also been the most productive time of Sewanee's life; professionally, personally, emotionally. She could feel everything, including her grief, settling now into a new, consistent normal.

"Sorry about Nick," Adaku murmured.

Sewanee huffed a forlorn sigh. "Please, don't remind me."

"Yeah, I wouldn't bring it up, it's a real sore spot," a sexy voice said, and they turned to greet it.

He was wearing the suit he'd been wearing in Vegas and the voice that had made him famous. "Maybe his flight wouldn't have been delayed if he'd flown into Burbank," he continued, as he came around to stand in front of the bar, "which someone definitely tried to tell him to do." He beamed down at her. "What a fart-head."

She reached over the bar and grabbed his face, bringing it to her own. She kissed him half as ardently as she wanted to and threw her arms awkwardly around his neck. He turned his lips to her ear and said, in his normal voice, "I'm so sorry. How are you holding up?"

She swallowed and pulled back. She smiled at him. "Better now."

With everything going on in each of their lives, they hadn't been together for the past couple of months, though they'd spoken nearly every day. In some ways, the distance had brought them closer. But now that he was here, in front of her, she wanted to close the door on everything and everyone else and lose herself in them. First, though: "I see you brought a date." She turned her attention to the dark-haired man standing next to Nick. "Something you want to tell us?"

"Aren't you the funny one?" He was back to the Brock voice.

Her laugh broke through as she said, "Jason, I presume?"

The two dimples that appeared on his olive-toned cheeks wrenched an almost imperceptible gasp from Adaku. *Wuh-woh*. "Sewanee." He held both hands out to her over the bar. "It's so good to finally meet you."

She clutched his hands and squeezed. "Finally is right!" The one time she'd gone to New York, they hadn't left Nick's apartment; all their other visits had been in L.A. because she hadn't wanted to leave a deteriorating Blah. By that point, Blah's original protestations had been forgotten, and Sewanee had been able to have the ending *she'd* wanted with her grandmother. "It was so nice of you to come." She released his hands and pivoted to Adaku, who already had her palm out, winning smile attached. "This is my best friend, Adaku."

"Best friends should always meet," Jason said, taking her hand. "A pleasure."

"Always," she parroted. She turned to Nick, cocked an eyebrow. "And hello to you, Mr. McNight. Nice to have you back."

"Please." He brought his hand to his chest. "Mr. McNight's my father. Call me Stiffy." He turned to Jason, saying, in his own voice, "Okay, I'm done. Never again."

Jason grinned ear to ear. "I told you not to bet."

Nick turned back to the women. "We played Choosies on the plane. I lost."

Jason said to Adaku, "We also listened to Sewanee's most

recent June project, the one you starred in." He shook his head, looking a bit awestruck. "Wonderful. You were incredible."

"Aww," Adaku cooed. "Thank you." She hip-bumped Sewanee. "It's all her brilliant direction."

Sewanee hadn't had a chance yet to tell Nick about the Broadway producer who had reached out to Adaku's people about doing a staged reading/workshop of the project. She'd give him the news later. She had many things to give him later.

Adaku clapped her hands together. "So what can I get you both?" She looked down at the bar. "We have a rum punch and all the martini ingredients available for purchase in this entire city." Nick said he'd have some punch and Sewanee ladled him a cup.

Jason leaned over to peruse the options. Adaku watched him avidly. "The punch looks great, but I'm sober, so—"

She clapped her hands again. "Ooh I got you covered!" She bent to a box behind the bar. "Do you like grapefruit? I started making this drink when I was in training for a job I ended up not doing, but the drink stuck! It's . . ."

Sewanee was sure Adaku's story was absolutely riveting, especially given the way Jason seemed to be hanging on her every word. But she was otherwise engaged. She was staring at Nick. And he at her.

She slipped out from behind the bar, but just as she was about to step into Nick's embrace, Stu and Marilyn descended upon them, clapping Nick on the back and yanking him into hugs. Sewanee, impatiently patient, waited for what felt like an eternity, as they caught him up on what seemed like every port of call they'd visited in the last eight months. Then Stu said, "Swanners sent us your new song! 'June's Bloom,' right? Terrific. And hey, I'm still waiting for that call to fill in on keys."

"Anytime." Through their laugh, Nick caught Stu's eye and said sincerely, "Cheers, mate."

Stu answered in kind. "Anytime, Nickster. Anytime."

"I think it's my favorite one, Nick. Just beautiful," Marilyn enthused, hands at her heart. "Is it going on the album?"

More eternity passed. This was cruel and unusual punishment. After Mark had stopped by, and she'd introduced Nick to Henry, and Mitzi had hobbled over to ask him, yet again, if he was single, Sewanee managed to extricate him. She dragged him around the side of the building, took his empty cup, set it on the ground, and pounced on him like a lynx.

After a minute of tender kisses and gently roving hands, he flipped her around until her back was against the wall and things between them, as they were wont to do, turned.

"I want to go," she breathed.

"But where?"

It was a good question. For the last three months, since Doug Carrey bought Mark's place, she'd been living in Adaku's two-bedroom bungalow with the thin walls. But now Adaku was back from filming. She was regretting their decision to invite Nick and Jason to stay with them there this weekend. They should have gotten a hotel.

"Austin?" she suggested, unseriously though desperately.

Nick chuckled. "Six of one." He and Jason had been living in their producer's tiny pool house while trying to finish the album.

"I want space," she whined, against his lips. "Hey. I just inherited some grazing land in Tennessee."

"Well, maybe that's where we should mooooooooove."

She laughed fully into his mouth. "But that doesn't help us right now."

"True. Back to the problem at hand."

She smirked. "The problem at hand. You know how I feel about euphemisms."

Nick brought his hand up between them. The one with the ring on his middle finger. "Who says it was a euphemism?" Then, not taking his eyes off her, he gave the ridge of the ring a familiar lick.

Sewanee's eye bulged. "Nick! No!" She looked frantically around. They were literally beside a dumpster. In the alley of an old folks' home.

He didn't say a word. He kept his gaze on her, as he slid the ring off his finger and reached down—

"Are you insane?!"

—And gently lifted her left hand. It floated up, suspended between them. He slipped his ring onto her fourth finger.

Sewanee's mouth opened, but nothing came out.

"I love you," he said. *"Sposami."*

Her mouth stayed open.

Eventually, he continued. "That's your cue."

Sewanee closed her mouth, swallowed. "I love you. I would love to marry you."

Nick knew the next word all too well. "But?"

"But. You're seriously proposing to me now?"

"All good Romance novels end with a proposal."

"But at Blah's funeral?"

"Can you think of a better way to honor your gran?"

"I . . . you . . ." Sewanee huffed a laugh, dropped her head to his chest, took a breath. She looked up, tears of laughter turning to so much more. "Yes."

The relief in his eyes. "Yes?" How could he have doubted her answer?

Sewanee grabbed his face and beamed. "Yes."

They kissed, and some time later Nick pulled back, looking serious. "How do I break it to Mitzi?"

"I think you're good, I saw her hitting on Jason."

They kissed some more and then Nick pulled away again. "Hey. You know where we could go?"

"Where?"

She saw the answer in the sparkle of his eyes. Like neon and snow.

Las Vegas.

She intertwined their fingers. "I know a great bar."

"Or we could find the nearest chapel as you're obviously mad for me."

Her heart switched places with her stomach. "Chapel?"

Nick grinned. "We might need some witnesses."

At that moment, Adaku's signature guffaw ricocheted around the building and echoed off the dumpster, making them both laugh. "I think we know where we can find them."

Nick dragged her even closer to him. Giddy, he brushed her hair back, gazed down at her face, searching for anything that wasn't real. He wouldn't find it. "Are we really doing this?"

She'd asked him the same question in a text message once, what felt like a lifetime ago.

She answered the same way he had then. "We're really doing this."

They kissed once more, and walked back out into the crowd, to their people, to share the news. To see who wanted to continue the party across state lines.

And by the way, in case you're wondering? At the end of it all, they lived happily ever after.

Six Years Ago

Seven weeks had passed since Nick came home to Prescott.

It felt strange, especially now that both of them were back in the house, Jason fresh from rehab, looking like an alley cat someone had put a bow on. Having them back made her miss them more than when they'd been away. Because she didn't know these new versions of them. These men.

She sat down at her desk to write the e-mail and recalled how much she'd fought with those two messy, boisterous, stubborn high schoolers. How she'd endured—not gracefully—hearing the same clunky chord progression over and over from the garage. How she'd done her best to tolerate the hours of basketball in the driveway while she tried to write. She'd never realized how much it had meant to her until it was gone. Until it was quiet.

She wanted their noise again. She wanted both boys to reclaim that spirit they'd once struggled to hush whenever she'd walked into the kitchen. A spirit that now seemed permanently damaged. Like her brother when he'd returned from Vietnam, lethargically dragging himself around with wounded stoicism. Until he left again. Permanently.

Sometimes she'd catch herself gazing at Nick, looking for the greasy-haired adolescent happily drying glasses behind the bar in Tom's pub. Looking for the little boy whose grin was so much like her little sister's that at times she had to turn away. But all those Nicks had disappeared.

She'd never been good at motherly concern. Her biggest personal failing—as Nick himself had once astutely and angrily pointed out—was that she saved all her emotional investment for her characters. In truth, she wanted another chance. To start over completely. To have the social worker set him down again on her doorstep, him and his ratty Eeyore.

A foolish thought, but one that took her back to memories of the precocious young boy who, a few years after his arrival, began endlessly asking "why" and to her frustrated attempts to answer him. To make him understand what the hell life was all about. Why she was his mother now. Why her sister had died and why she had made the choices that led to that worst possible outcome for him. Why life happened and why you simply had to live with it. Why there were no do-overs. Why we'd love to go back and change things if we could, but we couldn't.

We didn't get to live multiple lives and then choose the one we wanted at the end. Sorry.

His seven-year-old answer to all of this, staring her straight in the face, in all seriousness, had been, "Then I better do everything right the first time."

She'd sent him on a fool's errand.

And now look at him.

She knew there was no going back for a second chance, but worst of all, there was no going forward for one, either. Nick had stopped asking her why long ago; in fact, he'd stopped listening to her altogether.

So she wrote.

It was the only thing she knew how to do.

To: Westholme, Sarah
From: JF Admin
Date: April 23, 11:51 PM
Subject: For want of a catchier subject line: HELP

Hello, my dear,

I hope this email finds you well. Hell, I hope this email finds you. It's been almost a year since we last wrote, since you retired

Sarah Westholme, and I—for the life of me—can't recall your real name. Perhaps I never knew it? This is my only way of making contact, so I do hope it reaches you.

I'll get straight to it (you certainly know by now that's my way): I have a request. More to the point, a rather embarrassing request.

I will put you immediately at ease, this isn't a solicitation. (Though you know all you have to do is say the word and I'll give you as much work as you want.) No, I'm afraid this is a personal matter.

I have a nephew. I was given the chore of raising him. I use the word "chore" because I have never been good at taking care of anyone other than myself. A sad fact I now live with.

He's a good man (for which I take no credit). He has found himself kneed in the balls by life; repeatedly and recently. There are men I have known who deserve that. He is not one of them.

You once shared with me, quite early on, your own horrible circumstance. His return home has brought your accident to the forefront of my mind. Did you find your way back? Are you at peace with it? Have you accepted it? Do you feel whole again? I truly hope so, and if so, I must know how. He must know how.

Now comes the embarrassing request: may I put you in touch with him? I think it would help. Him. You? Please understand, I'm not matchmaking here. Call it writer's intuition. Hell, call it whatever you want, roll your eyes at my meddling, both of you, I don't care, so long as you connect with him.

Completely off topic, he might make a good narrator. He has an amusing voice he does in jest which if he ever took half-seriously could be quite good. But that's not my purpose in writing nor should you consider it relevant. Perhaps just a conversation starter?

I save groveling for my books, but short of that: Please talk to him. Listen to him. I've failed at both and here we are.

I realize you may never see this. If I don't hear back from you, I'll find another way.

Ciao,
June

ACKNOWLEDGMENTS

FIRST, THANK YOU TO THE INHABITANTS OF MY AUDIOBOOK PROFESSION. The storytellers. The storykeepers. The madmen and firewomen. I barely spoke about this book while I was writing it, but some of you were key to the journey for various reasons: Will Damron, Abby West, Andi Arndt, Erin Mallon, Amy Landon, Edoardo Ballerini, Sebastian York, and Sarah Mollo-Christensen.

In my last acknowledgments, I skipped my teachers for the sake of length. In this one, I want to feature them for the sake of rightness. From my fabulous elementary teachers to Mrs. Dewey, who first ignited my love of reading. To Caryl Pine-Crasnick and Barbara "Buzzy" Gogny, my studio teachers. Buzzela, you made me think I could write, and coming from a woman who was also a writer, man, did that mean something.

In college, Mary Ellen Bertolini informed me I was going to be an English major, which was very helpful, and then let me tutor her Jane Austen classes. To Paul Monod, for suggesting I apply to Oxford and making British History so entertaining I didn't begrudge an 8 A.M. Monday morning class. To my other professors, including but not limited to: John Bertolini, Larry Yarborough, Teo Ruiz, Eric Jager (technically never my professor, but it *feels* as if you were), Stephen Gill, and Peter McCullough. To Jeff Dunham for not flunking me in Physics for Poets when you absolutely should have; I enjoyed our chats about Jane Austen.

To my creative writing teachers over the years, in various settings, but especially: Rob Cohen, Summer Block, Chris Noxon, Laura van den Berg, Antonio Ruiz-Camacho, Mona Simpson, Don Mitchell, and my fellow students in their workshops, because that's how workshops work. And from those workshops, I'd like to single out Bri Cavallaro, who—a decade and a half later—not only writes fantastic books for me to narrate, but gave me early consult on the practicalities of Sewanee's disability. Finally, mostly, to Barbara Ganley, who taught tirelessly at a college that didn't deserve her (there, I said it) and whose wisdom, encouragement, advice, and sensibilities I think about—no exaggeration—daily. You taught me how to Read Like a Writer and that, more than anything else, has given me not one but two careers.

Teaching doesn't stop upon graduation. I continue to learn from other authors, those I record for as well as friends I've met along the way. Too many to name here, but particularly: Catherine McKenzie, Therese Walsh, Allison Winn Scotch, Emily Henry, Benjamin Percy, Philip Dean Walker, Amy Spalding, Kosoko Jackson, Thea Harrison, and, of course, Linda Holmes, who—of all coincidences—also wrote a Nick and a June into her sophomore novel. And a special thanks to those authors who, for this specific book, gave their time to an early read: Allie Larkin, Malcolm Brooks, Andrea Dunlop, Robinne Lee, and Taylor Jenkins Reid, Queen of Actually Everything.

Many thanks to Sarah MacLean and Jen Prokop for their fabulous podcast, *Fated Mates*, which helped me get up to speed on what I'd missed in Romance since I'd stopped recording it.

To my agent, Abby Koons: we started working together when I had nothing to show you and, when I finally did, it was at the beginning of a global pandemic and yet . . . it all worked. Sometimes you just know, I guess. To Alex Greene, whose editorial eye is just as keen as her legal one. To the rest of the Park & Fine team, but especially: Emily Sweet, Andrea Mai, Anna Petkovich, and Kat Toolan. And to our co-agents, especially Anoukh Foerg. And, for that matter, to the lovely people at Penguin Verlag for your faith and support.

To the HarperCollins/William Morrow/Avon team: Lisa Nicholas, Brittani DiMare, Robin Barletta, Julie Paulauski, Francie Crawford, Elsie Lyons, and Nathan Burton. Especially to Liate Stehlik at the beginning and to Erika Tsang at the end . . . *prayer hands*. And, mostly, to Elle Keck: I didn't want to do this book without you. Your DNA is in its marrow and I'm so glad we got to do it together.

On the personal side of things:

Ten years ago, Tim, Dana, Jeff, Pam, and Laura were all there for me so I could be there for my grandfather; and Marvin, Jolie, and Chris were there for my grandfather when I couldn't be. To everyone at his assisted living facility and Serenity Hospice, particularly Melinda, reverend and all-around Godsend.

Karen Gang for answering my questions about elder care, not only back when it benefited my real grandparents, but for this fictional one, too. And to Elena Hecht, for having such a wonderful mother in the first place.

To Laura Grafton, who began my audiobook journey; I could never have foreseen where it would lead. And to Ellen Steans for also having such a wonderful mother in the first place.

To Andrea Kaufman for giving me the GREAT news about Merriam-Webster adding a second pronunciation for areole.

To my Audm family for understanding I had to go write this book. To the spirit of Christian Brink: I told you this story was a Cyrano retelling, because, at the time, it was. It devastates and angers me all over again that you're not here to tell me, over gin and karaoke, how the Cyrano version would have been better.

To my actual family. Particularly Mom and Ken for their Zen

in the face of my . . . whatever the opposite is of Zen. Mom, I missed your hugs so much those eighteen months a pandemic kept us apart. To Gramps: it was an honor to escort you past the veil. To Dad: ten years later and I'm still pissed you're not here to see all of this and I guess at this point I always will be.

To my friends for putting up with my disappearing acts. Particularly Sarah, for letting me not only steal your name for this book (and, I just realized, your dog's!) but also your habit of watching golf for background noise. I only wish I could make Nick real for you.

And to my Nick: my Geof. The reason any of this works. For taking care of everything so I can pursue anything. For making our life so beautiful, so complete. As you say, enough is *always* enough. For feeding me, in every way: with your love and championing, with your freakish talent and earned insight, with your comic genius (on and off the page), and, literally, with your cooking. You know how fine you are to me?

About the author

About the book

Insights,
Interviews
& More . . .

Meet Julia Whelan

Kei Moreno

JULIA WHELAN is a screenwriter, lifelong actor, and award-winning audiobook narrator of over five hundred titles. Her performance of her own debut novel, the internationally bestselling *My Oxford Year*, garnered a Society of Voice Arts Award. Whelan is also a Grammy-nominated audiobook director, a former writing tutor, a half-decent amateur baker, and a certified tea sommelier. ⌇

On Autobiography

Here's what I've learned: No matter how many times you explain that your book isn't autobiographical, no one really believes you.

With *My Oxford Year*, the first-person possessive in the title didn't help. Nor did the fact that I had spent a year at Oxford. The default assumption, I've discovered, is that it's a memoir. I've even had *friends* who haven't yet read it say to me, years after the book came out, "Wait, it's *fiction*?"

With *Thank You for Listening*, I've already accepted that explaining the story to people will also require explaining how it's not *my* story, and admittedly, at first glance, there doesn't seem to be much daylight between myself and my main character: I used to be an on-camera actress; I am now an audiobook narrator; I once recorded a lot of Romance, under a pseudonym, which I did—in part— to help pay for a grandparent's care.

I also have a hunch that many die- hard audiobook fans will try to take my fictional characters and graft real narrators onto them (especially Brock). I will nip this in the bud: I specifically, intentionally, mindfully did not write my colleagues. Each character, from Alice to Mark to the engineers, are, if anything, pastiches of our industry's "types," or in the case of Ron Studman and others, whole cloth inventions. I learned this lesson with *My Oxford Year*. When my British friends knew I was writing the story and asked me—half ▶

excitement, half dread—if they were in it, I was able to truthfully say no, and it was such a relief.

I would also caution: Just as *My Oxford Year* was not *my* Oxford year, nor anyone else's for that matter, this glimpse into audiobooks is not the whole picture; it's not even a view from "the narrator's perspective." It is *one* narrator's perspective, filtered through the self-selective and self-serving lens of fiction.

In truth, the most autobiographical part of the novel is also the most universal. Like so many others, I had a beloved grandparent who suffered from dementia. By far, the most real-life moment in the whole book is when BlahBlah tells Sewanee what it feels like to lose her bearings in reality. I was gifted that exchange from my grandfather, after he called me at 4 A.M. from his room in an assisted living facility telling me he was at a conference at the beach waiting for my father (who'd been dead for three years) to pick him up. Six hours later, he was clearheaded enough to tell me what I've now told you (though I changed the particular examples to better suit Blah's backstory).

But I am not Sewanee. She is not me. Because, while the biographies might look similar, there's one major alteration (besides a missing eye), which, to quote Frost, "made all the difference."

When we speak of autobiography— or, really, autofiction—it seems to me there's more nuance in the concept than we acknowledge. After all, what defines a person? Is it what happens to them? Or is it who they are? Writers are encouraged to "write what you know," but "what you know" can mean anything. A profession, sure. A character, of course. A setting, obviously. But it can also just mean . . . an emotion. A feeling. A conviction.

The idea of writing a rom-com set in the Romance audiobook world came to me ten years ago, when I was knee-deep in the Romance audiobook world. It came when I was doing a dual narration with a narrator who's like a little brother to me, and the e-mails we were sending back and forth, the phone calls—*are you adding moans to the sex scenes? Just how growly are you making his voice?*—were, objectively, hilarious.

It's a weird job. There's no way around it. And it seemed like perfect fodder for something.

But what?

Over the years, this story lived as a screenplay. It lived, in my head, for a time, as a staged one-woman show. When I first began conceiving of it as a *book*, I thought Nick might be an author, writing under the June French pen name, who falls in love with his audiobook narrator, who, of course, doesn't know his true identity. That would have worked. But as audiobooks, and by extension narrators, became more popular, I witnessed the fandom that grew up around Romance audio's biggest male stars and I knew I wanted to write about that.

In the summer of 2017, when I'd turned in the final draft of *My Oxford* ▶

On Autobiography *(continued)*

Year and people were asking what I was working on next, this idea was leading the pack, but I had two problems. I didn't know if people cared enough about audiobooks to care about this book and I didn't know who my main character was.

Then audiobooks exploded in popularity and I felt confident that most people had at least *heard* of audiobooks, even if they'd never before thought about the narrators behind them.

But my main character was still a question.

I was, frankly, intimidated by that question. Because I knew, whoever I wrote, people would assume she was me.

So how would I differentiate her?

To start, I asked myself why she was narrating. If she were happy narrating, as I was, if she loved her life, as I did, where would the conflict come from? Many (probably most) narrators are actors, so maybe she was just biding her time, waiting for the next on-camera or theater gig? But that felt unsatisfactory. I wanted to give the professional, working-class, yeoman narrator their due. It's a job— a skill, a craft—in its own right, and it doesn't get enough attention as it is.

And then, MeToo happened.

I didn't want to write a MeToo book; this *isn't* a MeToo book, don't worry, you didn't miss something. But at the end of 2017, the entertainment industry that I had grown up in was rocked by scandal. Everything we'd always whispered was finally being shouted and it seemed— shockingly—that people might actually be held accountable. An outcome that, truthfully, had never occurred to me as a possibility. It was a time of reflection for me, and the realization that had me walking around for most of the winter of 2017-18 as one big ball of rage was how little control the business of acting affords and how that opens the door to predation. As an actor, you can't control when you work or with whom or in which role. You can't control when the opportunity arises or how it's handled in the execution. There's a pretty famous saying: sometimes the only power an actor has is saying no.

But who ever says no? To the potential money? Fame? Relevance? To the joy and satisfaction of getting to do what you love?

Well. I did. I decided around that time that I didn't want to act on the business's terms anymore. That any fun and fulfillment it might possibly bring wasn't worth the frustrations and dehumanization it reliably brought. I suppose it's like getting to that breaking point, finally, with that one boyfriend who just won't go away. Every time he leaves, and you think you're over him, he comes back with new excuses, new promises, and you say, *okay, well at least he's talking to his mother again* or *he has a job this time* or *maybe he finally sees my worth*. How many times do you let him come back? In the wake of 2017, I'd reached my limit. My life was so much better without Hollywood in it.

But it was my *choice* to walk away. What if it hadn't been? ▶

On Autobiography *(continued)*

What if "no" had been said for me?

What if the main character I'd been seeking had been kicked unceremoniously out of the pursuit of her dream, against her will, and *that* was why she was narrating?

I'd already written a book about choosing to walk away from an old dream and toward a new one.

This time, I wanted to write a book about accepting the absence of that choice. Nothing to overcome, nothing to be corrected . . . just something to accept.

It occurred to me, then, that I had explored this territory once before, albeit nascently.

Before *My Oxford Year*, I had been working on a YA novel about a seventeen-year-old girl growing up in Los Angeles, the daughter of a celebrity publicist. A pretty girl, a not-terribly-ambitious girl, a girl for whom doors opened simply because she was pretty and fame-adjacent. And one day, this girl skipped school and went skydiving with her friend and almost died. But she didn't. She survived, with half her face.

Her journey was accepting that while she may at first feel like an ugly duckling, she was actually a Swan.

So, I finally had my main character and, to borrow a line from her, I had her "why."

Finally, I was ready to write.

But first . . .

I had to promote *My Oxford Year*.

And attend to my day job of recording other people's books.

And then I got a job offer at an

audio-based tech start-up I couldn't refuse.

And then, after building the company to a place where I was able to step back, I finally, finally, sat down to write three chapters and a synopsis.

And then I flew to New York and met with my agent to discuss the pages.

And that meeting was on March 2, 2020.

The fact that this book about accepting all the things we can't change was written during the turmoil and upheaval of 2020/2021 seems fitting.

It was ten years in the making.

It was my pandemic baby.

It was my refuge from the madness.

Just when I would begin to think there was no empathy or laughter or romance left in the world, I'd open my computer and there were Swan and Nick, waiting for me to get cracking. Empathizing. Laughing. Romancing.

And it became autobiographical in a sense far deeper than occupation or history or family. It became the embodiment of all the hope for the future I wanted to have, but often found I couldn't muster. Just like my main characters. Into them, I wrote my fears as well as the antidote to those fears: the urging to take the risk. To trust in the outcome, an outcome that, whatever it may be, would at least be the result of action instead of inaction. That seemed worth writing about in these times. It seemed, as Sewanee observes at the end about Nick's voice, *something to believe in*.

Which, I suppose, is the very essence of Romance novels. ॰

Reading Group Guide

1. Throughout the story, Sewanee works toward accepting and embracing all that life has given, and taken away, from her. What do you think the turning point was for her to actually accept the way her life had changed? How do you think the future will fare for her now that she's no longer living in grief for her old self?

2. There's a lot of discussion about happily ever afters. Romance has them, but so do mysteries and thrillers (the bad guy is caught by the good guy). Why do you think they are important to so much of fiction?

3. Sewanee and Nick both have huge fans. Do you follow any audiobook narrators or podcasts? Why do you think people can connect so much to just a voice? Furthermore, how do you think this might change if audiobooks are synthetically narrated by AI in the future?

4. Are you an audiobook listener? Do you think it's a different experience than reading?

5. What did you think about June's last letter? Do you think Sewanee and Nick were meant to be or do you

think they were lucky to find each other?

6. Speaking of meant to be, do you find that Adaku's perception of life—that everything happens for a reason—is true? Or is Sewanee's belief that everything just happens more accurate?

7. We see many different sides of Hollywood in this book—from Sewanee, Adaku, and Blah Blah. Did any of their stories challenge your conception of Hollywood?

8. Sewanee loves her best friend and is genuinely happy for Adaku's success, but there is an admitted undercurrent of jealousy. If you feel "less than" someone else, do you think your admiration for them is truly honest, or is it only masking envy, resentment, and jealousy?

9. Sewanee and Nick fall for each other in two very different ways. Do you think it's possible to fall in love with a person without ever seeing them or meeting face to face?

10. If Brock hadn't turned out to be Nick, and Sewanee had found herself in a love triangle, who do you think she would have chosen? Who would you have chosen? ▶

11. Marilyn and Stu found each other later in life, but Marilyn assures Sewanee that she and Henry "had a good life together," that as difficult as he could be, "life is never one thing." Do you think it's possible to have an "unhappy" ending with someone and still find the life you shared to have been meaningful? ∿